MINDBENDER

TELEPATH: BOOK TWO

GORDON G. BOWMAN

BOWMAN
BOOKS

Published by Bowman Books.

www.bowmanbooks.ca

ISBN 978-1-0690302-0-7 (paperback - perfect bound)
ISBN 978-1-0690302-1-4 (hardcover - jacketed case laminate)
ISBN 978-1-0690302-2-1 (hardcover - case laminate)
ISBN 978-0-9936057-9-6 (EPUB)

For Jen'fer.

1

THE CELL

Zoe sat cross-legged with her eyes closed, floating two feet above the cement floor. She had been doing so since breakfast, and her goal today was to last until lunch arrived through the slot in her cell door. It was important to have goals in a six-by-eight-foot windowless room.

Solitary confinement, she knew, was a form of torture. Even a few days in solitary could cause serious mental health issues. She thought back to when she'd first woken up here 121 days ago. She hadn't cared about goals or mental health then. She hadn't cared what isolation could do to her brain. She had felt that she *deserved* this.

Every day, Professor Chao's last moments—in which he'd looked into her eyes—would play on a never-ending loop in her head. Every night, she would dream she was back at the Academy, walking through the aftermath of the Igigi assault. The fires had gone out, leaving only smouldering trees and ruins, and the air was still, the silence heavy and oppressive. No one was around, save for the bodies littering the bloodstained ground. So many bodies. She had to step carefully to avoid them, and all the while, students' lifeless eyes followed her. *It's your fault,* they said without words. *You killed us all.*

She would wake up sobbing, knowing in her heart that it was true. It had been her idea to wipe her memory and infiltrate the Academy. She disabled their security. She called in the attack, betraying everyone who had befriended and trusted her. It didn't matter that she ultimately switched sides. The damage had already been done. She deserved to be locked up forever. And so, she spent her days staring at the walls. Sitting on her bed, hugging her knees, and rocking back and forth. Oscillating between the agony of guilt and the numbness of loss. Never trying to escape. Just slowly allowing herself to descend into the madness she'd earned.

You're in a better place now.

She had to agree. Maybe her stubborn refusal to give Ragnar the satisfaction of watching her go mad had finally won out over her wish for punishment. Or maybe it was her desire to avenge her mentor.

Don't.

In any event, she'd eventually begun to work on herself. She lost herself in her memories of her childhood among the Igigi, examining her past through the lens of her new persona, formed during her time at the Academy. What had seemed normal to her then seemed monstrous now. Every waking moment had been spent in competition with the other Igigi children—training to fight, learning to infiltrate. They were taught to worship the god Marduk and to hate the Anunnaki, against whom they would one day wage war.

"The Anunnaki may capture you someday," Ragnar had said to the class when Zoe was ten. "If that ever happens, they *will* torture you. They will try to get past your shields and enter your mind to extract as much information as possible. They will try to break you—not just to gain information about your brothers and sisters, but because they will *hate* you. They will fear your superior strength and intellect. They will despise your moral superiority because it threatens their delusions of being the caretakers of this world. They will get sadistic pleasure from forcing you to plead for your life, to beg for mercy. You must *never* allow them that satisfaction."

He laid a plastic tarp on the dojo's floor and placed a chair in the centre. "If you've never been tortured before, they *will* break you. Therefore, torture resistance training is key. Who wants to go first?"

No hands went up.

"Well, that's disappointing. Zoe, come sit."

"I'll do it," Ethan said, standing.

"I've already chosen," Ragnar said, motioning for him to resume his seat. "Zoe?"

She rose and took the chair facing her classmates. Ragnar began strapping her ankles to the chair legs and her wrists to the armrests. Her mouth was dry, and her heart pounded. She hoped nobody could see her shaking.

"It takes years to build up resistance to torture," Ragnar said, "which is why we are starting now, years before you will go out into the world on your first missions." Once he'd secured her to the chair, he stood and addressed the class. "The trick to enduring pain is dissociation. Instead of fixating on the pain and letting your lizard brain react with screaming, crying, begging, let your brain's higher functions take over. Detach yourself from the pain. Observe it clinically and dispassionately, with interest and curiosity, as if it were happening to someone else."

He walked to the wall and opened a cabinet to reveal a wide array of torture devices. "The anticipation of pain," he said over the children's gasps, "is, in some ways, worse than the pain itself. There is a reason I put a plastic drop cloth beneath the chair—besides the blood, of course. Many of you will lose control of your bodily functions—but only if you let your fear control you. Before we begin, I want to make one thing clear to you all: I will not enjoy doing this. I do not believe in hurting children without an extremely good reason. My reason is this." He looked each student in the eyes. "It would be wrong of me to put you in a position where you might one day be captured without preparing you for it. We will start off small. We have excellent healers in this facility, so no one will suffer permanent damage. You are our hope for the future, after all. All you need to worry about is learning to overcome pain."

He nodded toward the back of the dojo, and Miss Gillespie came up to select an instrument from the open cabinet. Zoe thought of that fateful day with the frogs, when she had stopped Miss Gillespie's heart. The woman had hated her ever since.

"Zoe," Ragnar said. "I want you to raise your shields. Make them as strong as you can to stop me from entering your mind."

Zoe swallowed and did as she was told.

"Excellent. Now, I am going to try to get inside your mind, and you are going to do your best to stop me. As Miss Gillespie administers pain, you will find it increasingly difficult to maintain your shield. Years from now, though, you will be able to withstand any amount of pain without your shield wavering in the slightest. Are you ready?"

"Does it have to be her?" Zoe asked, nodding toward her former teacher.

Ragnar raised an eyebrow. "You think you will be able to choose your torturer?"

Zoe shook her head. "Never mind. It's stupid. I'm ready." But she wasn't. She was more terrified than she had ever been in her life, and she locked eyes with Ethan. Despite his obvious anguish, he nodded, trying to be her rock.

"Then let's begin," Ragnar said. Miss Gillespie smiled as she drew near.

Zoe let go of the memory. There was no point in reliving the actual pain of these torture lessons. Looking back, she marveled that she hadn't realized how abusive her teachers were. She had truly believed she would be tortured by the Anunnaki one day. She hadn't understood she was in a cult, because that was the only life she'd ever known. But now, she had a completely new life to compare it to, and seeing her childhood all over again with this fresh perspective helped her to properly integrate her two personas and feel a measure of peace.

She winced as the image of Professor Chao popped into her head again—on his knees and looking into her eyes as Ragnar delivered the killing blow. What right did she have to feel peace? She would never be able to forgive herself for his death. She hoped, though, that he had forgiven her at the end.

"I told you that I forgave you. Why is that not enough for you?"

She opened one eye to look at Professor Chao, sitting on the floor, his feet tucked beneath him in *seiza* position. She closed her eye. *Because you're not real, Professor. You showed up on day twenty-nine—the day I officially went mad.*

"You're not mad, Zoe."

No? What would you call it? Sane people don't see dead people.

"You brought me here to *keep* yourself sane," he said. "We are social creatures. We need interaction with other people. What they are doing to you is unconscionable."

So, you think I've been hallucinating my dead teacher just because I need company?

"It is *a* reason, yes, but not the only one. You carry a tremendous amount of misplaced guilt for my death. You want to be free of it, so you created me, but you are too stubborn to accept the forgiveness of a hallucination. So, my purpose is mainly to give you someone to see and talk to. Not that you ever speak to me with your physical voice."

It's the camera. I don't want them to know I've lost my mind.

"Perhaps that is what they are waiting for, Zoe."

What, to drive me mad? And then they'll let me out? She shook her head imperceptibly. *That makes no sense. What would be the point? No, they're trying to break me.*

"So, pretend to be broken."

She thought about that. It made sense, yet she balked at the idea. *I'm

. . . afraid to, Professor. I'm afraid that I'm barely hanging on and that if I pretend to break, even for a second, I'll break for real.

He was silent for a moment. "Very well," he said. "But you need a plan. And this—whatever you are doing—is not a plan."

This is too a plan. I'm meditating, just like you taught me. I've rid myself of my anger, learned to use my Abilities without it. I've become strong—look what I'm doing! I'm lifting my entire body off the floor and holding it in place for hours! How many others can do that?

"Not many," he admitted. "Certainly none as young as you."

And I've crushed and reformed that metal toilet using ferrokinesis a thousand times.

"It is very impressive, yes."

And I've learned to move air itself, just like Professor Martinov. A tornado of dust swirled around her.

"He would be most proud."

And then there's this. Blue electricity crackled around her hands. *I didn't even know this was possible until you showed me.*

"Electrokinesis is a most advanced technique, to be certain. You learned it quickly."

You see? I've used my isolation as a gift—to meditate and become stronger. I've even kept up my daily calisthenics, so that I don't wither away. I can do handstand push-ups now.

"Making the most of your time here is commendable, Zoe, but it is not a plan. What are you doing to protect my wife and daughter?"

She winced. *That's not fair.*

"Is it not? You have never tried to escape. You have never tested the strength of that door. You have never tried talking to the guards when they bring your food tray, let alone compelling them. You have never looked at the camera and demanded to see your father."

Zoe glared at her former teacher. *Don't call him that.*

"He called you his daughter. Whether he meant it literally or figuratively, it implies a bond—a bond that you can exploit."

The second I see Ragnar, I'm going to kill him.

"That would be unwise, Zoe. You are strong and fast, there is no denying it, but he is much stronger and has had many centuries to hone his fighting skills. You would almost certainly die."

You almost beat him.

"Almost means nothing. He killed me, and he will kill you, too, if you are not careful. Regardless, he is not the leader of the Igigi, merely a general. If you are going to defeat the Igigi, you need to learn the full extent of their plans and formulate a plan of your own to stop them. First, though, you need to do what you promised me. You need to find Mei and Lin and protect them."

I've looked, Professor. I've tried to reach Lin via mindlink. I've extended my broadcast way beyond what I used to be capable of, but she's not here— wherever "here" is.

"Exactly. You are no good to her here. Who knows what they have been doing to her and her mother while you sit here doing nothing? You are clearly scared of something."

I'm not scared!

"You are. And not just of talking to your dead professor or mentally breaking. You are clearly scared of escaping. Why?"

Zoe didn't answer.

"Why?" he pressed.

Why are you asking? she snapped. *You're me, so you already know the answer!*

"That is just it, Zoe—I do not. Which means you do not know, either. Whatever it is you fear, you are repressing it. You have convinced yourself that your best strategy is to meditate day after day and improve your Abilities, so that when the moment arrives, you will be ready. But it has been *four* months. At what point do you admit that what you are really doing is stalling?"

I need to be strong for when I face Ragnar—

"Enough!" Professor Chao yelled, rising from seiza to stand before her. "You *promised* me. You promised that you would protect my wife and daughter. I want to know why you are breaking your vow."

"Because it was my fault!" Zoe yelled back, dropping to her feet. Her hands clenched into balls of electricity. "Everyone trusted me, and I betrayed them! The headmaster, the professors, the students, my friends, you, Professor Yeoh, Lin—*everyone*!"

The professor's anger subsided. "You were in an impossible—"

"It doesn't matter! Excuses won't matter to any of them! I took down their security system, and I called in the attack. I'm responsible for everything that happened afterward, no matter whose side I fought on. People died! *You* died! How can I ever face Lin again?"

The professor was quiet a moment while he absorbed what she'd said. Did that mean *she* was absorbing what she had just said?

"So, you have been lying to yourself," he said at last. "Convincing yourself that biding your time was the best strategic move when, in fact, you have merely been afraid to face your friend?"

Zoe threw up her hands exasperatedly. "Yes? Maybe? I don't know!"

Professor Chao put his hand on her shoulder. It felt so real! "Zoe," he said, "Lin may, perhaps, find it difficult to forgive the person who called in the attack that led to her father's death. But you are *not* that person. That person was a child soldier indoctrinated in an extreme ideology. Lin was never friends with her. She was friends with a completely different person. It was this new Zoe whose persona ultimately dominated the old Zoe and who fought bravely alongside Lin and her family. I think my daughter is smart enough to understand this. No matter how she feels, though, she needs your help. It is time to leave this place."

Zoe took a deep breath and wiped a tear from her cheek. "Okay. Tell me what to do."

Professor Chao looked up at the camera. "They have been watching you speak out loud to me, so I suspect you may not have to do anything. I suggest you get some rest while I stand watch. I will let you know if anyone is coming."

Zoe didn't understand how her hallucination was going to do that, but she lay down on her bed and tried to sleep. It was difficult, because her mind was already formulating escape plans should a guard enter her cell, but eventually, she drifted off.

"Zoe," Professor Chao said, shaking her gently. "Zoe, wake up. Stay calm and do not do anything stupid."

"What?" Zoe said, sitting up and rubbing the sleep from her eyes.

"You are not going to like this. Promise me you will not do anything rash."

"What are you talking about, Professor?"

The cell door suddenly unlocked, and Zoe leapt to her feet. Ragnar entered, and he studied her as she stood frozen.

"You've looked better," he said. He sniffed in displeasure. "It stinks in here. Come with me." He turned and strode out, leaving the door open behind him. Zoe hesitated, hardly able to believe what was happening. After all this time, Ragnar was suddenly within striking distance, and he'd casually turned his back to her.

Do not attack him, Professor Chao warned. *We need to know what the Igigi are up to.*

Zoe stepped slowly into the hallway. After four months in solitary, everything felt unreal. It occurred to her that she might be dreaming. The hallway stretched in both directions with numerous doors identical to hers. There were no guards present—just Ragnar, climbing a set of stairs.

She hurried to catch up and entered what she assumed was the guardhouse. There were lockers, a kitchenette, a few couches, several tables and chairs, and a desk blocking the door to the basement. There were no guards, though. Ragnar exited through a door on the far side of the room, still not bothering to see if she followed. She ran after him and gasped. She was in her old school! The main foyer of the underground facility was utterly empty and silent now except for their echoing footsteps.

Zoe caught up, walking so close behind him now that she was tempted to attack. She might never get another opportunity like this, and he wasn't even worried. She clenched her fists and felt the electricity crackle.

Careful, Professor Chao reminded her, several feet behind them. *Right now, we need information far more than we need revenge.*

They finally came to a nondescript door and entered what Zoe assumed was Ragnar's residence. It was clean and tidy, tastefully decorated in a minimalist style, with antique Nordic furniture and sculptures of dragons and Norse gods. The walls were adorned with Viking art depicting seafarers and battles, as well as ancient Viking swords, axes, and shields. She wasn't sure what she had expected his residence to look like, but this wasn't it. This seemed like the home of a man of sophistication—not the shirtless, bloodied berserker of their last encounter.

He poured a drink from a decanter into a glass as she examined the weapons. They had all obviously seen battle.

"Would you like a drink?" Ragnar asked. "I know you're underage, but I won't tell if you won't."

When Zoe didn't reply, he shrugged and plopped himself lazily into a cushioned chair, putting his feet up on the wooden coffee table. Taking a sip, he motioned for her to sit. Zoe sat opposite him with her feet tucked under her and waited for him to speak.

"How is Professor Chao?" he finally asked.

Zoe kept her face blank, so as to hide her sudden stab of shame. She had stupidly blurted out everything for the camera to see, but she would be damned if she showed any embarrassment now. She arched her eyebrow at the professor, standing off to the side with his arms crossed.

He just nodded, and she turned back to Ragnar.

"He sends his regards, thanks."

Ragnar snorted. "He was a great man, your professor. Truly. I'd known he would be a formidable opponent, but I never thought I might actually lose to him. When I tossed that flying shield aside only to see a flying sword hidden behind it—brilliant." He took another sip. "Do you think he got the idea from you? I heard you almost decapitated poor Ethan with that little trick in your matchup against him in Doom."

When Zoe didn't respond, he continued, "Anyway, aside from his prowess in combat, I attended his memorial service and heard story after story about him. He was indeed a man of kindness and integrity. I can see why you liked him. I am sorry that I had to kill him."

"You didn't *have* to kill him," Zoe snarled. "You *chose* to kill him."

"Fine. I *chose* to kill him, because I *had* to kill him. He would never have become an ally, and he would always have been a danger to us. He needed to die so that his followers would surrender unequivocally and never plot to free him."

"Just to avenge him," Zoe said, coldly.

Ragnar shrugged again. "They're already plotting their revenge, but they'll never follow through. Enough pleasantries. You have questions, and this is your one opportunity to receive answers."

Zoe thought about it. Where to begin? She had so many questions.

"So, you're actually *the* famous Ragnar Lodbrok of the Viking sagas?"

He nodded.

"Didn't you die in a pit of snakes?"

Ragnar laughed. "You read that, did you?" He drank. "It seemed a good way to fake my death. It was getting difficult to hide the fact that I wasn't aging, so I left my people and wandered. But someone would always recognize me. So, I had my old friend King Aelle kill me. He and everyone around the snake pit saw what I wanted them to see, and afterward, someone who wouldn't be missed was in my clothes, swollen and unrecognizable at the bottom of the hole."

"Why did you call me your daughter?" she blurted.

Ragnar smiled. "It's funny, isn't it, how important it is to each of us that we understand our place in the world? Our roots. Where we come from. *Who* we come from." He sighed. "I always pitied you children for not having what most of us take for granted. On the other hand, I always envied your potential. We literally have no idea how powerful you children will become."

He thought for a moment, perhaps deciding where to begin. "You are aware that we have been researching human DNA ever since its discovery. Without laws to constrain our genetic engineering program, we progressed much more rapidly than the rest of the world. We learned how to create people who are smarter, faster, and stronger. We were also able to isolate the genes responsible for our Abilities. The idea of gaining your DNA from a single mother and a single father eventually became quaint. You children each have the DNA of hundreds of people." He pointed at Zoe. "Except for you. You are different."

He rose and poured himself another drink. "Since you've read your history, you'll know that I was first married to a shieldmaiden by the name of Lagertha. Historians got many things wrong about us, but this fact they got right: She was, and is to this day, the love of my life. A more beautiful, more ferocious woman has never lived. Losing her, through my own idiocy, remains my greatest regret."

He paused, deep in thought. "We had two daughters, she and I. Ragnhild and Åløf. They were the light of our lives. Precocious. Fierce. Had they grown up, I have no doubt they would have been shieldmaidens the likes of which the world has never seen." He fished something out of his pocket and placed it on the table. Zoe recognized her brooch instantly and snatched it up.

"Keep it," he said. "It's yours now. When I was a young man, it was tradition for a woman to place a lock of her hair in a brooch for her husband to wear into battle. Lagertha did me this honour, and I wore it around my neck for most of my life. Right until the day that I thought to ask our chief geneticist if it was possible to extract any DNA from a centuries-old strand of hair. To my surprise, it was. Not all the DNA was intact, of course, but enough was. I convinced him to work on a private project for me—combining my DNA with that of Lagertha's to create our third child. We still augmented your strength, speed, intelligence, and Abilities so you would have the same genetic advantages as your peers. But you are the daughter of Ragnar and Lagertha. I even drew pictures of our daughters and described their personalities to the chief geneticist, which he said could help guide him in the creation of your DNA. You're not either of them, but you are definitely their sister. The resemblance to them—and to your mother—is . . . uncanny." He shook his head. "You are so much like them, not just in appearance but in temperament and instinct." He paused, considering something. "Would you like to see them?"

"What?" she asked, stupidly. She could hardly believe what she was hearing. "How?"

Ragnar stood and walked behind her. He placed his fingertips atop her head, and she cringed. "Relax," he said. "Lower your shields, and I will show you your mother and sisters."

Zoe forced herself to do as he asked. Suddenly, she saw a small home with a thatched roof and walls made of wood and clay—exactly what she'd imagined a Viking home would look like.

This was my home as a young man. We built this house and farm ourselves.

Zoe saw a small field with assorted crops and several wandering goats and pigs. A woman emerged from the farmhouse, and Zoe gasped.

This was her mother.

Lagertha had long ginger hair and a beautiful face that lit up with her smile. The resemblance to the face Zoe had seen in the mirror her whole life was unmistakable. She was graceful and feminine, yet exuded the strength and confidence of a warrior.

Incredible, was she not? Ragnar asked.

Something caught Lagertha's eye, and she crouched down as a little girl of maybe three came running to show her mother a flower she had picked. Behind her walked a girl who looked to be several years older. Both had their mother's ginger hair.

The youngest is Åløf. The older one is Ragnhild.

Suddenly, the scene changed, and she was on a battlefield. It was cloudy and raining, and bodies were strewn everywhere. Lagertha was covered in mud and blood, her hair blowing in the wind. She held her shield in her left hand, her sword in her right. She looked over and nodded, then ran forward to meet an enemy, dropping down and to the side to avoid his swing while simultaneously slicing through his midsection.

The world has never again seen a shieldmaiden like my Lagertha.

The scene shifted once more, this time to a village. Ragnhild and Åløf fought each other with wooden swords. They were older now, around eleven and nine, and Zoe could see her resemblance to them much more clearly now. She could also see how skilled they were.

So much like their mother, Ragnar said.

They look like me, Zoe said, astounded. *I look like them. How did they die?*

She saw a flash of two graves before Ragnar wrenched his hands away and returned to his chair to drink.

"I wasn't there for them," he said. "I was off raiding, and when I returned, they were in the ground."

Zoe understood that no further details would be forthcoming. "I don't understand," she said. "Why didn't you ever tell me?"

"Two reasons." He held up a finger. "First, I didn't want you to be treated differently. Children of powerful or successful people almost inevitably become lesser versions of their parents. This is because they never have to struggle. Never have to endure hardships. Never have to become resilient. They grow up with all the comforts and privileges afforded to them by their parents. Ragnhild and Åløf were born to farmers and warriors. After I became chieftain, we tried to ensure that we didn't treat them any differently. But others did. Everyone was afraid to hurt them, so they wound up training mainly with each other. I didn't want you or your peers to think you were special. I wanted you to have the same struggles as all the other children, so that you would be strong."

He held up another finger. "Two. I didn't want you to become a target. Children of powerful people with enemies rarely live long."

Ragnar leaned forward, staring intently at her with his piercing blue eyes. "And this is why Marduk was not pleased. He was against creating you—he forbade it. After all, our enemies could use my child as leverage against me. When I created you anyway, in secret, he was angry. I had never known him to be so angry. He ordered you killed while you were still a small collection of cells. I refused and threatened to leave and undo all of our work if anything happened to you. It was the only time I've ever disobeyed him."

Zoe hardly knew what to say. "Why take such a risk?"

Ragnar was thoughtful for a moment. "My wife and daughters were . . . extraordinary. And once an idea forms in your head, it is sometimes difficult to let it go."

"So, why tell me months ago on the battlefield?"

He leveled his gaze at her. "I wanted you to understand the full extent of my disappointment in you."

Zoe blinked. Who did he think he was to be disappointed in her? A man who'd never claimed her as his daughter—who'd never shown her an ounce of kindness.

"Not only was I betrayed by my top student," he continued, "but I was betrayed by my own flesh and blood. I allowed you to go forward with your plan to infiltrate the Academy because you were so eager to prove yourself. I watched you in Toronto on the off chance that you might be discovered by Chao himself, and we got lucky. I thought I might be able to take him out in that restaurant and abort your mission. I nearly succeeded. I never thought that after less than a year with him, you would turn your back on me and your family."

"Wait," Zoe said, irritated by the audacity of this man and his *disappointment*. "You called me 'daughter' in public. I don't know if anyone else heard, but Ethan sure did."

Ragnar nodded. "Yes, it was a moment of recklessness. Do you think I should kill him?"

"What? No!"

"Are you certain? I don't care any longer if *you* tell people. But surely you wish that to be your decision, not his? Besides, you can't be very pleased with him. He betrayed you at the end, after all. You had your chance to kill me, and he stopped you."

"That doesn't mean I want him dead," Zoe said, eyes narrowed.

"Suit yourself," he said. "I had a word with him already, anyway. He won't reveal your secret to anyone without your permission."

Zoe didn't like the way this conversation was going. It was certainly good to know her origins, and there was a lot to process, but it didn't matter much in the grand scheme of things.

"Where is Lin?" she demanded. "And her mom, and the rest of my friends? What have you done with them?"

Ragnar raised his hand in a placating gesture. "They're fine, as is everyone who surrendered and swore fealty to Marduk. You'd be amazed at how easy it is to get someone to do that, you know. Just put a knife to the throat of the person they love most and tell them to swear allegiance. Sometimes the hostage heroically says, 'Don't do it!' But they almost always swear. And then you just swap throats and tell the hero to swear, and what are they going to do? Refuse and cause the death of the person who just gave up everything to save them? They swear allegiance quicker than the first."

Zoe was stunned. He sat there, well-dressed and drinking expensive scotch like he was civilized. But he wasn't. She had to always remember that.

"If they're fine, then where are they?"

Ragnar checked his watch. "I'd say they should be in the Great Hall eating breakfast about now."

Zoe shook her head slowly. "I don't understand. The Academy is still there? I thought it burned down."

"No, we put out the fires after the attack and spent the past four months fixing it up. You'd never know anything happened. Which is good, because as far as any Typicals are concerned, nothing *did* happen—except for the expansion wing, of course."

Zoe put it together. "So, that's why this school is empty. Your students are all at the Academy now."

"Not just mine—although, technically, they're *all* mine now, since I'm the new headmaster. I decided to integrate all the students together into one happy family. That's where you come in."

"Back up," Zoe said. "What happened to Headmaster Harrington?"

"Oh, he's dead," Ragnar said, matter-of-factly. "You can let almost anyone switch sides, but not the leaders. You could never really trust them, plus they'd always serve as a magnet for rebellion. No, he had to be executed, I'm afraid."

Zoe winced, remembering how the headmaster had defended her when she first arrived at the Academy. How she had spent countless detentions in his office and how he'd saved her reputation after she'd killed the soldiers pursuing Ethan. He was a good man. He hadn't deserved such a fate. She glanced over to see Professor Chao's head hung in sorrow.

"And what of former Minister Lafleur?" she asked. "Was she also executed?"

"Gabrielle? Absolutely not! Have you *seen* her fight? She taught your Professor Chao—did you know that? She and I met once, long ago, when I attacked Paris. Had it not been for her, I think I would have taken it. A warrior of her magnitude deserves better than an execution. And she was no longer their leader when I attacked, so I'm hoping she will come around." He shrugged. "We will see."

But Lafleur hated the Igigi with a passion. Zoe doubted she would "come around."

"You said that's where I come in," Zoe said.

"Yes. You," he said, pointing at her, "are the bridge between worlds. Ethan, too, to a lesser extent. Telepaths of the old breed are inferior to the New Gods, as Marduk likes to call you. They're still useful, though, and must be encouraged to join our cause willingly. If they're preyed upon, they will be less likely to feel like they are one of us. And that is exactly what has been happening since my students arrived at the Academy. You have been a leader in both groups. I want you to bring them together."

"Why would I possibly help you?"

"First," he said, sipping his drink, "you like your new friends at the Academy. You don't wish to see them suffer—and left to fend for themselves, they *will* suffer. Second, you *owe* me. Your mission was clear, and if you had just followed my instructions and kept your new persona buried after your awakening, you would have succeeded. Instead, you created a back door to merge your new persona, because you were so sure you could assimilate her. Your hubris not only resulted in you failing your mission, but you also literally betrayed us. I only managed to convince Marduk to spare your life by arguing that because you fought alongside the Anunnaki, they might still trust you enough to listen to you—which we can use to bring them to our side more willingly."

He leaned forward. "Third, do you actually *want* the world to end?"

Zoe was silent.

"Because it *will* end if we don't act soon. If nuclear or biological weapons don't kill us all quickly, climate change will kill us all slowly. Or perhaps not so slowly. It may already be too late. We would have made our move after the first atomic bomb was dropped if we could have, but we had to wait until we had the technology to build ourselves an army. It's mind-boggling that the Anunnaki let this happen."

"It's not that simple, and you know it," Zoe said. "Your plan to rule the world is clearly just mind control—compelling the world's leaders and turning them into your puppets. It's the only way. The Anunnaki refused to do that, because taking away someone's free will is wrong."

Ragnar snorted. "Tell that to eight billion people when they're dead. When did you become so stupid, girl? Besides, do you really think we need to compel everyone? The leaders are all that matter. Compel them and the rest will follow like the sheep they are. The free will of a few Typicals is not more important than our continued existence."

Zoe opened her mouth but found she had no good argument. "Is that where it ends?" she said instead. "With all of us living in a green utopia free of nuclear and biological threats?"

Ragnar laughed. "No, I don't imagine that's where it will end. Marduk is ambitious, for certain. But that's where it begins, and that should be enough for you."

He stood. "Oh, and there's a fourth reason you will cooperate. If you don't, I'll kill your friend Lin. Her mother too. Now, time's up. You've asked your questions, and I've given my answers. Time to go."

"Where?" Zoe asked, instantly knowing the answer.

"To the Academy, of course." He wrinkled his nose. "But first, you need to bathe and change into new clothes. I'm not going to spend six hours on a plane with your stink."

2

HOMECOMING

This time, the windows of the private jet were not blacked out and she wasn't drugged. As their plane rose into the sky, she watched the land below carefully. She had always known their bunker of a school was located in a tropical jungle, probably in Central America, but its exact whereabouts were a mystery. At first, she saw only treetops until they rose high enough that she could make out a coastline she recognized from her studies.

"The Osa Peninsula," she said. "Costa Rica."

Ragnar nodded across the aisle. They were the only two passengers. "A beautiful country. A shame you children couldn't have explored it."

"I understand," Zoe said. "We were prisoners, after all. You couldn't risk us escaping or giving away your location if we defected."

Ragnar scowled. "That's the new Zoe talking. You *never* felt like a prisoner. Your existence needed to be kept secret from the world, and you accepted that. Your childhood was nothing like mine, but it was necessary, and it was effective. It didn't prepare you for going out into the world, though—but that will be remedied now that we are no longer hiding from the Anunnaki."

"You know they don't call themselves that, right? Most of them have never even heard the word."

"It doesn't matter," Ragnar said. "They are what they are."

"So, you believe everything Marduk says? That he's an ancient Sumerian god? Does he even exist or is he just something you made up?"

Ragnar's eyes narrowed. "I will allow you to speak like this because you are my daughter and we are in private. But if you ever publicly question the existence of Marduk or his plan, I will put you back in solitary where your only entertainment will be listening to your friends scream in the neighbouring cells. Do you understand me?"

This time, Zoe scowled. "Fine," she said, reluctantly. "But since it's just you and me here, tell me: Is he real? Not just someone you made up?"

"Oh, he's real."

"And you've actually met him?"

"Many times."

"And he's an actual god? Not just a very old, powerful Telepath with delusions of grandeur?"

Ragnar took a deep breath. "It is . . . difficult to imagine him ever having been just a man," he said.

Had he just shuddered? What kind of man could scare Ragnar?

"Where is he, then? Why haven't the rest of us seen him?"

"The most powerful being in the world does as he pleases. He doesn't justify his decisions to anyone. As for where he is . . . you would do well to assume he is everywhere at all times. All knowing. All seeing. Always listening."

Zoe froze. "What does that even *mean*?" she blurted. "You're saying he can see us right now, even though he's not here? How is that even poss—"

"I've told you all I intend to tell you," Ragnar snapped. "Your stunt of allowing your temporary persona to persist has ruined you. You are not my star pupil, not my protégé—you are not even Igigi anymore. The only reason I have allowed you to live is because you are my daughter and

I believe you could still make yourself useful as a bridge between students."

He stretched his legs out into the aisle and crossed his ankles. "Now, I am going to take a nap. Remember, if you try to kill me and fail, I will kill Lin and her mother. And my men have standing orders to execute them, should I ever die for any reason. Enjoy the flight." He closed his eyes.

Zoe stared at him. He was utterly defenceless, his neck exposed. She was confident she could break his windpipe before he moved.

Do not dare.

Professor Chao sat two seats behind Ragnar. Had he been there this whole time?

I could do it, Professor. I could avenge you, then compel any crew on this plane to say nothing. I could reach the Academy before word of his death arrives and rescue Lin and her mom.

And what if they are expecting him to check in? Lin and Mei will be dead long before you get there. You need to put aside any thought of vengeance until they are safe. Besides, you do not kill a man while he sleeps. You are not a murderer or an assassin. Promise me.

Zoe winced.

Promise!

Fine! I promise!

Professor Chao relaxed. *Good. Lin is going to need you more than ever. You need to get your head straight.*

Zoe raised her eyebrows. *Says the hallucination.*

He nodded reluctantly. *A fair point. You were in isolation for a very long time, Zoe. No one endures that without repercussions. And your mind was already in a delicate state when you were captured.*

Do you think that's why I created you, Professor? My mind had been fractured. Segmented into two personas. When they began to merge, maybe the segmentation remained, making me more susceptible to hallucinating you, as though you were another full-blown persona in my head.

I have no idea, Zoe. Natasha should be able to help you, if she is still alive. But you need to listen now. You created me to keep yourself sane while in solitary confinement. Now that you are free, though, I am a liability. I will hinder your healing. Relying on me for advice will prevent you from learning to trust yourself and your own decisions. You need to let me go.

No! Zoe said. *I won't do that.*

Please, Zoe. You must—

I said I won't. You're MY hallucination, and I'll decide when you go. I'm not ready. She turned to look out the window.

The professor sighed. *Fine. We will discuss this at a later—*

Nope. Zoe imagined he was scowling but refused to glance back.

Try to get some sleep, Zoe. It is a long flight, and you have a long day ahead of you.

Are you kidding me? I'm finally out of that cell. I'm not sleeping until I drop from exhaustion.

. . .

They landed at the VIP terminal of Toronto Pearson International Airport. Ragnar stepped off the plane without a word, and Zoe followed, surveying their posh surroundings.

"Not at all decadent," she said. "Not like the Anunnaki."

Ragnar glanced sideways at her as he led her toward customs. "You think we should have taken a public flight? Maybe flown coach?"

Just as Zoe realized she had no passport, the customs agent's eyes glazed over and Ragnar handed her two passports, which she robotically stamped.

"The passports were simply for the benefit of cameras," Ragnar told Zoe once the woman had waved them on. "There is no record of us ever leaving or returning to Canada."

That made sense. It would be a simple matter for Telepaths to travel between countries undetected, but there were always cameras—and people watching those camera feeds—to worry about.

They got into the back seat of a nondescript black car and drove off in a convey of similar black cars. There were four men in black suits, sunglasses, and earpieces to each car—except for theirs, which contained only two. Despite his formidable fighting prowess, Ragnar clearly took his security seriously. Zoe doubted she would get another audience with him anytime soon, so this was her last chance to push him for information.

"What happened after the assault on the Academy?" she asked, getting down to business.

"What happened was that while the assault was ongoing, we finally put our plan—the one you delayed by months—into action worldwide. We captured or killed thousands of Anunnaki. The rest are in hiding, but we are hunting them down."

Zoe felt sick. All those people, dead and captured. It would have happened without her involvement, she knew, but the fact that her actions had put it all in motion was hard to swallow.

"If they're all in hiding, why the extra security?" She gestured at the convoy.

"One can never be too careful. As for what happened at the Academy, you can ask your classmates yourself. I will say, however, that I dragged you—unconscious—through our school to your cell so all your peers could see what a disappointment you have become."

Zoe turned away to stare blankly out the window. She didn't know what to expect upon returning to the Academy, but she suspected she would be a pariah, hated by everyone. Only one person mattered, though.

"So, what happens now?" she asked, as they slowed to a stop on the far side of an overpass. The infamous Toronto gridlock. "What's the grand plan? Are you already taking over governments or—"

Both Ragnar and Professor Chao tensed. She heard the distinctive whistle of a rocket-propelled grenade a split second before the security cars exploded around them. People in masks and flak jackets dropped from above and surrounded their car, brandishing automatic weapons. One jumped onto the hood and fired at the windshield. Another shot at Ragnar through the side window. Someone on the roof fired down on Ragnar's seat, and Zoe pushed herself as far from him as possible and covered her face, then realized the bullets hadn't pierced the vehicle.

Bulletproof, Professor Chao said in her head. *It will not last long, though.*

"Remember," Ragnar said, "if I die—or you escape—they die."

With a roar, he kicked out his door, exploding it into the man shooting at his window. He stepped into the road, as if in slow motion, and the two men up front followed suit, firing their pistols. The gunman on the roof aimed at Ragnar, but with a sweep of his arm, he bent the path of the bullets. He grabbed his assailant's ankle and threw him like a ragdoll into another masked man rushing in.

"To me!" Ragnar shouted to his men, who were crawling out of their burning vehicles. Some were immediately picked off by snipers, but others could clearly see the prescient yellow streaks, because they avoided the bullets. Returning fire, they ran toward Ragnar before engaging the enemy in hand-to-hand combat. But bullets flew everywhere, limiting their movement, and even with their obvious training, they were outnumbered.

Ragnar, though, was like a man possessed, rushing recklessly into the midst of his enemies, as though they had walked into *his* trap. He picked up a man and used him as a human shield as he charged into an onslaught of bullets, then hurled the man into a group of assailants, who Ragnar then attacked barehanded, screaming like a Viking berserker. If he intended to instill fear in his enemies, it was working.

Nevertheless, the sheer number of bullets and rockets soon took down all of Ragnar's bodyguards, forcing him to stop and erect a shield.

You must help him! Professor Chao insisted, now sitting in the passenger seat. *They do not know Lin will die because of this!*

Someone suddenly pounded on her window. "Zoe!" cried a familiar voice. "It's me, Gabriel! Come with me!"

Gabriel. Professor Chao's operative. She looked back at Ragnar, crouched down with bullets flying all around him. So many yellow streaks filled the air that it looked like a shimmering haze. Another missile suddenly exploded next to Ragnar, sending him flying. She rounded on Gabriel.

"They'll kill Lin!" she yelled. "And her mom! If I escape or he dies, they'll kill them! He said so!"

Gabriel's eyes widened in surprise, and without waiting for a reply, she launched herself from the car. Amid the flames and smoke, she spotted Ragnar getting to his feet unsteadily just as another missile raced toward him. Instinctively, she stretched out her arm and curved the missile away, but still, the force of the explosion hurled Ragnar into the air again. She looked for the missile's source and saw a woman reloading. A dozen or more people advanced on Ragnar, firing the whole time. Though on his knees and swaying, he still somehow managed to avoid the bullets. There was no time to warn them that Lin's life was in danger and no time to engage them all in combat.

Instead, she sprinted toward Ragnar and used all of her telekinetic strength to launch herself into the air. The last time she'd used this move was in an attempt to kill Ragnar before he could fight Professor Chao. He'd seen her coming, then. This time, though, he didn't seem aware of her at all. She landed between him and his opponents, electricity crackling between her outstretched hands. The bullets stopped abruptly as everyone looked at each other in confusion. Professor Chao walked slowly through the smoke and fire.

"Professor Chao's wife and daughter are his hostages!" Zoe yelled. "If you kill him, they'll be executed!"

But they didn't retreat. Two people aimed their rocket launchers at her. She assumed a fighting stance and clenched her fists, lowering them to her sides. Each fist was enveloped in a ball of . . . plasma?

"You think I don't want to kill him myself?" she screamed. "He killed Professor Chao! But you have to rescue his wife and daughter first! I promised I'd protect them!"

"Zoe!" Gabriel ran forward. "Step away from him."

Zoe couldn't believe it. Of all people, she'd thought that Gabriel would care. "They'll die," she said.

"I know," he said, slowly approaching with his palms up. "And I'm sorry, Zoe. Truly. I love them as much as anyone. I've known Lin for most of her life. I watched her grow up and watched over her. I don't want her or her mom to die. But as much as it pains me to say this . . . we have no choice." He pointed at Ragnar, who was clearly concussed and struggling to stay upright. "We *have* him. We've planned this for months and now we have him. I will *not* let him escape. He leaves here in a body bag. Now, stand aside."

Zoe's jaw clenched. "No."

Gabriel took a deep breath. "I know this is hard for you to understand. You're only a child. You haven't fought through wars. You've never had to make the difficult decision to sacrifice people for the greater good. There are thousands of lives at stake. He is simply too important a target to let slip away. So, I'll tell you again: Step aside."

"I won't let Lin and her mom die for the 'greater good,'" Zoe said, refusing to budge. "I don't care how important a target Ragnar is. I'll find another way. Professor Chao would never have approved of this."

"Well, he's dead!" Gabriel snapped. "Isn't he? And whose fault is that? His?" He pointed at Ragnar again and then at her. "Or maybe it's yours?" He stepped forward. "Yeah, I've heard rumours of what went down that day. You got Chao killed and now you're going to deny his family justice? You think Lin wouldn't gladly sacrifice herself to see her father's killer dead? You think you have some sort of moral authority here? *I* was Chao's right-hand man. *I* am the leader of the Resistance. And *I* am giving you a direct order. Stand aside. *Now.*"

"*You* do not command me, Gabriel. I don't want to hurt you—any of you—but I will."

"Enough! He's going to recover in a moment, so we're going to start shooting on the count of three, even if we have to shoot through you. One."

Everyone raised their guns. Zoe took a deep breath.

"Two," Gabriel said, stepping back and raising his own weapon.

Zoe didn't wait. Without pausing to consider if she could actually do this or if it would even work, she thrust her hands out and sent electricity into each and every weapon. Yelling, everyone instinctively dropped their weapons, which Zoe quickly yanked back behind her with telekinesis—except for a katana, which she caught in one hand.

"I may be just a child," she said, "but I'm pretty sure I'm more powerful than any of you. And I've been trained since birth to use this." She twirled her sword a few times, testing its weight and balance. "I've killed armed men in combat before. Don't make me do it again."

The Resistance fighters all looked to Gabriel, who glared at her. Behind her, Ragnar stirred. He was trying to shake off his concussion.

"*Go,*" she said, more forcefully. "Before he comes to his senses. I guarantee *he* won't spare your lives."

"Sir?" asked one of the Resistance fighters, eyeing Ragnar nervously. Zoe could almost see the wheels turning in Gabriel's head, wondering if they could all take her now that they were unarmed. How many would die in the attempt? Could they overpower her before Ragnar was able to fight back? His fists clenched.

"Sir!" another fighter said, as Ragnar opened his eyes and smiled.

"Abort the mission," Gabriel finally said. "Everyone into the trucks. Load the wounded."

"No, you should stay," Ragnar muttered while Gabriel's people scrambled. He rose to one knee, laughing. "I insist."

Gabriel shook his head at Zoe in disgust. "She'll never forgive you." He headed for the nearest truck. "Not for getting her father killed, and not for letting his killer go." He jumped in and glared at her before slamming the side door closed. The trucks roared away up the grass and onto another road.

Ragnar laughed as he got to his feet. She whirled and hit him in the face with all her strength, knocking him back down. "I hate you," she spat.

He laughed even harder.

...

Soon afterward, Ragnar's people arrived to clean up, and a helicopter spirited Zoe and Ragnar away before any authorities arrived. A healer tended to his concussion. There must have been so many witnesses to mind wipe and so many video recordings to erase. What if some people had driven away? Or live streamed it? It hadn't just been a crazy assault with automatic weapons and rocket launchers; it was a public display of their Abilities—and their faces, too. She was surprised the Resistance had taken such a risk. But if Gabriel was in charge, maybe it wasn't such a surprise. During their first meeting, he had made a lighthearted comment about being discovered by Typicals, and Professor Chao warned him against underestimating the threat Typicals posed.

In any event, she had her own problems to deal with now. She looked down at the Academy far below. You'd never have known it had been in ruins only months before. The lawns looked immaculate. The old, burned trees had been removed and new ones planted. All damage to the castle had been fixed and a new wing had been added, in the same Elizabethan style. It must have cost a fortune. Surprisingly, the barn still stood.

As the helicopter landed on the west lawn, she could make out the faces of students in the windows. This wasn't how she'd wanted to make an entrance. She had wanted to sneak in unnoticed and beg Lin for forgiveness. Instead, she looked like Igigi royalty, arriving in a helicopter with Ragnar Lodbrok.

While Ragnar disappeared into the castle, she stood beside the helicopter and stared at all the faces peering back at her. Was Lin among them? In a sudden panic, she began walking—not toward the castle but the barn. Her animal friends there wouldn't judge her. But as she drew near, she realized it was eerily quiet, and she entered the barn to find the stalls had all been cleaned out and the loft emptied of hay. Professor Chao sat up there, looking down at her. Zoe's heart sank. She'd wanted to hug Vincent and hear his goat noises.

"They're gone."

Zoe whirled to see Lin standing in the doorway.

"Ragnar apparently thought the animal sanctuary was stupid, so he shipped them all off somewhere. I have no idea what happened to them—or to Elizabeth."

At first, Professor Chao looked so happy to see his daughter, but his expression quickly morphed to one of concern. Lin looked different. She had grown taller over the summer, but it was more than that. Her eyes looked . . . cold. Haunted. Her hands were swollen and scabbed. Zoe tried to say something—anything—but no words came out. She was terrified. Literally trembling. "Hey," she managed to squeak.

"My mom sent me to bring you to the infirmary," Lin said. "Come on." She turned without another word, and Zoe hurried after her, Professor Chao following along behind.

"How are you?" Zoe asked, finally.

"I'm great," Lin said. "Why wouldn't I be?"

This wasn't the reunion Zoe had been hoping for, but at least Lin wasn't screaming at her. "And the others?"

"We're all great, Zoe. Everything is just great."

3
REUNITED

The foyer was empty, thankfully. Zoe didn't know what time it was, but she assumed classes were in session. She and Lin walked down the halls in awkward silence, and when they reached the infirmary, Zoe paused and readied herself. How would Professor Yeoh feel about her? But Professor Yeoh glanced up from her desk expressionlessly. She looked the same as Zoe remembered but with weary eyes. She rose and, without speaking, crossed to stand in front of Zoe.

"Mom—" Lin began.

Professor Yeoh slapped Zoe hard across the face, leaving her stunned. "That is for coming here to kill my husband."

Lin made no move to intervene.

She slapped Zoe again. "And that is for calling in the attack that got him—and many others—killed. Some of them children."

Zoe's eyes watered and her lower lip quivered.

Then, the professor's eyes softened, and she hugged Zoe tightly. "And this is for *not* killing my husband. For fighting alongside us and coming to the aid of my daughter and the other children." She tightened her hold. "And for trying to avenge him."

Lin's jaw dropped. Her expression quickly changed from

astonishment to anger, then she strode off without a word.

Zoe bawled. She hugged Professor Yeoh back and didn't let go. "I'm sorry! I'm sorry!" she sobbed. "I wish I could go back! I wish I could go back and change everything!"

"I know," Professor Yeoh said. "I know, Zoe." She held her until Zoe composed herself, then stepped back. "Now, let's look at you. Why are you covered in dirt and soot?"

"Something happened on the way here, ma'am. A failed attempt on Ragnar's life."

Professor Yeoh's eyes widened. "Was it Gabriel and his people?"

Zoe nodded.

"Is Ragnar still alive?"

"Yes, ma'am. Gabriel would have succeeded, but if he had . . . you and Lin would be dead by now."

"I see," Professor Yeoh said, quietly. "Ragnar told you this?"

"Yes, ma'am. He said his people have orders to execute you and Lin if he dies. I explained this to Gabriel, and he . . . reluctantly aborted the mission."

The professor scowled. If her own life was the only one at stake, Zoe imagined she would want to risk it. But her daughter's life was at stake, too.

Professor Yeoh changed the subject. "Come and sit. We heard you were in solitary. How long did he keep you there?"

"Until this morning, ma'am," she said, sitting on the examination table.

"What? He kept you in solitary for four months? Did you at least get time outside every day?"

"No, ma'am. I never left the cell. It was in our old bunker where I grew up. I was only able to count the days because the lights went out every night."

The professor shook her head. "That monster. To do that to anyone is abominable, let alone a child. I'll run some blood tests. You will definitely be deficient in vitamin D. I imagine the food wasn't great, so you're probably malnourished as well. Although . . ." She examined Zoe's arms. "Your muscle tone seems fine. Better than fine, actually."

Zoe nodded. "I tried to make the best of it, ma'am. Exercise was a way to keep myself occupied."

"Did you endure any physical punishment? Were you tortured?"

"Not physically, ma'am. But not seeing a single person for so long . . . that does things to you." She glanced at Professor Chao standing in the corner.

Professor Yeoh followed her gaze. "Hallucinations?"

Zoe hesitated, then nodded again.

"That is not surprising, Zoe. Did you experience panic attacks, depression, paranoia?"

"No, ma'am. I don't think so, anyway. I mainly just . . . saw . . . and heard things that weren't there." She hoped the professor wouldn't ask what it was that she hallucinated.

But Professor Yeoh didn't press. "I will speak with Dr. Sharapova about seeing you." Zoe gulped. "She is best suited to helping your mental recovery. *If* she will see you, that is. I realize that your time with us changed you, Zoe, but you are still responsible for the things you did before, and you must atone for them. You *wronged* Dr. Sharapova greatly."

Zoe nodded. "I know."

"For now, I want to do a full physical exam." She began taking Zoe's blood pressure.

Professor Chao slowly approached his wife. He lifted his hand hesitantly, as if to touch her cheek, then lowered it again.

"It's been hard for Lin," Professor Yeoh said. "Losing her father—and in the way that she did. Losing her best friend at the same time. She's lost. Fighting all the time. Your blood pressure is good. Let's listen to your heart and lungs."

As Professor Yeoh listened with her stethoscope, Zoe watched Professor Chao. He couldn't keep his eyes off his wife, as if he missed her so much. Her hallucination puzzled her. He was her creation, yet sometimes he seemed like a real person with real feelings.

"Sounds good, Zoe. Now, we'll draw some blood to test and get you into the MRI, like we did when you first came to the Academy."

...

An hour and a half later, Professor Yeoh pronounced her physically healthy.

"I heard about Headmaster Harrington," Zoe said, sadly.

Professor Yeoh took a deep breath and nodded. "Richard was a good man and a dear friend. He did not deserve his end."

"Ragnar said he was executed. How did it happen?"

"I don't know. We were all held captive at the time, being interrogated by nameless faces—being 'reeducated,' he called it. Ragnar himself visited me one day to apologize for taking my husband from me, to tell me that I should fully cooperate if I loved my daughter, and to inform me that he had executed our headmaster. He gave no details. I never saw Richard's body."

"What's it been like here since then?" Zoe probed. "With Ragnar as the new headmaster? I didn't think any of the professors would be kept on staff."

"I presume he needed qualified teachers for the upper grades. He only had teachers for the lower grades—the ones you had before coming here. They walk around like they own this place. That Miss Gillespie is a real piece of work."

Zoe shivered. She had no desire to see any of her Igigi teachers again. "And what's the end goal? I mean, the Igigi want to take over the world, basically. Have they already started?"

Professor Yeoh shook her head. "We're kept in the dark. Our phones confiscated. Internet access highly controlled. I have no idea what's been going on out in the world. We're all prisoners here. But the reeducation of students to understand and support the Igigi philosophy has begun. Professor Grant has been replaced by someone who teaches history with a decidedly different spin."

Zoe had no doubt. In all of her history classes with the Igigi, every bad thing that had ever happened—short of natural disasters—was always the fault of the Anunnaki. "What about Lafleur? Ragnar said she's still alive. Is she in the basement?"

"Your guess is as good as mine, Zoe. None of us are allowed down there, but the castle only has a few holding cells. We were all held somewhere else, an hour or so drive from here." Her eyes glazed over for a few seconds before she shook her head and smiled, as if nothing had just happened.

"Is there a plan to retake the Academy? Or are we just waiting to be rescued?"

The professor paused and met her gaze. "There is no plan. Security personnel are everywhere. Ragnar himself is here maybe half the time. But more importantly, no one knows whom to trust. Many of our own students have turned already. Some of the professors seem to have turned—or at least are pretending they have. Perhaps compulsion is at play, perhaps not. My memories of my time in incarceration are . . . fuzzy. I *think* I am the same person I've always been, but how can I know for sure? That is the nature of compulsion. Perhaps I was compelled to be more compliant and not rebel."

Zoe sighed. "So, no one trusts anyone. And I've been a prisoner the longest—plenty of time to have been turned. So, I can't be trusted, either."

Professor Yeoh said nothing.

"I understand," Zoe said.

"My principal concern, Zoe, has been to care for our students. The new Igigi children seem to hurt each other frequently in combat classes—and hurt our children even more frequently." She looked at the clock. "Off you go, Zoe. Good luck to you."

The halls teemed with students headed for the dorms after their last class of the day. Zoe tried to walk quickly without attracting attention, but everyone stopped to stare at her. She kept her head down.

"Zoe!" someone screamed in delight a split second before three teens mobbed her, all hugging her and asking questions. The Valkyries: Priya, Paige, and Makena.

"Let's get her to her room," Makena said. "Time for questions later."

They formed a protective circle around her, glaring menacingly at anyone who looked like they might want to cause trouble.

"Where's my room?" Zoe asked.

"Same as before, apparently," Priya said.

"You mean I'm still roommates with Lin?"

Priya nodded. Zoe was surprised. But then, maybe Lin didn't have a say.

"Everything is exactly how it was before," Paige said. "Can't you tell?"

. . .

Shortly after cleaning up and changing into her school uniform, Zoe ate dinner in the Great Hall with all the Valkyries—Lin included. She tried to ignore the staring and whispering. She told her friends everything that had happened to her since "the Battle"—as everyone now called it—minus the part about sharing her cell with Professor Chao. And the fact that Ragnar was her father.

"So, no people, no window, no Internet . . . nothing?" Paige asked. "How did you stay sane?"

"I . . . honestly don't think I did. I started . . . seeing things." She locked eyes with Professor Chao, standing at the window. He shook his head.

"Like, hallucinating, you mean?" Priya asked.

"I . . . don't think I'm well," she confessed.

"None of us are," Lin said, eliciting an awkward silence.

"So, tell me about you guys," Zoe said. "I have so many questions. What have I missed?"

"Well," Priya began, "your old classmates arrived soon after the Battle. Apparently, when you defected last year, they were told that you were a traitor, so they hated you. Then, they were told that it was all a ruse, so you were their hero. Then, you wound up defecting for real, so now they all hate you even more than before. As for everyone here, they know you came here to kill Lin's dad and that you called in the attack, so they hate you for that—but they also know you were fighting with us and that you tried to kill Ragnar. So, they don't know what to think."

Zoe nodded. She'd expected as much.

"Your old classmates . . ." Paige said, ". . . they're *scary*. Things haven't been easy for us since they got here. We outnumber them—unless you count the kids in the new wing—but we're still basically their punching bags. Especially Lin, since she's the daughter of the famous Professor Chao."

"In fairness, it's also because Lin keeps picking fights with them," Makena interjected.

Lin shrugged. "What do you want me to do? They taunt me, mock my dad . . . I can't just let it go."

Priya put her hand on Lin's shoulder.

Poor Lin. It couldn't have been easy for her. "Are you still the Valkyries?" Zoe asked.

"No," Makena said. "There's no more Doom. Ragnar says we have more important things to do."

Zoe wasn't surprised. It wasn't like she wanted to play games anymore, either. "Makena, I didn't even think you'd be here. You were in your final year."

"They wouldn't let any of us leave. Everyone has to take remedial classes in addition to regular classes, to teach us what they already taught the Igigi. At first, that included torture resistance training."

"Oh no," Zoe said.

"But after the first day," Priya said, "Lin's mom went ballistic. She and all the other professors revolted, saying they wouldn't teach anymore unless it stopped."

"The next day," Lin said, "Ragnar told us he'd 'reconsidered' and decided to abandon the practice altogether, since the Anunnaki are pretty much all defeated and the Typicals won't be a threat for much longer. So . . . yay, Mom."

"I'm so sorry you had to experience even one day of that, though," Zoe said.

"Hey, it wasn't the *worst* day of my life," Lin said, and Zoe winced.

"Anyway," Makena said, "the seniors are stuck taking nothing but remedial classes for another year. Mainly, though, they want us to be properly 'reeducated.'"

"Brainwashed, they mean," said Paige. "We're all prisoners here. The new school year officially starts tomorrow, with a new cohort of first-years arriving, but none of us were allowed to go home for the summer, or even to call our parents."

"I miss my family," Priya said. "My parents, my brothers and sisters . . . I missed my oldest sister's wedding in Mumbai. I hope they're all okay." Lin squeezed her hand comfortingly.

Zoe hadn't considered this. "You mean, *nobody* has heard from their parents? No phones, no Internet, not even letters?"

"We know nothing," Makena said. "They say our families haven't been harmed, but we have no way of knowing that. We don't know what they've been told, if they've been compelled, or if they're even still alive."

"I'm so sorry," Zoe said.

"It's not your fault," Paige said. "No one blames you. At least, *we* don't." They all nodded.

"Lin explained everything that happened," Priya said. "We get it. We're just glad you're on our side now."

Zoe was confused. If Lin had explained, then why didn't they hate her?

"That said . . ." Paige said, "I'd like to know how exactly you're different from the Zoe we all knew. I mean, I know you chose our side, but you're both the new you *and* the old you now, right?"

Zoe thought about it. "It's . . . strange. You wouldn't have liked me before. I was raised as Igigi. It's basically a cult. We spent our entire childhood being indoctrinated into its beliefs. And I *believed*. I wanted the world to be a better place, free from wars, free from suffering and exploitation, free from the threat of extinction. I wanted the rivers and oceans and air to be clean and the rainforests left alone. And I was taught that all this was possible except that the Anunnaki literally didn't care if the world burned so long as they got rich."

"Yeah," Lin said. "We've been listening to the same lectures for the past four months. What they always leave out, though, is the part about free will. It's kind of important." The others nodded.

Zoe took a deep breath. "Yeah, I agree that free will is important, but . . . I have to admit, I'm conflicted. I mean, is it more important than preventing the end of the world? If we had a crystal ball and we *knew* that some world leader was going to start a nuclear war, we would do *anything* to stop it, wouldn't we?"

"Wait," Makena said. "You agree with the Igigi?"

"No," Zoe said, "but not because I believe in absolute non-interference. We all know the world is in danger, but we stick our heads in the sand and pretend there's nothing we can do. Except, *we* actually can do something. And if we *can* save the world, then I think we have to try. My problem with the Igigi is that I don't believe their motives. Look at what they've done. They experimented with human cloning and genetic engineering for who knows how long, creating who knows how many failed attempts that they just . . . threw away, probably? They raised children in a bunker and trained them to be soldiers. They attacked this school, killed people, now are brainwashing everyone who's left. They say it's necessary for the 'greater good,' but it's really just about them being in power. They don't think Typicals are our equals. They want to rule the world like gods."

"So . . . you think both sides are bad?" Paige asked.

Zoe shrugged. "Basically, but for different reasons. Regardless, Ragnar—and his master, Marduk—have to be stopped."

"More than just stopped," Lin muttered, sparking an uncomfortable silence.

"Speaking of the Igigi kids," Paige said, changing the subject, "I guess I always figured they'd all look like you and Ethan—kind of Scandinavian. You know, since you were all created in test tubes or whatever. But they look like they're from all over the world, just like the rest of us. What's with that?"

Zoe shook her head. "I don't know for sure, but I always figured it was so we could be deployed as spies anywhere in the world. We were taught a lot of languages, and we each had some core languages that we were *forced* to learn really well. Ethan and I had to become fluent in German, Swedish, Danish, Finnish, and Norwegian, for instance, because we look like we could be from those countries. Other kids who look like they could be from China were forced to become fluent in Mandarin and Cantonese."

"By the way," Priya said, as an Igigi girl walked by, holding an Anunnaki boy's hand, "did you know they loosened the whole no-dating rule?"

"What do you mean?" Zoe asked.

"You told us that you guys weren't allowed to date each other at your old school, right? Well, they're fine with the Igigi kids dating us—and with us Anunnaki dating each other. Just no dating among the Igigi kids, for some reason."

Zoe thought about that. What a weird rule. They'd always been told that love was a weakness. It made you vulnerable. So why create rules about who could date whom?

"You haven't asked about him yet," Paige said, interrupting her thoughts.

"Who?" Zoe asked, knowing exactly who they meant.

"Ethan."

Zoe scowled. "I don't really care."

"He saved your life, didn't he?"

"He saved *Ragnar's* life. I would have killed Ragnar right then and there if Ethan hadn't stopped me."

"Yeah, and you would have died a second later," Lin said. "And I'd have been robbed of the chance to kill Ragnar myself."

Zoe couldn't tell which outcome would have bothered Lin more. "Ethan *betrayed* me."

"If so, he seems to have paid for it," Makena said.

"What do you mean?"

"He was locked up for as long as you were," Paige said. "Down in the basement. He was only released yesterday."

Ragnar hadn't mentioned that. She'd figured Ethan might have been disciplined for fighting alongside her, but he'd saved Ragnar's life. Surely that ought to have counted for something. Why lock him up for so long?

"So, how did he look?" she asked, reluctantly.

In response, Lin just nodded to where Ethan sat alone at a table on the other side of the room. He looked gaunt, and his hair was long and disheveled. His face was bruised, too, like he'd recently been in a fight. He met her gaze without any sense of recognition. He looked . . . defeated. He returned to his food, staring at his plate.

"I'm not sure if he's spoken to anyone yet," Priya said. "After the Battle, he disappeared, and word got out that his defection had all been a ruse—that the only reason he fought with us was because of you."

"So, all his old friends here abandoned him," Paige continued. "And the Igigi kids apparently beat him up as soon as he got out. I heard he didn't even fight back."

Zoe felt torn. For months, she'd been furious with him for saving Ragnar, but then again, she'd imagined him strutting through the hallways, the king of the Igigi kids—not in solitary, like her. Why did he look like he'd suffered more than she had? As she watched, a passing Igigi boy slapped Ethan hard on the back of the head, making his friends laugh.

"Yeah, that one's a real delight," Lin said. "I've had my share of run-ins with him already."

Zoe nodded. "Kyle. I've always disliked him." The boys took turns smacking Ethan, who did nothing except wince. What was wrong with him? "Wait, what sort of run-ins?" When Lin didn't answer, she turned to the others.

"The violent sort," Makena said. "The last was a full-fledged fight in the halls. Lin gave as good as she got. I doubt he'll pick a fight with her again."

"Not alone, maybe," Priya said, "but they travel in a pack."

"We do, too," Paige said.

"Yeah, to protect ourselves," Priya replied. "We don't pick them off if they stray from their pack."

"Maybe we should start," Paige mumbled.

"No," Zoe said. She looked at each of her friends. "That's not who we are. Defending ourselves is one thing. *Maybe* an immediate retaliation to discourage future attacks. But we don't *start* fights."

Kyle and his friends were just sitting down to eat when they caught sight of Zoe. Kyle stopped halfway to his chair, and then he smirked. Leaving their trays, he and his pack sauntered over.

"Here we go," Lin said, standing up with the others. Zoe, though, remained sitting and didn't even look up.

"Zoeeeeeee," Kyle drawled. "He finally let you out, did he? I'm surprised. If I were in charge, you'd still be rotting in there after what you did."

"Why would you ever be in charge, Kyle?" Zoe asked.

He scowled. "Because a lot has changed since you left, that's why." He seemed to be puffing out his chest.

Zoe sipped her water, seemingly unperturbed. She tried to channel Professor Chao, calmly drinking his tea when the godlings surrounded them in the restaurant. "And what exactly do you think has changed?"

"You and Ethan aren't the top dogs anymore," he said.

Zoe smiled. Kyle was a decent enough fighter, but he'd always been far too concerned about where he ranked. "You mean that with me and Ethan gone, you filled the void we created—a position you never could have risen to otherwise?" She kept eating without looking up at him, knowing he desperately wanted her to acknowledge his new standing.

Kyle balled his fists and stepped forward. "I'm a lot stronger than before, *Zoe*."

Strength was the only thing Kyle had ever respected, so time for a display of power. Rather than stand up, Zoe nonchalantly levitated herself out of her chair until she stood facing Kyle. Everyone stepped back in surprise, including her friends. "You think you're the only one stronger than before, *Kyle*?" She held out her hand, palm up, and willed a ball of crackling plasma into it.

"Whoa," Paige gasped, as everyone took another step back.

Zoe stared at the ball, transfixed, then began to roll it back and forth from her palm to the back of her hand while everyone watched, slack-jawed. She stopped, palm up at chin level, and locked eyes with Kyle.

"You have no idea."

Like blowing a kiss, she sent the plasma ball hurtling toward him. She dissipated it before it could touch him, but nevertheless, he scrambled backwards on his hands and feet. Zoe could feel the entire Great Hall watching. She stepped forward. Now that she had established her dominance, it was time to relinquish it.

She offered Kyle her hand. "It's okay," she said, when he looked hesitant. "We're not enemies." He took her hand, and she pulled him to his feet. "None of us are enemies. We're all prisoners here. We're all in this together, and we need to figure out what we're going to do—together."

Zoe sat back down and picked up her fork, as if nothing had just happened. Kyle and his friends slowly returned to their table, and after a moment, the Valkyries resumed their seats, too.

"So," Lin said, eventually. "You've come a long way. I remember when you couldn't lift a hundred-gram weight in Professor Martinov's class unless you were angry."

"Yeah, you also couldn't conjure balls of electricity like a freaking wizard," Paige said. "What the heck was that?"

"I had . . . a lot of time on my hands."

"Yes, it was very impressive," Makena said. "But I'm more interested in what you said to Kyle just now. You told us you were on our side, but now it sounds like you're not on *anyone's* side. You want to unite us?"

Zoe sighed. "Do you want the Igigi kids picking on you forever?"

"No," Makena snarled, "but I don't want to *join* them, either!"

"Do you know why Ragnar let me out? Or, at least, why he *said* he let me out?" She looked at each of them. "To unite us. To stop his New Gods from preying on you."

"And you're going to do what he wants?" Lin cried, incredulously.

"No!" Zoe said, quickly. "He wants me to unite us in *his* cause. I want to unite us in *mine*."

"And what cause is that?" Makena demanded.

"To stop him!" She looked to each of them in turn. "To stop Ragnar and Marduk from taking over the world and hunting down all the Telepaths."

"But how are you going to convince them to go against their masters?" Priya asked.

"Not just their masters," Paige added, "Marduk is, what, their *god*?"

Zoe took a deep breath. "I don't know yet. When I woke up this morning, I didn't even know the Academy was still here. But I do know that ideas are like viruses. They spread. We need to somehow show the Igigi kids that the attack on this school—and on Telepaths everywhere—was wrong. And that we have a plan that's better than Marduk's."

"Do we?" Paige asked.

Zoe shook her head. "Not yet. Just what we were talking about before. We're part of this world, so we should be allowed to make it better. But ruling it isn't the answer, either. There has to be a better way."

They sat in silence for a while. Finally, Lin spoke. "Okay, Zoe. I'll be part of this plan-to-make-a-plan. Except for one thing. You said you want to *stop* Ragnar." She shook her head. "That's not good enough. I'm going to *kill* Ragnar. Understood? Ragnar is going die by *my* hand."

The entire table grew very quiet and uncomfortable. Zoe hadn't seen this coming. She'd been so caught up in her own desire for vengeance that she hadn't stopped to think that Lin had even more reason to want revenge of her own. Lin's eyes burned with hatred. But she was no match for Ragnar and might never be. She would most likely get herself killed. Even if she somehow succeeded, how would the act of killing for the sake of revenge change her?

In that back of her mind, though, she was worried that maybe there was another reason she didn't like this idea. Ragnar was her father. Was it possible her feelings for him were changing? She had to admit, she felt more connected to the world and its history now. She found herself wondering what Ragnar's life had been like and if he had always been a bad man or if he had started out good. She wanted to know everything about her mother—and her sisters, who'd died so young. Was that why he'd told her? To cut through her hate and connect with her? To make her curious about her ancestry, which would forever remain a secret if she killed him?

Zoe finally nodded. "He dies by your hand, Lin. For what he did to your dad."

4

FREE TIME

Evenings were free time, but Zoe wasn't ready to risk any more confrontations just yet. She just wanted to chill in her room. As they rounded a corner on their way to the dorms, Zoe stopped in her tracks. Her jaw dropped.

"What's wrong?" Makena asked, looking worriedly at Zoe.

Zoe slowly approached the man mopping the hallway with his head down. "Fasil?" she said.

The man jumped. His eyes widened in recognition before he dropped his gaze to the floor again, clutching his mop tightly. "My lady," he said, nodding vigorously.

"I thought you were dead," Zoe said. As she drew near, the man cringed and hugged the broomstick close. "Do you remember me?"

"Yes, Lady Zoe, Worm remembers you." He nodded at the floor.

"You know him?" Priya asked.

"This is Fasil Nazari," she said, thrown off not only by the fact that Fasil was still alive but also referring to himself in the third person as "Worm." "He tried to kill me in the hospital last year. I took him hostage, but his people turned on him instead of standing down. He shoved them telekinetically while I ran. I assumed they killed him." She turned back to

Fasil. "How did you survive?"

"Worm fought them off for a bit, my lady, then threw his sword down and ran."

"So, how did you come to be the custodian here?" Lin asked.

"Captured, my lady. But Master Ragnar was kind. Worm deserved to be executed."

"For . . . trying to kill me?" Zoe asked, uncertainly.

Fasil looked like he desperately wanted to avoid this conversation. "For failing to bring you in, my lady. And for losing control of my subordinates. And for being a coward." He was nodding vigorously again. "Master Ragnar was very angry. Said Worm was pathetic and a disgrace. But Worm begged Master to spare his life, and Master was merciful. He said Worm could live and serve the lords and ladies. Worm is so grateful."

"I see," Zoe said, unsure how to feel about this. Fasil hadn't been punished for trying to kill her but because he'd been incompetent at it. He wasn't a good person, but did anyone deserve this? He had clearly been tortured and broken. But he was also alive, so was that better or worse than execution? She was curious about something, though. "Do you still have your Abilities, Fasil?"

"It's Worm now, my lady. And no, Worm was only a godling, so once the injections stopped, the Abilities faded away."

Zoe nodded. "Well . . . I guess we'll see you around, Fasil."

"Worm, my lady," he said, nodding obsequiously as they continued on their way.

"That was weird," Paige said after a long while.

. . .

After so long in solitary, Zoe's dorm room felt surreal. Honestly, nothing felt real anymore. The sounds and smells of the school felt like they belonged to a lifetime ago. She kept thinking she would blink and wake up in her cell.

Lin hadn't spoken since leaving Fasil and now packed a workout bag in silence.

"I'm sorry," Zoe blurted. "I'm so sorry, Lin. For everything."

Lin didn't look up. "For getting my dad killed, you mean?"

Zoe winced.

"Or for not killing him yourself after gaining his trust? That was your plan, right? That was what you came here to do."

Zoe hugged her chest helplessly.

"I was your *friend*, Zoe. And the whole time, it was just a joke to you. A way to get close to us, so you could betray us."

"No," Zoe said. "Lin, no. I *was* your friend. I *am* your friend."

"You're not my friend," Lin said, finally looking at her. The contempt in her tone was cutting. "A friend would never have done what you did."

"I'm sorry. I—"

"A *friend*," Lin continued, advancing on her, "wouldn't have spent an entire year lying to us, pretending to be someone she's not."

"I wasn't lying. I didn't remember anything."

"Yeah, by choice! The whole amnesia thing might have been real, but it was all part of the plan, right? *Your* plan. You weren't even following orders—the whole thing was your idea!"

Zoe nodded, tears rolling down her cheeks.

"You came here for the sole purpose of killing my dad. And why? To impress Ragnar?"

"I was a different person—"

"You were a *horrible* person!" Lin roared, forcing Zoe back against the door. "And yeah, I get that you became a different person while you had amnesia—but you're *both* people now, aren't you? The old and the new Zoe. Which means you're every bit as much the horrible person who came here to kill my dad as you are the person I thought was my friend!"

Lin punched the wall beside Zoe's head, making her flinch. Then Lin backed up, fists clenched, clearly trying to control herself. "You want to know the worst part, Zoe? Despite everything you did, everyone thinks I should forgive you. Makena, Paige, Priya—even my own mom. They don't say it outright, but they all make excuses for you, talk about how you joined us in the end, tell me how it isn't good for me to carry around this much anger."

"I don't deserve your forgiveness," Zoe said, staring at the ground.

"No, you don't. Because of you, my dad was executed on his knees. I saw it happen. And I can't *stop* seeing it. It replays over and over in my head. Do you have any idea what that's like?"

Zoe didn't know what to say. She knew exactly what it was like.

Lin grabbed her bag. "Get out of my way," she said. "I need to get away from you."

Once Lin had stormed off, Zoe huddled in a ball on her bed, rocking back and forth.

"Well, that could have gone better," Professor Chao said, startling her. He sat at the foot of her bed.

"You think?"

"She will come around eventually," he said.

"I'm not so sure of that. She has every right to hate me."

"She does not hate you. She just needs to understand that forgiving you does not mean betraying me. *I* forgave you, after all."

"Yeah, but I can't tell her that," Zoe said.

"Why not?"

"Because it would be manipulative!"

"The truth is manipulative?"

Zoe had no answer to that.

"I worry about her," the professor said. "She always used to smile and laugh. Her eyes would sparkle, and she would light up any room she entered. Now, her anger consumes her. She spends all her time training and fighting. She's in the dojo right now. I can feel her rage from here.

Ultimately, her fixation on revenge will get her killed. You cannot allow her to attempt to kill Ragnar. She will die."

"In one-on-one combat, sure," Zoe said. "But she could take him by surprise. Assassinate him."

"There is a saying that has been around for a very long time, in one form or another, about stabbing the devil in the back." He leveled his gaze at her. "What if you miss?"

Zoe thought about that. As far as she knew, she had never heard that saying. Was it just hidden away somewhere in her subconscious that her hallucination could access, or had she just made it up?

She stood up. "I'm going to the dojo."

"I doubt she wants you there," Professor Chao said.

"I'm sure you're right."

● ● ●

Zoe quietly slipped inside the deconsecrated church that was the dojo and walked to the back, keeping to the shadows. She hadn't been here since that fateful day when she'd meditated with Professor Chao, trying to pinpoint the source of her anger. She half-expected to see him walk through the door or drop down from the rafters, and she stiffened at the sight of him actually up there. A lot of students—both Igigi and Anunnaki—were training tonight, with no adult supervision. Professor Chao would never have allowed this, but it was the sort of practice that Ragnar had always encouraged. Training was no substitute for actual combat.

In the middle of the mat, encircled by cheering students, Lin squared off against Kyle. They had been fighting for a while already—judging by the blood dripping from their mouths and on the white tape Lin had wrapped around her hands like a Muay Thai fighter.

Kyle was much bigger than Lin, so he had the advantages of weight, strength, and reach. He also had the advantages of genetic engineering and an entire childhood spent training to be a soldier. By contrast, Lin was light and nimble and had the distinction of being the only person in the world to have been trained since toddlerdom by Professor Chao. Her biggest advantage, though, seemed to be her fury—she looked like she literally wanted to kill her opponent.

Kyle's eyes, on the other hand, were full of fear, like he deeply regretted starting this fight.

"Say it again," Lin demanded, sidestepping a punch and delivering a quick blow to the side of his head before dancing out of his reach. "I dare you to say it again."

"Your father—" But he was interrupted by a reverse roundhouse kick to the head.

"My father what?" Lin delivered a flurry of punches and kicks that Kyle tried his best to block—until his feet were swept out from under him. He curled up like a turtle as Lin rained blow after blow down upon him. "My father what? Say it! My father what?"

Suddenly, one of Kyle's friends tackled Lin. Makena—who Zoe hadn't even noticed—jumped in to pull him off her. Then, an Igigi girl hit Makena, who leveled her with an oh-it's-on look, and suddenly all hell broke loose and the dojo erupted into an all-out brawl.

Zoe darted into the fray and quickly found herself fighting back-to-back with Lin. She hadn't fought in so long, she had to admit it was kind of fun. It did not, however, serve to unite the Anunnaki and Igigi in any way. When the fighting slowed, Zoe smiled at Lin—who slapped her.

"I didn't ask for your help!" Lin screamed.

Zoe was stunned. Everyone was stunned.

Lin pushed her. "I don't *need* your help!"

"Lin—" Makena started, but Lin shrugged her off and pushed Zoe again.

"I've done just fine without you! Why did you have to come back?"

She punched Zoe in the face, and Zoe just stood there with her hands at her sides. "You were my friend! My *best* friend! And my dad is *dead* because of you!" She slammed her fist into Zoe's face.

"Stop it!" Makena yelled.

"Except, you know what, Zoe? It's actually *my* fault. Because I trusted you. When the old you returned and I caught you, I couldn't bear to never see *my* Zoe again. So, I made you open that stupid brooch. And once you were back, I couldn't imagine you ever hurting me, so I lowered my shields and let you escape. If I had just followed the plan and put you in a cell, where you belonged, maybe we would've been ready for the attack and my dad might still be alive!" She struck Zoe again, and this time, Zoe fell to her knees.

"No," Zoe said, shaking her head and spitting out blood. "It wasn't your fault. The attack was already coming. The security system was already down. If you'd done what I said, the new me would've been gone forever. Because of you, I was able to help during the Battle."

"A lot of good that did! You couldn't save my dad. You couldn't even *avenge* him. He's dead and you're still here, like nothing—" Another punch. "Even—" And another. "Happened!" And again. "Fight back!" She punched Zoe again.

Barely conscious, Zoe shook her head. She was pretty sure her nose was broken, and she could feel her left eye closing. "No," she managed to say. She deserved this.

Lin dropped to her knees in tears. "How am I supposed to forgive you? I want my best friend back, but I am angry *all the time*."

"It's okay," Zoe mumbled. "You don't have to forgive me. I'll always be your friend." She felt a hand on her shoulder and turned to see that it was Professor Chao, crouched between her and Lin, one hand on each of them.

Lin screamed and punched Zoe, and everything went black.

. . .

Zoe slowly came to in the infirmary. Given the dim lighting, she guessed it was very late. There was no one else here, save for Professor Yeoh, dozing off at her desk. Zoe sat up, waking her.

"They've all gone back to their dorm rooms," Professor Yeoh said, getting up and approaching Zoe's bed. "That was some brawl. I treated almost a dozen students, but you definitely got the worst of it." She shook her head. "My husband would have been horrified. Lin wouldn't say what happened. Just dropped you off and left. Wouldn't even let me treat her hands. Do *you* want to tell me what happened?"

Zoe looked at the empty chair beside her bed. There'd been a time when Lin would've been sitting there, waiting for her to wake up. She shook her head. "No, ma'am."

"Are you sure?" Professor Yeoh shone a light into Zoe's eyes. "I know you children have your code of honour, but whoever did this to you shouldn't get away with it. Follow my finger, please." After a moment, she switched off the light. "No lingering concussion. I fixed your broken nose and your loose teeth. The swelling should go down in a day or two. You can stay here for the night or go back to your room, whichever you prefer."

"Thank you, Professor," Zoe said, swinging her legs out from under the covers. "But I just want to sleep in my old bed. It's been a long time . . . and a very long day."

Heading back to her dorm, Zoe paused to listen. She could have sworn she'd heard someone else's footsteps. She looked behind her at the long, dark, empty hallway and waited a full minute before continuing. Maybe it was her imagination, but if not—and someone really was following her—she felt too physically and emotionally drained to deal with it.

She snuck into her room and closed the door gently so as to not wake

Lin. She crawled under her covers and closed her eyes, thinking back to this morning in her cell, when Professor Chao had assured her that Lin would forgive her. If she'd ever needed validation that he was, indeed, just a hallucination, she had it now. Her worst fear had come true. What should she do now? Keep trying to win Lin over? Give her space? Ask to switch rooms?

"I'm sorry," Lin said from her bed at the far end of the room.

Zoe caught her breath. "I didn't mean to wake you," she said.

"You didn't. I can't sleep, on account of just having beaten up my best friend."

"It's okay. We both know I deserved it."

"*No*, Zoe. It's not okay, and you *didn't* deserve it. Jeez." They were silent for a bit. "I don't understand what came over me."

Zoe made a decision. "Listen . . . I was going to tell you this later, but . . . there's something you should know. Your dad spoke to me at the end. In my head, just before he died."

Lin bolted upright in bed. "What? Why? What did he say?"

"He said, 'Protect them in the days ahead.'"

Zoe wished she could see Lin's face in the dark.

"Why would he say that?" Lin asked after a time. "Protect who? Why would his last words be to you and not me?"

"I was in front of him, in his field of vision," Zoe said. "He wanted me to protect you and your mom after he was gone. I'm sure that's what he meant."

Lin shook her head. "No, he wouldn't have said that to the person who had just betrayed him."

"He knew," Zoe said. "What the old me was planning. I don't know how, but he knew. After you woke up the new me, I was in a state of chaos. Two versions of me fighting for control. When the Battle started, I followed him. The old me wanted to stab him in the back and fulfill her mission, but the new me wanted to switch sides. Your dad had shown me nothing but kindness and was the closest thing to a father I had ever known. And then he turned to face me. He *knew* what was going on in my head, and he just . . . opened his arms wide, giving me the freedom to choose. I don't know if he really would've let me stab him, but if so, I was going to have to look him in the eyes while I did it. And his eyes were full of such compassion. That's when I chose to fight by his side."

Lin was silent, so Zoe went on. "I tried to save him. I really did. I tried to kill Ragnar before he could reach your dad, but he swatted me aside like a bug. I tried to kill Ragnar afterward, to avenge him, but Ethan stopped me."

"They'd have killed you," Lin whispered.

"But Ragnar would be dead. And I would've . . . atoned . . . instead of being here, feeling all this . . . guilt. I'd do anything not to have all this guilt—to go back in time and do things differently. I don't know if I can ever earn your forgiveness, Lin. I *want* it. More than anything else in the whole world, I want to make things right with you. But I want you to know that if you can't ever forgive me, I understand, and even if you hate me and want nothing more to do with me, you will always be *my* best friend. And I will do everything I can to honour your dad's last wish and to be the person he thought I could be."

5

PHYSICS

The next morning at breakfast, the first-years who had just arrived looked to be in shock. They had probably just learned of the Battle and that they might never go home again. Some looked like they'd spent the whole night crying. Some of the older kids consoled them, but others mocked them. Zoe figured this was probably a pretty good litmus test to determine who had fallen in line with the new establishment's dogma and who hadn't.

Lin ate her breakfast and watched the first-years impassively. There'd been a time when her heart would have broken for them, Zoe knew, but now, she was emotionless.

"We should train together," Lin said, out of the blue. "Now that you're a whole, integrated person again, are you better than you were before? At fighting, I mean. Before, you were good, but it was all instinctive. Now, you remember all your training. Does it help?"

Zoe thought about it. "I don't know. Maybe?"

"It should at least allow you to teach now, right?"

Zoe shrugged. "I guess?"

"Good," Lin said, nodding. "Teach me everything you know. I need to get better. Every time I fight an Igigi kid, I learn something, but it would be so much better to have proper instruction instead of always learning the hard way. You can 'make things right' by teaching me what you know."

Was this Lin's way of extending an olive branch? "Of course," Zoe said.

"Good. Hey, look, there's Pacha."

He wandered into the Great Hall with his tray of food.

"I hope the Igigi haven't been picking on him," Zoe said.

"Nope. Just the opposite, actually. They all seem to be in awe of him."

Zoe gaped at Lin. "Really?"

"Yup. He's the strongest telekinetic here. Stronger than any of them, even, despite their 'superhuman' DNA. Nobody touches him."

Pacha sat down at a table of other second-years. He noticed Zoe and lifted his hand in a subtle wave. He didn't smile, though. Zoe waved back.

"He hasn't been indoctrinated, right? He's one of us?"

Lin nodded. "I'd assume so. He's Pacha. A pacifist. Hard to believe he'd get on board with the whole taking-over-the-world thing. The Igigi are pretty impressed with Paige's telekinesis, too. Paige isn't at Pacha's level, but they're as strong as any of the Igigi. I think the Igigi kids were under the impression that all of us natural-born Telepaths would be weaklings."

They were silent a bit. "You're stronger now, too," Lin said. "Your Abilities. You levitated yourself—and without being angry. And the weird electricity thing. I've never even heard of that. You really just taught yourself?"

"It just . . . happened one day," Zoe said. She wasn't ready to admit that her hallucination of Lin's dad had taught her a new Ability. "It's called electrokinesis, I think." She wondered if she'd just made that up.

Suddenly, Lin looked up over Zoe's shoulder and smiled. "Hey, you!"

"Hey, yourself," Priya said, sitting down next to Lin. "You didn't come get me on your way down."

"Oh, I'm sorry!" Lin said.

"It's okay." Priya rubbed Lin's shoulder. "Old habits, I get it. What are we talking about?"

"Electrokinesis," Lin said. "Or whatever that thing Zoe can do now is called."

"You need to show me how you do that," Priya said. "It must be similar to what I do with ferrokinesis. I mean, I may not be *thinking* about creating an electromagnetic field, but that's what I'm really doing when I move or bend metal objects."

Zoe hadn't thought about that. "Huh," she said. "That's true. That would explain why I was able to start bending metal right around the same time I was able to generate electricity."

"Cool," Priya said. "You should've used that to bend your metal bars and break out."

Zoe scowled. "There were no bars."

"A door, then," Priya countered. "The door might've been metal, right? If not, you're strong in telekinesis—you probably could've broken the door down. Did you try?"

"Priya," Lin said.

"I'm just wondering why she didn't try to escape. I mean, after everything that happened that day and not knowing what happened to you . . . I would've tried anything to get back to you and make sure you were okay."

Zoe felt her anger rising. Who did Priya think she was, accusing her of not caring about Lin? She was behaving like . . .

Wait. She looked back and forth between Lin and Priya. Oh. She stood up with her tray in hand.

"I have to go," she said.

"Zoe," Lin began.

She cut her off. "It's okay. You two talk."

"What the hell, Priya?" Zoe heard Lin say as she went to drop off her tray. That was unexpected. Although, looking back, maybe not *so* unexpected? In any event, Zoe had more important things to worry about than teen drama. The problem was that she had no idea where to start. When all was said and done, she was a teenage girl trying to prevent a powerful Viking and his godlike master from taking over the world.

She decided to start with what needed to be done. Going back to class seemed weird after everything she'd been through, but she had to do it, so she went to the administration office to see if they had a schedule for her. They did. In a folder with her name on it in big letters, just lying on the counter.

She made her way to her first class early and found Professor Martinov staring out the window, alone. As always, he wore his trademark cape. Maybe someday it *would* come back into fashion. He turned when she entered and smiled. Not his usual exuberant smile but rather a sad, stoic one. He approached her with arms wide and wrapped her in a hug. Stunned, Zoe hugged him back.

"There are rough days ahead of us," he whispered. "He would want us to fight." He pulled back to look her in the eyes. "I am so glad you have joined us again."

"I'm so glad you're still here," Zoe said. "I was afraid you were dead."

"Me? No. One of them just got lucky and bonked me on the head, that's all."

"What did they do to you afterward?" Zoe asked. "Was it bad?"

"No, no, it was nothing. I barely remember it. Not like you. We heard about your incarceration. I am sorry you had to endure that."

"It wasn't so bad," Zoe said. "I wasn't tortured. Just . . . left alone."

The professor nodded. "Alone to go mad, yes. Simply a different type of torture." He held her shoulders. "But you persevered, and now here you are, back in school."

Zoe looked around the classroom. "It's surreal. It feels like I was here a lifetime ago, back when I was a child. How am I supposed to care about classes now, after everything that's happened? With everything that's *going* to happen?"

Professor Martinov nodded. "I understand. Despite your youth, you are no longer a child. Think of this as an opportunity to improve your Abilities as much as you can, while we bide our time."

"Is there a plan, though?" Zoe implored. "Does anyone have a plan? And can I help? Or is everyone just waiting, hoping an opportunity will arise? They tried to kill Ragnar yesterday, you know. But . . . they had to abort."

Just then, students began filtering in. "We will talk later," he said, gesturing for her to find a seat. He walked behind his desk.

Zoe chose a seat at random and watched the kids file in. As expected for Advanced Telekinesis, they were all Igigi—except for Paige and Pacha, who chose to sit on either side of her.

"It's good to see you again," Pacha murmured in her ear. "I'm glad you're back."

"It's good to see you again, too, Pacha," she replied. "I'm glad to be back."

Ethan entered with his eyes down and sat as far from Zoe as he could. Zoe could feel her former classmates' eyes boring holes through her, and she heard a lot of whispering.

"Traitor," someone coughed, eliciting laughter.

Zoe pretended not to notice. With her mind, she picked up a piece of chalk and began writing the word *TRAITOR* in big letters on the chalkboard while Professor Martinov tried to get the class to settle down. The Igigi kids assumed one of them was doing it and laughed even harder—until Zoe added a question mark at the end. She kept writing, as quickly as she could now. *THEY LIE TO US.* That caused a stir.

"Settle down!" the professor yelled, willing the piece of chalk to his fingers and putting it back in its place.

The intercom suddenly came on. "Professor Martinov, please send

Zoe to the office. Immediately."

Zoe sighed. "Well, that didn't take long." She stood and faced the class. "If you want to know why I switched sides, come talk to me privately sometime."

. . .

Zoe arrived back at the administration office expecting to be directed to a meeting with an angry Headmaster Ragnar. Instead, she was directed to the assistant headmaster's office. She hadn't even known there was such a thing. She opened the door and stopped in her tracks. Hands interlocked on the desk in front of her, Miss Gillespie smiled smugly.

"Hello again, Zoe. It's been a long time. Won't you take a seat?"

Zoe cautiously closed the door behind her and sat. "Miss Gillespie. You've been promoted, I see. But who will kill the frogs now?"

Miss Gillespie ignored the barb. "The headmaster was called away to attend to urgent matters and won't return until this afternoon," she said, stiffly. "I am in charge during his absence, and I have been given specific instructions pertaining to you."

"How long has it been since you attended the Academy?" Zoe asked. "I mean, I know it wasn't located here in Canada, but I assume you were a student once. Do any of the faculty remember you? They must be proud to see how far you've come."

Miss Gillespie took a deep breath. "That was a very inflammatory message you wrote on the chalkboard. Do you think that's what our headmaster meant when he said he wanted you to help unite the Igigi and Anunnaki students?"

"I don't know. He never gave me specific instructions, so I assumed I should use my best judgment."

"And your best judgment is to call us liars?"

Zoe nodded. "Yes. I mean, I just got here and haven't had time to formulate a real plan, but yes, that's what I was thinking."

Miss Gillespie smiled. "And what lies, exactly, do you think we have told, Zoe?"

"Calling them all Anunnaki, for one. You used to be one of them, right? So, you know that's a lie."

"I know no such thing. They *are* Anunnaki, whether they know their own history or not."

"They're not what you told us they were."

"No? How many of them have you met? The professors here, certainly. A few at a safe house. And the Council, who actually represent and lead them all. What was your appraisal of the Council, Zoe?"

"Much better after Professor Chao took over."

"Don't deflect. What did you think of former Minister Lafleur and the other Council members, other than Professor Chao?"

Zoe didn't reply.

"Exactly. They were *exactly* as we described. Corrupt. Using their Abilities to further their own wealth and power while refusing to help the world in any way."

"I don't disagree, but they don't represent everyone."

"They *do*, though. Every single Council member was voted into power by Telepaths from all over the world to represent the voters' interests. And what do you think their interests are?"

Again, Zoe remained silent.

"We know it's not to make the world a better place," Miss Gillespie continued. "They refuse to interfere. So, what else might their interests be?"

"Not to be exposed," Zoe said.

"Certainly. Is that it, do you think? Nothing else? Just don't interfere and don't get caught?"

Still, Zoe had nothing to say.

"Would it surprise you to know that virtually every Anunnaki in the world, after graduating from here, goes on to become rich? In the top 1 percent, in fact. Nice houses, nice cars, nice yachts. Decadent, exactly as we told you."

"Look," Zoe said. "I met the Council. I'm aware that they were horrible people. But that doesn't mean I'm okay with taking over the world."

"The world will end soon if we don't do something. So how would you, Zoe, in your infinite wisdom, prevent that?"

"Not by force! Not by taking over and enslaving Typicals! We could be subtle. We could identify key people in positions of power or influence and subtly change their way of thinking without them even knowing it."

Miss Gillespie nodded. "Exactly. This is the plan."

Zoe blinked. "What?"

"You've just described Marduk's plan exactly. Our primary goal has to be to prevent the end of the world. Everything else is secondary. Wouldn't you agree?"

Zoe sat still, stunned.

"Wouldn't you agree, Zoe?"

Miss Gillespie waited patiently for an answer, and eventually, Zoe reluctantly nodded.

"Excellent. We are on the same page, then. Exposing our existence, fighting with Typicals . . . this would not help us achieve our primary goal. It would do the opposite. No, we must be subtle and stealthy and surgical, exactly as you have described."

"Wait . . ." Zoe said, trying to mount a defence. "Even if we're on the same page about our primary goal, we're not on the same page afterward. I don't agree with taking over the world."

Miss Gillespie smiled. "Of course. You are young and idealistic. You believe that everyone is born equal, that no one is superior to another."

"That's not idealistic," Zoe said. "That's a fundamental truth. And attacking this school, killing people—that was wrong. Hunting them down all over the world—that's wrong. The Igigi are the bad guys. Pure and simple."

Miss Gillespie sighed. "Again, you are young and idealistic. As we all were once." She looked out the window. "Tell me, Zoe. Would you say that the end ever justifies the means?"

"No!" Zoe blurted. "That's just what people say whenever they want to justify doing something terrible—like torturing children and telling them it's for their own good."

"Hmm." Miss Gillespie nodded, ignoring the accusation. "And yet, you, no doubt, would agree that compulsion is also wrong, but you would be willing to compel world leaders and influencers in the name of saving the world."

"Only as a last resort."

"Of course. Only as a last resort, which is where we currently find ourselves. So, in this case, you agree that the end does indeed justify the means." She didn't wait for Zoe to reluctantly agree this time. "So, let's explore that thought further. What if you knew that the only way to put this plan to save the world into action was to forcibly take over the Anunnaki? Does the end goal of saving the world still justify the means?"

"But you *didn't* know that," Zoe said. "You never tried to persuade the Anunnaki. You just built an army in secret and then launched an all-out attack against them."

"But what if we *did* know?"

"You *didn't*. You didn't have a crystal ball. Unless . . . you're claiming that Marduk can see the future, which I can't believe."

Miss Gillespie shrugged slightly. "Well, precognition *is* possible. You yourself have experienced seeing the path of bullets before they are fired. So, theoretically, a sufficiently powerful being could see further into the future. If anyone were capable of that, it would be Lord Marduk. But no, Lord Marduk has never claimed to see the future. But would you agree that with age comes wisdom?"

"For some, maybe," Zoe said.

"How about for you? Do you think you are the sort of person who will grow wiser over the years? You've existed for only fifteen, and already you believe yourself to be wiser than us. What about after hundreds or even *thousands* of years? Surely you would be wiser than you are today."

Zoe saw where this was going. "I think *I* would be, yes. But clearly not everyone gets wiser over time. Maybe you need to be humble enough to admit you're wrong sometimes, in order to learn."

"I agree! So then, let me ask you this, Zoe. Assume you have observed Typicals and Telepaths for thousands of years and that you truly believe that exposing yourself to the Anunnaki and trying to persuade them is simply too risky. The fate of the world is at stake. Assume you believe, in your wisdom, that the best chance to save the world is to *not* take that risk and to instead preemptively subdue the Anunnaki. Would you not do so? Or would you really play dice with the lives of eight billion people just to protect the interests of ten thousand Telepaths who have, thus far, shown themselves to be perfectly willing to watch the world burn?"

Zoe furrowed her brow. "This is ridiculous. You're basically asking me if I would behave as Marduk does if I believed everything he believes. But *everyone* believes they're the good guy. *Everyone* believes their actions are justified, that they're in the right. That doesn't make it true. I'm *not* Marduk, I *don't* believe what he believes, and I *wouldn't* have done what he did!"

"So, you're saying that, knowing the world could literally end in thirty minutes if one man were to push a button, you would have rolled the dice?" Miss Gillespie folded her hands neatly in front of her once again. "Thank goodness you are not the one in charge."

Zoe crossed her arms. She'd always hated Miss Gillespie.

Miss Gillespie sighed. "In any event, what's done is done, and now we have decisions to make. I have an assignment for you. Or rather, Master Ragnar does. For whatever reason, he seems to have taken an interest in you. Personally, I would have had you executed on the spot for your betrayal." She smiled.

Zoe smiled back. "Thank goodness you are not the one in charge."

Miss Gillespie's eyes turned cold. "Your assignment is this. We are where we are, and now we must save the world. So, come up with a plan. Devise a mission. If Master Ragnar approves, he will let you and a team of your choosing go out into the world to execute it. As long as you have someone proficient enough in compulsion on your team."

Zoe gaped. "Just like that?"

"Apparently. The old rules of non-interference are gone. As long as you don't expose our existence and your actions are preapproved, you can go out and do some good in the world. This is what you've been trained for, after all."

"I thought I was trained to make people's hearts explode."

Miss Gillespie tightened her jaw. "You were trained to know *how* to do that, should it ever become necessary. If you think you can save the world more ethically than we can, now's your chance to prove it. Master Ragnar says to come back to him with a plan and, in the meantime, learn all you can. Classes are quite a bit different this year. Dismissed."

. . .

Zoe walked back to class, deep in thought. It had to be a trap, right? A way to get her on his side again. On the other hand, what if he actually let her leave this place? Once on the outside, she could communicate with Gabriel and the Resistance. Did she want to, though? Maybe Gabriel considered her an enemy now. If she could really pick her team, she could get Lin to safety and end Ragnar's hold on her. Although, that would leave Professor Yeoh at risk.

Professor Martinov arched an eyebrow when she returned, and she just nodded and sat quietly.

"For Zoe's benefit," he said to the class, "let me summarize what I have been saying. Increasing your telekinetic strength is achieved in the same way that you would increase your muscular strength. Weight training. Specifically, the overloading principle. You must increase the difficulty of your exercises if you want to increase your strength. That means always increasing the resistance, such as the weight of the objects you are lifting. Some of our classes will take place in the gym, where you will literally lift weights, just like a weightlifter. You can train for strength by lifting a lot of weight with fewer repetitions, or you can train for endurance by lifting less weight with more repetitions. Usually, one trains for a bit of both—not too many repetitions and not too few."

"Does the type of exercise matter, Professor?" Paige asked beside her.

He shook his head. "Not much, no. A weightlifter needs to do bench presses for triceps, curls for biceps. A Telekinetic, though, just creates force. If you can create a strong pushing force, then you can create just as strong of a pulling force. However, you should still get used to both pushing…" He pushed his heavy desk away. "And pulling." He pulled the desk back. "Also lifting." The desk rose into the air, then gently came back to the ground. "And … I'm not going to shove it down, because I like my desk and don't want to break it, but you get the idea." The class laughed.

"When lifting an object," he continued, "the distance of the object from you will affect how much you can lift—not just because our telekinetic force varies inversely as the square of the distance between you and the object, but also because leverage matters." He extended his arm out to his side. "I could easily hold a five-kilogram weight like this. But if I attached that weight to a ten-metre rod and tried to hold it up, I would not be able to, because the torque increases with the distance from the pivot point. This is why we invented the wrench. Hence, it is important to always do your weight training exercises in exactly the same way each time, so that you can chart your progress and ensure that you are lifting the same amount as last time—or hopefully more."

Zoe was only half paying attention. If she and Lin managed to escape, what would they do? How would they continue to learn and hone their Abilities without the Academy? It would be even worse for Lin, because she was only in her second year of studies, whereas Zoe had been training her whole life.

"Also," Professor Martinov went on, "as you progress with heavier objects, you will come to understand Newton's Third Law of Motion. Who can tell me what that is?" Several hands went up. "Kalisha," he said.

"For every action, there is an equal and opposite reaction," said a familiar voice from the back.

Kalisha had been Zoe's friend once, years ago. Or almost a friend. She had always been so competitive, though, and was never able to beat Zoe at sparring. Kalisha had become so resentful that eventually she stopped talking to Zoe. At least, that was how Zoe remembered it. Now that she had some perspective on her own past behaviour, though, she wondered if that was what had actually happened. Had Kalisha really been the overly competitive one? Except for Ethan, Zoe had never really had any friends before Lin, but Ethan had only stuck around because he was so lovestruck that he put up with her behaviour. She paused, thinking about Ethan. Her feelings for him were so complicated now. Anyway, it had taken becoming a new and better person to finally find a real friend.

"Excellent. That is exactly right," Professor Martinov said. "Forces come in pairs. The force of gravity is exerting a downward force on me right now. Why am I not falling through the floor? Because the floor is exerting an equal upward force on me. If I push a light object, I won't notice any resistance. If I push a heavy object, though . . ." With his hand, he pushed on his desk, but nothing happened. "Wait, my shoes have too much grip." He slipped off his shoes. "Plug your noses! My socks may be stinky!" This earned more laughter from the class.

"Now, with my slippery socks, if I push on the desk . . ." The desk remained in place while he slid backwards. "See? I exerted a force on the desk, and it exerted an equal force back on me. If the desk had feet like mine and was wearing the same socks, we would both move in opposite directions. It would move less than I would because it's heavier, but it *would* move."

"Why doesn't it move, though, Professor?" asked another voice Zoe recognized. Jacob had always been a sociable boy with lots of friends, but Zoe had never thought him particularly unique or distinctive.

"It has to do with the coefficient of kinetic friction. You will learn about it in physics class. Suffice to say that the desk's legs have a good grip on the floor, so a certain amount of force is required before the desk will move at all. Now, if I don't push on the desk with my hands but instead with telekinetic force . . ." He gestured toward the desk and slid back again as before. "You will see that I still slide back. So, how do I make the desk move and not me? By making myself as immovable as possible. First, I must get a good grip on the floor."

He took off his socks and wrinkled his nose. "Pee-ew! Don't get too close to me if you don't want to pass out! Second, a good, solid stance, low to the ground, hips forward. Now, when I push . . ." He thrust his hands out toward the desk, and it slid away. "The desk moved and I did not. But what if the desk is *really* heavy, you ask? Well, let's find out. Everyone up on the desk."

Nobody moved. "Up! Out of your seats! I want as many of you standing on my desk as can fit. Let's go! Go, go, go!"

Several students clambered onto his desk, shaking their heads and laughing. Those on the edges leaned outward, holding hands with those in the middle. Ethan stayed sitting, as did Zoe. She didn't feel especially social.

"That's it?" Professor Martinov laughed. "That's the best you can do? But you're only one level high! Let's see some people standing on shoulders!"

Soon, more piled on to make a wavering tower of students.

"Excellent! Excellent! Now, we need one more person at the top of the pyramid. Who wants to be top dog, huh? Zoe, how about you? Get on up there!"

Zoe sighed and approached the desk dubiously. "How am I supposed to climb up without knocking everyone down?" she asked.

"Do your levitating thing!" someone shouted.

"Yeah, do the levitating thing!"

"Whatever you're going to do, Zoe, do it quickly before our tower falls," Professor Martinov said, amid grunting and panicked shouts for her to hurry.

"Okay! Okay!" Zoe said. She took a deep breath and floated to the very top of the tower, where she crouched on the shoulders of the students on the second tier.

"Excellent!" the professor shouted. "Now, let's see what happens." He got into his low, solid stance and thrust his hands out like before. This time, the desk stayed still and he slid back.

"Now, even my most solid stance and sticky feet aren't enough to make the desk move instead of me. So, what do I do? Simple. I can do one of three things. One: I can apply telekinetic force to pull the floor toward me, like pulling on a rope attached to the floor. This makes me heavier, as far as the floor is concerned, thus increasing the threshold of force needed to move me." He gestured to the desk again and this time it—and all the students balanced precariously atop it—moved. "Two: I can instead apply telekinetic force to push against the wall behind me, thus counteracting the force of the desk pushing against me and keeping me in place. Be careful not to push against a window, though." He thrust his hand out and the desk moved further. "Three: I can push on an angle on the ground behind me, thus bracing myself." The desk slid away. "So, unless you are strapped in and don't have to worry about moving, you can never actually apply your full telekinetic force on a heavy object, because you will always have to use some of your power to hold yourself in place."

"Lift us, Professor!" someone yelled.

"Yeah, lift us!" others joined in.

Professor Martinov laughed. "Ha! Lifting is different. As I lift the desk, it pushes down on me. So, the only thing I have to do is make sure I don't collapse under its weight. Assume a horse stance." He spread his legs wide. "Keep your back straight, so you don't break it. Tighten your core muscles. Then lift." He spread his arms wide, then turned his palms to face the ceiling, and the desk rose into the air.

"Oh no! You're too wobbly!" The desk teetered back and forth, and the students screamed. "I hope I don't drop you all!" They tried their best to keep from toppling off the violently rocking desk. "I kid! I kid!" The desk settled and rose smoothly. "Now, you are all quite heavy. So heavy that my muscles and my bones cannot possibly manage your weight. I would hurt myself. So, I must use my telekinetic power to *strengthen* my bones and prevent them from breaking. Strengthen my muscles and tendons and prevent them from ripping. How to do this is difficult to explain. You just . . . do it. Some people need a lot of practice, to others it comes naturally. Pacha here, for instance, once lifted every table in the Great Hall, and I'll bet he never even thought about strengthening his bones and muscles. You just did it without thinking, didn't you, Pacha?"

Pacha was silent.

"Ah, he's humble, that one. But a powerhouse! If you still have trouble standing, push down on the ground beneath or behind you to brace yourself."

The bell rang, and Professor Martinov lowered the desk to the floor. The students leapt off, and as everyone scrambled for their books, the professor yelled, "Next class will be in the weight room! Wear your workout clothes and come prepared to sweat!"

6

THE TROLLEY PROBLEM

Zoe made her way to history class and claimed a seat at the last free desk. Moments later, Lin entered, spotted her, looked around to see what else was available, then took the spot next to her.

"Hey," Lin said.

"Hey." There was an awkward silence.

"We started dating two months ago," Lin blurted. "Priya and I."

Zoe nodded. "How's it going so far?"

"Good. I guess? I don't know. I've never dated anyone before, so I'm not sure how it's supposed to go. But . . ." She took a deep breath. "She was there for me, you know? After Dad . . . and after they took you, and all the chaos . . . I really needed someone, and she was there. And then things just . . . happened."

"I get it," Zoe said. "I'm happy for you, really. Priya is . . . a *little* old for you, though, isn't she? I mean, we're grade ten and she's grade twelve."

"Yeah, but we're only thirteen months apart," Lin said, quickly.

"Okay." She didn't know what else she was supposed to say.

"And it's not like I need your permission," Lin added.

"Of course not."

"She *does* get a little protective of me, though. And jealous. Like this morning. Sorry about that."

"Don't worry about it," Zoe said. "Listen, something happened this morning."

Just then, the professor strode into the classroom. She had never seen this woman before. She wore a multicoloured headwrap, blazer, and a long skirt, and she looked . . . intimidating.

"Please take your seats so we can begin," she said in a loud, no-nonsense voice. "Welcome to grade ten history, where you will be learning about World War One and onward. My name is Professor Dlamini." She wrote her name on the board at the front of the class. "This is my first time teaching at the Academy, but I have been a historian for many, many years. I was born in what is now called South Africa, where I lived for a long time before settling in London, England—as you can no doubt tell by my accent. I lived through Dutch and British colonization. I witnessed, from afar, the slave trade that fueled the colonization of North America, and I witnessed the genocide of its Indigenous peoples."

As she spoke, she moved from student to student, looking into their eyes, as if trying to pull them into the experiences she was relating. "I lived through the Great War, which resulted in the deaths of millions. I witnessed the genocide of Bosniaks and Croats. I watched the rise of Nazism in Germany and witnessed the Holocaust, in which the Nazis systematically murdered six million Jews, plus millions of Soviets and Poles, Serbs, Romani, disabled, and homosexuals. I witnessed the genocide of the Crimean Tartars at the hands of the Soviets. I lived through World War Two, which resulted in eighty-five million dead. I witnessed the U.S. drop atomic bombs on Hiroshima and Nagasaki. I witnessed Israel drive 750,000 Palestinians from their homes in the Nakba. Ethnic cleansing and genocides never end." She began counting on her fingers. "Guatemala, Zanzibar, Bangladesh, Ikiza, Acholi and Lango, East Timor, Cambodia, Bosnia, Rwanda, Hutus, Darfur, Sudan, Congo, Gaza. Untold atrocities all across the world. And I have watched us creep ever closer to the brink of extinction as nuclear weapons proliferate."

She took a deep breath. "And not once have our kind intervened."

The class was silent, transfixed by the power and intensity of the professor's words.

"We *could* have done something. We could have prevented it all. But we *chose* not to, acting as though we'd been issued some Prime Directive not to interfere in the natural development of an alien civilization—and all the while having the audacity to claim, among ourselves, that we are the *caretakers* of this world."

She straightened her blazer with a tug. "Well, I have been a vocal opponent of this policy of non-interference for most of my life. So, when the new management asked if I would be willing to teach history at the Academy—to tell you exactly what I believe we ought to have done in the past and what we should do going forward—I jumped at the opportunity."

Zoe raised her hand. "Professor? I don't mean to jump ahead, but in general, what do you think we should have done and should be doing? Assassinating world leaders and corporate leaders? Couldn't that just create temporary power vacuums that get filled again with people just as bad? Compel them to be more peaceful—less greedy and power hungry? I mean, it's one thing to look back in hindsight and know what the pivotal moments in history were and their key players, but without knowing the future, how do we make sure we don't accidentally make things worse?"

"What is your name, child?" Professor Dlamini asked.

"Zoe, ma'am."

"Ah. I've heard of you." She pursed her lips and paused dramatically, studying Zoe. "It has been said that history repeats itself roughly every eighty years. This is the case, in my opinion, because people only truly learn from experience, and Typicals have short lifespans of roughly eighty years. We do not. So, while we cannot see the future, we *can* recognize repeating patterns, like the rise and fall of fascism and authoritarianism. And we can recognize demagogues when we see them and not be fooled by their rhetoric. I believe that assassination should only be used as a last resort. It's a messy business, and if too many people are assassinated, Typicals will become suspicious. Plus, it offers no guarantee that the next person won't be the same or worse. Compelling influential individuals would indeed work much better."

"What about people's right to free will?" Pacha asked, loudly, surprising Zoe. "We wouldn't like it if compulsion were used on us."

"No?" Professor Dlamini asked, her eyebrow raised. "Tell me, how would you even know? That is the nature of compulsion—you would think every thought in your head is your own. The issue of whether it is morally right to compel Typicals is more of a philosophical question than a practical one. In the words of a fictional character I greatly admire, the needs of the many outweigh the needs of the few. One cannot argue that compelling Adolph Hitler into believing that all human beings are created equal—or that his true destiny lay in his painting—would not have had a positive effect on the world."

A hand shot up. "Why can't we argue that?" Kyle asked. "How do you know someone else wouldn't have risen to power and done exactly the same as him, except better? Maybe the Nazis would've won."

"And why does it even matter?" Jacob interjected. "They're Typicals. As long as they don't threaten us or ruin the planet for us, why do we care about their wars and their genocides?"

The professor looked back and forth between the Igigi boys. "I will answer you first," she said, addressing Kyle. "Yes, it is certainly possible that someone even worse than Hitler could have risen to power—or that a peaceful Germany would have resulted in an alternate timeline that was ultimately worse. Perhaps if all of their scientists had stayed, they would have invented the atomic bomb, and *then* if the Nazis rose to power, no one could have stopped them. Or perhaps another country entirely would have tried to take over the world. But we are not talking about time travel, where we make one single change in history and hope for the best. We are talking about using our wisdom, gained through centuries of experience, to recognize potential dangers and steer events in a better direction. And if it inadvertently results in something worse, we steer the ship *again*."

She pointed a finger at Jacob. "As for you. I understand that you Igigi children grew up isolated from the rest of the world, and were taught that you are superior—not only to Typicals but to Anunnaki, as you call us— but I will not tolerate that sort of rubbish in my classroom. A person's worth is not determined by their strength or their intelligence or by their lineage or the society into which they were born. Every creature on this planet has a right to exist and to live in peace. You had better hope the Typicals think so too, should our existence ever become known to the world."

She addressed the entire class again. "But we were discussing the ethics of using compulsion. I am a utilitarian. I do not believe that actions are inherently moral or immoral. I believe that what truly matters is whether or not an action benefits more people than it harms. Have you all heard of the trolley problem?"

Some students nodded.

"The trolley problem is a classic thought experiment in ethics. Imagine a trolley—that's a streetcar running along a track, for those of you who have never seen one—is going to collide with a group of five people up ahead, who, for whatever reason, cannot get out of its path. The driver of the trolley has the option, however, to pull a lever and move the trolley onto an adjacent track, where only a single person stands. Do you pull the lever or not?"

Hands went up while other students shouted their answers. Professor Dlamini raised her hand for silence. "A utilitarian would pull the lever, arguing that it is morally acceptable to intentionally kill one person in order to save five, because this guarantees the maximum benefit. Therefore, the end justifies the means. A deontologist, however, would argue that the morality of an action does *not* depend on the outcome but rather on a series of rules. To them, the greater good doesn't matter. They would not pull the lever because such an action would intentionally kill someone, which is inherently immoral."

She walked behind her desk. "Of course, people always try to complicate this thought experiment. What if the one person is the victim of the other five, for instance? As a utilitarian, it can sometimes be difficult to determine the maximum benefit. But all else being equal, I would pull the lever. Not just because fewer people would die, but because I think it is inherently flawed to think that pulling the lever is an action that requires moral justification, while *not* pulling the lever is a *non*-action and so requires *no* moral justification. It's nonsense. The actions themselves are irrelevant. They are just the means by which we implement our choices. Our choices are what matter. Choosing *not* to do something is every bit as much of a choice as choosing *to* do something. We could be healing people whose injuries are beyond current medical science, but instead, we let them die. Pretending that inaction absolves us of the consequences is cowardly. And that is what we Telepaths have collectively been for centuries. Cowards."

She stared at the class, letting her words sink in and daring anyone to challenge her. "Now, would you all be so kind as to take a textbook from the back of the room and open it to chapter one?"

■ ■ ■

"It's a trap," Lin said, stuffing her face full of fries. "It has to be."

"In what way could it be a trap?" Paige asked. "He's letting her *leave*."

"Why would he let her leave, though?" Priya countered. "No one else can."

"So that he can get her on his side," Makena said. "Let her do something she wants to do anyway so she'll start thinking maybe he and Marduk aren't so bad after all."

"Exactly," Lin said. "A trap."

Zoe swallowed and wiped her mouth with a napkin. "I know it's a trap. But it's also an opportunity. He's been threatening Lin to keep me in line. This is a chance to get her to safety."

"What, so I can spend the rest of my life hiding while everyone else learns how to become powerful Telepaths?" Lin shook her head. "I don't think so."

"It wouldn't be for the rest of your life," Zoe said.

"How long would it be, Zoe? Just a few years? When I'm too old to come back to school? Besides, my mom is here. And we already agreed I'm going to kill Ragnar. So, I'm not running away."

Zoe took a deep breath. "Fine. It's still an opportunity, though. Maybe we could contact the Resistance. Find out what's happening out there. At the very least, we could do some good in the world. Play along with Ragnar, make him think we're on his side, earn his trust so someday we're in a position to betray him."

"I don't know," Lin said. "I get what you're saying, but it kind of sounds like you're justifying doing what Ragnar wants. My mom would not approve of this. Neither would my dad."

Everyone fell silent. "I'm not talking about killing anyone," Zoe finally said. "Just making horrible, influential people do the right thing."

"What if they were *really* bad, though?" Paige asked. "We could be like assassins in black spandex with masks and swords, jumping from rooftop to rooftop."

"What would we want to do, exactly?" Priya asked, ignoring Paige. "Getting rid of nuclear weapons seems a little beyond us—unless you know how we can get up close to major world leaders."

"Climate change, maybe?" Zoe offered. "Find the worst offending private company, break into the CEO's home during the night, and give them a new perspective on what they're doing to the world?"

"Or we could become superheroes!" Paige cried. "Dress up in colourful costumes with capes and spend our nights in downtown Toronto, beating up bad guys and mind-voodooing them into becoming better people."

"You're forgetting something," Makena said, also ignoring Paige's excitement. "None of us know how to perform compulsion on someone. Even in grade twelve, all I learned was how to erase someone's memory if they saw us using our Abilities. It's always been one of those things that we know is possible but forbidden. Unless you learned how at Igigi school?"

Zoe squirmed. "A little. I was never very good at it, though. Forcing someone to do something against their will is one thing. I could get angry and brute force it." She remembered doing that to Ethan in the alley. "Getting inside someone's head, though, and making them *think* differently is like a posthypnotic suggestion. It takes . . . finesse."

"Who was best at it?" Lin asked.

Zoe looked to Ethan, sitting alone in the corner.

"Oh," Lin said. "You know, you're going to have to talk to him eventually. I don't even understand what your issue is with him. He came here because he was worried about you, he fought on our side in the Battle, he even attacked Ragnar for you, then saved your life when you tried to kill Ragnar after . . ." She took a deep breath to steady her quavering voice. "No one wants Ragnar dead more than me. But if Ethan hadn't stopped you, you'd be dead, too. He did the right thing. And he's been paying for it ever since. I don't know what they did to him in solitary, but just *look* at him. He clearly needs help. So, go help him."

...

The third class of the day was—perhaps not so coincidentally—exactly what she needed: Compulsion 101. It was a mix of Anunnaki second-years and Zoe's former Igigi classmates. When she spotted their new professor, wearing a stylish white pantsuit, she froze.

"Hello, class," the professor said without a smile. "For those of you who are new to this school, I am Professor Sharapova. You may also call me Dr. Sharapova. I am a trained psychologist and psychiatrist and have served in this capacity at the Academy for many years. I have never taught a class here, though. I certainly never thought I would be teaching *this* particular subject to children. However, I was . . . persuaded." She paused and closed her eyes tightly for a moment.

"Compulsion is . . . wrong. It is one of the most invasive things you can do to a fellow human. It robs them of their free will and should only be employed as a last resort. It comes in two forms. The first is to impose your will upon someone, forcing them to consciously act against their will. They become your puppet. Usually, they will feel you inside their mind and will fight you—even Typicals. It then becomes a battle of wills. If you are extremely skilled, however, they won't feel your presence at all, and the experience will be akin to an inexplicable compulsion of their own that just feels easier to carry out than to fight against. One might force an enemy to drop their weapon and kneel, for instance."

Hands in her pockets, Professor Sharapova strolled casually through the classroom. "The second type of compulsion is far more insidious. Planting thoughts, suggestions, *values*, so deeply in a person's mind that they don't realize they are not their own. They will experience this as a eureka moment, and these thoughts will stay with them even after you are gone. We sometimes refer to this as 'mindbending,' because you are bending their mind to your will. It fundamentally changes the person. For those of you with parents, I am ashamed to say that this has been done to all of them."

There was a sharp intake of breath from half of the class. Professor

Chao had told Zoe this a year ago, on her first day at the Academy, but she had never mentioned it to anyone.

"It's subtle—just a suggestion to never reveal our existence to the world—and perhaps it's necessary for our survival, but nevertheless, I have never approved of it." She took a deep breath. "It's quite similar to hypnosis, actually—a technique invented by Typicals. The power of suggestion is an incredibly powerful tool."

Professor Sharapova looked directly at Zoe. "There is a third type of compulsion. It's not normally even thought of as compulsion, because it's simply not taught." A chill ran up Zoe's spine.

"You can create a new persona for someone," the professor continued, slowly advancing on Zoe. "One in which they are your slave, for instance, and you can activate it whenever you wish. They'll go about their life, never realizing that they are your slave, never remembering being activated and doing your bidding, never remembering how they betrayed all their friends and got some of them killed. Not unless they are *allowed* to remember later, perhaps because a particularly sadistic individual thought it would be amusing."

Professor Sharapova stood directly in front of Zoe's desk, looking down on her. The class had fallen completely silent. "You would have to be a truly evil person to do that to someone, wouldn't you, Zoe?"

Zoe gulped, and her hands trembled. But then, the professor turned away abruptly.

"But we aren't evil, are we? We will only use compulsion for *good*. We will only employ it on *bad* people. 'Guiding mankind with a firm but loving hand to bring about a new golden age.' That's our mantra now, right? So, let's begin."

7

THE ANGER PARADOX

When class ended, Zoe practically ran out of the room, refusing to make eye contact with Professor Sharapova.

"You okay?" Lin asked, as they hurried down the hall.

"No." Zoe felt sick to her stomach. What she had done to Professor Sharapova was unforgivable. She was a monster. And now she wanted to go out into the world and use compulsion on Typicals, justifying it as a necessary means to an end. Had she changed at all, or was she still the same person she had always been? Lin was offering no words of comfort, because she knew Zoe was a monster.

They soon found themselves in the dojo, waiting for whoever would be their Advanced Combat teacher. Zoe glanced up, and as expected, there was Professor Chao sitting among the rafters.

Most of the students were Igigi, and everyone was either stretching or practicing. Her former Igigi classmates had obviously improved over the past year. She wondered if she had missed out on any important lessons, or if she had the advantage, having trained with Professor Chao.

As Ragnar entered, the class rushed to sit down. Lin glared at him with barely concealed hatred and remained standing a full two seconds longer than everyone else. A subtle act of defiance. Ragnar raised an eyebrow and the corner of his mouth turned up.

"Lin," he said. "You can be my volunteer for today's lesson."

Oh no.

Lin rose and went to stand six feet away from Ragnar, facing him.

"Despite my duties as headmaster," he said to the class, "I will be your professor of combat whenever I am present at the Academy. Other duties will often pull me out into the world, however, so I am arranging for numerous guest instructors to help round out your training. Today, we will not be focusing on technique or sparring. Instead, we will be putting Professor Martinov's lessons into practice. Using telekinesis to both increase your power . . ." He regarded Lin. "And your ability to take a punch."

What? No way. She couldn't let this happen.

Don't interfere, Zoe, Lin said, preemptively, in her head. *I don't need your protection.*

"We'll start with power." Ragnar turned to face Lin, his stance casual, his arms at his sides. "Hit me in the stomach with everything you have."

Lin clenched her fists, then she stepped forward quickly and hit him with all the power she could muster. He didn't flinch or budge. She stepped back.

"Again. Like you mean it this time."

She did, this time clearly aiming at a spot behind him, trying to drive her punch through him. Again, he remained unmoved.

Ragnar addressed the class. "No matter how much Lin may wish to harm me, she is a little girl and simply not strong enough to do so. Not with physical strength, at least. That's why telekinesis is the key." He faced Lin again. "This time, I want you to think about your telekinesis before you attack. Build it up like a coiled spring, then let it explode out of your fist at the moment of impact."

Lin closed her eyes for a moment, then stepped forward and delivered a punch that was clearly much stronger than before. She stepped back, shaking her hand.

"Good. But you hurt your wrist, didn't you? Now, when you coil your spring, I want you to also use your telekinesis to strengthen the bones in your fist and arm. Imagine them becoming unbreakable."

Lin readied herself, then punched again. This time, Ragnar stiffened and expelled his breath when struck.

"I felt that one. You'll have to do better than that, though. Again."

Lin yelled and punched again, rocking Ragnar back a foot.

"There you go. Still not enough to hurt me, but enough to move me. Unfortunately for you, I can employ telekinesis, too. If I were blocking, I could strengthen the bone in my arm. Or if you were aiming for my face, I could strengthen my skull, even my teeth. With a blow to the midsection, though, I can't strengthen my abdominal muscles in the way that we can strengthen our bones. That just doesn't work. I can create a shield in front of my midsection, though, timed for the precise moment of impact. Again."

Lin drove her fist with much more power than before. But Ragnar didn't flinch this time.

"You'll need more power if you want to hurt me now. Try again."

Lin hit him again. And again. And again. Each time, he remained unmoved, and she seemed to grow angrier and more frustrated.

Ragnar smiled. "Good. Get angry. But keep your anger focused. Let it fuel your power."

Lin paused and closed her eyes. When she opened them, Zoe saw pure hatred there. Lin stepped forward and hit him again, this time forcing him back half a foot.

"There you go! Now, you'll notice that when you hit me, not only did you knock me back a bit, but you knocked yourself back a bit, too. This time, use your telekinesis to ground yourself, so that you don't budge at all. And roll your shoulder into the punch."

This time, Ragnar was forced back two feet. "Good. But in combat,

I would assume a fighting stance to ground myself, like this." He assumed a typical Aikido stance, his hips and front foot facing forward, his back foot facing sideways. "Again."

Lin's punch was loud, but he didn't move an inch. "More power. Again."

Lin hit him over and over. Each blow seemed more powerful than the last, but each one was just as ineffective. She finally stopped, sweating and out of breath.

Ragnar shook his head in disappointment. "Lin, I thought you, of all people, would have more anger than this. How are you ever going to avenge your father with such a pathetic display of power? It's like you don't even care that I killed him in front of you."

Zoe gaped at him, as did everyone else.

Lin's eyes widened in shock. Then, a calm seemed to come over her, as though her hatred for this man had just reached a new level and was scarily focused now. She moved faster than Zoe had ever seen her and delivered a blow that slid Ragnar back a full two feet.

"Excellent!" he exclaimed. "Now—"

She hit him again, shoving him back three feet.

"That's enough."

She hit him again—four feet.

"I said that's enough!"

She tried once more, but this time, he stepped in quickly and struck her in the chest with an open hand, sending her flying backwards.

"Lin!" Zoe yelled, scrambling to her feet, but Makena held her back. Lin got to one knee and held up a hand.

Don't, she said in Zoe's mind as she slowly climbed to her feet, fists clenched.

"Now, it's time to learn to take a punch," Ragnar said. "Come closer."

Lin faced him in a ready stance.

"You've wanted this for some time, haven't you? To go toe to toe with me. But it's not enough to be powerful. You must also be tough. Punches as strong as your last few can kill someone who is unprepared. Do what I did. Use your telekinesis to brace yourself so you don't slide back too much. But most importantly, use it to shield your midsection. Not beforehand, only at the moment of impact. Telekinesis takes energy, and we only have so much of it before we need to rest and recharge. You can either use it in a prolonged way or all at once in a much more powerful burst. Expel your breath just as you normally would, tightening your abs in preparation for a punch, and time your telekinetic burst with that. Here's the trick, though. It takes time to go from zero to a telekinetic burst. Time that you might not have. So, you need to summon your telekinesis at the beginning of a fight and use it in your body at a very low level. That way, you won't drain yourself, but you can create a burst in an instant. Now, ready yourself."

Lin took a deep breath, then nodded. Ragnar stepped in and punched her in the stomach. She winced and grunted and slid back a foot.

"That was a very weak punch. Your burst needs to be stronger and better-timed or you'll get hurt. Ready?"

Zoe didn't like this at all. She tensed, ready to jump to Lin's aid.

Lin nodded, determined, and Ragnar punched her again. This time, she cried out and slid back three feet, dropping to one knee and clutching her stomach. Ragnar shook his head.

"Pathetic," he said, crouching down to look in her eyes. "You know, your father was a great fighter. How disappointed he must have been in you. How sad he must have been, in his final moments, knowing that his only child would never be able to carry on his legacy. All those years of training you, only to finally have to admit that, deep down, you're weak. You have no mental fortitude. No well of strength to draw upon in the face of adversity. How do you not even have a well of *anger* to draw upon after what I did?" He indicated the rest of the class. "No one else here has reason to be as angry as you. I forced your father to his knees and cut off his head while you watched. I have given you a gift, Lin. *Anger* should be your superpower. *Hate* should be what gives you strength beyond what your classmates can ever hope to achieve. Only by embracing both can you ever hope to one day be capable of defeating me." He leaned in close. "If you loved your father, this shouldn't even be a question. So, stand up, channel your hatred, and use it to defend yourself."

Ragnar stood and returned to his position. Lin closed the distance and stood in ready stance. Zoe had never seen such an expression of cold hatred in anyone before. Lin nodded and Ragnar stepped in with his punch.

Now, Lin didn't flinch and didn't budge. Her eyes never left Ragnar's.

He nodded his approval. "Good." He stepped back. "Again." He punched her harder. Again, Lin held firm. "Excellent. Again." He punched even harder, and Lin slid back two feet but still didn't flinch. "Again." She slid five feet.

Ragnar smiled. "Last one. Let's see what you can handle." He stepped in quickly and punched. The sound of the impact was loud. Lin slid back fifteen full feet and staggered but stayed upright, her eyes still locked on his. Ragnar nodded again.

"There's hope for you yet, Lin Chao." He turned back to the class. "Everyone, find a partner and practice. Try not to kill anyone. Increase the power of your punches gradually to make sure your partner can handle it. A dead student is useless to me."

Zoe glanced up at the rafters, where Professor Chao looked down at his daughter with worry.

. . .

Professor Yeoh had gone ballistic. Apparently, she stormed into Ragnar's office and threatened to disembowel him if he ever hurt her daughter again. Then, she ordered every student to the infirmary so she could check for internal injuries, which a few had.

"She worries too much," Lin said that night in their dorm.

"Internal injuries are serious," Zoe replied.

"Not that. I mean, she worries too much about me. She's afraid I'm going to get myself killed."

"You don't think she has reason to worry?" Zoe asked.

Lin sighed. "Not you, too. First my mom. Then Priya. I'm not an idiot, Zoe. I'm not going to go and challenge Ragnar to a duel. I know I'm not at his level yet. He'd swat me like a bug, just like he did to you. But if an opportunity to take him by surprise presents itself, or if we could come up with a solid plan . . . well, that would be a different story. Meanwhile, if he's arrogant enough to train me to be good enough to fight him someday, I have no problem with that."

"Lin," Zoe began, trying to articulate what she needed to say. "What you did in class today was impressive, but it went against everything your dad believed."

Lin sat up in bed. "What are you talking about?"

"The day of the attack on the Academy, soon after my old persona woke up, I sat with him in the dojo. He spoke with me about my anger."

Lin cocked her head.

"He warned me about relying on it. He said that while anger *does* make you stronger, it becomes addictive. It clouds your judgment and makes you reckless. More importantly, though, it makes you easy to manipulate."

"How am I being manipulated, Zoe? What have I done that you think is part of Ragnar's grand plan to use me?"

Zoe considered her words carefully. "He knew exactly how to push your buttons in class today. He played on your emotions to make you angrier than I've ever seen you. And he focused your anger to allow you to do things you never thought possible."

"That doesn't count!" Lin protested. "Yeah, I know he intentionally made me mad, but it made me *strong*, Zoe! You have no idea how strong I felt. I'll bet my telekinetic Abilities were ten *times* their normal strength. If he's stupid enough to make me strong enough to kill him one day, I'm going to let him. I'll learn everything he has to teach, I'll bide my time, and then I'll kill him."

"You don't get it, Lin. Ragnar did the same thing to me when I was little. He found whatever it was that I was angry about and nurtured that anger. Showed me how much stronger I could be if I just let myself be angry *all* the time. So, I did. And I became a zealot. I have no doubt he had plans for me. He probably intended to make me his attack dog. But your dad changed all that, and now Ragnar can't control me anymore. So, now he's set his sights on you."

"I'm not going to do his bidding," Lin said.

"Yes, you will. You already said you'll bide your time. So, until you're ready to challenge him, you'll do what he says. It'll start off innocently enough. He'll tell you to do things that you have no ethical problem with, so you'll do them. I mean, why not? Then he'll tell you to do something you're not entirely comfortable with, but you'll go through with it because you're not ready to go up against him yet. And he'll keep moving that ethical line until you're doing things you wouldn't dream of doing today. And the whole time, you'll be thinking that you're using *him*, but in reality, he'll be using *you*. He'll slowly turn you into his loyal puppet, just like I was."

Lin squeezed her eyes shut and clenched her fists before forcing herself to relax. "Even if what you say is true, I'll never become his loyal puppet. I have more reason to hate him than anyone. Nothing will ever make me forget that."

"Okay." Zoe relented. She didn't want to push too hard. "Listen," she said, changing the subject. "There's something I've been meaning to tell you. It's . . ." She exhaled. "It's really difficult to say, but you need to know this. I don't want there to be any secrets between us."

Lin reclined on her bed. "I'm listening."

"You know how I said I started hallucinating in solitary? Well . . . I saw your dad."

Lin leaned forward again. "Excuse me?"

"I know. I was so lonely and desperately needed someone to talk to. And then he just appeared one day. Sitting next to me, talking to me, seemingly as real as you are." Lin stared. "He admitted that he was just a hallucination, but it was so easy to forget sometimes. He would spar with me, have deep conversations with me, meditate with me. He taught me how to improve my Abilities."

"Wait." Lin stood up. "Did he teach you electrokinesis?"

Zoe reluctantly nodded, and Lin dropped her head in her hands like it was about to explode. "It was really just me teaching myself, Lin."

"Who teaches themselves an advanced Ability, Zoe? Did he *tell* you it was called electrokinesis, or did you come up with the name yourself?"

"He's not real, Lin. He's my hallucination. There's no such thing as ghosts."

Lin paced back and forth as she absorbed this. "You're lucky," she said, finally. "I wish I could see him, whether he's real or not. Do you still see him? Is he here right now?"

Zoe shook her head. "He's not here now, but I still see him sometimes. He just appears randomly."

"Can you tell me the next time you see him?"

"If you're sure you want me to. It's a little weird. I mean, he's your dad."

Lin nodded. "I know. I just . . . just tell me, okay?"

"There's something else, Lin. Something big. Honestly . . . I'm really afraid to tell you. But I have to."

Lin looked incredulous. "What could possibly be bigger than my dad haunting you?"

She took a deep breath. "Ragnar is my biological father," she blurted.

Lin stared blankly. "What?"

"He called me 'daughter' after I tried to kill him. I spent the whole time in solitary wondering why. I was created in a test tube, just like every other Igigi kid. But when he finally let me out, he told me." She hugged her knees and rocked back and forth on her bed. Would Lin ever be her friend again after this? "He said that while I have the same special genes they used to make the rest of the Igigi kids, he used his own DNA for me, plus whatever DNA he could salvage from a strand of his dead wife's hair. He *showed* her to me. In my mind. He showed me his daughters, too. They looked so much like me."

Utterly terrified, she waited for Lin to react.

"So . . . your dad killed my dad?"

"He's *not* my dad. He's a monster. He was never a father to me, never treated me any differently. I might share his DNA, but he's not my dad."

Lin stared into space. "I need to process this," she said, grabbing her workout bag and striding out the door. Zoe got to her feet.

"And don't follow me, either!" Lin yelled from down the hall.

Zoe paced the room. Had it been a mistake to tell her? All these months, she had been worried that Lin would never be able to forgive her for what she'd done. Now, it seemed maybe Lin wouldn't be able to forgive her for who she was.

She opened the door, intending to follow Lin anyway, and was immediately sucker punched. She staggered, dazed, as masked people forced their way into her room and began pummelling her. She tried to fight, but she was barely conscious, and someone had shielded her. She curled into the fetal position and endured kick after kick.

Then darkness.

. . .

"It's okay, Zoe," she heard Lin say in the distance. "It's going to be okay." Then darkness again.

She opened her eyes. She was in the infirmary. Again. This time, Lin sat at her bedside.

"Mom, she's awake."

Professor Yeoh gently touched her shoulder. "How are you feeling, Zoe?"

"I've been better," she said through swollen lips. She could taste blood. "How bad is it?"

Professor Yeoh shone a light in her eyes. "You know the drill," she said. "Follow my finger, please." Zoe did. "You have a slight concussion. It should be minimal, though, because I've healed what I could. Three broken ribs, which I've also mostly healed. Your nose was broken, so I've reset it. The swelling in your face should go down in the next day or two. All in all, you're lucky it wasn't much worse."

"I'm sorry, Zoe," Lin said. "I should've been there."

"It's not your fault. There were too many of them, anyway. They took me completely by surprise, so I didn't even get a single punch in. It would've been you against all of them, however many there were."

"Six," Lin said.

"How do you know that?"

Zoe followed her gaze. Six Igigi kids lay in the other hospital beds. "Did you do that?" she asked.

Lin shook her head. "Wasn't me."

"So, who?"

...

The next morning at breakfast, Zoe saw him sitting alone, as usual. Taking a deep breath, she sat next to him.

"Hello, Ethan."

Ethan froze midbite.

"I hear that I have you to thank for last night?" When there was no reply, she took one of his hands and examined his knuckles. "Thank you. You didn't have to do that."

He nodded without meeting her eye.

"Why did you?" she asked. "I said some pretty mean things the last time we spoke."

When he didn't answer, she continued, "I'm sorry. I wasn't thinking straight, then. I was the old me and the new me but not . . . combined yet. I was confused. And I guess I've just been stubborn and avoiding you since I got back. I know you only came here to make sure I was safe, and that you literally betrayed the Igigi for me, and that you only stopped me from killing Ragnar to save my life. What I said to you wasn't fair."

But he remained frozen.

"Ethan? Are you okay?" She touched his shoulder, and he flinched. "What did they do to you in solitary?"

This time, when he still didn't respond, she waited patiently.

Finally, he whispered, "It was . . . bad. I know it must've been for you, too. I'm sorry I didn't come rescue you. I tried."

"What?" Zoe couldn't believe he was apologizing. "Don't be ridiculous. There was nothing you could possibly have done. I wasn't even on the same continent."

"I had plans . . . for escaping and making my way to our old school, where I thought he might be keeping you. But they caught me. They . . ." He scrunched his eyes shut. "Did things." He tapped his skull. "To my head." He looked at her. "I don't know what, but I'm not . . . myself anymore."

Zoe felt horrible. She should have gone to him the moment she arrived. "I'm sorry," she said. "We'll get to the bottom of this, okay? Whatever they did to you, we'll figure it out and we'll fix it. We'll make you better."

Ethan nodded, and his lower lip quivered. She pretended not to notice, in case he was embarrassed. Boys were funny that way, always wanting to project strength. "How did you even know I was in danger last night?" she asked.

He composed himself before speaking. "I've kind of been keeping an eye on you, since you got back. Not stalking," he hurried to add. "More like watching out for anyone who might want to hurt you. Nobody notices me anymore, so I can just sit and listen. I overheard some of them talking about taking you out yesterday. So, I kept watch on your dorm last night, from a distance. I saw Lin leave and almost immediately afterward, a bunch of kids in masks ran in. I would've gotten there sooner, but Kyle was standing guard and he was surprisingly good. Took me a full ten seconds to take him out. By then, they had already done a number on you."

So, he'd taken out five of them all at once, single-handedly. Whatever they'd done to Ethan's mind, it hadn't affected his fighting skills. She squeezed his hand. "Thank you."

After a little while, he asked, "What are you going to do about Lin?"

"What do you mean?"

"Ragnar's up to his old tricks again. Just with Lin this time. We can't let him get his hooks into her."

Zoe nodded. "I don't know. We talked about it, but it didn't go well. That's why she stormed off last night. But I won't let him manipulate her. I'll find a way."

After swallowing another bite, Ethan broached another subject. "Is it true? What he called you?"

You are such a disappointment, daughter.

"Apparently," she said. "I'll tell you all about it later. But, Ethan, you shouldn't be sitting here alone all the time. Do you want to sit with us?"

Ethan looked hesitant—scared, even—but he nodded. Together, they started across the Great Hall to the Valkyries, but she paused at her assailants' table. They all looked like they'd been through a war. Most stared at her defiantly. Kyle, though, looked ashamed and wouldn't meet her gaze. Zoe was surprised to realize she didn't feel angry. Instead, she felt sad. These kids had been her friends—or classmates, at least. She'd grown up with them, shared so many experiences with them. And now, they hated her so much they'd attacked her in the middle of the night. She couldn't help but feel like she had failed them.

"It didn't have to be this way," she said. "It *doesn't* have to be this way."

She continued to her table, where her friends greeted Ethan with smiles. She would find a way to fix everything.

...

Zoe and Lin exchanged shocked glances when Lin's mom entered the dojo and sat in seiza in front of the class, her eyes closed and hands folded neatly on her lap.

"Umm, Lin . . ." Kalisha said. "Why is your mommy here?"

The Igigi kids snickered. Professor Yeoh waited until the students settled down, then turned and touched her head to the mat, bowing to the photos of Morihei Ueshiba and Ip Man that still hung on the wall. The students followed suit. Then, she turned and bowed to the students, who bowed back.

"Hello, everyone," she said. "I am Professor Yeoh. I teach healing, and I run our school's infirmary, where I have patched up many of you already. I will be your guest instructor this week." She stood and walked to the wall of weapons.

"Ma'am?" Jacob said, raising his hand. "This is *Advanced* Combat." The Igigi kids laughed again.

"Yes, I'm aware," Professor Yeoh said, selecting a wooden staff and twirling it faster than the eye could see. She ended with an overhead strike to Jacob's head that she pulled at the very last second, so that she only lightly tapped him instead. "You can be my demonstration partner. Go grab a metal practice sword."

Professor Yeoh returned to the front of the class. "My specialty is the staff," she said, moving through some basic techniques—overhead swing, forward and reverse figure eight, uppercut, and chop. "I learned from Shaolin monks a long, long time ago. If you are in this class, then you already know how to use a staff." She put her staff back in its spot on the wall. "Some of you even have experience with this." She pulled out a foot-long metal tube from within her uniform. Zoe recognized it immediately. Professor Yeoh clicked a button with her thumb, and in the blink of an eye, the tube expanded to a six-foot metal staff. "I am told that this is the weapon of choice among the Igigi, and I have to say . . . I am impressed. It is much more concealable than a sword. And much more versatile, allowing you to incapacitate your opponent—who may be a Typical—without killing or seriously injuring them."

She moved through various forms again. "The weight is excellent. It is made of titanium, making it as strong as steel but much lighter—just over a kilogram. It will never break, and it will deliver a lot of force." She struck the mat so hard the dojo shook. "The balance is also excellent," she added, twirling the staff as fast as she could. "Something that I did not expect from an expandable staff. And when you are done . . ." She dropped to one knee and slammed the staff into the ground, collapsing one side, then rotated it in her hand and slammed the other side into the ground behind her. "It collapses quickly, so you can hide it in even a short jacket."

She rose to her feet. "Now, since I am only your guest instructor for this week, we do not have time to ensure your basic skills are up to par. I will make myself available to you every evening this week, though, if you wish to learn more. As always in martial arts, your base techniques must be solid or else your advanced techniques will be sloppy. My focus for this week's lessons will be using a staff against a sword."

She nodded to Jacob, standing off to the side with his metal practice sword.

"The advantage of a sword, of course, is that it is sharp, capable of killing your opponent with a single slice or thrust." She glanced at Jacob. "Lunge at me, please." Jacob lunged, aiming for her midsection. The professor stepped back and struck with her staff, pulling the blow an inch from his head. "The advantage of a staff is its longer reach. He is fully extended, yet still unable to hit me while I am able to hit him. The strategy of the swordsman is to get inside my reach. The strategy of the staff wielder is to maintain enough distance to strike without getting hit. Come at me again, Jacob."

Jacob began to attack with a series of feints and slices and thrusts. "It is imperative," Professor Yeoh said, "to be mindful of your surroundings and to never allow yourself to get backed into a wall. If that happens . . ." She intentionally backed herself up against the wall. "You might be able to keep the swordsman at bay, but if he slips inside . . ." She allowed Jacob to get past her defences, then stepped forward and to the side as he lunged so that she was standing beside him. "You don't just stand there and let yourself get hit. You close the distance, like I have done. At this point, you can either step behind your opponent and regain your distance, or you can strike at close range. A head strike, perhaps." She tapped Jacob on the head. "But a foot sweep would also work well." She swept him off his feet with her staff, and he landed on his back.

She helped him up and took his sword. "Another advantage of the staff is that it requires much less body movement. A sword can attack from many angles." She began slicing through the air. "But it requires a lot of motion from your body to do so, which takes time and telegraphs your intention to your opponent." She returned the sword to Jacob. "With the staff, though, I can make a pivot point with one hand and hold it from the top with my other hand. Notice how with merely the slightest movement of my top hand, I am able to strike my opponent anywhere from many angles. Not only is it faster than a sword, but it requires less work, so I will grow less tired over a prolonged fight."

She stepped away from Jacob. "The staff also has an advantage over the sword when dealing with multiple attackers. With a sword, you never want to leave your back exposed. You often stay in motion, choosing a single opponent and moving toward them while trying to keep all of your opponents in front of you. The same is true for the staff, if possible, but if you find yourself surrounded and get attacked from behind . . ." She turned her back to Jacob, who then attacked. She quickly slid the staff through her hands so that her back hand became the front hand. "See? Without even needing to move, I am able to keep my attacker at bay, simply by sliding the staff through my hands."

She bowed to Jacob, and he bowed back, placing his sword in her outstretched hand before resuming his seat. "Everyone, find a partner and grab a sword and an expandable staff. We will start with learning to keep your distance."

Zoe looked at Lin, who was staring at her mom with unmistakable pride.

8

PULLING THE STRINGS

"As you might expect, compulsion is impossible to perform on anyone who has their shield up," Professor Sharapova told the class. "You must either catch them before they can raise their shield or force your way through their shield, which is a whole other technique that maybe you will be taught later. I don't know. Hopefully, not by me."

Zoe winced as she remembered interrogating Ethan under Miss Gillespie's direction.

"We're going to try something simple today. You're going to make your partner raise their hand. That's it. Nothing more. No pranks. You will make them raise their hand up high, as if asking a question, and then lower their hand. That's it. Anything more and I will kick you out of this class. Does everyone understand me?" She paused to look around at the students. "Pair up with whoever you're sitting beside. Choose which of you will be the compeller first. Afterward, you will switch roles."

"You do it first," Lin said.

"You sure?" Zoe asked, hesitantly.

Lin nodded. "I want to know what it feels like before I do it to you."

Professor Sharapova slowly walked along the aisles. "The first thing to understand is that this is *not* telekinesis—at all. You are not *forcing* your partner's hand up. You are overpowering your partner's will and forcing them to lift their own hand up. Since this is our first lesson, if you are the one being compelled, do *not* resist. You will do so instinctively, every bit as much as you would resist trying to breathe underwater, so you will have to force yourself to relax, keep your shields down, and let yourself be controlled."

Zoe felt nervous. She had only just started learning this when she left the Igigi. Some had figured it out for themselves before that, though. She looked over at Ethan, who was staring off into space. He had always been the best. She *had* managed to overpower him, though, in the alley, making him walk toward her like a marionette. And it had felt so *wrong*. She shuddered.

"Slowly enter your partner's mind," Professor Sharapova said. "Gently. Try to slide in as unobtrusively as possible. You don't even want them to notice you're there. Don't do anything. Don't read their thoughts, don't rummage through their memories, don't do anything other than just *be* there."

Zoe did as she was instructed. She and Lin had done this many times before when they were first learning how to read each other's memories. This time was different, though. Lin's mind was . . . chaotic. Zoe kept seeing images of Professor Chao on his knees as Ragnar delivered his killing blow, but from a different angle than the one she knew. She felt immense rage and frustration everywhere, barely contained, and yet Lin looked so calm on the outside.

"The next step is a little difficult to explain," Professor Sharapova said. "Try to transplant yourself into their body. Allow yourself to feel their heartbeat, their breathing, and then their limbs and fingers and toes, as if they were your own. Don't try to move them yet. Just feel them. Imagine what it would feel like to twitch your new fingers, but don't actually do so. Spend a few minutes getting acquainted with your new body."

This felt strange. As Zoe allowed her consciousness to extend into Lin's body, she could feel Lin's limbs. And the more she became aware of Lin's body, the less she became aware of her own.

This feels so weird, Lin said in her mind. *I can feel you inside me. It's taking all my self-control not to throw you out.*

Sorry, Zoe answered. *I'm trying to be gentle.*

No, it's okay. You are. It's just . . . super uncomfortable. I don't like it.

"Focus on their right arm," Professor Sharapova said. "Focus on it until it feels like it's your own arm. Now, gently raise your new arm into the air."

Ethan's partner's arm shot high into the air, and he shrieked, "No! Get out! Get out! Make him stop! Make him stop!"

"Ethan, let him go!" Professor Sharapova barked.

Ethan did so immediately, and his partner's hand dropped. The boy fell off his chair as he scrambled away from Ethan. Professor Sharapova ran to his side. "It's okay. It's okay. Gently, everyone! Slowly and gently!"

Zoe tried to ignore the commotion. *I'm going to move your fingers first, okay?*

Okay, Lin said, nervously.

Zoe twitched her new fingers, and Lin gasped.

Oh, I really don't like this, Lin said. *This is so messed up.*

Want me to stop?

No, let's just get this over with.

Okay, I'm going to raise your arm now. Here we go.

Lin's arm raised slowly into the air and reached toward the ceiling.

Cool, Lin said. *Cool, cool, cool. Now, let me go.*

Zoe left Lin's body and mind, and Lin's shield shot up into place as she yanked her arm down and rubbed it vigorously.

"I did *not* like that," Lin said.

"If your partner throws you out, just reset and start over," the professor said. "Once you have successfully raised their hand, switch roles."

Once Lin had composed herself, Zoe relaxed. When she felt Lin touch her mind, though, she instinctively threw her out and raised her shields.

Sorry! Zoe said. I didn't mean to. You okay?

Yup. Let's try again.

On the third attempt, Zoe was finally able to force herself to tolerate Lin's presence in her mind. *Sorry, I don't know why I'm finding this so hard.*

Trauma, Lin said. *Ethan did this to you once against your will. But you're safe now. I'm your . . . friend . . . and we're doing this together, willingly. I'm going to raise your arm and that's it. Nothing else. Okay?*

Zoe took a deep breath and nodded. It was the first time Lin had called them friends since Zoe came back to school. Her arm lifted on its own, and she wanted to scream. *Okay, great*, she said, her panic rising. *You can leave now.* She felt Lin's presence depart, and she, too, raised her shields and dropped her arm, breathing heavily.

Lin touched her shoulder, and Zoe nodded. "I'm okay."

"When you have both had a chance to do this," Professor Sharapova said to the class, "and you have both been successful, you can either just relax until the end of class or you can try again with the other arm. Do *not* do anything other than raising a single hand. In our next class, we will attempt to manipulate multiple limbs at the same time, and we will eventually progress to making your partner walk and perform complex tasks. But not yet. Please do not practice this outside of class. And if I *ever* hear of anyone compelling someone against their will, I will kick them out of this class. Am I understood?"

▪ ▪ ▪

Zoe told Lin that she was staying behind after class and then grabbed

Ethan's hand and pulled him toward Professor Sharapova's desk. Professor Sharapova looked up from her notes to realize they were the only ones left, and her expression turned to one of both fear and loathing.

"Hello, Natasha," Zoe began, looking as contrite as possible.

"You will address me as Professor Sharapova," she snapped.

"I'm sorry," Zoe said, quickly. "Professor Sharapova. We . . . want to apologize. I'm so sorry for what we did to you. It was wrong . . . and horrible. I was a different person then. A zealot, brainwashed since birth. I know it doesn't excuse what we did to you, but I just want you to know that I'm not that person anymore. And if I could take it all back, I would."

"Whose idea was it?" Professor Sharapova demanded.

"It . . . it was mine. I was a pathetic, loyal minion wanting to impress Ragnar, and I asked Ethan to help me."

"So, neither of you were following orders. You didn't fear punishment if you didn't do it. You *chose* to violate me. Correct?"

"Yes," Zoe said. "Again, I'm—"

"You're sorry. I know. Anything else?"

Zoe squirmed. This could have gone better. She could hardly blame Professor Sharapova, though. But they needed her help, so Zoe's next words had to be straight to the point. "They did something to Ethan's head. Something bad, I think. We didn't know who else to turn to."

Professor Sharapova looked at Ethan. "What did they do?"

He wouldn't meet her eye—and hadn't for the entire conversation. "I don't know. I don't remember much. It's all hazy. But I remember being strapped to a chair—repeatedly, I think—and injected with something to prevent me from fighting back while someone did things in my brain. I don't know the person, I don't think. I don't feel like me now. I feel . . . off. Like I'm constantly under attack, jumping at shadows. I sometimes even catch myself thinking things that feel like . . . someone else's thoughts. I think I'm losing time, too. I never find myself somewhere else or anything, but I keep catching myself in a daze. And sometimes little things are off afterward. Like an object has moved, or my laptop isn't how I left it. I just have this overwhelming feeling that I'm losing my mind."

Professor Sharapova regarded him. "I see," she said, clearly conflicted. "And you would like my help."

Ethan nodded, embarrassed. "I know I don't deserve it." His voice cracked a little. "But I really need it."

Professor Sharapova ran her fingers through her hair and sighed. "Ethan, are you sorry for what you did to me? Would you do it again?"

Ethan nodded. "I *am* sorry. Truly. But . . . yes, I would do it again, if Zoe asked me to."

"Ethan!" Zoe blurted.

"Are you serious?" Professor Sharapova snapped.

"I wouldn't *want* to!" Ethan said, raising his hands. "I'd hate every second of it! I'm good at compulsion, but I hate doing it. But . . . I would still do it, if Zoe asked me to."

The professor looked like she could hardly believe what she was hearing. "Why?" she asked, incredulously. "*Why* would you do that to me again, just because she asked?"

Ethan shrugged. "Because . . . I love her."

Zoe looked helplessly back and forth between Ethan and the professor. "I would never ask that again! And even if I did, you shouldn't do it, Ethan! You shouldn't do something you know is wrong just because I asked you to!" She faced the professor. "I'm sorry, Professor! He doesn't know what he's saying. He's not in his right mind. He needs help. Please."

Professor Sharapova stared at Ethan for a long time. "I'm free tomorrow. My office, after last class."

"Thank you," Zoe said. "We'll be—"

"Not you." She rounded on Zoe. "Just Ethan. I haven't forgiven either of you, but I won't turn away a student in need. We'll figure out what they did to you, Ethan. Don't breathe a word of this to anyone, though. Neither of you. Not a soul, do you understand? Don't even let on to anyone—especially Ragnar—that you know they did something to Ethan's mind. If he discovers we know what he did and that we are actively trying to undo it . . . well, I can't imagine he will be pleased."

· · ·

With Ethan now a part of the gang, the Valkyries filled him in on Ragnar's offer to Zoe.

"You know he's manipulating you, right?" he said. "He wants you to do something he wants, which aligns with what you also want, so that the idea of obeying him isn't so repulsive. He'll keep moving the line until you're doing things you never would've thought you'd do for him."

"Gee, where have I heard that before?" Lin asked.

Zoe ignored her. "I know. But as long as I'm aware of that, I can use *him*. He'll think he's using me, but in reality, I'll be using his authority to allow me to do some good out in the world without compromising my principles."

"Wait, I thought it didn't work like that," Lin said, pointedly.

"It's not the same thing, Lin."

"If you say so."

"If you insist on doing this, I'm going, too," Ethan said. "I'm the best one here at mindbending. I've never implanted a thought or a value system before, so I should practice first, and maybe I can convince Professor Sharapova to give me a few pointers. Do you have a plan yet?"

Zoe didn't know what to say. Lin refused to come along, so she had to admit, taking Ethan did make sense. The others nodded like they thought so, too.

"Not yet," she admitted. "I was just thinking I'd start small. Somewhere close by—so, Toronto. Someone highly influential but with no security and who lives alone. That way, we can just enter their home and spend all night doing what we have to do."

Ethan nodded. "That makes sense. So, a politician who's not too high up. Or a CEO. Or maybe a journalist."

Zoe squirmed in her chair. "I don't know. Targeting a journalist doesn't seem right to me. I think they should be off-limits."

"What about a talk show host?" Lin suggested. "One of those yelly people on those cable news shows that old people watch?"

"Hey, that's not bad," Paige said.

"Oh, but I don't think they live in Toronto." Lin sighed.

"New York City," Ethan said. "Not too far from here—if they'll let us go. I'm sure those guys have some security, but I doubt it's anything we can't handle."

"That could make the world a better place," Priya mused. "Providing a different perspective to viewers used to hearing only one viewpoint. But it could just get them fired, I suppose. And it won't help prevent the end of the world or anything. I thought we wanted to do something big."

"Think of it as a trial run?" Paige offered.

"You *could* go big," Ethan said. "I mean, this is Canada. The prime minister lives in a regular house without much security. There's no Secret Service. We could get in there at night."

"Are you serious?" Zoe asked. "I wasn't thinking of going *that* big for our first attempt. Besides, he's not exactly a horrible person."

"He's the same as all the rest," Makena said. All eyes turned to her. "He pretends to be woke, but he's just another rich, powerful man leading a settler colonial state. In a way, he's worse than those blatantly racist, anti-intellectual politicians. At least you know where *they* stand."

"Anti-intellectual?" Paige asked. "Is that a thing? People against . . . being smart?"

"I didn't know you were so into politics," Zoe said.

"I'm not," Makena said. "I just know how the world works. My mother is a human rights activist in Kenya. I grew up attending protest marches. We're sheltered from the world here at the Academy. Taught that we exist separate from the world of Typicals. It's easy not to interfere with their world when we're not even aware of what's wrong with it. It's crazy, though. We spend the first fourteen years of our lives living as Typicals and then suddenly we're supposed to just abandon our people and switch our allegiance to the Telepaths. Some of the kids here come from really oppressed places, and they're supposed to go home after graduation and *not* use their Abilities to help their people? Anyway, Professor Grant taught history from a very Western colonial perspective. I doubt he was even aware of half the injustices he never taught us. Professor Dlamini, though . . . *she* sees the world as it really is."

Zoe nodded. "I was literally raised in a bunker, so I wasn't exposed to any perspective except that of the Igigi. According to them, Typicals are brutal to each other and unfit to rule themselves. And to back up that claim, they taught us about every war, genocide, occupation, and injustice throughout history—including current ones. So, I agree with what you're saying. I'm just worried about setting our sights on a world leader for our first mission."

"So, let's lower our sights instead," Lin said. "Like, a really popular, toxic, social media influencer."

"Oh, I like that even more than talk show hosts!" Paige cried.

"I like it," Zoe said, as the others nodded. "We won't change the world, but it's a start. Probably not much security. Let's do a little research and pick our target. The most popular, most toxic influencer nearby."

9

CONDUCTING RESEARCH

The Academy still prohibited cellphones, and the firewall was even more sophisticated and restrictive than before, preventing virtually all outbound traffic beyond search engines. Students could still access social media on their laptops, though they couldn't create posts of their own. After some digging, the Valkyries chose their target.

"So, we're agreed?" Zoe asked. "Andre Taggart?"

Huddled in their little private corner of the library, the others nodded.

"He lives in Toronto," Zoe said, counting off on her fingers. "So, that's convenient. Alpha male, racist, misogynist, homophobe, transphobe, anti-science, climate change denier. Anything else?"

"He's a self-made man," Paige said, "whose parents just happen to be uber rich."

"He has millions of followers, and he's super popular with gamer boys," Lin added.

Makena grinned. "He's perfect."

The first step was to learn his address and his schedule, so they could be sure he would be home. Despite all their Internet sleuthing, though, they couldn't do it. Apparently, rich and famous people were pretty secretive about where they lived. In the end, they decided to inform Miss Gillespie of their plan and ask if Ragnar's intelligence network could provide the address. Meanwhile, Ethan went off to his first session with Professor Sharapova.

"Good luck," Zoe said, squeezing his hand.

...

When Ethan didn't show up for dinner, Zoe went looking for him. She knocked on his door, but his roommate Phillip said he hadn't seen him. She tried Professor Sharapova's office but there was no answer. She couldn't find him at the dojo or barn, either. Finally, she reached out with her mind. They had always been able to communicate over long distances.

Ethan? Where are you?

He didn't answer, which meant he was either unconscious or ignoring her. Worried, she kept searching, and finally, she found him in the woods, sitting behind a large tree. He was crying. She sat next to him and wrapped her arm around him. She didn't say anything. Something terrible must have happened during his session with Professor Sharapova.

After a few minutes, he wiped his eyes and tried to steady his breathing.

"She said she wanted to start earlier than when I was imprisoned." He could barely control his voice. "Asked me to think back to when I first started having feelings for you. I didn't understand why, but she said she had a suspicion and that it would help her figure out what they did to me. We went back to when you and I were little. The time when you got in a fight with a bunch of kids—too many for you to handle—and they beat you up. I found you and took you to the infirmary."

"I remember," Zoe said.

"Ragnar was furious. He demanded to know what had happened and why I hadn't helped you. I said I wasn't anywhere nearby when it happened. He looked at me for a long time. I never remembered anything more about that incident. But there was more. Sharapova uncovered a memory that was hidden."

His lower lip quivered, so Zoe waited patiently until he composed himself.

"Ragnar told me to sit in a chair. The doctor injected me with something that made me feel weird, like I had no willpower. Then, Ragnar sat in front of me and went into my mind. I was so scared. He told me you were reckless and that it might get you killed before you could grow up to reach your potential. So, he wanted you to have a protector. Someone who would watch over you and always have your back, no matter what, just in case you got yourself into more trouble than you could handle."

A chill ran up Zoe's spine as a horrible thought occurred to her, and she feared what he would say next.

"He . . . *made* me love you, with every fibre of my being. An overpowering, all-encompassing love for you that would become the tentpole of my life—the defining value that all my thoughts and actions would be built around from that moment on. And along with it, he gave me an overwhelming compulsion to keep it a secret from you and everyone else." He sobbed, "It was never *real*, Zoe."

She hugged him close. "I'm so sorry, Ethan," was all she could think to say.

"The thing is," he continued, "even now that Sharapova undid Ragnar's compulsion, it doesn't matter. I *still* love you, as much as ever. It might as well be part of my DNA now. It happened so early in my childhood that all the neurons in my brain have wired themselves around this artificially implanted suggestion. I'll never know if it's real or not."

Zoe hardly knew what to say. She was furious at Ragnar. To do this to anyone was horrifying, let alone a child. No one deserved this. And yet, wasn't she planning to fundamentally change the value system of another man, arguing that it was for the greater good—for *his own* good? Was she really so different from Ragnar?

"I can't even let Ragnar know that I know what he did to me, or he'll know Sharapova's been in my mind."

"We'll figure it out," Zoe said. She kissed his cheek and then rested her head against his. "It'll be okay."

■ ■ ■

Ragnar must have approved their mission because they had a hand-delivered dossier on their target the very next day. The guard looked none too happy as he handed it over to Zoe in the library, grumbling something about not being a delivery boy for children.

Everyone gathered around as she opened the large brown envelope and pulled out photos. She placed them on the table.

"Pictures of his home," Lin said. "A penthouse apartment, of course."

"Whoa, they even got floor plans," Paige said. "It's like we're freaking spies."

Zoe skimmed the dossier. "We have an address. No immediate travel plans, so he should be in Toronto. The surveillance report says he has two bodyguards stationed outside his door and four bodyguards whenever he goes out."

"Now we have to decide who's going," Makena said. "I'm the only one old enough to drive, so I'm coming."

"I'm the best at mindbending," Ethan said, "so I'm in."

"I am *so* in," Paige said. "But I want a ninja outfit. We *all* get ninja outfits. Oh! And gadgets. We should ask for spy gadgets."

Zoe looked at Lin, who bit her lip. "I'll ask my mom," she said. "But I don't think she'll like this."

"I'll go if Lin goes," Priya said. "And I'll stay if she stays."

Zoe nodded. "And I'm going. So, now we just need to learn how to turn a horrible person into a good person."

"I assume Sharapova will teach us eventually," Makena said.

"Yeah, but we need to know now."

"I have an idea of how to do it," Ethan said, adding privately to Zoe, *Now that I remember what Ragnar did to me as a child.* "I'd like to ask Sharapova for some pointers, though." He looked at the clock on the wall. "And my next session with her is now, so . . . I'll let you know how it goes."

"Broach the subject very carefully," Zoe cautioned. "Professor Sharapova clearly doesn't approve of compulsion and might react very badly if she learns what we're planning. Best to ask theoretically, if possible."

■ ■ ■

"Yeah, she wasn't happy," Ethan said, when he got back to the library. Only Zoe had stuck around to wait for him. "I couldn't keep pressing her for details, so I switched to asking what she thought of the ethics of using compulsion on horrible people in positions of influence. I brought up what Professor Dlamini said about compulsion being better than assassination and the end justifying the means." He shook his head. "I don't think Professor Sharapova is a utilitarian."

"What about your mind?" Zoe asked. "Does she know what Ragnar did to you while you were imprisoned?"

Ethan shook his head. "No, but she said it's like nothing she's ever seen before, which can't be good. At first, she didn't notice anything obviously wrong, but then she saw what looked like new neurons growing. A *lot* of them, apparently."

"Whoa. Any recovered memories of the person actually doing it?"

"No. It's weird. I can remember someone being in the cell with me but not any details about them. She figured that my memories must've been blocked, but she couldn't find them. Now, she's wondering if maybe the memories were destroyed somehow."

"She hasn't given up, though, right?" Zoe asked. "She's going to keep trying to figure out what's wrong?"

"That's what she said."

"Good. Hey, let me show you what I found while you were gone." She held up a book. "*The Art of Mindbending.* It's pretty old. The author doesn't even call it compulsion. But there's a chapter on what we want to do. What Professor Sharapova said in her first class is true: It's a lot like hypnosis. You talk to the person and make a suggestion—in this case, about how we want them to behave. Where it differs is that we're inside their mind when we make that suggestion—and we can immediately see where in the brain that new suggestion conflicts with long-established values. We can then block off those areas, so that the suggestion is better able to take hold."

Ethan nodded. "Yeah, that jives with what I was thinking. I still wish I could practice before we try this for real, though."

"I have an idea," Zoe said.

■ ■ ■

Zoe knocked on the door. It opened, and there stood Fasil, looking shocked.

"My lady!" he blurted before backing away, bowing deferentially. Zoe and Ethan slipped into the custodian's office, shutting the door behind them.

"Hello, Fasil," Zoe said. "Do you remember my friend Ethan?"

"Yes, my lady. Worm watched you both grow up during my visits to the Centre when other agents and I were trained to use our new Abilities."

Zoe cocked her head. "The Centre? Is that what you called it? We never even had a name for it. It was just . . . home . . . or school."

"Is there something Worm can do for my lord and lady?" he asked, clearly nervous about their presence in his office—and between him and the exit.

"It's more like something we can do for you," Zoe replied. "Why don't you have a seat, Fasil?" She gestured toward his chair.

He began to shake.

"It's okay," Zoe said, quickly. "We're not going to hurt you. I promise. It's just the opposite, in fact. Please just sit, okay?"

Fasil retreated until the backs of his knees touched the chair, then he dropped into it. His lip quivered. The poor man.

Ethan stood behind his chair and placed his hands on Fasil's head. "You too, Zoe. You need to see what I'm doing, so you can learn how to do it yourself. Guide him to the moment."

Zoe sat on the edge of the desk and gently touched Fasil's head. She let herself enter his mind. She could feel Ethan in there already. What a *strange* sensation, she thought.

Fasil, do you remember when you were captured after we fought? You said Ragnar was angry with you.

"Yes, my lady. I remember. Very angry."

Zoe could see his memories of Ragnar looking furiously down at him.

He took you back to . . . the Centre?

"Yes, my lady." She saw the inside of a cell. In fact, it looked like the exact same cell she'd spent four months in.

What did they do to you there? As soon as she asked, she saw his memories and flinched.

"Torture, my lady. It's okay, though, yeah? Worm deserved it."

No one deserves to be tortured. I'm so sorry that happened to you. Now, I want you to remember the moment just before you became Worm.

He was strapped to a metal chair in the middle of the cell. Ragnar loomed over him. Fasil was crying and begging him for mercy, and then . . . he was walking out of the cell behind Ragnar.

The memory has been blocked, Ethan said. *Can you see it? Watch. I'll repair it.*

Zoe watched as a neural pathway regrew.

There we go.

Ragnar placed his hands on Fasil's head and closed his eyes. *You are pathetic,* she heard Ragnar's voice echo in his mind. *Worthless. You are not even a man. You are a worm. In fact, that is your name now. Worm.* As he said this, areas of Fasil's mind fought back against the suggestion.

Pause, Ethan said. *Watch what he did. All these areas that are lighting up now are rejecting being called Worm. You can see that the neural pathways to these areas have been broken. So, we're going to fix them.*

Zoe observed each pathway repair itself.

Here, you try to repair the next one, Ethan said.

How? she asked.

It's the same as healing a cut. You just focus on it and imagine it regrowing to be the way it should be.

Zoe willed the neural pathway to repair itself and was astonished to see it obey.

There you go, Ethan said. *Nice. Let's repair the rest of them together.*

It took only a few minutes. *What's your name, Fasil?* she asked.

"It's Fasil, of course," he said.

Of course. What did Ragnar say next, Fasil?

From this day forward, Ragnar said, *you are the lowest of servants. You live only to serve me and the New Gods. You will bow and scrape and show deference at all times. Like a serf from olden days, you will refer to the children as lords and ladies. You will endure their abuse and thank them for it, because you know deep down that you deserve it. You will spend every waking hour cleaning our filth. The only joy you shall ever experience for the *rest of your miserable life will be the joy of serving us.*

Oh, this poor man, Zoe thought. She and Ethan worked quickly to repair all the pathways that were lighting up during Ragnar's compulsion. *How do you feel, Fasil?* she asked once they had finished.

"I . . ." Tears streamed down his face. "I feel . . . like I've just woken up from a nightmare that wouldn't end." He started to sob.

You tried to kill me, Zoe said. *I can't ever forget that, but no one deserves what Ragnar did to you.*

"Thank you," he said, his chest heaving. "Thank you. I regret what I did to you. I was under orders to bring you in, but I got carried away. I don't know why. I wasn't always like that. I was a good man once."

Zoe looked at Ethan, who raised an eyebrow. *What do you mean?*

"I grew up in Beirut," he said. "My father was killed during the civil war when I was young, so it was just me and my mother. We had nothing, but she raised me to be honourable, like my father. When I was old enough and the war ended, I wanted to do my part to ensure that no one ever invaded our country again. I became a skilled operative. But . . . it wasn't what I'd thought it would be. I'd thought I would be fighting for a noble cause, but I kept being pushed to do things I thought were wrong. I came to realize I was no better than any of my counterparts in other nations. Espionage is simply not an ethical profession. So, I quit. My employers were not happy. I planned to take my wife and children and mother far away, where they would be safe from retaliation. But . . . I didn't. Instead, I left them behind and joined the cause of the Igigi." A confused look contorted his face. "I never understood why I did that."

How did you learn of the Igigi, Fasil? Ethan asked.

"From Master Ragnar," he said. "I was having a drink in a bar with some old friends to say goodbye, when suddenly, everyone put their head down and went to sleep. Everyone except for a large Scandinavian man leaning against the bar. He told me he'd heard about me, that I was exactly the sort of man he was looking for, and that he could offer me the noble cause I was looking for."

Zoe could see and hear this meeting through Fasil's eyes and ears. "He said I had to come with him right away, that I must leave my family behind and never return." As Ragnar spoke, Zoe and Ethan hurriedly repaired neural pathways to the parts of Fasil's brain that had rejected this. "He was so persuasive," Fasil continued. "I remember his eyes boring into me. I felt like I would follow him to the ends of the earth. So, when he got up and left . . . I followed him. I never even said goodbye to my family. I've . . . *hated* myself ever since. But not once did I ever consider going back to them. I don't know if they were punished by my employers for my absence. I don't even know if they're alive or dead."

I think we've repaired them all. What do you think, Zoe?

Let's see. She withdrew her hands from Fasil's head. "Fasil, looking back at that meeting with Ragnar, would you still make the same choice to go with him?"

"No!" he cried. "Never! I don't understand what came over me that day or . . . every day since." He looked utterly horrified. "What have I done? I abandoned them!"

"It wasn't your fault," Zoe said. "None of this was your fault. You've been under his control since the day you met him. He compelled you to be his loyal servant and further compelled you to never even entertain the thought that you were acting under compulsion."

Fasil stared at her with haunted eyes. "I'll kill him," he whispered.

"I wouldn't advise it," Ethan said, lifting his hands from Fasil's head. "He'll almost certainly kill you."

"But maybe you could escape and go back home," Zoe said. "Getting off the Academy grounds will be the hardest part. We're all prisoners here. But I think we can help you. We're going on a mission soon. We're literally going to be driving out of here. If you can be patient a little while longer—and keep playing the part of Worm—we can try to smuggle you to Toronto. After that . . . I honestly don't know. I'm assuming you don't have a passport or anything."

"I can handle that," Fasil said. "How long?"

"A few more days, at least," Zoe said, standing up. "I know it won't be easy, but I think it's your best chance to escape. We'll let you know more details as soon as we have them." She touched his shoulder. "I'm really sorry this happened to you."

Fasil nodded, and Zoe and Ethan peeked out into the hall before sneaking out of the custodian's office.

Zoe, Ethan said, as they walked, *you realize we can't just let him leave, right? He knows about the existence of Telepaths. He has no reason to keep that a secret.*

Zoe didn't answer.

And while we got some practice at undoing compulsion, we didn't even try to compel him to be a good man.

We didn't have to! He already was a good man!

Agreed, Ethan said. *I never saw that coming. I always just assumed all the godlings were morally bankrupt Typicals who jumped at the opportunity to gain powers and help take over the world. Regardless, we still have a problem, and it still requires the same solution.*

Compel him not to reveal our existence, you mean?

Exactly. You heard Professor Sharapova. They do it to all the Anunnaki parents already. No big deal.

It's still a big deal, Zoe protested.

We could just erase his memories?

That's years of his life!

Well, do you have a better idea?

I don't, Zoe admitted, *but I don't like either of those options.*

Well, he knows everything, thanks to us, so if he escapes—with or without our help—he's a huge liability.

I know, Zoe said, as they reached the dorms. *Let's sleep on it and ask what the others think in the morning.*

When Zoe entered her room, Lin looked up from her desk and shook her head. "She went ballistic."

"Your mom?"

"Yeah. She said it was not only dangerous but highly unethical, going against everything we believe in. She won't let me go. So, Priya won't go, either. Sorry. It's just the four of you, I guess."

...

The next morning, Fasil was gone. They first suspected as much when security escorted Zoe and Ethan from the Great Hall to Ragnar's office.

"What did you two do?" he asked, pointedly.

Zoe and Ethan looked at each other and shrugged.

"You'll have to be more specific, sir," Ethan said.

"You were both in the custodian's office yesterday."

"How could you know that?" Zoe asked. She'd been absolutely certain no one had spotted them.

"I told you once that you would do well to assume *he* is always watching, Zoe."

Zoe was fairly certain he was just trying to scare her by invoking Marduk. It seemed far more likely that he had cameras hidden everywhere.

"You spoke with Worm yesterday. This morning, a guard was found incapacitated near the outer wall and Worm is nowhere to be found. Which means he is no longer Worm but rather Fasil. Care to explain how that happened?"

"It's my fault," Ethan said, quickly. "I wanted a test subject to practice on before we head out on our mission."

"No, it was my idea," Zoe confessed. "I wanted to see how you did . . . what you did to him. But it just seemed so sad . . . so I undid it. I couldn't help myself."

"I see," Ragnar said. "That would explain why Fasil returned, but not why he then fled. He should still be a loyal godling."

"He fled before, though," Zoe pointed out. "After he failed to capture me last year, he fled."

Ragnar thought about this. "That is true. His fear overcame his loyalty."

"The problem with ruling through fear," Zoe muttered.

Ragnar stared at her with that unnerving gaze of his. Was he deliberating whether to believe her or punish her? "That's all you did to him? You didn't undo anything else? Or implant some other suggestion?"

"No, sir," they both said in unison.

"Because that would be very bad, if you did. All of the godlings have been compelled to keep our existence secret from the Typicals. If you removed that and he exposes us to the world . . . that is something even your precious Professor Chao feared."

"We didn't," Zoe lied.

After a long silence, Ragnar said, "Go. No more experimenting on my godlings. Experiment on each other if you must."

"Yes, sir," they said, hurrying from his office.

This could be bad, Zoe said to Ethan.

Very.

10

LESSONS IN POWER

"Maybe it won't be so bad," Lin said, as they headed to their first class. "I mean, who would believe him? A secret society of superpowered immortals who run around with swords and control people's minds? That all sounds a bit ridiculous, don't you think?"

"But if he convinces even one person to investigate . . ." Zoe began.

"Then they'll be discovered, and someone will do mind mojo on them to make them think they never found anything."

"But if they're not discovered, or if they capture video proof and upload it—"

"No one will believe it! Have you seen how many fake videos are on the Internet? People supposedly levitating and moving things with their mind?"

"But that's different from a video taken by a credible intelligence agent," Zoe argued.

"Whatever. What's done is done, Zoe. You did a good thing, helping Fasil like that. Now it's out of our hands. We have our own problems to worry about."

Zoe couldn't argue with that. They were hardly going to escape the Academy just to hunt him down. Ragnar had his own people doing that, anyway—and she hoped Fasil would be able to elude them. Still, she and Ethan had narrowly avoided becoming Lafleur's lab rats, and she didn't want that to happen to Telepaths en masse if their existence was exposed to the world.

"Oh, here," Lin said, fishing in her backpack and pulling out a bagel, which she offered to Zoe. "Thought you'd be hungry after those stupid security guards made you miss breakfast. I hate how they strut around like they own the place, trying to intimidate everyone. I wonder if they realize how many of us could kick their butts?"

"Thanks," Zoe said, munching the bagel. "See you next class."

"Actually—" Lin followed her into the classroom, "I'm in Advanced Telekinesis now, too."

"What? For real?"

"Yup. Apparently, getting angry has it perks. It unlocked a telekinetic potential I didn't know I had. Professor Martinov moved me here."

Zoe wasn't pleased. It was bad enough that Ragnar was encouraging Lin to tap into her anger, but now Professor Martinov was, too? He'd always said that being angry all the time was a terrible way to live.

"Everybody up!" Professor Martinov yelled. "Today's lesson is outside. Follow me!" He spun, twirling his cape, and led them through the Main Hall and out the front entrance. Parked outside under the largest tree was an enormous off-road vehicle—the sort you might need on a jungle adventure. It looked like an old model, but in immaculate condition.

"This," said the professor, "is our new headmaster's personal vehicle. It weighs two metric tonnes. I am told he is very fond of it. Who would like to try to lift it?"

Everyone glanced at each other.

"Does he know we're doing this?" someone asked.

"Of course," Professor Martinov answered, innocently. "Do you think I am the sort of person who would just allow his students to play with—and potentially damage—a terribly expensive, classic vehicle that means the world to his employer?"

"Why is it under a tree?" another student asked.

"Lest any spy satellites be looking down at us. We must *always* take care not to expose ourselves. No matter what."

"I *hate* having to hide like this," Jacob grumbled in the back. "What are we afraid of anyway? They should be freaking worshipping us."

"You in the back, thank you for volunteering. Come to the front, please."

Jacob made his way to the front and gestured at the vehicle. "No one can lift that. What's the point of this?"

"What, you think my lessons don't have a point? That we're just messing around with someone's truck for no good reason? Just try your best. Get into a solid stance, use your telekinesis to strengthen your bones—particularly your spine—and try to lift the truck."

Jacob did just that. The truck's suspension visibly moved up a bit, but the tires never left the ground.

"Come on, you can do better than that!" Professor Martinov yelled. "Really try! Give it everything you've got!"

Grunting with effort, Jacob finally surrendered.

"A valiant attempt!" the professor said. "Now, look at your feet."

Jacob looked down, confused, and everyone laughed. His feet were buried in half a foot of dirt.

"And this, Jacob, is the *point* of today's lesson. It takes a great deal of force to lift that truck. And the farther away from it you are, the more force it requires. This is known as torque. Your physics professor should really be paying me for all these lessons." He raised his hands defensively. "I kid, I kid," he said. "But . . . it's true. Anyway, as we know from Newton, for every action, there is an equal and opposite reaction. So, all that force you use to lift that truck up pushes *you* down. It isn't something to worry much about on a concrete floor, but outside, on the grass, it becomes a problem. Especially when you're in combat and need to be able to dodge quickly. So, how can we fix this problem. Anyone?"

Paige raised their hand. "Snowshoes," they said.

His face lit up. "Exactly!" he cried. "It is *exactly* like snowshoes! Why do snowshoes let us walk on snow without sinking?"

"More surface area," Zoe blurted.

He clapped his hands and pointed at Zoe. "There you go! More surface area. If you spread the force over a larger surface area, then each square centimetre of snow has less force on it, so you don't fall through. The same is true here. So, the trick to heavy lifting is to use your telekinesis to create a flat, circular platform beneath you to spread out the force. Paige, since it was your idea, you can try first!"

Paige stepped up and assumed a solid stance. Their eyes narrowed. They spread their arms out at their sides with palms facing up, as though about to physically lift something heavy. Then, the vehicle's chassis rose. Zoe watched the grass compress in a four-foot circle beneath Paige. Slowly, the front wheels lifted and hovered shakily an inch off the ground before Paige gasped and dropped the car.

"Magnificent!" Professor Martinov cried. "Very impressive, Paige. Who's next?"

Three Igigi students tried, but only Kyle was able to lift the front tires off the ground. When Pacha stepped forward, everyone held their breath. The diminutive boy closed his eyes a moment, then assumed a casual stance and lifted. The truck moved but didn't leave the ground. His brows furrowed, and he solidified his stance and spread his arms wide. No noise escaped his lips, but he breathed heavily and sweat beaded his forehead. Slowly, the truck began to rise. First the front tires, then the back tires, until, finally, the entire truck floated unsteadily an inch off the ground. He held it for five seconds before it fell.

Everyone cheered. Professor Martinov nodded approvingly. "I knew you were a powerhouse, Pacha, but I wasn't sure even *you* could do it. *Very* nice. Zoe, your turn."

Zoe stepped forward. A year ago, she'd barely been able to levitate a hundred-gram weight unless she got angry—and only then did she become strong. She had been like that her entire life. Even now, it was what she was known for. But this time, she was determined to prove—to herself and to Lin—that anger wasn't the only way. She had spent four months in solitary, under the tutelage of her hallucination of Professor Chao, relearning how to achieve telekinetic strength without anger. But she had never attempted anything like this before, and she didn't know if she could do it.

She sat cross-legged on the ground and blocked out the others' murmuring. She closed her eyes and reached into herself, searching for the source of her strength. The source of her willpower. Perhaps it was just her imagination, but during her many hours of meditation and self-reflection, she had begun to picture her willpower as coming from a well within herself. By drawing upon that well slowly, she could levitate for hours; so, theoretically, if she drew upon it quickly, she ought to be able to levitate a truck for a few seconds.

Once she found it, she created a circular shield beneath her and strengthened her skeleton. Then, with a deep breath, she reached out to the truck and began to lift it. At first, it didn't budge, so she increased her force, imagining the flow of her will doubling, then doubling again. Soon, all four wheels of the vehicle lifted off the ground. The downward force on her body was so immense she was sure that if she lost her concentration for even a fraction of a second, her spine would snap. But she lifted the vehicle unsteadily another inch. Then another. The higher it rose, the more force it took to hold it there. She wouldn't be able to keep it up much longer, so she gave it everything she had. The truck was a full three feet off the ground before she knew she was done. She let it drop quickly but controlled its descent until the tires touched the ground again. Then she released it and relaxed.

After a long time, she heard Paige say, "Whoa," as if from very far away. Zoe opened her eyes and got to one knee, but her legs felt like rubber and the world spun. She realized she was leaning against Lin, who was somehow crouched next to her, with Ethan supporting her other side. Professor Martinov knelt in front of her with her head in his hands, looking into her eyes. She tried to say something funny but was fairly certain it was just slurred gibberish.

"Paige, please run to the infirmary and fetch Professor Yeoh. Zoe, can you hear me?"

She nodded. She felt so dizzy. What was wrong with her?

"Well," the professor said, "*you* have certainly come a long way since our first class a year ago. Who taught you how to do that?"

"Professor Chao," she slurred.

Puzzled, he looked at Lin, who shrugged. "Well, I have never in my life witnessed such a display from a student. But you overextended yourself. What you are now experiencing is glycogen depletion. Glycogen fuels your muscles and your brain. Long-distance runners sometimes experience this after several hours. They call it 'hitting the wall.' You managed to deplete your glycogen stores in under a minute because you were lifting a two-tonne vehicle, using an incredible amount of energy in a short period of time. You'll be fine, though. You just need rest and lots of food and drink to restore your energy. We'll still have Professor Yeoh check you out, but your breathing seems good, so I don't think you've injured your brain in any way. I think we can continue. Lin, would you like a turn at lifting Ragnar's vehicle?"

Ethan helped Zoe to the side, where she promptly sat back down on the grass and watched Lin assume a stable stance. She looked at Zoe and nodded, then began lifting. But nothing happened.

You can do it, Lin, Zoe said in her mind. *You don't need to draw on your anger for power. It's already there in you, you just have to find it.*

Still, the vehicle didn't move.

I can't, Lin said.

You can! You saw me do it. Don't get mad—just get really calm and focus on finding where your power is coming from.

Students started giggling.

Your way isn't working, Zoe.

Be patient. You don't need to be able to do this today. It's more important to do it the right way and fail than to do it the wrong way and succeed.

No! Lin yelled, and the chassis began to move. *I tried it your way. Now I'm doing it my way. I hate this stupid truck!* Lin severed their connection and stepped forward, eyes full of rage. Zoe watched incredulously as Ragnar's vehicle rose off the ground. How could Lin have become so powerful so quickly? How could she ever convince her that this wasn't the way when it was working so well for her?

Lin took another step and began to shout as the vehicle rose a full two feet off the ground. She yelled louder, sending it a foot higher. Suddenly, it began to crumple.

"Lin, that's enough!" Professor Martinov cried.

Lin roared and the headlights exploded.

"I said that's enough!" He pushed in front of her, and Lin threw her arms down and the truck slammed to the ground. She stood there, panting.

"Uh-oh," Ethan said, nodding toward the school entrance, from which Ragnar had just emerged. He did not look happy.

"What is the meaning of this?" he bellowed, as the students parted to let him pass. Lin faced him with murder in her eyes.

"My fault, my fault." Professor Martinov stepped between them, arm outstretched placatingly. Suddenly, he clutched his throat and dropped to his knees. Lin stared at him, bewildered, then looked up as Ragnar bore down on her.

"No!" she screamed, and thrust her arms out, shoving Ragnar back several feet. He shrugged it off and sent her flying into the grill of the vehicle. She collapsed.

Zoe leapt to her feet and joined Ethan, Paige, and Pasha in blocking his path to Lin. Her fists crackled with electricity, but really, she could barely hold herself upright.

"Get away from my daughter," Professor Yeoh roared, racing toward them. Ragnar turned, and Professor Martinov got to his feet, rubbing his throat. Ragnar seemed to weigh his options. Did he really want to pick a fight with two of his professors and four of his students—in front of an entire class? Or would that make him look weak—like an ineffectual leader?

"I. Expect. Obedience." His gaze swept across everyone. "An attack against me has *severe* consequences."

"She was defending her teacher," Zoe said.

"Was this your idea of rebellion?" Ragnar spat at Professor Martinov, as security arrived. "Show your students that they can disrespect my property and they'll soon begin to disrespect me?" Ragnar jerked his head at the guards. "Put him in a cell."

"No!" Paige yelled, stepping forward.

But Professor Martinov raised his arms. "It's fine," he said. "I'll go." He allowed himself to be escorted back to the school.

"As for your daughter," Ragnar said, addressing Professor Yeoh, "see to her injuries. The rest of you, go to your next class." He strode past her as if she no longer existed.

Professor Yeoh ran to Lin, and as she examined her, a look of concern crossed her face. "Someone help me get her to the infirmary."

. . .

"So, this is what it's like from the other side," Lin said, waking up to see Zoe—and Priya—at *her* bedside for once. "Are you okay?"

"Me?" Zoe asked. "Oh, right. Yeah, your mom sent me to eat some bread and bananas in the kitchen. I guess it restored my glycogen. I'm fine now."

Professor Yeoh appeared at Lin's side instantly and clutched her hand. "How do you feel?" she asked, smiling but worried.

"Okay, I think," Lin said.

"Can you wiggle your fingers and toes?"

Lin did just that. "Yup."

"Oh, thank goodness!" Professor Yeoh breathed a sigh of relief.

Lin looked alarmed. "Why? Did you think I wouldn't be able to?"

"You sustained injuries to your spine. Were you in a Typical hospital, you could have been left paralyzed. Fortunately, because I arrived just after the injury occurred, I was able to repair the damage before it was too late."

Lin seemed at a loss for words. "Thanks, Mom," was all she could say.

"You're welcome. We will speak later about your actions. Now that I know you're all right . . ." Her eyes narrowed, and she suddenly looked dangerous. "I need to have a chat with that brute. Stay here until I return."

She strode from the infirmary like someone on a mission.

"Zoe?" Lin asked, rattled. "Can you follow her, please? Make sure she's okay?"

Zoe squeezed her hand. "I'll keep her safe," she promised.

Ethan, I need you at the office.

She followed at a distance until Professor Yeoh pushed through the large oak door to the administration office.

"You can't just barge in without an appoint—" Miss Gillespie started, and then Zoe heard a loud smack. She raced inside to find Abby, the assistant to former Headmaster Harrington, sitting stunned at her desk and a bewildered Miss Gillespie on the floor, tenderly touching her jaw. The door to the headmaster's office was ajar.

"First you kill my husband," Professor Yeoh growled, "then you try to kill my *daughter*?"

Zoe crept over to peek in unseen. Lin's mom stood with fists clenched in front of Ragnar's desk. Suddenly, Ethan showed up, surveyed the scene, and joined Zoe in flanking the door.

"If I was trying to kill her, she would be dead," Ragnar said, very calm.

"She almost became a paraplegic today! She *would* have if I hadn't been there."

"Then it's a good thing you were there."

"She's a child!"

"She attacked me. I couldn't just let that stand."

"Yes, you could! You were in no danger. She posed no threat to you. If you were a man of honour, you would know that you *defend* yourself against children—you don't *retaliate* against them. You don't intentionally *hurt* them. If you knew how to actually lead people and inspire them, you wouldn't have to resort to violence like a barbarian!"

"You think I don't know how to lead?"

"I *know* you don't. *Everyone* knows. The only thing you know about *real* leaders is how to kill them."

"I would watch your tongue—"

"Or what?" she snapped. "You'll kill me, too?"

Ragnar was silent.

Professor Yeoh stabbed her finger at him. "If you hurt my daughter again, it will be the last thing you ever do."

"Mei," Ragnar said slowly, "despite what you may think, I bear no ill will toward you—and especially not toward your daughter. Indeed, I have come to feel personally invested in her well-being, since I am the reason she lost her father. I shudder to think how she would feel if she lost her mother, too. Should such a tragedy ever come to pass, though, I swear to you here, on my life, that I will raise her as my own."

A stunned silence filled the office as the enormity of his words sank in.

"You are correct," he continued, "that my leadership style is different from that of your late husband. I have no patience for inspiring loyalty. I lead through fear. I allowed you and the other professors to live because you are useful to me. Should any of you ever become more trouble than you are worth, however, I will either imprison you or I will execute you. I do understand your maternal instincts that led to this confrontation, but if you wish to remain in a position to protect your daughter, you would do well to keep those instincts in check. Now, is there anything else?"

Zoe could hardly fathom Professor Yeoh's dilemma. Surely she wanted to kill Ragnar more than ever, but if she failed . . .

Finally, Professor Yeoh asked, "Where is Alexey?"

Ragnar stared blankly. "Oh, Martinov?" He laughed. "I didn't even know his first name. I haven't harmed him. He's just in detention, thinking about what he did. I'm sure he will apologize soon, and then he will be released. Are we done here?"

"Stay away from my daughter," Professor Yeoh snarled, then stormed out, sweeping past Zoe and Ethan in the doorframe.

"Zoe, Ethan, a moment, please," Ragnar called. They shuffled into his office. "The mission you have planned: I approve of your target, and I approve of your team. This will hardly change the world, but it's a good, local, low-risk trial run. Your car is ready, and you will find appropriate outfits in your rooms. You can go tonight, if you wish, or any night this week. If anything goes wrong—if any of you are caught—say absolutely nothing until we come for you. Dismissed."

Zoe didn't budge. "You knew Professor Martinov moved your vehicle under the tree today, didn't you? Security must have reported it to you, and yet you allowed his class exercise to happen."

"Is that a question or an accusation?"

"Did you let it slide because of Lin? So you could reinforce her reliance on anger by giving her the chance to hurt you? Or at least something you value? What is your sudden fascination with her?"

Ragnar shrugged. "Every leader needs a protégé. I had high hopes for you, before you meddled with your own mind."

"You told me you'd kill her if I stepped out of line. But you just told Professor Yeoh that you would raise her as your own daughter."

"Ah," he said, "yes. I thought her greatest value to me was as a hostage. But I've come to realize that she has great potential. She will make an excellent attack dog one day."

"So, you no longer intend to kill her if I leave?"

"Oh, I'll still kill her if *you* misbehave. She's my only leverage against you. We both know she's the only person you truly care about." He looked pointedly at Ethan. "Sorry, I know that must sting a little."

"Leave her alone," Zoe said. "She's not yours."

"Are you offering to repledge your loyalty to me?" Ragnar asked, cocking his head.

"What? No! I'll never be the person I used to be."

"Well then." He leaned back in his chair, his hands behind his head.

Zoe scowled. "I won't let you do this to her."

Ragnar just smirked. Zoe turned on her heels, and together, she and Ethan walked down the hall in silence.

"It's not true," Zoe said, at last.

"What's not true?"

She took his hand. "What he said. It's not true."

■ ■ ■

After checking in with Lin—who was under orders to stay put in the infirmary—Zoe discussed the mission with Makena, Paige, and Ethan over lunch.

"Is there any reason to wait?" Paige asked. "We have our plan. I say we do this."

"Agreed," Makena said. "Tonight's as good as any."

"But . . . is what we're doing right?" Zoe couldn't help but ask.

"Jeez." Paige sighed. "It's a little late for that now, don't you think? This was *your* idea."

"I know, but this is our last chance to back out, so let's make sure we all agree on what we're doing."

"I don't like the idea of doing Ragnar's bidding," Makena said. "But I *do* want to make a difference in the world. If we had been asked to do something like this last year, before all this happened, I still would have jumped at the opportunity. This man is scum. I'm in."

Zoe looked at Ethan.

"I have no qualms about it at all," he said. "I'm with Professor Dlamini. This will benefit far more people than it hurts."

She turned to Paige.

"I like this plan," Paige said, nodding vigorously. "It's a good plan."

Zoe took a deep breath. "Okay, then, we'll head out at dusk."

11

THE OPERATION

They stared at the car waiting for them outside. It was a BMW.

"Hardly inconspicuous," Makena quipped.

Paige shook their head. "What was it the Igigi said about the Anunnaki being decadent?"

They all took turns hugging Priya and Lin, who'd finally been freed from the infirmary.

"I don't like staying behind like this," Lin said, squeezing Zoe's hands. "You be safe, okay?"

"Of course," Zoe said, squeezing right back. "Don't worry—nothing can go wrong."

They stowed their gear in the trunk and piled in. In the driver's seat, Makena adjusted the mirrors.

"Let's go," she said, putting the car in gear and stepping on the gas.

As they made their way to the highway, Zoe punched their destination into the navigation system. "Let's remember to delete this as soon as we get there," she said. "In case anything *does* go wrong, we don't want to leave any evidence."

Half an hour later, they exited onto the Don Valley Parkway and then onto Bloor Street. Suddenly, lights flashed behind them.

"What the—? I wasn't speeding," Makena said, looking at the speedometer. "There's no reason to pull us over."

"What do we do?" Paige asked from the back.

"We pull over, of course," Zoe said.

Makena pulled onto the shoulder and put the car in park. The police car blinded them with its headlights and then just waited.

"What's he doing?" Paige asked.

"Running our plates," Ethan said. "Seeing who the car's registered to."

Eventually, the officer got out and approached their vehicle. He tapped on Makena's window, and she rolled it down.

"Is there a problem, officer?" she asked.

"You failed to signal your lane change back there," he said.

Makena cocked her head. "I don't think I did."

"This is a very expensive vehicle for such a young lady to be driving," he said. "Is this your car?"

"No, sir, it's my father's," she lied.

"Well, let's see. License and registration."

"Why am I really being pulled over?" Makena demanded. "I know I signaled back there."

"License and registration," he repeated, more forcefully.

Makena raised an eyebrow at Zoe.

She felt stupid. How had she never considered this possibility? Was this car even registered—and if so, to whom? Why didn't they all have fake IDs? She'd been so caught up in planning the actual mission that she'd never stopped to think about common hazards they might encounter on the way there.

"Ethan?" she whispered.

He leaned forward. "You don't *need* to see her license and registration," he said, waving his hand.

A funny look came over the officer's face. "Actually, I don't need to see your license and registration," he said.

"You can't just pull people over without justification," Ethan continued.

"I . . . shouldn't have pulled you over."

"You feel terrible that you did this."

The officer hung his head. "I'm really sorry, miss."

"We can go on our way now," Ethan said, sitting back.

"You can go on your way now, miss. Sorry for wasting your time." He returned to his vehicle, and Makena drove off.

"*That* was totally awesome!" Paige said.

"Ethan," Makena said, "I like to fight my own battles . . . but that was seriously impressive." Her face split into a grin, and she stuck her fist over her shoulder for Ethan to bump. "You need to teach me how to do that."

• • •

They arrived minutes later at a luxury hotel and condominium on University Avenue. They parked on the street and headed to the main entrance.

"That's a tall building," Paige said, looking up. "Can you imagine actually living on the sixty-fifth floor, looking over the city? How rich do you have to be?"

"Very," Zoe said. "Okay, let's do this."

They entered the extravagant lobby and were greeted by a smiling young woman at the front desk. "May I help you?" she asked.

"You certainly may, Debbie," Ethan said, reading her name tag. Then, with a subtle wave of his hand, he added in a soft voice, "You can tell me where your security control room is located. And don't worry, you're totally allowed to tell me, but try not to let anyone else hear."

"What's with that little hand wavy thing he does?" Paige whispered to Zoe.

Confusion swept over Debbie's face before it was swiftly replaced by a smile. "It's in an employees-only section on this level," she murmured.

"Could you bring us there without arousing your colleague's suspicion?"

She glanced at a woman speaking with a guest at the opposite end of the desk. "Umm, maybe?"

"Why don't you call her over? Tell you need help with something."

"Janet, could you come here for a sec? I need your help with something."

"Excuse me one moment, sir," Janet said to her guest and walked over.

"Hello, Janet," Ethan said, motioning for her to come closer. "Debbie is going to take me and my three friends somewhere, and I want you to notice nothing, okay? As far as you are concerned, it's totally normal and you will think nothing of it. In fact, you won't remember this conversation, or Debbie leading us anywhere, or even seeing us at all. And when Debbie returns, you won't notice that she was ever gone."

Janet looked at all of them before shrugging and saying, "Okay."

"Thank you. You can go help your guest now." Ethan turned back to Debbie. "Is there anyone else who might notice us going where we don't belong? A security guard, maybe? A manager?"

Debbie nodded. "Yes, Phil over there." She pointed to a large security guard in a white shirt and black tie. "He'll be suspicious for sure. And my manager, Debra, is around here somewhere. My name is actually Debra, too, but she makes everyone call me Debbie, which I hate."

"That is so *unfair* of her," Ethan said. "Can you take us to see Phil, please?"

Debbie led them across the lobby to Phil, who watched them warily.

"Hello, Phil," Ethan said, waving his hand again.

"There it is again!" Paige hissed at Zoe.

"I want you to not notice me and my friends here, okay?" Ethan repeated his spiel.

Phil nodded. "Yeah, I can do that," he said in a rich baritone.

"Thank you so much," Ethan said. "Debbie, do you see your manager yet?"

Debbie looked around, then pointed at a woman across the lobby. "Oh, there she is!

"Zoe, you wanna try?" Ethan asked as they approached.

"Me? I've never done this before. Learning on the job doesn't seem wise."

"When else can you learn, though? It's a lot easier on Typicals, but unless you want to ask Ragnar to bring some to the school for us to experiment on, this is your only chance."

That was certainly true. And it would be helpful if she could learn, so future missions wouldn't rely so heavily on one person.

"Don't worry. I've got your back."

"Hello, Debra," Zoe said. She reached into Debra's mind and tried to exert her influence. "I'd like you to not notice us here. Can you do that?"

Debra regarded her quizzically. "Why wouldn't I notice you? Debbie, what's this all about?"

Paige nudged her in the back. "Do the hand wavy thing."

Focus on her prefrontal cortex, Ethan said in her mind. *That's the area of the brain responsible for willpower.*

Zoe slid her consciousness to the front of Debra's brain.

"Don't worry about Debbie," Zoe said. "She's not even here, she's still at the front desk." Now she could see areas of Debra's brain lighting up, resisting her words, since she could clearly see Debbie right in front of her. Zoe clamped those areas down.

"Do you know where Debbie is?" she asked.

"She's over there," Debra said, pointing to the front desk. "The woman on the right. But what did you mean about not noticing you?"

Zoe tried again. "I *really* want you to not notice me and my friends here." She pushed back against Debra's willpower, bending it to her own. "At all. You won't notice us going into a restricted area, and you won't notice us coming back out or leaving. Later, you won't be able to recall us ever being here. Can you do that for me, Debra?"

Debra nodded. "Certainly. That will be no problem whatsoever."

"Thank you," Zoe said. "And one other thing. Are you aware that your concierge hates being called Debbie?"

"Oh, I know," Debra said with a sly smile.

"Well, from now on, you are going to call *her* Debra and *you* will be Debbie. Understood? You can switch name tags right now."

Debra clasped her name tag in horror.

"Go on," Zoe said, exerting pressure where it was needed in Debra's mind.

Reluctantly, the manager swapped name tags with her concierge, who giggled. In the back of her mind, Zoe was aware that she had just done more than the mission required. She had chosen to right a perceived wrong—and she had done so easily, with no moral qualms. What if she was wrong about who was the bully in this situation? Even if she was right, should she really have intervened in something so trivial?

Ethan nodded. "Nicely done." He turned to the concierge. "Now, *Debra*, please lead the way."

The concierge took them down a hall to a nondescript door and swiped her badge to enter. They descended a flight of stairs to the basement and went down another hall.

"Here it is," she said, stopping at a door.

"Thank you, Debra," Ethan said, eliciting another giggle. "Please go back to work now and forget all about this. Forget you took us here, forget you left your desk, forget you ever saw us. And if you see us again on our way out, don't even notice us."

Debra turned without a word and walked away.

Zoe knocked on the door. After a long pause, she knocked again.

Finally, the door opened, revealing a cross woman in a white security uniform.

"This is a restricted area. You kids shouldn't be here. How did you get down here?"

"It's okay," Ethan said, taking charge again. "We're allowed to be here. Would you let us in, please?"

The woman's demeanour abruptly changed. "Oh. All right, then." She opened the door wide and stepped back to let them enter. Two men rose to their feet in alarm. Zoe approached the one on the left while Ethan took the one on the right.

"It's okay," they said in unison. "We're allowed to be here."

The men nodded and sat back down.

"Who's in charge here?" Zoe asked.

"That would be me," the woman said.

"What's your name?" Ethan asked.

"Lois."

"Lois," he continued, "we're going to need your help. I realize this is all very unusual, but I assure you, it's all okay. I need you to turn off all the cameras in the building, both interior and exterior. Can you do that, please?"

She nodded and returned to her desk, where she began clicking and typing. Then, she said, "Done."

"She should delete all footage of us, too," Makena said.

"Right," Ethan said. "Lois, please delete all footage from the past fifteen minutes."

Lois nodded again and got to work. The men startled again when they realized all the screens were blank. Zoe motioned for Makena and Paige to pay attention.

"It's okay," she said to both men. "The screens are working just as before, showing footage of the hotel just like they always do. Nothing is out of the ordinary." The men sat back and watched the blank screens.

"There you go," Lois said. "Erased."

"Now, listen carefully, Lois," Ethan said. "You're going to forget that we were ever here. If you ever see us again, even in a picture, you won't recognize us at all. You're going to forget you erased the footage. After we leave, you will sit here and continue to watch the monitors like your colleagues over there. You will continue to see footage of the hotel as if the cameras are on. Nothing out of the ordinary will happen. In thirty minutes, you will turn the cameras back on. You won't notice anything amiss throughout this transition. Can you erase all electronic evidence of you turning them off and back on again?"

Lois thought about it. "I think so."

"Good enough. You will forget that you turned them off and turned them back on. You will forget that we were ever here. This will be just another boring, uneventful evening. Do you understand?"

Lois nodded, and Zoe repeated the relevant instructions to the two men.

"Do you have a stopwatch, Lois?" Ethan asked, and she pulled out her phone. "Good. Start a timer for thirty minutes. When that goes off, you will turn the cameras back on."

Zoe's team set their wristwatches—which had been provided as part of their mission gear—to count down from thirty minutes.

"Just one more thing, Lois. Will your security card get us up to the penthouse?"

"Yes."

"Take us to the elevator now."

She led them down the hall to the elevators, and they piled in. Lois swiped her card and pressed the button for the sixty-fifth floor.

"Thank you, Lois," Ethan said, putting his hand out to stop the door from closing. "Now, head back to your station, erase any logs of your recent card swipes, and forget any of this ever happened."

Lois nodded and returned to the control room. The doors closed, and the elevator rose rapidly. Unfortunately, it stopped at the ground floor, and a man stepped in.

"Excuse me, sir," Zoe said, tapping him on the shoulder as the elevator continued its ascent. He turned to her. "I'm going to need you to forget you ever saw us."

...

At the sixty-fifth floor, the elevator doors opened, and they stepped out into the hall. Two large, bald men in suits stood outside a distant door. Their jackets were unbuttoned—a telltale sign they were carrying firearms. Without hesitating, the four students approached.

"Good evening, gentlemen," Zoe said. "Is your boss home?"

"Who wants to know?" asked the suit on the right.

"And how did you get up here?" the other asked. "You're not expected."

"It's okay," Zoe said, "we're allowed—" She stopped abruptly, and Ethan assumed a fighting stance.

"What's going on?" Paige asked as both they and Makena assumed their own fighting stances.

"They're shielded," Zoe said. "How the hell are you shielded? Who *are* you?"

The men exchanged alarmed glances, then reached into their jackets.

"Oh, I don't think so." Zoe pinned her man's hand inside his jacket, just as Ethan did the same to the other guard. "You're going to tell me why two Telepaths are guarding a Typical."

Too late, she realized she'd gotten cocky. The man grabbed her wrist with his free hand and twisted, breaking her hold, then shoved her back and pulled out his gun. He pointed it at the ceiling—though obviously not of his own volition. Paige must have used telekinesis. He flung out his left hand, and Paige flew backwards. But Makena stepped in to deliver vicious blows to his face and groin before spinning around on his partner, who Ethan had been trying to subdue on his own.

How had this gone so wrong so quickly? Zoe dashed forward and leapt up and over her friends. She grabbed her man's gun arm and channeled all of her telekinetic force into an elbow strike to the top of his head. He dropped. She turned to help Ethan, who was pinned to the wall and struggling. His opponent pushed his forearm into Ethan's throat, ignoring Makena's blows. Suddenly, the man rose into the air and floundered, helpless. Behind them, Paige had both arms outstretched. Ethan rubbed his throat, then delivered a telekinetically enhanced uppercut to the man's chin, knocking him out. Paige lowered him gently to the ground.

Then, they heard a noise, and a couple of people peeked out of the two neighbouring apartments. Ethan put on a big smile and advanced with his hands up. "It's okay, folks. Everything's good. Actually, could I ask you a question?" Both doors slammed shut.

"Well, crap," Paige muttered.

"They're going to call security—or the police," Makena said.

Ethan looked at Zoe. "We don't have much time. Do we abort?"

This was a disaster. "No, we can still salvage this."

Makena raised her eyebrows. "What's our exit strategy?"

"We'll figure it out. I'm not going back to that man having failed. Let's just hurry. Ethan, can you make sure they don't wake up anytime soon?"

He bent down and placed his hand on each man's head, and a moment later, he nodded.

Zoe tried the door. Of course it was locked. She rummaged through the nearest guard's pockets and found a security card. She swiped it, and the door unlocked. Turning the handle quietly, she brought a finger to her lips. "Drag them inside," she said, then slowly opened the door.

Zoe had never seen such a lavish apartment. It was massive, with high ceilings and a winding staircase to the second floor. Floor-to-ceiling windows provided an incredible view of the Toronto skyline. The white interior walls were covered in framed paintings, and the centre of the room featured a roaring gas fireplace.

Ethan and Makena dragged the guards inside, and Paige locked the door. They all spread out, moving stealthily. There was no sign of their target, so they crept upstairs.

"Out here," a voice called from the patio. Stunned, they exchanged glances. Paige shrugged, and together, they walked out onto the rooftop patio. There, sitting by the pool and flanked by two beautiful women, was Andre Taggart, wearing a silk robe and smoking a cigar. Taggart and his companions stared blankly, saying nothing as Zoe and her team approached. A man sitting with his back to them rose.

"Hello, Zoe," Gabriel said, smiling impishly, his hands in his pockets.

Zoe gasped. "Gabriel!" she exclaimed. Then, she tensed. Their last encounter had not exactly gone well. "What are you doing here?"

"Waiting for you," he said. He seemed to pick up on her wariness. "Relax," he said, holding up a hand. "We're good. I hope the guards didn't give you too much trouble."

"They did, actually. Were you aware they're Telepaths?"

"Well . . . telepath-*ic*."

She cocked her head. "They're Ragnar's godlings?"

"No."

"Wait." Ethan stepped forward. "Zoe, who is this man?"

"Gabriel, these are my friends, Ethan, Makena, and Paige. Everyone, this is Gabriel. Gabriel worked for Professor Chao's intelligence network."

"Actually," Gabriel said, scratching his scraggly, week-old beard, "I was the *head* of his intelligence network. I am now the de facto leader of the Resistance. We have a lot to talk about."

"The neighbours saw us taking out the guards," Zoe said. "We don't have much time."

Gabriel pulled out his cellphone and texted someone. "I have people in the building. We'll handle them."

"What if they called security?"

"Then we'll handle them, too. Trust me, Zoe, I've been doing this a long time." He motioned toward their target. "I assume you're here to turn this miscreant into some semblance of a decent human being? Professor Chao would not be pleased. Free will, yeah?"

"How'd you know we would be here?"

Gabriel turned to Zoe's friends. "Are you three capable of completing your little mission on your own? I need to talk to Zoe, and no offence, but I don't know any of you." He looked at Ethan. "Although I have heard of *you*."

"Ethan, can you take care of things?" Zoe asked. He nodded, and she followed Gabriel downstairs to the kitchen. They stood on opposite sides of the granite island.

"We should probably talk about what happened last time," Gabriel said.

"What's there to talk about? You want to kill Ragnar, and you're willing to sacrifice Lin and her mom to do it. I'm not."

"I'm not happy about it," Gabriel said, "but if you hadn't interfered, he would be dead and we would be in a much better place right now."

"And Lin and her mom would be in the ground. The end justifies the means, huh? You would really like my new professor."

He studied her. "I'm trying to figure out whose side you're on, Zoe. I'm aware of your unique situation. Raised in a cult. Sent on a mission to infiltrate the Academy and assassinate Professor Chao. Word is you literally called in the attack on the Academy and then inexplicably switched sides. Even tried to kill Ragnar and went to prison for it. But then you saved his life. And now you're doing missions for him."

Zoe sighed. She hated having to explain herself to everyone. Did she even *want* to explain herself to this man who would happily sacrifice two innocents for his cause?

"He is a good man," Professor Chao said, startling her. He perched on a stool at the end of the counter. Zoe glanced at him nonchalantly. "However, he is unaccustomed to leadership and feels the weight of so many lives on his shoulders. I am not pleased he would sacrifice my family, but such a decision could not have been easy for him."

Zoe wasn't so willing to forgive Gabriel, but Professor Chao *had* trusted him. "I'm here because Ragnar offered me the opportunity to 'help the world.' He said I could choose my own target. I know what he's playing at, trying to slowly lure me back to his side." She took a stool and dropped her elbows on the counter. "I'm playing along, because I thought we could maybe do some good in the world while also getting off of school property. I wanted to learn what's been happening in the outside world since Ragnar took over. I never expected you to find us. How did you know where we'd be?"

"It's best if you don't know. Suffice to say, I have eyes and ears everywhere," Gabriel said. "Not as many as in the past but enough." He leaned against the counter. "You need to understand something, Zoe: Your little 'mission' tonight is a joke."

Zoe was taken aback. "I know it won't make much difference in the grand scheme of things, but we're just trying to get our feet wet before we choose a more influential target."

He shook his head. "You don't understand. Do you think Ragnar made his move—took out Chao, Harrington, Lafleur, took over the Academy—only to wait for his students to tell him what targets to hit? To wait for his students to grow up into the operatives he needs? He's been planning this for decades."

Zoe didn't like where this was going. "But . . . he created generations of genetically engineered Telepaths to be his army. Are you saying he never intended to use us to take over the world?"

"Oh, I think that was exactly his plan in the beginning. But something made him accelerate his plans. Maybe he thought the world wouldn't last much longer if he didn't act. I don't know. But I *do* know that the minute he attacked the Academy, he put a carefully thought-out plan into action. His godlings were stationed all over the world. At exactly the same moment, they attacked *all* of us *everywhere*. His goal wasn't to kill us. No, he wanted to capture us—and mindbend us."

Oh no. "He told me that he compelled teachers to work for him just by threatening their loved ones," she said.

Gabriel sighed. "I don't know. Maybe he did that, too. Maybe that was faster. All I know is that two-thirds of us now work for him—and not under duress. They are fully committed to his cause. Friends I've known since I was your age—who I *know* would never have turned against us—are now hunting us. Others have been actively infiltrating the governments of every major power, though they seem to be focusing on the superpowers: America, Russia, China—any nation with nukes."

Zoe raised an eyebrow. "To . . . begin the process of nuclear disarmament?"

"One can hope, but it's more than a little scary to have one man in charge of the entire world's nuclear arsenal—not to mention its most powerful militaries. Anyway, you can't just get access to the leader of a superpower, so they're working their way up from the bottom. But here's the weird thing." He paused. "Those who have been captured and turned are suddenly *really* good at mindbending. We were never taught compulsion at the Academy. The powers that be didn't want the average Telepath to be able to do it. Too much temptation. We had operatives who were trained in it, who would clean up messes and prevent our accidental discovery. But now, all the released captives are amazing at it. It's inexplicable."

"He taught them?" Zoe suggested.

Gabriel shook his head. "No. It takes a long time to get good at it. I know you're learning how to do it yourself. We saw you downstairs in the lobby. But it's one thing to compel someone to do what you want or to forget they've seen you; it's another thing entirely to fundamentally change a person's morality and loyalty. That takes a *lot* of skill." He looked up the stairs. "I'm surprised your pal Ethan thinks he can do it, to be honest. Anyway, here's the thing. I've interrogated low-level government employees who have been compromised. All of them Typicals. They haven't just been compelled into giving access to the next level of government, thinking it's no big deal. They are fully aware that they're giving access to *Telepaths*—the greatest security risk the world has ever known—but they don't care because they're completely *loyal* to Ragnar." He shook his head. "It's like they've become a secret organization infiltrating governments all over the world."

Zoe didn't know what to say. She just sat there, stunned.

"And you want to hear the *really* weird part? I'm pretty good at compulsion. As an intelligence agent, it's my job. But when I looked into the minds of compelled government employees . . . it's like nothing I've ever seen before. Their neural pathways weren't just altered in key, strategic locations, like any skilled mindbender would have done. They were altered *everywhere*. It was like they had become fundamentally different people. And that's not even the strangest part." He took a deep breath. "When you spend enough time in people's minds, you come to realize how unique everyone is. Everyone's neural pathways develop differently due to their unique experiences in life. But when I looked into the minds of two compelled government workers, a small piece of both brains was absolutely identical."

A terrible cold crept through Zoe's bones. Was someone *inside* each of these people? What had Ethan said? That he sometimes felt like his thoughts belonged to someone else?

"When I eventually capture a Telepath who has been compelled," Gabriel said, "I'm willing to bet I'll see the exact same pattern of neural pathways. I don't know if I'll be able to undo whatever's been done to them, though. This scares the living hell out of me, Zoe. I can't begin to explain what's happening to these people. I only know of one person who might have some insight."

"Professor Sharapova," Zoe said.

"Exactly. Only we can't get to her."

"I thought you had a mole at the Academy."

"I never said that."

"How else could you have known we'd be here tonight?"

"We *can't* get to her, Zoe. I need you to do it."

"She hates me."

He snorted. "Yeah, I don't doubt that. So, apologize. Do whatever you need to do. But make her hear everything I've just told you. If she can somehow escape—maybe with your help—we have subjects she could examine. If not, hopefully she can find someone there to study."

"And then what?" Zoe asked. "The professors at school all seem to think the Resistance has a plan to save us. Do you?"

Gabriel ran his fingers through his hair. "I'll be honest with you, Zoe. It's bad. At the moment, we're just trying to survive, to stay one step ahead and avoid capture. These people used to be our *friends*; they know all our hiding spots. If we want to fight back, we *need* to understand what they're doing to us and how. Until then, all we can do is try not to get caught and throw whatever wrenches we can into Ragnar's plans."

Zoe looked at the guards lying unconscious near the entrance. "Like that? They're godlings. But if they're not Ragnar's, then how did they get ahold of the drugs to give them Abilities?"

Gabriel looked sheepish. "Yeah . . . I'm not entirely proud of this, but . . . we intercepted a large shipment of their godling drugs. And we need money to run our operations, because they cut off all access to our funds. So . . . I started selling their drugs to extremely wealthy people, who use it on themselves and, apparently, on their bodyguards."

Zoe's jaw dropped. "You're creating your own godlings?"

"No," he said, quickly. "No, no, no. They're not mine."

"So, they're just rogue Telepaths? How many?"

He bit his lip. "A lot?"

Zoe could hardly believe it. "How long before Typicals learn about this? If they haven't already?"

"Like I said . . . sowing chaos, yeah? I figure Ragnar will hunt them down to keep our existence secret, and any effort spent hunting *them* is effort not spent hunting *us*." He looked at his watch. "How much time until the cameras come back on?"

She looked at her own wristwatch. "Five minutes."

"Time to go, then." He handed her a small piece of paper. "Here's my contact info. For now, at least. Memorize it and get rid of it. Try to keep going on missions, so we can hopefully meet again and exchange more info in person."

Zoe looked at the paper, memorized Gabriel's phone number and email address, then nodded and handed it back.

"You sure?" Gabriel asked. "You don't want to keep this?"

She tapped her head. "I've got it."

Gabriel shrugged. "Go get your friends. Give Lin my best."

■ ■ ■

The ride back was awkward. At first, they were excited to have pulled it off. According to Ethan, Andre had vowed to be a new man. He would tell his millions of followers that he'd had an epiphany, that he was ashamed of all his hate-filled videos, and that, going forward, he would dedicate his life to helping people. They couldn't have hoped for a better outcome. Plus, they'd made it out before the cameras came back on, so, assuming Gabriel's people handled the neighbours, there should be no evidence they'd been there at all.

But when Zoe told them what Gabriel had said, their excitement gave way to stunned disbelief.

"Jeez," Paige said, after a while. "Kind of makes what we did tonight seem pretty useless."

Zoe could only nod. A glance at Ethan told her exactly what he was thinking. He was worried about what might have been done to his mind.

"What do we do with this info?" Makena asked. "Do we tell people at school? Do we continue these missions?"

"I don't know yet," Zoe said. "I think we just tell Lin and Priya, for now. We definitely can't let Ragnar find out what we've learned."

Nobody was waiting for them at school. Zoe made her way through the darkened halls to her room and found Lin reading in bed, despite the late hour.

"How'd it go?" she asked, sitting up.

Zoe dropped her bag on the floor and tried to figure out where to start. "Well, Gabriel says hi."

12

THE SUBSTITUTES

Word spread quickly throughout the school. Everyone wanted to know all the details of their successful mission and how they could become as good as Ethan at mindbending and go on missions, too. Even Professor Dlamini heard about it.

"I hear we have some celebrities in our class today," she said. "Andre Taggart, hmm? I can't say he would have been my pick, but he certainly deserved some 'readjustment.'"

"Who would you have chosen?" Kyle asked, and the class erupted with speculation until the professor quieted them.

"Who would I target?" Professor Dlamini sat on a stool and crossed her legs. "Why, the oligarchs, of course." When it was apparent that nobody knew what she meant, she elaborated. "Politicians do not actually run the world, you see. They are puppets. Those who pull their strings are called 'oligarchs.' These are immensely rich and powerful men who help politicians get elected in return for favours, which help them become even more wealthy."

Professor Dlamini was a powerful speaker; every student listened intently.

"Another way oligarchs preserve and increase their power is through controlling the media. They buy up all the news outlets and control public opinion—quite effectively—by selecting which news stories to cover, which to hide, and which to spin in a light favourable to their purposes."

"But Professor Dlamini," Pacha said, "democracies don't work like that. We elect our leaders. We could just elect someone who isn't controlled by billionaires."

The professor smiled. "I'm sorry to have to be the one to tell you this, child, but democracies are really oligarchies in disguise. Plutocracies, to be more precise, because the oligarchs are all rich. The United States, for instance, is run by a handful of oligarchs who collectively possess more wealth than the entire bottom half of the population. They select each party's political candidates, giving voters the *illusion* of choice."

The professor stood. "So, to answer your question, if I had to choose a target, I would choose the most influential oligarchs of the most powerful nations. Once you control them, you control the world."

"But wouldn't they be hard to get to?" Kyle asked.

"Not nearly as difficult as you might expect," she answered. "Certainly not as difficult as getting to, say, the president of the United States. Billionaires have their own security, certainly, but it's nothing like the Secret Service. Now, on to business. We were discussing the events that led up to the Second World War."

. . .

Zoe pulled Ethan aside in the hallway after class.

"Hey, you okay?" she asked, grabbing his hand. They hadn't had a chance to talk privately since Gabriel's revelations.

He turned, and it was like he didn't even recognize her. Like it wasn't *him* behind those eyes. She yanked her hand back, and then he blinked and smiled and he was Ethan again. Had she just imagined it?

"I'm fine," he said. "Worried, but fine. Hopefully Sharapova can shed some light on what's wrong with me."

"I'm going to talk to her today," Zoe said.

"I was thinking about that, actually. Why don't you let me talk to her at my session today? I can relay everything Gabriel told you."

"Are you sure?" Zoe asked. "I know she hates me, but I'm sure she'd at least listen to what I have to say."

"I just think she'll be more receptive to me, that's all."

"Okay." Zoe didn't really have a good reason to argue. "Just let me know what she says."

"Of course."

They took their seats in Advanced Telekinesis and waited. Zoe hoped Professor Martinov would sweep through the door, as usual, but instead, an old man with a shaved head and red robes shuffled inside.

"Nice dress," Jacob said from the back. The class snickered.

The old man jerked his fingers up and down, and Jacob shot up through the ceiling and back into his seat.

"Good morning, children," the man said to the suddenly silent class. Plaster dust drifted from the ceiling, and Jacob groaned. "I am Tenzin. I have been instructed to teach what I am told is an advanced class in telekinesis while your professor is imprisoned. I know you all must be as worried about him as I am."

"He's a traitor," Kyle shot back. "He tricked us into ruining Master's truck. I hope he gets what's coming to him."

"I hope you get what's coming to *you*," Lin spat, "when we kick you and your friends out of our school. Who cares about your stupid master's truck?"

"It's *our* school now," Kyle yelled back, "and he's your master, too!"

"He will *never* be my master!" Lin leapt up, knocking her chair over. Kyle did the same. Alarmed, Zoe jumped between them with both arms outstretched. This had certainly escalated quickly.

Tenzin raised his hands and struck them together in a deafening thunderclap. Everyone covered their ears. "That is quite enough," he said, quietly. "Take your seats, both of you."

Glaring at each other, Lin and Kyle picked up their chairs and sat. Zoe stared worriedly at her friend. Lin seemed to be spiraling.

Tenzin went on, "I have fond memories of Professor Martinov. He was one of my better students. Always so enthusiastic. I hope he returns to you as soon as possible."

"You *taught* Professor Martinov?" Zoe asked.

"I did."

"How long ago?" Pacha asked

Tenzin gazed up at the ceiling. "It was during the Russian Revolution, so 1917. He was so worried."

"You're a monk?" Paige asked.

"I am," Tenzin said. "Now, what I will be teaching you is not explosive power, but rather endurance. Specifically..."

He rose up into the air and crossed his legs. "Levitating yourself is not so difficult. Some of you may be able to do it already for a brief time. Technically, it is no different than jumping high by pushing on the ground. The difference is that you are not pushing for a split second—you are pushing continuously. When I first began practicing levitation, my goal was to be able to do so not for seconds, or minutes, but *hours*. It took me a very long time to be able to do this, and I accomplished it through meditation. Anger helps telekinesis, but only briefly, explosively—unless it's become such a part of your life that a slow-burning hatred is always there to draw upon. But that does not sound very fun to me. For sustained levitation, I needed to find my strength someplace else. Somewhere deep inside. It's essentially willpower, and willpower is like a muscle that can become stronger through exercise."

Kalisha raised her hand. "Professor, what's the point of this? I mean, I get that Zoe thinks she's really special, but isn't levitating kind of useless?"

Tenzin arched an eyebrow. "I am not a professor. You may just call me Tenzin." He looked around the room. "Which one of you is Zoe?"

Zoe reluctantly raised her hand.

"Zoe, can *you* think of a reason levitating could prove useful?"

"Infiltration," she said without missing a beat. "If you can move without touching the floor, you're less likely to make noise or activate a pressure pad." She thought about that. "Although, I guess if you're pushing down on the floor, that *would* be the same force as walking. You could spread the force out over a bigger area, though. Or . . . I guess you could pull on the ceiling and push on the walls to avoid the floor altogether."

"You guess correctly," Tenzin said. "Anyone else?"

"Calisthenics," Pacha said. "It's like weight training to build up your telekinetic strength, but without the weights."

Tenzin nodded approvingly. "Indeed."

"How high can you levitate?" Lin asked. "Can you rise up the side of a skyscraper, for instance?"

"No. Your Professor Martinov may have explained this to you already, but our telekinetic force gets weaker the farther we are from the object we're pushing or pulling. If I am doing this for hours and want to conserve my strength, I will stay less than a foot off the ground. But I can go higher for brief periods." He rose to the ceiling.

"Can you fly?" Paige blurted. "I mean, if you pushed on the ground at an angle instead of straight down, wouldn't you fly?"

Tenzin smiled. "You mean like this?" He suddenly shot across the room, zigzagging from corner to corner above the students, laughing the whole time.

"Superhero," Paige whispered, wide-eyed. "How fast can you go?"

"Surprisingly fast," he said, coming to a stop. "I only have to overcome air friction, so when I assume an aerodynamic flying position and apply constant telekinetic force to the ground, on an angle, it does not take long to get up to the speed of a car."

"How did I not *know* about this?" Paige cried, pounding their desk. Zoe wondered much the same thing.

"Not many of us can levitate, much less fly. It takes more effort and practice and sacrifice than most people are willing to put in. I spent many years building up my strength and endurance. Most people have better things to do—unless they happen to be a monk in a mountain monastery. Or . . . imprisoned."

"But wait," Paige said. "Couldn't you fly high in the same way a plane does? By pushing against air?"

"In theory, yes," Tenzin said. "But unlike the ground, air does not push back on you very much. So, you would need to emit an extraordinary amount of telekinetic force. We do not have that much power. Now, if one were to someday discover antigravity and create an antigravity field in the same way one creates an electromagnetic field, *that* would be a different story."

He clapped his hands. "Now, everyone, get up and sit on your desk, cross-legged." The students eagerly piled onto their desks. Zoe didn't love the idea of showing off in front of the class, but she doubted she had much choice.

"I want you to close your eyes and rest your arms on your knees, palms up. Block out the outside world and focus inward. Try to find the source of your strength. Then, push down on the desk to make yourself rise. Don't try to rise too high. Just a centimetre or so is fine. The point of this exercise is not to see how high you can go but rather to stay in the air as long as you can."

Zoe heard a lot of thumps and giggles and curses as people levitated for a second and then fell. She let herself rise a foot into the air. She hadn't practiced in a while, and it felt good. She opened her eyes and caught Tenzin regarding her with respect. Glancing at Lin, she was incredibly surprised to see her hovering in the air, too. She was a bit unsteady, but she was definitely doing it. But her face betrayed just how. She was clearly drawing from a pit of deep, burning hatred of the kind Tenzin had warned against.

Pacha and Paige were strong telekinetics, but they weren't having much more success than when Zoe had first started trying to levitate in her cell. Tenzin rose another foot in the air and grinned at Zoe, as if challenging her to follow suit. She rose, too, and Tenzin gave her a quick nod of approval, then jerked his head toward the bookshelves along the wall. Two books slowly flew over to hover in the air above his hands. He nodded toward the bookshelf again. Zoe raised an eyebrow and pulled two books from the shelf, levitating them just above her hands, too. She had never tried anything like this before—splitting not just her strength but her focus. She was amazed she could do it at all.

Tenzin's books rose and started to circle around his head. Zoe mimicked him, but this time, she started to wobble. This was harder than it looked.

Another book flew from the shelf to join the others circling Tenzin's head. He smiled innocently and levitated himself down the rows of desks, helping each student—his crown of books still spinning. Zoe pulled another book and sent it spinning around her head with the others. What was it Professor Martinov had said last winter, when he had taken all their snowballs and spun them into a tornado? The trick was to think of them not as multiple objects but rather to connect them all via telepathic strings and treat them as a single object. She had done this intuitively as a child with wooden blocks.

Just when she was starting to feel like she was getting the hang of it, though, Tenzin floated over again. Now, he was *juggling* his books. He waved and drifted off again as Zoe watched in awe. It was one thing to connect the books in a string above her head, but to *juggle* them like that? She would have no choice *but* to keep them separate. She was supposed to split her telekinesis four ways? She gave it a try, and her books instantly tumbled to the ground. She picked them up and tried again and failed spectacularly.

"The problem," Tenzin whispered behind her, "is that you do not know how to juggle. A juggler only has two hands yet can juggle many balls. How is this possible?"

Zoe thought for a moment before it clicked. Trying to control the flight of each book would be like a juggler holding all the balls at all times and moving them in an arc—but a juggler would *throw* the balls, one or two at a time, and let gravity take care of them until they needed to be thrown again. So, she didn't need to split her awareness into four; she just needed to throw one book at a time. And levitating while doing so would be like if the juggler were also balancing on a unicycle—something skilled unicyclists could do without needing to think about it.

She gave it a try—and still failed miserably, her books falling to the floor over and over again.

"You have the idea now," Tenzin said, "but your problem is still that you do not know how to juggle. Learn with your hands first, and then you will be able to do it with your mind."

After class, Tenzin asked Zoe to stay behind.

"Your levitation is very impressive," he said. "I have never known one so young to be so skilled at it. How long were you imprisoned?"

Zoe blinked. "Four months, sir. Solitary."

He shook his head sadly. "It is a horrible thing they are doing to us. I have spent many years alone in a cave by choice, so solitary confinement does not bother me the way they seem to think it should. But for a child … this is not right. I am so sorry you had to endure that."

"Thank you, sir," Zoe said. "I'm fine now, though."

He smiled. "For the record, it took me ten years in that cave to accomplish what you managed in just four months. I do not know what our future holds …" He sighed. "But I am glad you are on our side."

"Tenzin!"

Professor Yeoh appeared in the doorframe and rushed to hug the old man.

"When I heard a monk in red robes was here, I knew it had to be you," she said, releasing him and wiping tears from her eyes.

"It is good to see you, Mei," Tenzin said. "I was so sorry to hear about Ling. How are you and your daughter?"

"You saw her," Zoe said. "Lin was sitting next to me."

"*That* was little Lin? Oh, Mei, she has so much anger in her."

Professor Yeoh nodded. "I know. Come," she said, offering her arm. "We will have tea and talk about better times."

"I would like that very much," he said, locking arms with her and starting for the door. "But there is much to discuss besides the past."

...

Combat class had a substitute teacher, too. A middle-aged military man, judging by his stance and demeanour.

"My name is Professor Smith," he said. "I am a former Green Beret and current paramilitary operations officer in the Special Operations Group of the US Central Intelligence Agency. To answer the obvious question, no, I am not a Telepath. I am what you call a Typical. I am extremely good at what I do, though, which is why I was recruited into your organization. I am here today specifically to begin your training in firearms."

Everyone exchanged glances. Was he being compelled? Was he was taking the drugs that would give him Abilities, like the godlings?

Zoe raised her hand. "We don't use guns," she said.

"Yes, I heard your former teacher was a skilled swordsman who did not like guns. I am told they are ineffective against your kind, because you can see the path a bullet will take before it is fired. That is *quite* a skill.

With all due respect to your former teacher, though, guns are *highly* effective against Typicals, who you *will* be up against. Unlike a pistol, a sword is difficult to conceal. A pistol also has the advantage of range. You can dispatch a room full of enemies in a matter of seconds. A rifle can dispatch an enemy in a position that you cannot easily reach, like a guard tower. Even against your kind, guns can be useful. In close combat, a Telepath might not have time to avoid a bullet. At the very least, multiple guns firing from multiple angles could be used to pin you down. I'm told guns and even rocket launchers were used to take this facility last spring. The rebels also have guns. Even if a blade is your weapon of choice, you may find yourself captured one day, and the only weapon available is the gun you take from the enemy. Every operative *needs* to know how to use a gun. It's that simple."

He gestured to a table at the far end of the dojo. "We will start with the basics. You will learn the safe handling of a pistol, to ensure you do not accidentally shoot your classmate. You will learn how to load it, how to properly draw it from standing and kneeling positions, how to properly grip and aim, how to holster it, how to clean it. Then you will learn how to shoot."

. . .

"I hate this," Lin said, as they walked back to their dorm after class. "My dad hated guns. I hate guns. I hate that they're making us do this."

Zoe nodded. "I know. I feel the same way. But I get that soldiers need to know this stuff."

"We are *not* soldiers," Lin said.

"We *are*, though. I've been trained to be a soldier—or at least an operative—my entire life. And now you and everyone else are being forcibly trained, too. I have no doubt they'll teach you everything they taught me. Situational awareness, threat assessment, infiltration. They'll teach us everything they teach spies. He was right about one thing: The Resistance did use guns that day I came back. And Gabriel was your dad's right-hand man."

Lin said nothing.

"I don't want to use guns," Zoe continued. "But I guess . . . I kind of want to know *how* to, just in case I ever need to use one."

"I still hate it," Lin said. "I feel like I'm betraying my dad."

Zoe wrapped her arm around her. "I know."

13

INFECTED

E than froze with his mouth full of food. "What?"

"I said," Zoe repeated, "what did Professor Sharapova say?"

Ethan stared blankly.

"When you told her everything Gabriel told me?"

"Oh." He swallowed and wiped his mouth. "Right. She . . . thought it was interesting."

"Interesting?"

"Mm-hmm," he said, taking another bite.

"That's it?" she asked, incredulously. "She didn't have *anything* else to say?"

"Not really."

"Did she . . . think it might be related to whatever they did to you?"

"No," Ethan said. "She said I seem to be fine now. No signs of anything wrong with my head. Whatever they did, she thinks I've self-healed."

Zoe was stunned. "Wow." That couldn't be possible, could it? Her mind raced. Had Sharapova been compelled to say that? Every professor had been held prisoner after the Battle, and their memories were blurry. What if they had all been compelled or had alternate personas created, to be triggered whenever necessary? Wait, Sharapova already *had* such a persona, so it was probably still there, just waiting to be activated. But why would Ethan believe such an implausible lie? Unless . . .

She needed to tread carefully. "That's . . . that's great news. How could that have happened so quickly, though?"

Ethan shrugged.

"Well, what did she say about escaping to help Gabriel?"

He shook his head. "She said she's needed here. Students are still shell-shocked from the Battle. So, she's staying put."

"PTSD," Zoe said.

Ethan cocked his head.

"Post-traumatic stress disorder. No one says 'shell shock' anymore. That was coined back in World War One."

"Right. It's been called a lot of things over the centuries," Ethan said. "The ancient Assyrians called it Spirit Affliction. They thought the spirits of those they killed in battle had come back to haunt them."

"I didn't know that," Zoe said, slowly. "Ancient Assyria. That's . . . Mesopotamia, right?"

"Northern Mesopotamia. Their empire arose maybe . . . four thousand years ago? They lasted almost a millennium and a half before the Babylonians conquered them. Empires rise and fall."

A chill ran up Zoe's spine. "It must be so interesting for Telepaths who have lived through the rise and fall of all those empires. I mean, we read about it in history books. But to have actually *lived* through it all. What a different perspective you'd have."

Ethan looked at her for a long time before smiling. "I have to run," he said, standing up with his tray as Lin and Priya approached. "Talk to you later, Zoe."

Zoe stared after him as Lin and Priya sat.

"Zoe?" Lin said, looking from her to Ethan's retreating form. "What is it? You look like you just saw a ghost."

Zoe's blood ran cold, and her hands trembled. "I have to go."

．．．

Zoe knocked on the door.

"Come in."

She hurried into the office and shut the door. A very angry Professor Sharapova leapt up from her desk.

"You are *not* welcome in my office," she said. "Get out."

"Was he here?" Zoe asked.

"Was who here?"

"Ethan. Did he come to his session today?"

"Other students' sessions are none of your business. Now leave."

"He skipped it, didn't he? He told me he spoke to you about Gabriel, but he didn't, did he?"

"Gabriel?" Professor Sharapova paused and seemed to really look at Zoe for the first time. "You're shaking."

It was true. Zoe had never been so scared.

"Please don't make me leave," she whimpered. "I need your help."

The professor closed her eyes and breathed deeply. "Sit," she said.

Zoe sat on the couch and rocked back and forth.

"Start from the beginning," Professor Sharapova said.

"First things first," Zoe said. "Would you like me to make sure that you're . . . still you? That your alternate persona hasn't been activated? I could say a phrase and bring the real you back. If you're already you, it shouldn't have any effect, I don't think."

Professor Sharapova stiffened. "If you betray me again, Zoe—"

"I won't. I promise."

The professor thought for a moment, then nodded.

"The password is . . . tulips," Zoe said. "It's time to go to sleep now, Natasha." Nothing seemed to happen, and Professor Sharapova breathed a sigh of relief. "What's the password, Professor?"

"Tulips," she replied.

Zoe told her all about their mission and their unexpected meeting with Gabriel. How he had looked into the minds of the compelled and noticed the same neural patterns over and over again. How he had asked for Professor Sharapova's help in making sense of it all.

"The first thing I thought of was Ethan. What if he has this same neural pattern in *his* head? I wanted to tell you everything and ask for your help, but Ethan insisted he would do it. But when I asked him how it went, he lied. He claimed you said his mind was fine now—that there were no traces left of whatever was done to him. He said you wouldn't help Gabriel because you're needed here to treat students suffering from 'shell shock.' When I corrected his terminology, he started talking about what the ancient Assyrians called it—which is not how Ethan talks. And that's when a horrible thought came to me."

She rocked. Was she being ridiculous? Did she dare speak this out loud? She felt like saying it would somehow make it real, and she desperately wanted this to just be in her head.

"When Ragnar freed me from solitary, I asked him if Marduk was really a god—or even real. He insisted Marduk was very real and that I would be wise if I assumed he was always watching and listening. I never understood what he meant by that. Is Marduk so powerful that he's actually omniscient somehow?"

She pulled her knees up and hugged them to her chest. "I always thought it was odd that they know what happens around here. I've never noticed security cameras anywhere, so I assumed they had hidden cameras. But maybe that's not it. What if . . . what if Marduk can get inside people's minds? Not to observe . . . but to *live*? What if all these repeating neural patterns are his, giving him just enough consciousness in each mind to communicate with other copies of himself? He could be a decrepit old man somewhere—or he could have died a long time ago, but he lives on in the minds of others. Like a virus."

She looked out the window. "I don't know what Ethan told you, but he told me he has thoughts that don't feel like his own. He sometimes wakes up and things aren't where he left them. And sometimes when he looks at me, I swear it feels like there's someone else behind his eyes."

She closed her own eyes tightly and went back to rocking. "I think he's Marduk." Her voice broke. She started to shake. Saying it aloud made it suddenly much more real. "I think Marduk has been growing in Ethan's mind and now has full control. And he *knows* that I know. Please tell me I'm delusional. Please tell me I went mad in solitary and none of this is real. Did you know I saw Professor Chao in prison?" She started laughing. Why was she laughing? Professor Sharapova looked alarmed. "Yeah, he kept me company for months. He still does. So, clearly, I've lost my mind a bit, and I'm imagining things and arriving at conclusions without merit, and Ethan isn't really Marduk. Right?"

Professor Sharapova was clearly unnerved. After a long time, she said, "No one should ever be held in solitary confinement, Zoe. Certainly not a child. It's barbaric." She took a deep breath. "It's my job to care for the students here, and I should have been there for you when you returned. I'm sorry. In my defence, what you did to me made me feel . . . violated. And I have been trying to deal with my own trauma from that, without anyone to help me, because *I'm* the person people come to for help."

"I'm sorry, Professor. I'm so sorry—"

She held up a hand to stop her. "I know. I would like to know more about your time in isolation and your visions of Professor Chao. I will help you as much as I can. But as for the problem at hand . . . I have to be honest, this scares the living hell out of me. There's never been a Telepath strong enough to do what you're suggesting, but . . . I don't have a better explanation, either. What Gabriel has described is unprecedented."

"So . . . what do we do?" Zoe asked, quietly.

"I don't know, Zoe." Professor Sharapova shook her head. "I need to examine a subject with these repeating neural patterns. Two subjects, so I can see for myself and compare. I don't like the idea of leaving, if I can even escape, but I'm not sure what else to do."

"What about Ethan? Can you help him before you go?"

"I honestly don't know. Perhaps if I had another subject, I could compare their neural pathways and destroy any that are identical . . . maybe? But unless someone else here is . . . infected, helping him would be exceedingly difficult. I could destroy any memories that are not his, but that would still leave neural pathways responsible for behaviour, morality, ideology. I have never heard of anyone replicating neural pathways in another person. Did they create new ones or rewire existing pathways? If the latter, I don't know how I could ever repair them, because I wouldn't know how they used to be. Also, if these new pathways were created while Ethan was a prisoner, then why is his condition getting worse over time? I don't understand how these pathways could be *growing* on their own, unless his tormenters installed some sort of blueprint, causing the pathways to develop naturally on their own."

Poor Ethan. How had he felt as another consciousness grew inside of him? What could it feel like now? Was he still conscious in there, watching someone else take control? Or was he just . . . gone? It wasn't fair. He had been through so much already.

"I just had another horrible thought," she said. "You told Ethan that Ragnar made him fall in love with me, right?"

Professor Sharapova nodded.

"Well, that struck me as weird. If the idea was to give me a protector . . . why? I'm as strong as any of the other kids. What do I need a protector for? But what if Ragnar *knew*—a long time ago—that Marduk would claim Ethan someday? What if Ragnar made him love me so as to offer me some measure of protection against Marduk?"

"But why you?" Sharapova asked.

"Because I'm Ragnar's daughter."

"You're *what?*"

. . .

"You're *what?*" Makena, Priya, and Paige cried in unison at their spot by the lake.

Priya punched Lin's shoulder. "You knew? Why didn't you tell me?"

Lin scowled and punched her back harder, making Priya wince. "Because it wasn't my secret to tell."

Zoe filled them in on the details of her DNA and on her theory that Marduk was inside Ethan's mind.

"Whoa," Paige said. "So . . . what do we do now? What do we do the next time we see Ethan? Are you even sure about this? Can we trick him into revealing himself? Get him to pretend to remember something that never happened, maybe?"

"Do we even *want* to do that?" Makena said. "We're talking about a god here—or at least the most powerful Telepath of all time. I don't think tricking him into revealing himself is the right strategy."

Zoe shook her head. "I don't think it would work anyway. Marduk would still have access to all of Ethan's memories. Maybe we could trick him into saying something that only Marduk would know, like I tried earlier."

"Do you think he suspects that you know?" Lin asked.

"Maybe? I'm not sure," Zoe said. "When I pushed a bit too far, he smiled, as if he knew I was trying to trick him into revealing himself. I don't know what I'll do or say when I next see him. I think I'll have to play it by ear. Ethan said he'd been having blackouts, so maybe I just caught him during a rare moment when Marduk was in control? As for how to help him, I only see two choices. We can find someone here who has been infected and get them and Ethan into a room with Professor Sharapova, so she can compare their minds and destroy any identical neural patterns. Or we can go on another mission and sneak Sharapova out with us—and hope Gabriel shows up."

"What, like we sneak her out in the trunk?" Paige asked.

"They didn't check the trunk last time," Makena said.

"Yeah, maybe because Ethan was with us, and he's unwittingly been their eyes and ears this whole time."

"Well, I don't have a better plan," Zoe said, "so let's start thinking of our next target. Meanwhile, don't let on that I told you anything about Ethan."

"So, we're just supposed to pretend that the dude sitting with us at meals isn't an ancient, evil god?" Paige asked.

"It would've been easier if I hadn't told you anything, but I thought you needed to know, just in case." Suddenly, a thought occurred to her. "Except . . ."

They all waited. "Except?" Paige prompted.

"I just thought of something," Zoe said, "and honestly, I feel really dumb that this never occurred to me until just now."

"What?" Priya demanded.

"We . . . can't actually trust anyone." Zoe looked each of her friends in the eyes. "Not even each other. Hell, not even ourselves."

Their quizzical expressions quickly gave way to understanding.

"Oh," Lin said.

"Yeah," Zoe continued. "The professors—even Lin's mom—all said that their time in prison is fuzzy. We were *all* captured. Any one of us could be under the influence of compulsion and never even know it. Or we could have an alternate persona that wakes up occasionally. Or we could even be infected with Marduk's . . . consciousness or whatever. We could be reporting to Ragnar or Gillespie regularly for all we know."

Paige looked around suspiciously. "So . . . what would you suggest we do about this?”

“I think we get Sharapova to check us all out.”

. . .

“This is not wise,” Professor Chao said, as the Valkyries marched to Professor Sharapova’s office. “She could be compromised herself.”

I already made sure her split persona wasn’t active.

“She could be compelled. She could be infected. It is dangerous to have her in your minds.”

Well, I don’t have a better plan. We need to be able to trust each other.

When there was no answer at the office door, they found her quarters instead. She looked quite surprised to find five girls waiting in the hall outside her door.

“We need your help,” Zoe said. “Can we come in—quickly, before anyone sees us out here?”

The professor shooed them in and shut the door. “You shouldn’t be here. What’s all this about?”

They explained their concerns. “Can you look in our heads and make sure we’re all okay? Not infected, not compelled, not split?”

I do not like this, Professor Chao said in her head.

You don’t have to like it, Zoe snapped. *You’re not real.*

Professor Sharapova took a deep breath and ran her fingers through her hair. “Not a word to anyone. If I get caught . . .” She sighed. “Who’s first, then?”

Not you, Professor Chao said. *If you insist on doing this, go last in case something goes wrong.*

Okay, that sounded reasonable enough. “I’ll go last,” Zoe said. “If any of us are infected and suddenly turn violent, I want to be able to subdue them.”

“I’ll go first,” Makena said. She sat in a chair, and Professor Sharapova stood behind her, placing her hands on Makena's head. They both closed their eyes. After several minutes, their eyes opened.

"I can't find anything suspicious," the professor said. Paige went next and was also cleared. "I didn't see any similar neural patterns like Gabriel mentioned, either."

Priya was next, then Lin. When it was Zoe's turn, she sat and closed her eyes.

All right, we've done this sort of thing before, Zoe. Just relax and let me do a bit of probing.

After a minute, the professor gasped.

What? Zoe asked, alarmed. *What is it?* But there was no answer—for several long minutes.

Sorry, Zoe, Professor Sharapova said, at last. *I didn't mean to alarm you. It's all good.* She pulled her hands away and slid out of Zoe's mind. "You're all clean," she said.

Zoe regarded her suspiciously. What had just happened? Why did the professor look so rattled?

"Now go," Professor Sharapova said, shooing them out. "And be careful. Don't get yourselves killed."

"Wait, there's one more thing," Zoe said. She explained their plans to either smuggle the professor out to Gabriel or to find another infected person in the school.

She just nodded and shoved them into the hall. "Let me know," she said, shutting the door and locking it.

They looked at each other.

"Did that end . . . weirdly?" Paige asked.

"She seemed spooked," Lin said. "Did something happen while she was in your head, Zoe? We heard her gasp."

"I don't know," Zoe said. "I heard it, too, and then she just stopped communicating."

Everyone looked uncomfortable. Were they suspicious of her?

"Well," Lin said. "She said you were clean . . . and coming here was your idea, so I can't see *you* being infected by Marduk."

"Unless she is and doesn't know it," Priya said. "And Marduk just did something to Professor Sharapova."

The mood changed. Bloody hell. Now no one trusted her—*again*. It *was* suspicious, she had to admit. Something had definitely happened back there. But Marduk couldn't be inside her, could he? Zoe didn't feel the way Ethan had described, with someone else's thoughts inside her—

Oh.

. . .

"Your hallucination of my dad can't possibly be Marduk," Lin said that night in bed. "He's been helping you. Why would Marduk help you?"

"He *did* caution me against killing Ragnar," Zoe said. "And he taught me electrokinesis. You thought that was pretty weird."

Lin was quiet. "I guess I've secretly been hoping he actually is my dad. His spirit or whatever. Dumb, huh?"

"It's not dumb," Zoe said. "That's what I wish, too. That would be a whole lot better than Marduk."

"We still don't know he's Marduk. He could still just be a hallucination, like you've always said."

"Yeah," Zoe said. "Could be."

"Zoe," Lin said, sighing, "I think I should tell my mom. About Ethan, I mean. This is too big."

Zoe nodded. "Sounds good. Maybe she can talk to Professor Sharapova, too. Find out what spooked her."

. . .

The weeks that followed were uncomfortable. Zoe's friends were awkward around her—even Lin. Whenever she joined them, the conversation would abruptly stop or change topic.

Ethan continued to hang out with them, but he also kept disappearing. It was weird. He still seemed like Ethan, for the most part, but every now and again he would say something slightly out of character. Was he Marduk all the time now or just sometimes? He seemed to realize that everyone was treating him differently, too, but he never said anything about it. Zoe was too afraid to confide anything in him for fear she would be telling her secrets directly to Marduk. Sometimes she wondered if they were all just being paranoid. It wasn't like they had any proof of any of this.

Meanwhile, they continued to look for another target as an excuse to smuggle Professor Sharapova out of the school. This time, they decided to go bigger and chose the premier of Ontario, who could improve the lives of millions of people while still having minimal security. Their mission, however, was denied, due to being "too risky." So, they asked if they could go after the mayor of Toronto and were told to stay away from politicians altogether for now. Nobody else's missions were getting approved, either, but only because they weren't skilled enough at mindbending yet. It wouldn't be long, though.

On the plus side, Tenzin's levitation classes were a daily dose of fun. Every day, Paige, Lin, and Zoe would go outside and practice flying. Just like Tenzin had said, if she pushed on the ground at an angle, she would move horizontally and keep gaining speed. So, it was like they were flying, just really close to the ground. It was comical but also a blast. Paige was especially good at it and seemed to be fulfilling some long-held superhero fantasy by flying in a Superman pose. Zoe, on the other hand, preferred to zoom around cross-legged.

One day—two weeks after the Sharapova incident—they arrived at Advanced Telekinesis and were surprised to see Professor Martinov grinning at them.

"You're back!" Zoe cried.

"I'm back!" he exclaimed, stretching his arms out wide.

"Are you okay?" Lin asked.

"Me? Oh, I'm fine. I'm fine. I just needed a little attitude adjustment, that's all."

Oh no. "What do you mean?" Zoe asked, her heart sinking.

He leaned in close so that only she could hear. "You *know* what I mean, Zoe. Your Professor Martinov is mine now."

Zoe shivered. He leaned back, still grinning, then looked momentarily confused, before returning to normal, as if nothing at all had happened. "Take your seats, everybody! It is so good to be back. Let me start by apologizing for my actions during our last class together. What I did was deeply disrespectful to Master Ragnar, and I am very ashamed. I simply did not understand Lord Marduk's plan and how he wants to save us all. But I do now. And I will do everything in my power to prepare you all for the days ahead."

Zoe sat still, too stunned to speak. Then she got angry. Leaning over, she whispered in Lin's ear, "We have our subject for Professor Sharapova."

■ ■ ■

The trap was set. Everyone was in position. From her hiding spot in the trees, Zoe could see Professor Sharapova standing by the shore of the little lake, illuminated by the full moon. She couldn't see her friends, though, so hopefully Professor Martinov wouldn't be able to see them, either. Footsteps crunched down the gravel path. It was him.

"Natasha," Professor Martinov said.

"*Privet, tovarisch,*" Natasha said in Russian. She hugged him tightly. "You got my message. Thank you for coming. I am so sorry. Two weeks. Are you all right? What did they do to you?"

"I'm fine," he said. "It was like a vacation. Just me and my thoughts."

"Did they . . . ?" She pointed to his head.

He shrugged. "I don't think so. It was just punishment, not . . . reeducation." He looked around. "Am I early for the secret meeting or is it just us?"

She smiled. "You *are* early, actually. Mei is joining us. I thought it best to keep the group small, for now. It's so hard to know who to trust. I assume that's why you're shielded."

"One cannot be too careful in these troubling times."

Shoot. Plan A had been for Sharapova to shield him before he could resist. Time for plan B. Zoe emerged from her hiding spot. "Professor!" she yelled.

As Professor Martinov turned, Professor Sharapova reached into her jacket, pulled out her collapsible metal staff, and hit him in the back of the head.

It bounced off, like his skull was made of metal.

Professor Martinov smiled, cold and sinister. Without looking, he forced Professor Sharapova to the ground. He pointed at Zoe.

"You," he said. "This was your idea, no? Zoe, always with the troublemaking." He shook his head in disappointment. "You think I did not expect a trap?"

Crap. Plan C.

Zoe extended her own metal staff, intending to charge him, but Martinov stomped his foot, and the earth between them erupted, flinging her into the air. She landed on her feet and found her friends already attacking him from all sides.

They had known this would be a tough fight, if it came to it. They were taking on a master of telekinesis. He was stronger than all of them and far more experienced. Weapons would be almost useless against him. But Ragnar had shown them he had a weakness.

He needed to breathe.

As Lin attacked with her staff and Paige tried to lift him off the ground telekinetically, Zoe reached out a hand and tried to strangle him with telekinesis. Unfortunately, he must have strengthened his neck, because he was utterly unfazed. He was still smirking at Zoe's troubled reaction when Makena rose out of the water behind him and threw a plastic bag over his head. Lin and Paige seized his arms to prevent him from ripping the bag. The original plan had been for Makena to put him in a rear choke hold, but they figured if Zoe's telekinetic choke didn't work, then neither would a physical one. But now they had to be careful—they didn't want to kill him.

Professor Martinov flailed, no doubt panicking from lack of air. Telekinetic explosions radiated outward from his body. Though dazed, everyone held firm. Then, he stopped fighting. Was it working? He was still standing, so he wasn't unconscious yet. What was he—

A telekinetic explosion emanated from his head, bursting the bag open, and he gasped for air.

Makena quickly applied a choke hold while Zoe swept his feet out from under him. Lin punched him as hard as she possibly could in the solar plexus, hoping to wind him. Then, she and Zoe grabbed his arms while Paige clamped a hand over his mouth and pinched his nose. Then, Paige was flying away from him, and Lin and Zoe were flying into each other, knocking heads so hard that they both saw stars. Makena suddenly screamed and dropped the professor, her arm broken.

Professor Martinov rose to his feet, disheveled and furious. That was it. They were out of plans.

"Alexey!" someone yelled. An old man in a red robe approached the lake, Professor Yeoh at his side, staff in hand.

"Tenzin," Martinov said. "I thought you had left already. Your presence is not needed here."

Tenzin walked forward, his hands in his robe. "Is that how you greet your old master after so many years?"

"Forgive me," Martinov said, "but now is not a good time. You should both leave. This does not concern you."

"Are you all right, Lin?" Professor Yeoh asked. Lin lay on the ground but nodded. "Makena?"

Makena winced. "I'll live."

"You think this does not concern me, Alexey?" Professor Yeoh said.

"Your daughter and her friends attacked *me*," he said.

"Why would they do that?" Tenzin asked.

"He's under compulsion," Professor Sharapova said, getting to her feet. "I wanted to try to help him."

"Nonsense," Martinov said. "I have . . . seen the light. That is all."

"He's lying," Zoe said.

"Girls, leave us," Professor Yeoh said.

Zoe shook her head. "No."

Professor Yeoh scowled. "Lin, go. That's an order."

"Sorry, Mom," Lin said, getting to her feet. "I'm not leaving, either."

"Kids today." Professor Martinov grinned. "No respect for their elders. Tell you what, Mei. I do not wish to get your daughter in trouble, so I will leave this matter for you to deal with. I won't even tell Master Ragnar." He began to walk away, but Tenzin blocked his path.

"I am afraid I cannot allow you to leave, Alexey."

Martinov cocked his head. "Are you challenging me, Tenzin?"

"I am afraid so." Sighing, he motioned for everyone to stand back. "Do not interfere, no matter what." He took a ready stance, as did Professor Martinov.

Zoe could hardly believe this was happening. When was the last time two masters of telekinesis had dueled like this?

Martinov flicked his wrist, and the ground beneath Tenzin erupted upward, utterly engulfing him. Martinov piled more dirt and rock on top of him, squeezing it tightly from all sides. Just when Zoe started to worry the duel was already over, all that earth exploded outward. Martinov erected a shield just in time to protect himself, causing him to lose sight of his opponent, so he didn't see Tenzin hurtling down from above until it was too late. With a loud cry, Tenzin drove Martinov down into the ground. But a split second later, the ground exploded again, hurling Tenzin high into the air over the lake. A gust of wind caught him and delivered him softly to the opposite shore.

Martinov crawled out of his crater, and the two men faced each other. Martinov roared and sprinted toward the lake, his cape billowing behind him. He jumped, so high that he clearly would have made it to the other side—if a water funnel hadn't suddenly reached up and sucked him down under the water's surface.

For a moment, the lake was silent. Then, the water began to churn and Martinov's head surfaced. He gasped for air, but Tenzin only piled more water on top of him. Then, the ground beneath Tenzin abruptly gave way, uprooting a tree behind him and knocking him into the lake, which pulled him under, too.

For almost thirty seconds, both men battled underwater. Then, the water stilled and Professor Martinov emerged. He waited at the edge of the lake, and after several minutes, he nodded.

"*Dasvidania, tovarisch*," he said, quietly, and turned. "Now, how to deal with you all?"

Zoe raced for the lake and dove in. She couldn't just let Tenzin die. She saw a shape deep in the water and swam toward it. Then, she saw him—sitting cross-legged within a bubble of air. He pressed his finger to his lips.

Zoe surfaced.

"I couldn't find him," she lied, despondently.

Professor Martinov shrugged. "He will turn up eventually." Suddenly, he grabbed his ears. His eyes bulged, and his mouth opened soundlessly. He seized his throat and searched for his opponent—but it was fruitless. Spying Zoe, he hurled her, then Paige, away before dashing from the lake. Suddenly, he stopped, turned ninety degrees, and took off again before stumbling to his knees. At last, Zoe realized what was happening. While Tenzin was tucked safely underwater, he had somehow created a vacuum bubble around Professor Martinov—and no matter which way he ran, he couldn't escape.

The professor strained, probably trying to pull air into the vacuum bubble, but it was too late. His eyes rolled back, and he collapsed.

Tenzin emerged from the lake and bent down to take Professor Martinov's pulse. "He will be fine," he said. "I would suggest you do whatever it is you intended to do quickly, Natasha, before he awakens."

"That was incredible," Ethan said, slow-clapping, as he strolled down the path toward them.

Zoe and Professor Sharapova locked eyes, like two deer caught in headlights. Capturing Professor Martinov had only been the first half of the plan. Now they were supposed to capture Ethan—by surprise.

"I am truly amazed," Ethan continued. "I don't think I've seen two humans display that amount of raw power in over a millennium."

Everyone froze.

"Don't be afraid," he said. "I'm not going to hurt any of you. Not as long as you behave."

Time seemed to slow. This couldn't really be happening. What should she do? Attack him?

"Don't," Ethan said, looking at Zoe. "I'm nowhere near as powerful as I once was—not yet—but I'm still the most powerful being alive." He strode onto the surface of the lake and turned to face them. "This was always one of my favourite party tricks," he said. "Almost as much as this." He raised his hands, and the water parted before him.

"You must be the infamous Marduk," Tenzin said. "I must admit, I did not think you existed."

"I am," Ethan said. "You would do well to bow to me. All of you."

Everyone dropped to their knees. Even Tenzin. Zoe felt absolutely terrified. Was this Marduk's doing? Compelling her to be afraid? Or was she just scared to be in the presence of the god she had been raised to fear her whole life? He seemed to emanate power, but maybe it was just his demeanour. She couldn't raise her shields.

"I am Marduk," he said. "And I am a god. The only god left in this world." He regarded Zoe. "But I'm also Ethan. The same Ethan you have always known. I have all the memories of our childhood together. All of my . . . feelings . . . for you. Even if they did stem from compulsion."

"So, Ethan is still in there?" Zoe asked. "Just not in control?"

"It's . . . not really like that. It's more accurate to say that we've merged. The part of me that's Marduk has been growing for months until he—I—finally became the dominant personality. And I will continue to grow as the part of me that is Ethan diminishes. But I will always keep Ethan's memories and values, to honour his sacrifice."

"It's not a sacrifice when it's not freely given," Zoe growled. "Why Ethan? Why not, say, Ragnar?"

"He's too old. And too useful to me as my general. I wanted a *new* body, and Ethan was perfect. Young, intelligent, strong—both physically and in his Abilities. Particularly mindbending. You were also a surprisingly strong candidate, Zoe, but you damaged your mind, and to be honest, you were never really in the running, regardless."

Zoe wondered what he meant by that. Because she was a girl? Or because she was Ragnar's daughter? "Have you done this before? Is this how you've survived for so long? By taking over other people's bodies?"

"I am a network of thousands of people throughout the world. Soon, that network will include all the world's leaders, too. In each mind, I exist as a shallow copy of myself, just enough to observe and control and communicate with other instances of myself in the network, relaying important information back to me. I would hardly want to have multiple *deep* copies of myself in existence, though. They would be a threat and would go to war with one another. No, Ethan is special."

"Is your original body still alive? Are you somewhere nearby?"

Ethan smiled. "Such probing questions, Zoe. It would be in your best interest to abandon all hope of defeating me. I am a god, and you are a human child. It would be a shame if I were forced to kill you. I want you to rule by my side, after all. We can make the world a utopia together. And your friends here—your Valkyries—you can all be my disciples. My lieutenants."

"I want my Ethan back," Zoe whispered.

Ethan spread his arms wide, and the waters closed beneath him. "I'm still here, Zoe," he said, crossing the lake's surface to meet her. "I'm still Ethan. Just . . . so much more. I *want* this. I'm *stronger* than I was before. Wiser. I remember events from *thousands* of years ago. I can make this world *better*."

"I don't believe you," Zoe said. "This is Marduk talking, not Ethan. My Ethan didn't want his mind to be taken over any more than I would."

Ethan sighed. "I understand this is difficult for you, Zoe. But ultimately, you *will* have to accept it. Otherwise . . ." Shrugging, he approached Tenzin. "Not used to being shielded and paralyzed, I imagine." He placed his hand on Tenzin's head. "Sleep."

Tenzin collapsed.

Marduk gestured at Professor Yeoh. "You as well," he said, and she collapsed, too. Next, he turned to Professor Sharapova, who was quaking. "What to do with you, hmm? Are you more trouble than you're worth? I know!" He snapped his fingers. "I'll wake up your alternate persona. The one in which you are unconditionally loyal to me. And I'll change the deactivation phrase so that you can never ever come back. Would you like that?"

Professor Sharapova timidly shook her head.

"I can't hear you."

"No, sir."

"No what?"

Sharapova swallowed. "No . . . my lord."

Ethan drew so close their noses nearly touched. "No more chances, Natasha. There are worse things than death."

Sharapova nodded vigorously.

Ethan moved on to Professor Martinov. He touched him, and Martinov stirred and sat up. "You fought well, but you failed. Next time, I expect better of you, understood?"

"Yes, my lord. I am so sorry."

"Go get security. Have them escort Tenzin to a cell."

"So, you can infect him, too, you mean?" Zoe asked. "Why? He's a harmless monk who was minding his own business before you dragged him from his monastery. Just let him go home."

Ethan looked thoughtful, and Zoe hoped he was weighing the advantages of infecting Tenzin with those of winning her over to his side. "Very well," he said. "I am a merciful god, after all. Alexey, have security gather his things, escort Tenzin to the airport, and put him on a plane home."

Professor Martinov nodded, then strode back up to the school.

Ethan looked at Professor Yeoh, then at Lin. "I expect better from you, too, Lin." He faced the rest of them. "I have much to do. We'll talk again soon."

He strolled past them and . . . *flew* away.

Everyone remained on their knees for some time afterward, shaking uncontrollably.

"This is very bad," Lin whispered, at last.

14

A GOD RETURNS

They sat in their corner of the library, staring blankly.

"Did that really just happen?" Paige asked.

"Afraid so," Priya said.

"I'm so sorry, Zoe," Lin said. "We'll get Ethan back. Somehow, we'll get him back."

"*How*?" Paige exclaimed. "We just saw the most epic telekinetic battle ever, and then Marduk handled Tenzin without even trying. He *flew* away like some bloody superhero! High in the sky! How much strength must that have taken? And he just . . . did it. Like it was nothing."

"I don't know," Lin said. "But we'll find a way."

"Did you all feel it, too?" Zoe asked. "Like you were terrified and had no strength? No willpower at all?"

Everyone nodded.

"I wonder how he did that," she mused. "I don't think it was just that we were scared of a really strong Telepath. And that's all he is—he's not a god. I think it was another of his tricks. We need to figure out how he does it and how to defend against it."

Makena spoke. "Zoe, this is a whole other level. Before, we were up against a powerful Viking Telepath. But Marduk? If he's not actually a god, he may as well be. I *felt* his power. He could have killed me with a stray thought. I know he could have. And he said that wasn't even close to his full strength. If we go up against him, we may all die. *All* of us. Now, if he wanted to destroy the world, I'd say we try our best to kill him, because what would we have to lose? But he says he wants to *save* the world. Using the same strategies you yourself have advocated. I *hate* that he's taken Ethan from us, but right now, we don't even know if what he's done to Ethan is reversible. Are we *sure* we want to go against him? Is this worth dying for?"

An uncomfortable silence followed.

"If it were you that he had taken over," Zoe asked, "would you want us to save you?"

"No," Makena replied. "I don't think I would. It's too dangerous. I wouldn't want you to risk your lives for me."

Zoe thought about that. "Well, Ethan would risk his for me. So, I'm going to do the same for him."

"I'm going to help you," Lin said.

"Lin . . ." Priya began.

"I'm scared to death," Lin continued. "I don't want to die, but Ragnar killed my dad under Marduk's orders. And you're my friend. It's that simple for me."

Zoe gave a quick nod of appreciation—Lin always had her back. "No one needs to commit to anything right now. We're all terrified. And I don't actually know what to do yet, anyway. Once we have a plan, you can decide if you want to help or not. For now, I need more information. I think I'll have to talk to Ragnar."

. . .

Zoe knocked on Headmaster Ragnar's chamber door. He looked surprised to see her.

"I really need to speak with you," she said. He arched an eyebrow and opened the door wide enough to let her step into his living quarters. She'd never seen it during Headmaster Harrington's day, but it now resembled Ragnar's quarters in their old school, with Viking swords and shields adorning the walls.

"This is unexpected," he said, sitting in a chair and gesturing for her to do likewise. He picked up a glass of scotch that he must have just poured. "To what do I owe the pleasure of a visit from my estranged daughter?"

Still trembling, Zoe sat. "So, I just spoke with Marduk."

"Ah," Ragnar said. He pointed at her trembling hands. "He has that effect on people."

"Any advice on how to minimize it?"

He raised his glass. "I've always found that alcohol helps."

Interesting. "He just visited you, too, then? I thought by now you'd be immune to whatever type of mind control he uses to induce fear."

"If it's mind control," he said, taking a sip, "then he is always controlling the minds of everyone near him. I think it's possible that humans are just wired to be frightened in the presence of a god."

"You really think he's a god? Not just someone with a god complex? I mean, he's scary powerful, but he's still just a dying old man hiding in his sarcophagus or whatever in the basement."

Ragnar smiled. "We both know he never told you that."

Shoot. It was just a theory, but she'd been hoping for some confirmation or denial. "Well, I don't believe he's some incorporeal being who can just make his memories and Abilities appear in Ethan's mind as new neural pathways. He didn't just appear in Ethan—he's been *growing* in Ethan. I think his memories have been getting transferred into Ethan, somehow, which means Marduk—old Marduk—is here somewhere."

"What can I do for you, Zoe?"

Zoe sighed. Clearly, she wasn't going to get much out of him. She changed tack. "When did you meet him?"

"When I was fourteen years old," Ragnar said. "He wandered through my village. An old man claiming to be a *seiðmaður*. A seer."

"Can I see?" Zoe asked. "Like how you showed me my mother and sisters?"

Ragnar mulled this over. "No."

"Why not?"

"Because it's not my decision to make. I'll pass along your request to Marduk the next time I see him. If he agrees, I'll show you."

"So, he trained you to be a Telepath?"

"He did. Up in his cave, out of sight. He taught me how to fight, too. Old, long-forgotten fighting styles. But his greatest lesson to me was to hide from other Telepaths, lest they take me away."

"An old man living in a cave. He doesn't sound like much of a god to me."

"Well, he's not the capital G god that so many people believe in these days. He didn't create the world and the entire universe. But I grew up believing in the Norse gods. I was convinced he was one of them, despite his claims that he was far older."

"So, you never attended the Academy? No one even knew you existed?"

Ragnar shook his head. "Marduk was my master. No other. A few Telepaths have discovered me over the centuries, but none lived to tell of it."

Zoe let that sink in. The only Telepath who had ever influenced Ragnar was Marduk. "So, why are you working for him? Out of loyalty, because he was your teacher and companion for, what, twelve hundred years? Or is it out of fear? Or do you genuinely want everyone to be just another version of him, spreading like a virus, until the whole world is some sort of . . . hive mind?"

He considered this. "Call it strategic self-preservation. Choosing the winning side."

"But why?" she pressed. "I mean, I don't want to die, either, but I'm not afraid to risk my life fighting for something I believe in. You're a bastard, but you don't seem like a coward to me, so . . . why?"

Ragnar was silent, perhaps trying to decide if he should be offended, or else how much to reveal to her. "I have been around for a long time, Zoe. I have watched Typicals develop technologies over the centuries. One invention leading to the next. But they never grow *themselves*. They are still, most of them, like children fighting for control of the playground. Only now they have the means to lay waste to that playground. It's not a question of *if* they will destroy the world but rather *when*. You talk of Marduk being a virus, but it's the Typicals who are the virus. They number almost eight billion now and use up all the resources wherever they go without any thought for the future. Marduk offers a solution—the only foolproof solution anyone has ever offered. It's the only version of the world that is guaranteed not only to survive, but to *thrive*. The Typicals' only purpose in life will be to turn the world into a paradise for *us*. When it comes down to it, I would much rather live in his world than die in theirs."

"But they'll fight," Zoe protested. "Once they realize what's happening, they'll fight."

"They won't know what's happening until it's too late. But even if they do fight, so what? What other choice is there? What would *you* do?"

"I would leave them alone!" Zoe shouted.

"Is that why you went on your recent mission? To leave them alone?"

Zoe said nothing.

"You want the same thing—you're just not able to do it on the same scale that Marduk can. Or maybe *you* just want to be the one in charge."

"I *don't* want to be in charge. But I don't trust *him* to be in charge, either. I wanted to influence a few key people, not turn everyone into mindless zombies."

"They're not mindless, just loyal."

"Would *you* want to be one of them?" Zoe demanded.

"No." He shrugged.

"But you think it's all right for them?"

"Yes," he said, slowly, as if speaking to a little child. "Because they're not me."

"So, you're a hypocrite."

Ragnar smiled. "Zoe, this isn't me saying one thing and doing another. This is me not adhering to your simplistic moral philosophy of the Golden Rule. I follow Marduk because he's immensely powerful, so I would need a very good reason to risk going against him. And I don't *have* such a reason, because he actually offers a world I can live in that Typicals won't ruin. You just don't like him because he took your precious Ethan."

Zoe glared at her father. "How long have you known he would do this to Ethan?"

"I've known for *certain* ever since he did it several months ago. But I've known it was *likely* since you both began pulling away from the pack at five years old. Luckily for you, you are my daughter, otherwise he might have chosen you for his host body." He sipped his scotch. "You're welcome."

"Why us? Why not capture some other Telepath?"

Ragnar cocked his head. "I thought you would have figured this out by now. Why do you think you were all created in the first place?"

Zoe gulped. "What do you mean?" she asked, stupidly.

"It was always going to be one of you. He needed a new body—one with a mind that had the potential to contain his, so that he wouldn't become a lesser version of himself. There *are* no such Telepaths in the world, so he created them—using his own DNA."

Zoe sat there, stunned. How had this never occurred to her?

"You also make up his army, of course. But the primary reason you—

and your failed forebears—were created was so that one of you would serve as his host body. In the beginning, he simply tried to clone himself, but it never worked. We didn't know if it was because our cloning technology was flawed or because human eggs were somehow incompatible with the DNA of a god. Time was running out, so he tried a different approach—hybrids. You are my daughter. Half of your DNA comes from me, some comes from your mother, and the rest from many others. But *none* of your DNA comes from him. Your peers, though, are all his children, with a random sampling of 50 percent of his DNA. Well, not completely random, otherwise they'd all *look* like half siblings. He didn't want that—he wanted them to look indigenous to regions all over the world, for the purpose of infiltration. The other 50 percent comes from as wide and diverse a sampling of people as possible, in the hopes of maximizing the probability of creating a viable host. You all, of course, have the genes that we believe to be associated with our Abilities."

"So . . . except for me, all the Igigi are half siblings. Is that why you forbade romantic relationships? Why didn't you just tell everyone they're related?"

"You'll have to ask him," Ragnar said. "I just follow orders."

"So, he just . . . copies himself into Ethan and calls that immortality? It's not *him*, though. It's a *copy*. There are two of him now. Is he close to dying or something?"

"That's just it, Zoe. Ethan *isn't* a copy." He paused, trying to figure out how to explain. "Imagine you could clone yourself, but its mind is a blank slate. You get old or you get some terminal illness and you want to survive, so you upload your brain into that body somehow and then realize, wait . . . I'm still here. *I'm* not in that body. A *copy* of myself occupies that body. I didn't think this through at all. That's your point, right?"

Zoe nodded.

"Well, did you know that most of the atoms in your body are

replaced every year? You don't think of yourself as being a different person from who you were a year ago—well, maybe you're a bad example, given how you were *quite* a different person a year ago—but in general, we don't believe we become new people as we age, because we experience continuity of our consciousness. Marduk experiences that same continuity as he grows inside Ethan's mind, because he experiences what his consciousness in Ethan experiences. His two minds are linked. Each knows what the other is thinking and feeling. You keep refusing to accept Marduk as a god, but what human has ever been able to do this?"

"So, when he's done taking over Ethan, he'll just exist in two bodies until the old one dies?"

"You're fishing again," Ragnar said. "He'll do whatever he wishes."

"How do I get my Ethan back?" she blurted.

"You don't. It's too late. Just be glad Ethan has been in love with you for most of his life. Remnants of that should stay with him. If Marduk ever thought you were an actual threat, he would kill you without a thought."

Zoe was livid. Poor Ethan had been used as a pawn for most of his life. Doomed to love her because of Ragnar's compulsion, doomed to lose his body and mind because of Marduk's unwillingness to accept death as a fact of life. She stood.

"Yeah, Ethan still loves me. In fact, he wants me to rule the world by his side. I imagine then I could get revenge on anyone who's ever wronged me."

She'd hoped to scare him, but he just smiled and looked . . . wistful? Melancholy? He stared off into space. "I imagine," he said, "that you would be in a unique position. You'd be the only person in the world with direct access to Marduk, with *influence* over him." He stared into her eyes intently. "The only person in the world close enough to keep an eye on him—and to *do* something, should it ever become necessary."

Zoe started as she realized what he meant. Had this always been his plan? To create a daughter a god would love—who could manipulate him and perhaps get close enough to kill him should things get out of hand?

"Don't do anything to jeopardize the position you find yourself in," Ragnar warned.

...

"So, those were quite the revelations," Zoe said, lying back on her bed. She had just told Lin everything Ragnar had said.

"At least you're not related to Ethan," Lin offered. "That's good to know—for after we get Marduk out of him, I mean."

"But do I tell everyone they're all related? They deserve to know."

"Absolutely," Lin said. "You have to."

"And now I know why he made Ethan love me. So that I'd be close enough to influence him and even kill him if things ever got out of hand."

"I wonder what Ragnar considers 'out of hand,'" Lin said.

"I have no idea, but he must have some concerns about Marduk's plan to save the world. The thing is, though, Ragnar doesn't know that Ethan learned the real reason *why* he loves me. I can't imagine Marduk is pleased with Ragnar for compelling Ethan like that."

"Well, Ethan found out a while ago, and Marduk hasn't done anything to Ragnar yet. So, maybe he doesn't care."

"Or maybe he still finds Ragnar useful, so he plans to keep him around until he's not needed anymore."

"Couldn't happen to a nicer fellow," Lin said. "But I don't want Marduk stealing my revenge from me."

"On the plus side," Zoe continued, "at the lake, Marduk said he still has feelings for me, so either he doesn't care that those feelings were implanted or he just can't help himself. Either way, we should use that to our advantage."

"Get close enough to knife him, you mean?"

"What? No! He's in Ethan's body, Lin. I want Ethan back, not dead."

"Right. So, how do we do that? Even if it's possible, I can only think of two people who might be able to remove Marduk from Ethan's head. Professor Sharapova . . ."

"And Marduk himself," Zoe finished. "I think he's here, Lin. Old Man Marduk. I think he's here somewhere. It's the only thing that makes sense. There's no way you could somehow compress everything that makes you who you are—all of your memories, your personality, your Abilities—into something that you could just implant in someone and then let grow. I think it would all have to be transferred, bit by bit, day after day. Ethan complained that he kept waking up to discover stuff had moved. What if Marduk was taking over during the night and sneaking off to visit his old body for late-night mind transfer sessions?"

"If so, he must still be doing it. He said he wasn't at full strength yet."

"Which means we can follow him. If he's still here, that is."

"He wouldn't just . . . still be in Ethan's room, would he? Like, with his roommate?"

Zoe's eyes went wide. "Phillip."

They tore through the hallways to Ethan's room and found commotion outside his door. Kids milled about, looking confused and scared and keeping a good ten feet away from Ethan's door. Zoe approached it and a sudden wave of fear rushed through her.

"You feel that?" she asked Lin, who nodded, trembling.

Zoe knocked. No one answered, but someone whimpered within, so she tried turning the knob. It was unlocked. She slowly opened the door, and they both peered inside.

At the far end of the room, Ethan levitated above his bed—cross-legged, eyes closed—within a sphere of blue light. Phillip sat as far from him as possible, hugging his knees and shaking. He reeked of urine. Zoe and Lin pulled him out into the hall, shutting the door behind them, and then kept dragging him until they left the range of the fear bubble.

The poor boy seemed catatonic, utterly unaware of his surroundings.

"Take him to the infirmary," Zoe said to the wide-eyed kids around her. No one moved.

"*Now,*" Lin snapped with authority, making four boys jump. They picked up Phillip and carried him down the hall.

"I'll go tell my mom," Lin said. "What will you do?"

"I don't know," Zoe said. "I guess . . . I'll try talking to him. This is crazy! He can't be here, affecting everyone like this."

Lin nodded. "Be careful. I'll be back as soon as I can."

She ran off, and Zoe faced the crowd of kids.

"Everyone stay away from Ethan," she said, taking a deep breath. No sense trying to keep this a secret. "He's Marduk now."

She returned to the door and felt that same fear again. Steeling herself, she entered once more, closing the door behind her.

"Ethan." Her voice trembled. He didn't respond. "Ethan!" she yelled, forcing herself to step closer. He still didn't respond. Was he asleep? Could he even hear her within that blue energy bubble? She reached out to touch it and gasped.

She found herself in front of a stone temple sitting atop a . . . pyramid? No, a ziggurat. But it wasn't a ruin. Rather, it was in its prime, towering over a sprawling city. Thousands of people filled the streets surrounding the ziggurat, stretching as far as she could see. They were all on their knees, chanting.

Maaarduk. Maaarduk. Maaarduk.

Welcome to my temple, Zoe. Welcome to Etemenanki.

This is . . . Babylon? Seen through your eyes?

Yes. Roughly 3,400 years ago. This was my home for a time. I lived here with my wife, Sarpanit.

This was incredible. She was literally seeing the world as it existed thousands of years ago.

The people here actually worshipped you? A living man, not the usual mythical god?

A living god, he corrected. *Life was simpler then. The world wasn't rife with so many religions worshipping their false gods. How many wars have been fought in the name of religion? How many people have suffered and died? I can't wait to rid the world of it all.*

Wait, Zoe said. *You want to get rid of religions?*

Of course. I don't want them worshipping their imaginary little sky god. I want them to worship me.

Marduk and Zoe stepped off the edge of the ziggurat and drifted to the ground far below. They walked among the people, all prostrated and quaking, unwilling or unable to look up.

They're terrified of you.

Nonsense. I am a benevolent god. They are my people. I love them.

You love being feared. Look at them—they're shaking. Just like you did to us at the lake.

I didn't DO anything, Zoe. Humans are simply frightened when in the presence of a god.

We're currently in your dorm room, Zoe said. *No one out in the hallway knows you're in here or that you're Marduk, but they're still terrified and they have no idea why. You're clearly emitting some sort of electromagnetic field or something that's stimulating the amygdala in our brains and creating a fear response.*

Marduk was silent.

And whether you're aware of it or not, Zoe pressed, *you're still doing it. And if after thousands of years you've never investigated why and tried to stop doing it, then there can only be one reason—you love being feared. That doesn't sound like a god to me. That sounds like a weak narcissist who needs to feel strong and important.*

His anger suddenly washed over her, leaving her terrified—and just as suddenly, she was curled up in a ball on Ethan's dorm room floor. He towered over her.

"You think I am weak?" he asked.

Zoe nodded. *I know you are. A strong person would never intentionally instill fear in others. Ethan would never do what you're doing to me now. Not to anyone, but especially not to me. That's how I know you lied when you said you're still Ethan.*

A myriad of emotions played across his face. Anger and contempt were momentarily displaced by . . . disgust? Self-loathing? Self-awareness?

"Zoe?"

The fear vanished. Ethan dropped onto the bed and ran his fingers through his messy hair. He stared at her with what seemed to be a mixture of love and despair. He was Ethan again.

"I'm sorry," he murmured. "He's just so powerful." He closed his eyes, and when he opened them again, Marduk looked back at her. But . . . calmer. More reflective. "I don't want you to be afraid of me, Zoe."

Ethan *was* still in there. He had fought back and gained control, if only for a few seconds. That had to mean he could still be saved. It had to.

"You shouldn't want *anyone* to be afraid of you," she said, sitting up. "A kind person doesn't do that. A benevolent god certainly wouldn't."

He nodded. "I am . . . unaccustomed . . . to being challenged. I would typically kill anyone who dared speak to me thusly."

"Which is another thing a kind person wouldn't do. You're a fifteen-year-old boy I've known my whole life," Zoe said. "I used to beat you up. I'm not going to start treating you differently just because you have a god complex now. Also, you really need to stop speaking 'thusly.' You sound ridiculous."

Marduk laughed.

"Seriously, though," Zoe said. "If you really mean it when you say you're benevolent, you must know that what you're doing to Ethan is wrong. Everyone dies someday. It's not right to steal his life to prolong your own."

Marduk's smile faded, and his eyes narrowed. "You are important to me, Zoe. But if you think I will let myself die so that you can have your beloved Ethan back, you are mistaken." He stood. "Ethan is mine. The sooner you accept that, the better."

He strode from the room, brushing past concerned students huddled outside the door. They didn't recoil this time, so clearly he wasn't triggering anyone's fear response now. Had she just won a small victory? More importantly, had Ethan? Regardless, she'd come here so she could follow Ethan to the real Marduk. She hurried out into the hall, but there was no sign of him.

"Which way did he go?" she asked the crowd.

They stared blankly.

"Which way did Ethan go?" she repeated.

She received nothing but confused looks. Had he made them forget his presence? Or not notice him in the first place? Why would he bother doing that? She picked a direction and ran. She ran down the stairs and all the way to the Great Hall. Then on to the Main Hall and out the front doors. But she'd lost him.

15

THE ROOF

"Maybe he flew away," Paige suggested after Zoe had updated them over breakfast the next morning.

"Maybe," she conceded, "but I was only a few seconds behind him. Unless he was running, too—which seems out of character for a self-professed god—I don't see how he could have made it to the ground floor and out the side door before I caught up to him. It's like he just vanished."

"Maybe he can make himself invisible," Priya offered. "Bending light around himself. That would be a neat trick."

"It's more likely he just made everyone not notice him," Makena said. "That's a much easier trick. And it worked—you wanted to follow him to his lair, and you couldn't."

"I need to find it," Zoe said. "He *must* be down there. Besides, I've been wanting to get into the basement since I got back here. There may be prisoners we could free down there. But there's only one way in, at the end of a long hallway, and it's guarded. I didn't notice a security camera, though."

"You've been down there?" Lin asked, cocking her head.

Zoe nodded. "Just before the Battle. My two personas were struggling for dominance, and I wanted to speak with Lafleur. The guards immediately called someone." She glanced at Lin. "But Professor Chao ordered them to let me through, and they led me to a room where Lafleur was being held. It *did* have a camera."

"So, even if they haven't installed security cameras in the hallway, the guards would have plenty of time to tell people we're coming."

"We?" Zoe asked.

Makena nodded. "I've had time to reflect. I like the idea of saving the world—and I'm okay with mindbending a few bad people to do it—but Marduk scares the hell out of me. He can't be allowed to rule the world. The time to stop him is now—not later, when he's at full strength. And Ethan is our friend. He doesn't deserve this. I'm with you."

"Me too," Priya said, squeezing Lin's hand.

"Me three," Paige said.

"You know," Lin said, "I still remember when the Academy moved here, back when I was little. My mom and dad told me this place used to be a private residence back in the mid-1800s—and that it was rumoured to have not only a hidden chamber somewhere but also a tunnel that runs all the way to Lake Ontario."

"Secret tunnel!" Paige sang, excitedly.

"Is this for real?" Zoe asked. "Or just a myth?"

Lin shrugged. "I don't know. If they exist, nobody's ever found them. But if you were super rich and building yourself a castle, wouldn't *you* make some secret passages?"

"So, there *might* be a secret tunnel that would presumably lead to the basement," Zoe said, "but even if it exists, it could have collapsed at some point in the last century and a half. And there *might* be a potentially unrelated hidden chamber. I don't know how we would go about finding either of those."

"Talk to an elder," Makena said, and they cocked their heads. "Someone old who knows about this castle."

"Like an . . . old headmaster?" Priya suggested.

"Or an old caretaker," Paige said.

"Or a Telepath," Zoe said, "who was actually alive at the time the place was built and lived nearby."

"Oh, well, that's Professor Grant," Lin said. "He's Canadian. And a historian. I'm pretty sure he's the one who recommended this building when the Academy moved from Brussels."

"Do we know what happened to him after the Battle?"

Everyone looked at each other.

"Let's ask your mom, Lin. Maybe she knows something."

...

"I have no idea," Professor Yeoh said. "I don't even remember seeing him during the Battle. Why do you ask?"

Zoe told her about her last encounter with Ethan and watched as Professor Yeoh's eyes grew wide.

"You saw the Tower of Babel," she said.

"Excuse me?"

"Etemenanki is thought by many historians to be the legendary Tower of Babel. It lies in ruins now, just south of Baghdad. And you saw it in its glory." She shook her head. "Regardless, it was dedicated to the Mesopotamian god Marduk—and you literally *saw* him there, being worshipped by the Babylonians. This means he's no fraud. He is, for all intents and purposes, a god. And you want to try to find him and kill him?"

"What other choice is there?" Lin asked. "Escape isn't an option when he plans to control the minds of everyone in the world. We either join him or we kill him. It's that simple."

"So, first you want to kill Ragnar and now you want to kill Marduk."

"Well, what's *your* plan, Mom?" Lin snapped.

"My *plan* is to keep you safe!"

"*Nowhere* is safe!" Lin took a deep breath and calmed down. "Mom, I get that you want to protect me. But we can't just wait this out and hope that someone saves us. No one is going to save us. It's all up to us. We either let Marduk take over the world or we stop him."

"My goal right now," Zoe said, interceding, "is to save Ethan. I suspect Marduk's body is old and near death. He's probably weak and vulnerable. If I can find him before he finishes transferring his entire mind to Ethan, I can threaten him into leaving Ethan."

"He won't go for that," Professor Yeoh said. "If he's as weak as you think, then you could just kill him even after he cooperates. He won't risk it."

"Well, I don't have a better idea," Zoe cried, throwing her hands into the air. "Sharapova is the only person—other than Marduk himself—who *may* be able to get him out of Ethan's brain, but she'd probably need to examine Martinov, and look at what happened last time we tried that. She's terrified now."

"We don't even know if Marduk is *capable* of leaving Ethan," Professor Yeoh said. "I know this isn't what you want to hear, Zoe, but there's no guarantee that we can even get Ethan back."

"No," Zoe said. "I *saw* him. For a brief moment, he was able to regain control."

"Zoe," Professor Yeoh said, "I know how much Ethan means to you, but I don't want to see my daughter—or you—get yourself killed trying to save him. If you are hell bent on going after Marduk, then assassinating him is the safer route by far."

Zoe's eyes narrowed and she stepped forward. "If anyone tries to kill Ethan, they're going to have to go through me."

Professor Yeoh arched her eyebrows. "Are you threatening me, child?"

"Easy," Lin said, stepping between them. "Nobody's going to hurt Ethan. Right, Mom?" She looked at the professor. "*Right*, Mom?"

The standoff lasted a few more seconds before Professor Yeoh relented. "Fine. But, Zoe, if it turns out that we can't remove Marduk from his mind . . . we will be left with a very difficult decision."

"If that happens, the decision will be *mine* to make," Zoe said.

The professor nodded.

"Well," Lin said, "now that's settled, how do we find Professor Grant?"

"I'd start by looking in the basement," Professor Yeoh said.

"Are you serious?" Zoe blurted. "The whole point of finding him is to find a secret tunnel *into* the basement."

She shrugged. "What can I tell you? If he's still alive, he's either in the basement or off-site."

"Or he's been infected by Marduk and is out there somewhere advancing his cause." Zoe rubbed her temples. She needed help. "I need to talk to Gabriel. I need to warn him about Marduk's hive mind—and ask about Professor Grant. I have his contact information, but I can't reach him through our firewall. I wish I just had a phone, so I wouldn't have to rely on online texting services. With cellular signal, I could bypass the firewall entirely."

The professor crossed to the far wall, from which she removed a brick. She reached through the gap and pulled out something, which she tossed to Zoe. It was a phone with a charger and cable wrapped around it.

"You've had this the whole time?" Lin gasped.

"It's useless. I've tried. There's a high-powered cellular jammer somewhere nearby."

"But if I could either find and disable the jammer or get outside school grounds, would it work? Is there still an active cell phone plan?"

Professor Yeoh nodded. "My husband believed in planning for the worst. It's prepaid through the year. It's untraceable, as is the SIM card, so don't worry about losing it. And it has never been connected to the Wi-

Fi, so once charged, it won't automatically connect. Don't manually connect, either, or they'll notice a new phone on their network. The passcode is 3956. It's meaningless, so it's unlikely anyone will guess it."

Zoe put the phone and charger in her pocket. "Thank you, Professor. I'll put this to good use."

"Be careful," she said. "Don't get my daughter killed."

...

"Sorry about my mom," Lin said on their way to class. "She's just a little overprotective."

"It's okay," Zoe said. "I get it."

"But, Zoe . . . what you did back there was not cool. I know you were defending Ethan, but getting in my mom's face like that? Threatening her? You can't do that. I mean, you're my best friend, but if you ever make me choose between you and my mom, you know I'm choosing her, right?"

Zoe winced. "Of course. I'm sorry. I didn't mean to act disrespectfully. I just . . . I'm all he has. I'm his *only* chance. No one else is going to save him. And if our roles were reversed—if Marduk had chosen me as his host—I know Ethan would be doing everything he could right now to save me. I *can't* fail him." She wiped away an unexpected tear.

Lin wrapped her arm around Zoe. "I get it. We'll save him, okay? We'll find a way."

Kyle stopped them at the classroom door. "Zoe, hold up. I need to ask you something."

She cocked her head.

"There's a rumour going around that you said Ethan is . . . well, Marduk now, somehow."

Zoe nodded. "It's true," she said. "Marduk was dying, so he transferred his mind and power into Ethan."

Kyle shook his head. "For real? You're saying Ethan is a god now?"

"Marduk isn't a god," Zoe said. "He's just a really old, powerful, insecure Telepath."

Kyle scowled. "You shouldn't talk about him like that."

"What would you call someone with an overwhelming need to be feared and idolized?" Zoe asked. "Strong, secure, confident people don't behave like that. Anyway, there's something else you should know." She took a deep breath. "Marduk fathered all of the Igigi. He created us to find a host for himself, and he eventually chose Ethan." She didn't want to admit who her father was just yet. "That's why we've never been allowed romantic relationships except with the Anunnaki—because the Igigi are all half siblings."

They entered class, leaving a slack-jawed Kyle hanging back in the hall.

■ ■ ■

That night, while everyone slept, Zoe and Lin crept from their dorm to the upper floor of the central part of the castle. They climbed an old, easy-to-miss stairway to a small trapdoor in the ceiling—leading to the roof, presumably. Unfortunately, it was padlocked.

"Now what?" Lin whispered. "Do we force it open?"

"Not without making a lot of noise and alerting security. Fortunately . . ." She pulled two paper clips from her pocket. "I came prepared."

Zoe bent one paper clip at a forty-five-degree angle. "This," she said, "is our pick, which we'll use to push the pins up." She straightened the other paper clip, then bent it in half and squeezed both sides together. She inserted the looped end a few millimetres into the bottom of the keyhole, then bent it ninety degrees to the side. "This," she said, "is our tension tool, which we'll use to turn the cylinder." She put a bit of tension on the cylinder, then held the tool in place with her left hand. She pushed the pick all the way into the top section of the keyhole. "We can either push each pin up individually or just rake backwards a bunch of times like this until . . ." The locked popped open. "Voila."

Lin looked suitably impressed. "They taught you that?"

Zoe nodded, pulling the padlock free and placing it on the top step. "Spy school, remember? I assume they'll teach you, too, in remedial class. They gave us clear locks to practice on so we could see the pins. What I want to learn, though, is how to pick a lock using telekinesis. I can open my brooch lock because I know the combination, so I can turn each tumbler inside to the right spot. Lock picking like this would take a lot of finesse, though."

She pushed upward and swung the trapdoor open. They stepped out onto the flat gravel roof. The view was amazing. You could see all the turrets of the castle and all the lights of the nearby town. Zoe often forgot how close they were to civilization. How had the Battle—with its guns and rocket launchers and helicopters—not attracted attention? The Igigi must have had to do a lot of damage control. Did they mind wipe everyone in town or just whoever came to investigate? She made a mental note to look up the headlines in the Typical newspapers.

"This is so cool," Lin sighed. "I'll bet kids have been sneaking up here for over a hundred years."

Zoe pointed at something on the roof. "I don't actually know what a high-powered signal jammer looks like, but I'm betting it looks an awful lot like that."

They walked over to inspect the equipment. It looked like a large metal box mounted on a stand with wires running from the bottom to what she assumed were three stand-mounted antennas. It had a locked panel and was connected to a large black battery.

"I assume that's a battery backup, in case of a power outage," Zoe said. "So, even if we *had* thought of knocking out the power, it wouldn't have worked."

"But now we can just disconnect it from both power sources, right?"

"Step away from the equipment," a man's voice made them jump. They whirled around, but no one else was on the roof. "You're on camera," the voice said. "And you're both in a lot of trouble. Make your way downstairs—now."

Zoe and Lin exchanged glances. "Yeah, I don't think so," Lin said.

Zoe searched for the source of the voice and spotted the camera. She yanked it free of its wires and inspected it. "I don't think it has a microphone, so I doubt they heard why we're up here—though I don't think we said anything incriminating, anyway." She tossed the camera off the roof. Then, she pulled out her trusty paper clips and began picking the lock on the jammer.

Lin returned to the trapdoor, which she closed with her foot. Then, she positioned herself beside Zoe. "No hurry," she said.

"Almost got it, I think. There." The panel popped open.

"I don't suppose there's an off switch?" Lin asked.

"Actually, I think there is." She flipped a switch and some lights turned off. She pulled out the cellphone. "There's a signal! It's trying to connect." She shut the panel door. "The message to Gabriel is all ready to go. As soon as we're connected, hit send and wait for a reply." She held the phone out to Lin. "I'll hold them off."

"Nah, I got this." Lin started stretching.

"Lin . . . this isn't a game. We don't know how much force they'll use. They could try to kill us." She held out the phone again. "Take it and let me handle them."

Lin calmly cracked her neck in an admittedly badass show of confidence. "I said I've got this, Zoe."

Zoe scowled. "Lin, you're good, but I promised your mom that I wouldn't get you killed. Let me do this."

Men were yelling at the bottom of the stairs.

"You're welcome to put down the phone and join in the fun if you want," Lin said, turning her back to Zoe and approaching the trapdoor, "but I've been wanting to do this for a long time."

The trapdoor burst open, and Lin kicked the first security guard in the chin, immediately knocking him unconscious. The second guard blocked her next kick but went down when she caught him with a spinning kick to the side of the head. She slammed the trapdoor closed, leapt up, and kicked down on it, catching the fingers of a third man, who cursed.

As soon as she was connected to the network, Zoe sent the message. A burst of golden light shone through the trapdoor, and she shouted, "Get back!"

Lin jumped back as a shotgun blast from below blew the trapdoor to pieces. She looked at Zoe in astonishment. "I saw golden streaks!"

Zoe put the phone in her back pocket. The man with the shotgun came tearing up the stairs, and before Zoe could react, Lin had already grabbed the barrel of the shotgun with one hand and delivered a vicious elbow to the man's face. He dropped, and Lin kicked him down the stairs. She casually threw the shotgun off the roof and stepped back to rejoin Zoe.

"Nice," Zoe said.

"Thanks."

"I imagine they're regrouping."

"You know we can't run, right?"

"I know," Zoe said. "They'll hurt those closest to us."

"You think they'll try to kill us?"

Zoe shook her head. "I doubt they have orders to. We're just a couple of students on the roof. But we *did* attack them, and they *did* escalate things pretty quickly, so I don't think we can trust them to make sound decisions. In my experience, godlings always feel like they have something to prove."

"The feeling is mutual," Lin said. They could hear a lot of running and yelling from downstairs, as well as from the grounds below. Zoe's back pocket pinged, and she looked at the phone.

"Professor Grant is alive! Gabriel's trying to reach him."

"Maybe let him know it's kind of urgent?"

Zoe quickly typed a reply, muttering, "Hurry . . . guards . . . coming."

"*All* the guards," Lin corrected.

"All . . . the . . . guards." She hit send and stashed the phone again. "Once we get an answer, we can always surrender." A thought occurred to her. "And you know what will happen if we do?"

"What?"

"They'll probably put us in a cell . . . in the *basement*."

"Ha," Lin said. "Nice. But that'll probably happen whether we surrender or not. So, the way I see it, I finally have an opportunity to beat up as many of these guards as I can with literally no consequences."

Zoe grinned. "I like the way you think." She peeked down the stairs again. "They're too quiet. Something's about to happen. Get ready."

A small object flew up the stairs. "Gas!" she yelled and instinctively reached out telekinetically to knock it back downstairs. Some tear gas had already escaped, though, so she backed up.

"Hold your breath!" Lin yelled. Zoe spun around to see gas everywhere—they must have thrown canisters from the lawn too. Men in full riot gear—with shields, batons, and gas masks—stormed the roof. She hadn't inhaled any gas yet, but her eyes were on fire and she could barely see. She couldn't believe they were using chemical weapons on a couple of kids—but then again, she totally could.

She tried to disperse the gas with telekinesis but had to abort when the guards rushed them.

Rip their masks off! Zoe said.

She and Lin ran to meet the attack. The guards were packed together with their riot shields touching. Their shields didn't extend all the way to the ground, though, so Zoe dropped at the last moment and slid under them while Lin flipped over them. Lin ripped off one guard's mask as she landed, and Zoe punched her two men in particularly vulnerable areas, then pulled their masks off as they collapsed. Another guard bludgeoned her with his baton. She strengthened her bones with telekinesis, but would no doubt have a lot of bruises. With one arm shielding her face from his blows, she managed to put on a mask and finally took a deep breath.

Getting to her feet, she held out the other mask to Lin, only to realize she was already wearing one—and already taking out two more guards with a stolen baton. Zoe threw the extra mask over the roof's edge and seized her attacker's baton. She stepped in and delivered a flurry of strikes, then pulled off his mask and threw it over the ledge. The two men she had unmasked earlier were on their knees, gasping for breath. She knocked their heads together and grabbed their batons, throwing one to Lin. Now armed with two batons apiece, they went to work.

Zoe had always believed that due to her genetic engineering, she was inherently faster than Typicals and natural-born Telepaths. But looking at Lin, she wasn't so sure anymore. They were both whirlwinds. She knew Lin was an exceptional fighter, but she hadn't realized just how fast she was—*preternaturally* fast, like the Igigi. Within ten seconds, two dozen men lay collapsed on the ground, either unconscious or unmasked and gasping.

As the guards who were still conscious and retching dragged themselves down the stairs to escape their own karma, Zoe and Lin wandered into the gas clouds to find the canisters. They tossed them back to whoever had thrown them below and then did the same with the shields, masks, and batons. Then, they sat cross-legged in the middle of the roof, amid the dissipating gas cloud. Zoe pulled out the phone.

"Here we go," she said. "Professor Grant says he actually knew the original owner way back when. The man built a tunnel all the way to Lake Ontario in order to evade taxes. The tunnel entrance is supposed to be somewhere in the woods off Highway 401, right where it connects with the creek that feeds a harbour."

"Well, that's that," Lin said. "Mission accomplished."

Zoe started typing. "Thanks. Ditching . . . this . . . phone . . . now." She hit send, deleted the conversation, and then initiated a factory reset to make sure nobody would be able to retrieve the conversation with Gabriel. Then, she turned the jammer back on. Wiping the phone for fingerprints as best she could, she held it with her sleeves and placed it inside the metal box.

"Pretty sure they'll find it there," Lin said.

"Yeah, but I don't see anywhere else to hide it up here. Who knows? It's so obvious that it might just be the last place they'll look. Besides, if they do find it, it's just a wiped, untraceable phone. And if they don't find it, maybe we can use it again someday."

Zoe closed the panel, then pulled out her paper clips yet again and got to work locking it while Lin kept watch. When she finally got it locked, Zoe stepped back and hit the jammer with a baton hard enough to dent it. Lin raised an eyebrow, and they sat down in the middle of the roof again.

"Our story," Zoe said, "is that we came up here on a lark, because we've always wanted to see the castle roof. That's it. Simple."

Lin nodded. "Sounds good."

"If they noticed the jammer stopped working for a few minutes, we feign ignorance. It got hit during the scuffle with the guards, so maybe that just caused it to go out for a bit."

"Makes sense—if they didn't notice that it stopped working *before* they came up here."

"And if they ever discover the phone, we don't know anything about it. It's not ours."

"Never seen it before," Lin said.

"And if, somehow, they *do* manage to link it to us, our story is that I found it in the washroom, I never told you exactly where, and I just wanted to contact Gabriel to ask for news of what's going on out there with the Resistance."

Lin nodded again. "You're good at this."

"So, now we have a decision to make. We have the information we wanted, and we had a lot of fun beating up the guards. But the next person coming through that trapdoor is probably going to be Ragnar. We could fight him, but we'll lose. We'll be at his mercy, and if he wants to hurt or kill us, he will. The last time you confronted him, he almost paralyzed you."

"You think we should surrender?"

Zoe sighed. "If we had a good plan to take him down and I thought there was a reasonable chance of success, I'd say we should try. But fighting him now seems kind of pointless. I don't want to see you get hurt for no reason."

"I don't want to see *you* get hurt, either," Lin said. "But . . . there *are* more guards down there we could beat up." Zoe could tell from her eyes that she was smiling impishly behind her gas mask. It was the first time Zoe had seen her smile since the Battle, and it genuinely warmed her heart. If beating up guards was what it took, then so be it.

Just then, an imposing figure emerged from the stairs to stand in the dissipating gas cloud.

"You two," Ragnar said, standing before them in bare feet, wearing only pyjama pants and a T-shirt, "are in so much trouble."

Zoe and Lin stood up and retreated to the edge of the roof.

You know how to do this? Zoe asked.

There's a first time for everything, Lin replied.

Waving to Ragnar, they both stepped backwards off the ledge and plummeted. Zoe waited until the very last moment before using a blast of telekinesis to slow her fall while bracing every bone in her body to withstand the impact. Lin landed a fraction of a second later. They had both, Zoe noticed, performed perfect superhero landings—on one knee, punching the ground.

"Paige would be so jealous," Lin laughed.

They wandered out of the gas cloud to see six frightened guards grouped together. They drew their pistols as the girls advanced, and Zoe saw golden streaks of light. She and Lin both dodged the streaks and were about to attack when suddenly Ragnar landed between them and the guards.

"Fools!" he bellowed, yanking the guns out of the guards' hands telekinetically and lifting every man off the ground by their throats as they kicked wildly. "Useless! Incompetent! My students are worth a thousand of you! You would use lethal force against them?"

"Don't kill them!" Zoe blurted, yanking off her mask. Ragnar looked back at her. "It's not their fault," she said. "They only do what you've compelled them to do, right? You must not have been specific enough."

Ragnar scowled. "They should still have some common bloody sense!" he yelled, knocking their heads together and dropping them all in a heap. He rounded upon the girls. "Now, *what* is the meaning of this?"

Lin pulled off her mask, and they both smiled innocently.

"We were just exploring," Lin said, sweetly.

"We always wanted to see what was up on the roof," Zoe added.

"But we didn't realize there would be a camera up there."

"And they were, like, 'come downstairs immediately,'" Zoe said in her best impersonation of a guard's deep, authoritarian voice.

"And we were, like, 'no, I don't think so,'" Lin said, shaking her head.

"And then the guards came up and attacked us."

"So, naturally, we defended ourselves."

"And then they used tear gas on us for *no reason.*"

"So, we had to take them out, because we needed their gas masks."

"And that's when you arrived, all scary-like in your pyjamas."

"So, we jumped."

"And then they started firing at us."

"And then you saved us," Lin finished. They both put their hands behind their backs, hung their heads, and twisted left and right in their best imitation of chastised students.

Ragnar stared at them like they were from another planet. A vein throbbed in his forehead, and he rubbed his temples with one hand. He started to say something several times and stopped. Finally, he shook his head. "Come with me."

He led them through the front doors, down to the basement, and into a holding room containing an empty cell with plexiglass walls.

"The only reason you're not each in solitary is because we don't have any more cells available," Ragnar growled. He slammed the door shut and turned his back on them. "I'm going back to bed."

He strode away, leaving them alone in the silent cell.

"So," Lin said, folding her arms and looking around, nodding. "Our cunning plan to infiltrate the basement worked."

16

THE BASEMENT

"I have to get out of here," Zoe said, pacing the dimly lit cell.

"That's the plan, right?" Lin said.

"No, you don't understand. I *need* to get out of here." Professor Chao sat on the bed looking at her in concern. "I hadn't counted on this."

Lin cocked her head. "Are you okay?"

"Something's wrong with me." Zoe's heart pounded, and she struggled to breathe. It felt like the walls were closing in. She hit the cell door with the palm of her hand. "What is wrong with me? I spent *months* in solitary!"

"Maybe that's the reason," Lin said. "Try lying down on the bed."

"I can't." Zoe shook her head.

"Why not?"

"Because it's *taken*."

Lin looked puzzled, then she understood. "Oh. You mean . . ."

"Yeah."

"I'm sorry. You haven't mentioned him in a while. I thought he was gone."

"I thought so, too." Zoe squeezed her eyes shut, then opened them and jumped back in alarm. Professor Chao was suddenly right in front of her.

"You are experiencing a panic attack," he said.

"Yeah, you think?"

"Breathing is the key to making it subside."

"No, getting *out* of here is the key to making it subside." She hit the door again, hard, strengthening her arm and putting a lot of telekinetic force into it. The walls shook with a loud boom.

"I thought you wanted to sneak out of here," he said.

"That was before. Now, I just want out of here—*period*." She hit the door again, harder than before.

"The guards will come if you keep that up."

"So what?"

"So, there is a better way to achieve your goal, that is what." He put his hand on her shoulder. "Please, Zoe. Let me help."

She brushed his hand off. "How are you going to help? You're not *real*. You shouldn't even be here. Lin's over there thinking I've gone mad, thanks to you."

Professor Chao held up his hand placatingly. "Just . . . give me a moment." He closed his eyes. "There is a guard standing in the hallway, right outside the door."

Zoe stared at him. "You can't possibly know that."

He smiled, then suddenly he was on the other side of the plexiglass. He put a finger to his lips, walked toward the door to the hallway, and disappeared.

Lin followed her gaze. "What's . . . going on?" she asked.

"I don't know." Zoe shook her head. "He wants us to be quiet. He says there's a guard outside."

Lin's jaw dropped. "How could he—"

"I don't know. I guess because my subconscious knows. Or is pretending to know. I have no idea. I've gone mad, remember?"

"You're not mad, Zoe."

"Well, I've seen saner people."

There was a camera mounted in the corner of the visitor section, and its red light suddenly switched off. Zoe and Lin exchanged glances. A moment later, the door to their holding room opened, and a guard entered, closing the door quietly behind him. He put a finger to his lips, pulled out a set of keys, then opened their cell door and stepped inside. Placing the keys and a security card in Zoe's hands, he smiled, lay down on the bed, and closed his eyes.

Lin looked at Zoe like she'd seen a ghost. "What the actual—"

But Zoe wasted no time fleeing the cell. She felt better immediately but still needed to sit and try to slow her heart rate. With shaking hands, she held out the keys to Lin, who found the one to lock the cell door again.

"Zoe, what just happened? You said he's a hallucination."

"He is. I don't know how to explain this. But we can figure it out later. Right now, let's do what we came here to do."

Zoe cracked open the door and peered into the dimly lit hallway. No one was around, presumably because it was the middle of the night. They snuck down the hall, using the guard's keys to open the next door over. They hurried inside.

In another cell behind plexiglass lay Headmaster Harrington. He had long hair and a long beard now, but it was definitely him.

"You said he was dead!" Lin hissed.

"That's what Ragnar told me."

"Why would he lie about that?"

"Maybe so we wouldn't try to rescue him?"

They opened the cell door, and Zoe crouched in front of the former headmaster. "Headmaster?" she said, touching his shoulder. When he didn't respond, she shook him gently. "Headmaster!"

"What's wrong with him?" Lin asked.

"He's drugged, I think." She snapped her fingers in front of his face and shook him again. "Headmaster? It's Zoe. Can you hear me?" His eyes opened, but there was no recognition in them.

"This is horrible," Lin said. "What have they done to him? He's like a zombie."

"Antipsychotic medication," Zoe said. "To keep him confused and docile."

"But . . . why? Why not just mindbend him? Or do what they did to Professor Martinov?"

"I don't know." Zoe shook her head. "This doesn't make any sense."

"We have to get him out of here," Lin said.

"Agreed. But how? I doubt he can walk. Even if we can somehow sneak him upstairs, what then? Where do we stash him while he recovers?"

"Well, we can't just leave him here!"

"If we can find the castle-side entrance to the secret tunnel, maybe we could smuggle him out—or get word to Gabriel to attempt a rescue." Zoe stood up. "For now, I think we have to keep searching for that tunnel and for any other prisoners. And for Marduk's real body."

Lin nodded, and they locked the cell once more and snuck back out into the hall. In the next cell, they found Gabrielle Lafleur. They couldn't wake her up, either.

"Shoot," Zoe said. "We could really use her help. She's certainly not my favourite person in the world, but she did fight alongside us in the Battle. She's *good*."

They entered the next room and stopped dead in their tracks, staring dumbly at Professor Grant.

"Oh no," Zoe moaned.

"Gabriel lied," Lin gasped. "Why would he lie?"

"I don't know," Zoe said, trying to process the implications. "I can only think of one good reason."

"He's been compromised," Lin said. "Infected."

"Which means the entire Resistance—if it still exists—is now just a trap to catch all the remaining Telepaths."

"Why tell us about the tunnel, though?"

"Maybe it's not real?" Zoe suggested.

"Or it's a trap. But for whom?"

"I don't understand what's going on," Zoe said, "but if Gabriel is infected, then Ethan knows what we were doing up on the roof, even if Ragnar doesn't yet."

"I guess we should see if we can wake up Professor Grant," Lin said.

But they couldn't, and continuing down the hall, they found nothing but empty cells, storage rooms, and the boiler room.

"Sorry, Zoe," Lin said. "Marduk doesn't seem to be down here."

"It makes no sense," Zoe said. "Even if Marduk isn't down here, I thought for sure there would be more than *this*."

"Maybe we can find the entrance to the secret tunnel—or that legendary hidden chamber?"

They kept searching but without any luck.

"If it's anywhere, you'd think it would be behind one of these stone walls," Zoe said, searching behind the shelves in a storage room. Out of the corner of her eye, she saw a face peering through the little glass window in the door. She jumped, but it was only Professor Chao. He turned and walked away down the hall. Curious, Zoe followed him, and found him waiting for her at the end of the corridor. Then, he turned around and stepped through the wall.

Zoe hurried over to push on the stone wall.

"What is it?" Lin asked, coming up behind her.

"Maybe nothing, but . . ." She pulled out the security card. So far, they had found no reader for it, but she moved it around against the wall. Suddenly, something electronic beeped, and the wall opened inward on a hinge, revealing a stone stairway leading down. Professor Chao slipped out of sight around a bend in the stairs below. Zoe looked at Lin.

"Well, we can't very well *not* go down there, right?" Lin said.

As they crept down the curving stairway, the hidden door closed automatically behind them. Fortunately, electric lights on the walls lit their way.

"I hope that card opens the door from this side, too," Lin mumbled.

"I don't think this is new," Zoe whispered. "I mean, that hidden card reader obviously is, but these walls and stairs look like they were chiseled a long time ago."

As they descended, they heard what sounded like men shouting in the distance. The stairs brought them to another passageway, at the end of which stood Professor Chao, resting his hands on a railing, gazing out at something. Approaching the railing, Zoe stared in disbelief at the massive cavern deep below. Powerful electric lights illuminated construction workers and a framework of metal girders rising from the ground.

"So . . . maybe this is the legendary hidden chamber," Lin said. "I figured it was just a room somewhere in the castle, if it existed at all. Not . . . *this.*"

"They're building a secret complex down here," Zoe said. "Another underground bunker, like the one I grew up in. Do you think Harrington and everyone else knew this cavern was here?"

"I don't know. I mean, you'd think my mom would've mentioned it."

"But how could they *not* have found it? The Academy has been here for years, and Ragnar clearly found this place right away."

"Their memories of this place were erased," Professor Chao said.

"Oh."

"What do you mean? Oh . . . you weren't talking to me, were you? What did he say?"

Zoe wished she hadn't responded to him. Poor Lin. "It's nothing— just my subconscious making stuff up."

"What did he *say,* Zoe?"

She sighed. "He said their memories of this place were erased."

"Huh," Lin said. "That actually makes a lot of sense."

"Even if it's true, it's just me guessing, Lin."

"Ask him how they got all these long metal girders in here. They didn't come in the same way we did, that's for sure."

"Through the tunnel," Professor Chao said, pointing. "You cannot really see from here. We spent many years widening and fortifying it to allow trucks to drive through. We intended to use this space ourselves and keep the Academy here for longer than usual." He walked toward another staircase carved into the rock along the wall of the cavern. Zoe reluctantly relayed what he'd said to Lin.

"Ask him if he's real," she said. "I want to know what he says."

"He's not real, Lin. Besides, he's not over here anymore. He's walking down the stairs."

"Well, follow him, then."

They descended the second stone stairway, grateful they'd dressed in black and could blend into the shadows. Soon, they realized that the ground level of the facility was already finished while construction continued above. They made it to the bottom, where Professor Chao waited.

Lin pointed out the tunnel, where two guards were stationed. "Big enough to drive a truck through."

The only entrance to the facility was a large metal door with a card reader.

"How do we sneak past the workers?" Lin asked. "And those guards over there?"

"Follow me," the professor said. "They will not notice you." He strode out of the shadows and past the workers.

"Umm, he wants us to follow him," Zoe said. "He says they won't notice us."

"How can they possibly not notice us?"

"Well, your dad did it to a crowd of people when we escaped from Ragnar in that restaurant. And the godlings did it to the hospital staff. There's clearly a trick to it.

"And do you know how to do this trick?"

"No," Zoe admitted. "I mean, not without talking to them and getting inside their minds, like we did at the hotel."

"Then how is your hallucination going to do it?"

Professor Chao was halfway to the door, motioning for them to follow. Zoe looked at Lin helplessly. Lin muttered something about a leap of faith, sighed, and then resolutely strode out of the shadows.

"Lin, don't!" Zoe cried. But it was too late. The workers would surely see her. Except . . . they didn't. Professor Chao smiled and went to wait for Lin at the door. Zoe gaped. How was this possible? At the door, Lin shrugged at her. Finally, Zoe shook her head and walked toward them, expecting to be caught at any moment. But she reached Lin and Professor Chao unnoticed.

"I don't understand what's happening," she said.

"Like you said, we'll figure it out later. Think that card will work?"

Zoe fished the card from her pocket and held it to the reader. It made an error noise and flashed red. The door remained locked.

"Give me a moment," Professor Chao said. "There must be someone inside who can help us." He disappeared, and Zoe waited uncomfortably.

"He says he'll be right back," she said.

Lin just nodded, as if this were totally normal. Before long, the door opened, and a man in a white lab coat held the door open for them without ever seeming to notice them.

Inside, Zoe and Lin gasped. They stood in a massive laboratory with dim lighting and high ceilings. The walls were lined, top to bottom, with what appeared to be artificial wombs—small vats with glass fronts, each containing a fetus immersed in liquid.

Thousands of vats.

"He's creating an army," Lin said. "Is this . . . how you started out?"

"No," Zoe said, shaking her head. They walked along the edge of the room, peering into the vats. Dozens of lab technicians did the same—checking vitals, presumably. Sometimes, one would look at Zoe and Lin in astonishment only to immediately turn away, indifferent. "I started off in a test tube but was then carried to term by some random woman, I guess. The same with all my classmates. This is something new and cutting edge. I don't think artificial wombs even exist yet for Typicals. Something is weird, though. The Battle wasn't that long ago. These children are too far along. Unless they're growing faster than normal, they must've started off in a lab somewhere else and been transported here. Why would they take such a risk?"

"Maybe their old lab was discovered," Lin suggested. "Or was about to be."

"There is something you need to see," Professor Chao said, leading Zoe toward a vat that was set apart from all the others. "This child is not like the rest. Marduk is still trying to clone himself."

Zoe let that sink in.

"What's happening?" Lin asked.

"This is Marduk's clone," Zoe said, softly. "But that means . . . Ethan is just a temporary host. Just until Marduk succeeds in creating a viable clone. So, what'll happen to Ethan then?"

Professor Chao shook his head. "It will take at least fifteen years, I think. But . . . I do not imagine Ethan will be allowed to live once Marduk copies himself to his clone host. Killing Ethan would be far simpler than extricating himself from Ethan's mind."

"Wait," Zoe said. "How could you possibly know this? Up until now, everything you've said and done has had a plausible explanation, even if it was hard to believe. But you walked right over to this vat, knowing it was different. *I* didn't know that, so how could you?"

Professor Chao said nothing.

"You are *not* my hallucination. And I don't believe in ghosts. So, who are you, and how did you get into my head?"

"Dad?" Lin stepped forward to face whoever it was Zoe was speaking to. "Is that you?"

The professor sighed. "Let her see through your eyes," he told Zoe.

After a moment's hesitation, she stepped behind Lin and touched her head. "Close your eyes. I'm going to try to do what Ragnar did to me—except instead of seeing my memories, you'll hopefully see what I'm seeing right now."

Lin did as instructed. And then she gasped.

"Dad," Lin murmured, a tear running down her cheek.

"No," the professor said, shaking his head sadly. "I am sorry, Lin, but I am not him. However, I *was* a part of him for a very long time. So long that he will always remain a part of me."

"I don't understand," Zoe said.

"Do you remember the myth about Marduk? How he slew the goddess Tiamat?"

She nodded.

"Gods are notoriously difficult to kill. Unbeknownst to him, I survived . . . in the mind of another."

"You're saying . . . you're *Tiamat*? And you currently exist in my mind? How?"

"I've survived for thousands of years by jumping from one Telepath to another. Never without permission, and never taking control— existing only as an observer and a companion. A passenger. For the last 450 years, I existed within the mind of Ling Chao. He was a lost soul when we met, wandering aimlessly after having brutally avenged his family. My host was dying, and I asked Ling Chao if he would allow me sanctuary within him. I offered whatever wisdom I could impart, and he agreed."

"He told me that he'd met someone who guided him," Zoe said.

"Who taught him how to overcome his anger and take control of his life again. I assumed he meant Lafleur."

"No, he was referring to me. I remember that conversation—it was at that moment that I left him and entered you."

"What? Why would you do that? And without my permission?"

"I *saw* you, Zoe. Sitting in the dojo beside us, I saw who you really were. I warned him that your previous persona had returned, so full of anger and plotting to kill us. I advised him to have you arrested before you called in the attack. But he refused. He thought forewarning had given him the advantage. More importantly, he said you needed to be free to choose your own path, so that you could become the person he knew you could be."

"He should have stopped me. If Lin hadn't discovered me and forced me to integrate my two personas, I might have killed him. I almost did anyway. And in the end, it didn't make any difference."

"It made all the difference. He was a stubborn man but one of the wisest I have ever known. He saw in you a kindred spirit. A lost soul full of helpless rage—just as he had once been. He knew there was a chance we would not survive, that we might meet our end either by your hand or Ragnar's. He knew you would need help afterward. So, he asked me to save both myself and you."

The professor—no, Tiamat—stepped aside as a lab technician came to check on Marduk's clone. "I had never before entered someone without their permission, but he argued that if he survived the coming attack, I could simply jump back to him without you ever learning of my presence. And if he didn't survive, you would need me. He said that once I helped guide you in overcoming your anger and integrating your personas, I could reveal myself and find another willing host, if you so desired."

"In his last moment," Zoe said, "he said to 'protect them in the days ahead.' Was he talking to me or to you?"

Tiamat smiled. "He was speaking to both of us."

"Why the charade?" Zoe asked. "Why present yourself to me in the form of Professor Chao? Why make me think I was hallucinating?"

"If Marduk looked into your mind and discovered that I was still alive—and in you—he would have killed us."

"Show us what you really look like," Lin said, still seeing through Zoe's eyes. "It's not right to keep looking like my dad."

The professor nodded, and suddenly a Mesopotamian goddess stood before them, tall and beautiful with long, curly black hair. A long white skirt wrapped around her body and was belted at the waist.

"So, why reveal yourself to me now?" Zoe asked.

"Because you are in danger," Tiamat said. "Not just you, but the entire world. Marduk cannot be allowed to succeed. To defeat him, you may need more than my guidance—you may need my *power*."

"What do you mean?"

Tiamat seemed to consider her words carefully. "I was a very powerful being, in my day. When I cheated death, it was not at the last moment. I knew that Marduk might defeat me, so I distilled and compressed my mind—its trillions of neural connections—into a small package that could be transferred to another if needed. This is something Marduk clearly never learned how to do. I exist as a shadow of my former self, resisting the urge to decompress my essence. If I did, I would once again possess all of my memories and all of my powers . . . but at what cost to my host? They would cease to be their own person. We would merge. I could never ask that of anyone. And could their body handle my power? I do not know. What I *do* know is that you intend to go up against Marduk. And if you fail, he will try to kill you. What remains of Ethan will not be able to stop him. If that comes to pass, you will need not just my guidance but all my power in order to survive."

Zoe considered this. Tiamat's power could save her, but if her body couldn't handle it, she could die. And even if she could physically survive the decompression, what of her mind? Integrating her two personas had taken so much time and effort. She would have to start all over again—but this time with the persona of a god! How could she compete with that? Would there be anything left of her?

"You won't do that unless I give my permission?"

"Never. Even now, if you want me gone, Lin's mother has agreed to host me, should you wish. Ling and Mei spoke about it at great length, even if she did ask to forget, lest she be captured and interrogated."

"But then . . . she would be the one in danger of being discovered, right? And *she* would be the only one with the ability to fight Marduk." Zoe shook her head. "I couldn't ask that of anyone."

Tiamat nodded.

"So, what now? I came here looking for Marduk's old, dying body and instead found his new, unborn body. Is this child destined to become him?"

"If we lose, undoubtedly. Assuming this clone survives and is without genetic defects, he will copy himself into it before the child ever grows powerful enough to challenge him. But if we defeat Marduk before that, then this child could yet grow to become a good person. Or a bad person. But dangerously powerful, regardless."

"So, how do we defeat Marduk?"

"You already have the plan. It may not work, but it is sound. Unfortunately, I do not know where his ancient body is, either. I had hoped to find him here."

"If we can't find him, it's hopeless. He'll never leave Ethan."

"Then we must keep searching. For now, you both need to return to your cell. Don't let them know you escaped, let alone came down here." Tiamat paused. "It was so good to finally meet you both."

They left the laboratory and made the long trek back to their cell. The guard rose from the bed when they entered and took the keys and security card. He locked them in and left, and Zoe pushed down the immediate feelings of panic. A minute later, the little light on the security camera turned back on.

Lin sat on the bed with her back against the wall and hugged her knees.

"You okay?" Zoe asked, joining her.

Lin shrugged. "It's stupid. I just thought . . . for a moment, that maybe somehow . . . it really was my dad."

"I'm sorry," Zoe said, wrapping her arm around her.

"Seeing him again, before she showed us her true form . . ." She sighed and hung her head. "I just really miss him."

"I know. I miss him, too."

"Wait," Lin said. "What about you? Are you okay in here?"

Zoe forced a nervous smile. "No, but . . . I'm not by myself, at least. Not that I *want* you to be locked up in here, but . . . I'm glad you're with me."

They leaned against each other in silence, eventually drifting off to sleep.

. . .

They woke to the sight of Ethan on the other side of the plexiglass.

"Looks like I missed out on some fun last night," he said. "What, I don't get invited to these things anymore?"

"Not since you became a weird little god dude," Lin said, groggily.

"Hmm. Fair, I guess," he said.

"What are you doing down here?" Zoe asked. "Visiting your old, desiccated vampire body in its crypt?"

He cocked his head. "Is that what this is about? You wanted to get put down here so you could find my original body?"

Zoe feigned surprise. "No, it was about sneaking up to the roof for fun, like regular schoolkids do. You still remember what fun is?"

"I remember," he said, sitting down. "I remember when we were kids, we'd sneak up to the surface at night and climb a tree to see the stars. We were allowed up top so seldomly."

"It was your decision to keep us all imprisoned in a bunker, *Marduk*."

He scowled. "The cameras were out last night."

"I don't like being spied on."

"How did you turn them off?"

She held up a hand and electricity danced across her fingertips. "I have my ways."

"They were *all* off. And now they're all on again."

"Okay," Zoe said, simply.

"And one of the guards went wandering last night. I know because the logs show he used his security card to go somewhere he had no reason to be."

"What are you asking?"

"I'm asking if you two were wandering around here last night."

"No," she lied. "We were here. In a cell."

"I can just look into your mind, you know. Or Lin's."

Zoe fixed him with her most dangerous glare. "The day you try to force your way into my mind—or into the minds of any of my friends—is the day you abandon all hope of ever winning me over, and the day I abandon all hope of there being anything left of Ethan inside of you."

Ethan looked annoyed. "Fine," he sighed. "I don't want to punish you, but there must be consequences to beating up the guards, or else *everyone* will start beating up the guards, and it'll be anarchy. So, you two can spend the day here and . . . think about what you did."

He opened the door to the hallway and paused. "That camera," he said, pointing, "stays *on*."

Professor Yeoh visited them shortly afterward. It was hard to tell if she was angry because they'd been imprisoned or because they'd gotten themselves into this predicament in the first place. She *had* given them the phone, though. At one point, she got very quiet, and her eyes went wide in astonishment. Zoe realized she and Lin were talking privately, mind to mind.

"I am told that you will spend the rest of the day and another night here," Professor Yeoh said, standing, "and that I will not be allowed another visit." She fixed them each with a stern look. "Just . . . stay here. Be safe."

What did you tell her? Zoe asked Lin as soon as Professor Yeoh left.

I told her how Gabriel lied about Grant and that we found him down here, drugged, along with Harrington and Lafleur. I asked her if there's any way she can swap their drugs with something harmless, so they can come to their senses.

That's a really good idea, Zoe said. *That way, they can either escape on their own or at least be easier to rescue.*

Thanks, Lin said. *She doesn't know if she can do it, since she'll have to learn what drug they're getting and where it's being stored—plus, she's not sure she has anything that looks similar enough to fool the guards. But she's going to try.*

You didn't tell her about the cavern? Or about Tiamat?

No, I figured I was already risking enough as it was. Maybe they're only letting her visit so they can look in her mind and check our story. I sure hope not.

That day, Zoe kept herself as busy as possible in order to keep herself from panicking. She started by trying to teach Lin to conjure electricity. That proved difficult, as she had no idea how to actually do it, other than just *willing* it to happen. They also practiced *chi sao*—sticky hands—with each other, like they'd done the first time they met. Now, though, they were both a flurry of punches and blocks. Zoe kept increasing the speed until she was going as fast as she could, and was astounded that Lin could keep up.

That night, they just slept, too afraid to break out again. They needed to rescue Harrington, Lafleur, and Grant somehow, and the tunnel was the most feasible way to get them out. However, they'd need to be capable of walking, unless the Resistance could sneak in with stretchers—but was that even an option anymore? Not if Gabriel was under Marduk's influence.

In the morning, they were set free. They got cleaned up in their dorm before heading to the Great Hall for breakfast. Their friends had a million questions, and Zoe and Lin told them all about their adventure and what they'd found in the cavern. They left out the part about Tiamat, though.

"Lin," said Priya, who'd been oddly quiet throughout their story, "could we have a word in private, please?" Lin looked perplexed but followed her to a corner, and Zoe and the others watched on in uncomfortable silence. She couldn't hear what was being said, but from their body language, it was serious. After a minute, Priya walked off and Lin returned to the table and her breakfast. They all exchanged glances.

"Well?" Paige said, finally. "What was that all about?"

"Oh," Lin said. "Priya isn't very happy with me. I think we just broke up, actually."

"Oh no!" Zoe exclaimed. "I'm so sorry, Lin. What happened?"

She shrugged. "I guess she didn't like that I went off on a dangerous mission with you without bothering to tell her, and that after we got released, instead of going straight to her, I just took a shower and came to breakfast. She said it doesn't feel like she's particularly important to me."

"Oh," Zoe said. "I'm sorry! This is all my fault."

"Nah," Lin said. "It was my idea as much as it was yours. She's right, though. It never even occurred to me to tell her or to wonder if she was worried." She nodded to herself. "I guess I need to think about that."

No one knew what to say.

"I guess one of us should go talk to her," Paige said, uncomfortably. "You know, so it doesn't get all . . . awkward."

When no one moved, Makena rolled her eyes. "No, stay," she said, getting up. "*I'll* talk to her."

"I wish I had some advice," Zoe said. "I guess relationships can be pretty complicated, huh?"

Lin rolled her eyes. "You have no idea."

17

BEST LAID PLANS

Weeks passed, and Zoe was getting desperate. She couldn't find Marduk's ancient body anywhere, and she couldn't follow Ethan because he no longer attended classes and she didn't know where he was most of the time. Whenever she did catch sight of him, he'd just disappear as soon as she tried to follow. She couldn't figure out where he was sleeping, and she didn't know if Marduk had finished transferring his mind into Ethan. For all she knew, she had failed Ethan already.

"He must be using the same trick Tiamat used," Lin said, as they searched the empty barn. Zoe'd had the crazy idea that maybe there was a secret bunker under it, too. "Making everyone just . . . not notice him."

"I was hoping that wouldn't work on someone who's shielded," Zoe protested, "but lately, I've been walking around with my shields up *all* the time."

"Well, maybe that's how he stays hidden from most people, but he literally hides behind furniture when he sees you coming. Or jumps up and hangs from the ceiling."

Or he is simply not here, but out in the world, Tiamat said. *A possibility I have mentioned numerous times.*

"Anyway," Lin continued, "there's no bunker here, and I don't think he's hiding up here in the hay loft."

"I know," Zoe said. "I was just grasping at straws." Lin laughed at her unintended pun as she sat down and dangled her legs over the edge. "I feel like I'm failing Ethan, Lin. Like I *have* failed him."

"Let's start from the beginning." Lin took the spot next to her. "Maybe we can see a pattern. When was the first time he pulled his disappearing act?"

"Right after he showed me ancient Babylon," Zoe said. "In his dorm room. He was angry at me and generating his fear field. I was curled up on the floor. He left, and I gathered myself for just a few seconds before running out into the hallway after him. But he was gone, and nobody had even seen him."

"So, does he just walk around invisible all the time? Or did he not want you following him?"

"I've seen him walking around before and since, so it's not *all* the time. He does it deliberately when he—" An idea popped into her head. "Oh, wow."

"What?" Lin asked.

"I can't believe I never thought of this!" Zoe shouted, jumping down off the loft.

"Where are we going?" Lin hollered, scrambling after her.

"The dorms!"

"Ethan doesn't live there anymore!"

"I'll bet he does," she yelled, bolting through the entrance to the dorms. "And not just Ethan. Marduk too."

"What? You think Old Man Marduk is living in the dorms?" They ran up the stairs.

"Think about it," Zoe said. "When this all started, Ethan thought he was sleepwalking at night because things were out of place. My theory was that he was waking up for late-night mind transfers. But if he was doing that every night, why risk being seen when he could just occupy the room next door or across the hall?"

They sprinted up the last flight of steps and looked down the hallway. "You think an ancient Sumerian god is hiding out in the boys' dorm." Lin said.

She nodded. "I do. It's the last place anyone would think to look." She knocked on Ethan's door and waited. Phillip answered, looking surprised to see them.

"Hi Phillip," Zoe said. "How are you doing?"

"I'm okay," he said, nervously. The last time she'd seen him, he was catatonic.

"I'm glad," she said. "Listen, I have a question for you. First . . . I'm assuming you haven't seen Ethan lately?" He hurriedly shook his head. "Didn't think so. Second, do you know who all of your neighbours are?"

"Well, Eli and Miguel are on that side," he said, pointing to the left, "and Logan and Jack are on that side." He pointed to the right.

"Thanks," she said. "Do you know who else lives on this floor?"

Phillip listed off the names of everyone else in the other rooms. "Why do you want to know?" he asked.

"She's looking for an all-powerful Sumerian god," Lin said.

Phillip's face went white.

"I'm sorry!" Lin said, quickly. "I forgot! I'm so sorry, Phillip."

"It's okay," he said, closing the door, but Zoe stopped it with her foot.

"Actually . . ." Zoe said, "maybe you should go somewhere for a bit. Like, for an hour or so. Somewhere far from here." There was no need for the poor boy to go through that again.

Phillip didn't ask questions, and he didn't need to be told twice. He took off down the hall.

"Wait, Phillip!" Zoe called, pointing at the door across the hall. "Who did you say is in this room?"

A puzzled look came over him, and he turned from her without a word and kept walking away.

"Well, that was weird," Zoe mumbled.

"What was weird?" Lin asked.

Zoe opened her mouth to speak, then paused. "I . . . don't remember." She shook her head. "Right, then. Let's start knocking."

"What do we do if we find him?" Lin asked.

"We'll worry about that when the time comes." She knocked on the first door.

"I don't know," Lin said, skeptically. "Seems like the sort of thing we should worry about beforehand."

Before long, they had knocked on all the doors and were lucky enough to find everyone home—but there was no sign of Marduk.

"I don't understand," Zoe said, frowning. "I was so positive."

"Are we sure we knocked on every door?"

"I think so. Let's double-check." They wandered the entire floor, counting on their fingers as they passed each door and rattled off the names of those inside. At the end, Zoe looked quizzically at her nine upraised fingers. "Aren't there ten rooms per floor?"

Lin nodded. "You must've forgotten to count Phillip."

"No . . . I definitely counted him. Let's do this again. Slowly."

They methodically wandered the floor again.

"Nine," Lin said, counting her fingers. "Something feels . . . wrong."

"I feel it, too," Zoe said. "I have an idea. This time, let's focus on one side of the hallway at a time and keep ourselves one door apart. They started counting again.

"Wait," Lin said at one point. "Did you miss a door?"

"I don't think so . . . but you do seem unusually far away. I have an idea. Close your eyes."

"Closed."

"Mine too," Zoe said. "Now, walk toward me, touching the wall with your hand. When your hand feels a door, stop. I'll do the same. One, two, three."

Zoe walked toward Lin, feeling the painted brick wall on her fingertips. "Ow!" she cried, as she bonked her head against Lin's. She looked at the wall and . . . struggled to process it. "What's happening?"

"This isn't a wall . . ." Lin said. "What are we doing again?"

Zoe sat on the floor so she wouldn't wander off. "We're looking for Old Man Marduk," she said.

Lin staggered away. "Something's wrong with me."

Zoe started crawling toward her, then forced herself to stop. Why was she on the floor? She'd sat down for a reason. *Tiamat, help me!* There was no answer. *Tiamat?*

I am . . . disoriented, Tiamat said, finally. *I think we have found him.*

Who? Zoe couldn't remember.

The man who killed me.

Marduk is here?

Close your eyes again and touch the wall.

Zoe did what the voice in her head said.

It feels smooth, does it not? This is a door, not a brick wall.

So?

So, find the doorknob.

"Zoe?" Lin called from down the hall. "What are you doing down there? Why are you on the floor?"

Zoe felt for the doorknob but couldn't find it. "Lin? Am I still in front of a door?"

There was a pause. "Yes?" Lin squeaked. "I mean . . . I think so? It's like . . . I can barely look at it."

"I need you to force yourself to look at it and tell me when my hand is on the doorknob."

"Okay . . . up . . . right . . . more right . . . up . . . right . . . stop. You're touching it."

"I'm touching it? Are you sure?" This was crazy. She could swear she was touching the wall.

"It's hard to look, but your right hand is literally touching the left side of the doorknob. I'm coming to you."

"No!" Zoe shouted. "Stay there. You're farther away, so you're less affected. We can trust your senses more than mine." It didn't feel like there was any resistance to moving her hand to the right, so maybe she was pulling it back to slide overtop without realizing it.

"Your right hand is literally on top of the doorknob," Lin confirmed. "Just close your fingers."

Zoe did so. It felt like she was just clawing the wall, but her nails weren't digging into her palm, either, so maybe that meant she *was* holding something. This all felt so dreamlike.

"Good," Lin said. "Now turn."

She rotated her hand. "Did it work?"

"I don't know, try pushing it open."

Zoe pushed and tried walking forward. "Is it working?"

"No," Lin said. "You look like a video game character trying to walk through a wall. Stop."

"Hmm. Maybe it's locked."

"You have your paper clips on you?"

"Ha. No. They wouldn't be much use anyway, since I can't feel anything. I'm going to open my eyes."

She opened her eyes, and she was visibly touching a wall. Except, she knew she wasn't. So, she forced herself to look at her hand. *Really* look at it as she squeezed something she couldn't feel. Nevertheless, whatever it was prevented her hand from forming a fist and from rotating. She began to feel sick. "I'm pretty sure it's locked."

"What now?" Lin asked.

Break it down, Tiamat said.

What?

You have finally found what you came for, and you will never be able to pick the lock. He may even be aware of you already. If Ethan is not inside, he may be on his way. It is now or never.

She was right. Zoe had come this far and might only have seconds until Ethan arrived. Time to act. She took a half step back and stared at the brick wall that was really a door. She drew on her telekinetic strength, letting it build inside her until she felt like she would burst. Then, she raised her shields, telekinetically braced the bones in her body, stepped in quickly, and struck the wall with all of her physical strength, channelling all of her coiled-up telekinetic potential into her palm.

The wall exploded inward. Except, it really wasn't a wall but rather the remains of a broken door. She stepped into the dark room. One of the student beds was missing, replaced by a hospital bed. And lying in this bed was the shriveled body of a very old man.

Marduk opened his eyes.

Zoe dropped to the ground, so utterly overcome with fear that she vomited.

YOU DARE?

Zoe tried to crawl toward the dying god.

Tiamat, how do I fight this?

Get angry.

You taught me to overcome my anger!

So that it would not control you—but it is still a weapon. And right now, it is your only chance to overcome this fear. Let him fear YOU!

She was shaking violently, her body flooded with adrenaline and cortisol, and she was reacting not with fight or flight but with paralysis— the worst option, at this juncture. But she tried. Zoe remembered every horrible event of her childhood—trained from birth to be a weapon. She remembered the anger she'd felt all the time. She remembered the Battle and all the lives lost. She remembered Professor Chao's last moment and the hatred and blinding rage she'd felt when Ragnar murdered him. Marduk was responsible for all of it, and now he was taking Ethan from her, too. She was Ethan's only chance, and here she was, collapsed on the ground. She needed to get angry and fight!

But it was no use. The anger just wasn't in her anymore.

Poor Zoe, Marduk mocked. *All this effort to find me and save your boyfriend, and it is all for naught. You thought you could be a hero? A god slayer? Look at you, grovelling on the floor in fear. You are a weak, pathetic little girl with delusions of grandeur.*

I'm not afraid of you, Zoe said, rising to her hands and knees. *This is a trick.*

Ah, if only it were so. You so wish to see yourself as brave. Yet, in your heart, you know the truth—you are nothing more than a coward.

Zoe laughed. *I know who I am. I was locked up for months with nothing to do but reflect. No, this fear isn't real. But yours is. You've been afraid your entire life. Afraid people will discover what you really are.*

What I am, child, is a god.

No. You're a fraud. She slowly pushed herself to her feet, legs trembling. *You're desperately afraid of what people would truly think about you if they were allowed to think for themselves. So, you don't let them. You bend the minds of everyone around you so that you'll never have to find out if you're actually worthy of being loved, or liked, or even respected.*

She stepped forward. *Deep down, though, you've always known the answer—you're NOT worthy. You have nothing to offer the world except pain and suffering. If you allowed everyone to see the real you and the free will to judge you, not a single person would have anything good to say about you.*

Another step closer. *You don't even trust them to fear you, so you generate your little fear aura and pretend, even to yourself, that this is just how puny mortals react in the presence of a god. Everything about you is fake. You're a joke. If you weren't so evil, I'd even feel sorry for you.*

She reached his bedside. The rage behind his eyes was unmistakable, but so was the panic. He was clearly too weak to even lift his arms, and he wasn't trying to attack her with his Abilities in any way. His tricks of instilling fear and staying hidden were all he had left.

"Zoe," said a familiar voice behind her. "You shouldn't be here."

"Ethan?" She turned, remembering the alley when her new persona had met him for the first time. He had said those exact same words. And here he was now, looking at her with the exact same eyes. But only for a moment before Marduk returned, and his eyes turned cold.

"You *shouldn't* be here," he said. "What's your plan? To threaten to kill my old body unless I relinquish my new one?"

Zoe placed her hand on Old Man Marduk's head, her fingers crackling with electricity. "Yes."

Ethan laughed. "All right," he said, crossing his arms. "Do it."

"It's not a bluff," she said, increasing the amount of electricity in her hand. He winced, as if he too felt it.

"If you say so." He wandered over to the window and opened the blackout blinds. "You've killed people before, right? Your first time was with me, in fact, right out there on the snow-covered lawn. That must've been a sight to see from up here." He turned back to her. "It's a whole lot different when it's not in self-defence, though, isn't it? I mean, look at him." He gestured to his older self. "He can't even lift a finger. It would be cold-blooded murder." He smirked. "Are you a murderer, Zoe?"

She didn't like how this was playing out, at all. "I'll do whatever I have to do to get my friend back."

"I know you will, Zoe. I'm touched that you care enough to risk your life for me. But I don't *want* Marduk to leave me. I *like* who I've become."

"Stop talking like you're Ethan. We both know this is Marduk talking. If you don't leave Ethan, I *will* kill your old body, and you can say goodbye to any memories or Abilities you haven't transferred over yet."

Ethan sighed. "Fine."

"I mean it, Marduk." She increased the electricity flowing from her fingers. "I'll kill him."

Ethan lithely hopped up to sit cross-legged in thin air and rested his chin on his hands. "Not the way I thought he'd go out, but you have my rapt attention."

Now, Zoe didn't know what to do. She didn't want to murder anyone, no matter how evil. She wanted Marduk to beg for his life. "You expect me to believe you don't care?"

"Of course I care," he said. "I lived in that body for thousands of years. It's important to me that I be here at the end."

She increased her electrical output even more, and Old Man Marduk arched his back. "Don't make me do this. Just leave Ethan. Find someone else. A willing host."

"I'm not *making* you do anything, Zoe. But I'm not going anywhere, either. So, if this is what you feel you need to do, then do it. Become the killer we both know you can be. Hello, old friend."

Zoe looked up to see Ragnar in the doorway.

"Master," he said.

"Come for the show?" Ethan asked. "Your daughter here says she's going to kill me. Well, *old* me."

Ragnar seemed to assess the scene immediately. He looked worried. For Old Man Marduk or for her? He caught Zoe's eye and shook his head almost imperceptibly. Behind him, Lin appeared—with a knife in her hand. Where had that come from? Did she just walk around with a hidden knife now? She locked eyes with Lin.

No, Zoe told her, via mindlink.

"Would you like me to handle this, Master?" Ragnar asked.

"Oh, no need," Ethan said, waving a hand dismissively. "This is an important life lesson for Zoe. A teaching moment."

"About what?" Zoe asked. "Not threatening to kill someone unless I'm prepared to go through with it? I could argue this isn't murder at all. You exist in two bodies simultaneously, your consciousness connected between both. You would still exist afterward, so killing him would be like cutting off a finger."

"Sounds like you have the ethics of this all figured out," Ethan said. "Go on, then."

Damn. Her bluff had failed, and she had no backup plan. She had been so desperate to help Ethan that she hadn't thought this part through. Or maybe she'd just avoided thinking about this possibility because she had no better plan. It was just this, all or nothing.

"I *want* you to do it," Ethan said.

Zoe hesitated. She had lost. She had never intended to kill the old man, but if he was pretending not to care, then maybe she should just do it. Maybe it would teach *him* a life lesson about being so arrogant.

"Here, I'll help you," Ethan said. He raised his hand and made a fist. Old Man Marduk's eyes went wide, and a small sound escaped his lips. Lifeless old eyes stared up at her. She turned to Ethan in shock.

"Not with a bang but a whimper," he murmured, lost in thought. He snapped out of it. "We finished our mind transference a week ago. We kept going to see if maybe there was anything we'd missed, but really, we were just waiting for the end. It was undignified, though." He nodded to himself. "This was better." He lowered himself to the ground. "Ragnar, please take care of the body like we discussed."

"Of course, Master."

Ethan sauntered out without another word and without even a backward glance.

Ragnar didn't say anything to her, either, just arched an eyebrow and turned to see Lin standing behind him. His gaze darted to her knife, then to his four guards surrounding her with swords drawn. He motioned them inside and whispered something to one of them, who nodded and ran off. Ragnar turned his attention back to Zoe.

"Out," he said. "Both of you."

18

UNEXPECTED DEVELOPMENTS

Zoe was depressed. She had moped about for weeks, doing the bare minimum for her classes and hardly talking to anyone. She felt utterly defeated. She had *been* utterly defeated. She had failed the one person who had loved her his whole life, and now he was gone, probably forever. She had no plan to get him back. No plan to defeat Marduk. No goal, really. She was rudderless.

Lin was sympathetic, but she had her own problems to deal with. Namely, a seething anger that just kept growing by the day. She was as fast and strong as most of the Igigi now, and she fought them at every opportunity, whether in the dojo or in the halls. They were growing scared of her, and rightfully so. Even Zoe didn't hold back anymore when she and Lin sparred. Lin fought Ragnar every chance she got during combat classes, more aggressively than anyone else dared. She was testing herself, Zoe knew, to see how close she was getting to his level. Ragnar seemed to love it, both amused by her hatred and proud of her progress.

Even Tiamat hadn't been able to snap Zoe out of her funk and eventually receded to whatever corner of Zoe's mind she lived in, doing whatever she did to occupy herself. Zoe wondered what such an existence must be like—a passenger in someone else's mind. How did she resist the urge to decompress herself? To take over and have her life back? Zoe doubted she could do anything to stop Tiamat—any more than Ethan had been able to stop Marduk—if she decided to take over, especially since it sounded like it would happen a lot quicker. Zoe wasn't too worried, though, since Tiamat had resisted the urge for thousands of years. Maybe she should just give up and let Tiamat take over. In a way, it was selfish of her *not* to. Tiamat was the world's best chance to defeat Marduk, and here Zoe was, putting her own needs above those of the entire world.

Zoe didn't even know what was going on in the outside world anymore. For all she knew, Marduk had already infected the minds of all the world leaders, and it was all over. She doubted it, though, because it seemed like everyone was going on little missions these days, in teams of four—two Igigi and two Anunnaki—targeting local celebrities and social media influencers, forcing them to be better people and patting themselves on the back for having made the world a slightly better place. Zoe was ashamed to have led the first mission; she'd been so convinced that what she was doing mattered. But nothing mattered anymore. Marduk would infect everyone of importance.

She actually told people what he was planning, and word quickly spread. But no one cared. If anything, they thought it was brilliant and were relieved that soon they wouldn't have to worry about the world ending. Ethan strutted around like a rock star, clearly happy to be young and have followers again. Should she even call him Ethan anymore, she wondered. For all intents and purposes, he was Marduk. If Ethan was still in there—still existing as a distinct entity—then he was just the passenger now. Or, he might be utterly merged with Marduk, with Marduk the dominant persona. Regardless, now that Marduk was at full strength, she saw no way to help Ethan. No way, save one.

Maybe that was why she was so depressed—because she hadn't just failed Ethan, she was actively failing *everyone* with every breath Zoe took instead of Tiamat. It didn't help that she couldn't talk about it to anyone other than Lin, either. She had sworn not to reveal Tiamat's existence to anyone.

"Do you think your dad would've done it?" she asked Lin one night as they lay in their beds, trying to fall asleep.

"Done what?" Lin mumbled.

"Let Tiamat take over. Knowing that it was our best—maybe only—chance to beat Marduk, do you think he would've let her take over?"

Lin rolled over in bed. "What are you talking about?"

"Forget it," Zoe said. "Just thinking out loud."

"No, I don't think my dad would've let her take over. She was inside his head for centuries, apparently, and he never asked her to decompress. Is this what's been bothering you? I thought it was just that Marduk beat us, but all this time, you've been thinking about letting Tiamat take over your mind?"

"Your dad was brave. A hero. He would've sacrificed himself in a heartbeat if he thought it was the only way to save your life. He never knew that Marduk is real. He never knew the danger Marduk presents. If he had, don't you think he would've sacrificed himself to save the world?"

"I think he would've tried to save the world all by himself."

"Come on, Lin. He was an amazing fighter. But he wasn't godlike powerful. How would he have taken on Marduk? No one can challenge him physically."

"Why? You think he's immune to a sword in the gut?"

"Yeah, maybe! We have no idea if he can heal. Or if he can use telekinesis to strengthen his skin as well as his bones. But I don't think he'd ever let a sword come anywhere near him. I think his mindbending is so powerful that he'd just turn his enemies into his servants. He could do that to all of us anytime he wanted to."

"But he hasn't," Lin said. "So, there's a reason. Maybe it's hard for him to have too many copies of himself out there. Or maybe he wants a world full of worshippers, not mini-clones. Or maybe he's just lazy, or careless, or overconfident. It doesn't matter. As long as there are people who aren't infected by him, he's vulnerable."

"I suppose," Zoe conceded. "But you still have to admit that Tiamat stands a better chance of beating him than any of us do."

"She's a last resort, Zoe." Lin sat up and jabbed a finger at her. "I mean it. A *last* resort. Promise me."

Zoe bit her lip.

"*Promise* me, Zoe."

"Fine! I promise. She's a last resort. Are you happy?"

"Yeah," Lin said, lying down again. "I'm happy. A promise is a promise. I can't believe you were ever even *thinking* about leaving me."

. . .

A promise was a promise, but that didn't mean Zoe could stop thinking about asking Tiamat to take over her mind. What constituted a last resort anyway? Did she have to wait until her life was in imminent danger? Or Lin's? That seemed unnecessarily reckless. If Zoe was going to do this, she should do it well before putting herself or anyone else in danger, and then Tiamat would have the added benefit of taking Marduk by surprise.

Stop.

Zoe stopped midstep, tray of food in hand. *Tiamat?*

Don't stop what you're doing. Go sit. I mean, stop this line of thinking.

Zoe joined Paige at their usual table. *I thought you disappeared.*

I did. I thought if I went away for a time, you would stop fixating on me. But that clearly didn't work.

How am I supposed to stop thinking about a goddess living inside my mind who could solve all our problems with the snap of her fingers?

It wouldn't be that easy. I have never decompressed, so I have no idea how powerful I would actually be. In any event, I don't understand why you are agonizing so much over a decision I never asked you to make. So, I am going to make this easy for you. I won't do it. Not unless you are moments away from death and you give me permission.

Why? Zoe asked.

Because your life matters! You are only fifteen years old. You have centuries ahead of you. And even if you weren't so young, everyone's life matters.

But it wouldn't be the same as dying, would it? I thought it would be like merging with you, not being replaced by you.

Yes, I would ensure that it's a merging. You wouldn't cease to exist. But even so, it's not . . . right. I've had my time. I'll return if needed, but this is your time. You are just beginning to figure out who you are. I have no desire to take that away from you.

"Hello, Earth to Zoe," Paige said, snapping their fingers in front of Zoe's face. "Come in, Zoe."

Zoe shook herself alert. How long had she been talking with Tiamat? "What?" She looked around the table. The Valkyries were all staring at her. Hadn't it been just her and Paige a second ago?

"Did you hear *anything* I said?" Paige asked.

"Sorry," she mumbled. "My mind was somewhere else. What were you saying?"

Paige sighed exaggeratedly.

"They were saying they have a plan," Lin said, gently touching Zoe's arm.

"For what?"

"Escaping," Paige said.

Zoe cocked her head. "Why?"

"Because . . . we're prisoners here?"

"Yeah, but Lin already said she's not leaving, right?" She looked at Lin, who nodded. "And besides, I want to stop Ragnar and Marduk, not run away and let them win."

"We could join the Resistance out there, Zoe."

"The Resistance is compromised. And even if it weren't, it must be spread thin all over the world. If I were in a cell, I'd agree that escaping was my best option. But I'm not, so I have way greater access to Ragnar and Marduk here than out there."

Paige mimed pulling their hair out.

"Hey," Zoe said, "don't get me wrong. If you want to escape, I'll totally help you." She looked around the table. "Any of you. But so long as Lin is here, I'm staying put."

"I have an idea," Priya said. All eyes turned to her. "Not about escaping. About stopping Marduk. You know how nobody knows where he sleeps? Well, someone must know, because he doesn't eat here—which means someone must bring his meals to him."

"Amelia," Zoe said, standing. She hadn't spoken to the head housemaid since returning, which in hindsight was dumb—she would know everything that went on in the school.

"Wait," Priya said, pushing her back down. "That's only half the plan. Amelia can tell us where his room is, but more importantly, she can put something in his food."

"You mean poison him," Makena said.

Priya squirmed. "Or sedate him, yeah."

"It's not like we can keep him a prisoner in our dorm," Lin said. "Sedating him would only have one purpose. To allow someone like Professor Sharapova to remove him from Ethan's mind. If it's not too late for that."

Zoe didn't want to get her hopes up, but this felt like the beginnings of a plan. And a spark of hope. "I'll go speak with Amelia Zehringer."

She dropped off her food tray and headed to the kitchen, where she found the head housemaid, who was none too pleased to see a student there.

"Please," Zoe said, raising her hand placatingly. "I need to speak with you. It's important."

Amelia scowled, then ushered Zoe into a side room.

"I am very angry with you," Amelia said, simply.

"I'm sorry—"

"Yes, I have heard you are sorry. So very sorry. But that won't bring Ling back, now will it?"

Zoe winced.

"I knew him when he was just a boy first starting at the Academy. So homesick, he would cry every night. Other boys would bully him for it. I took him under my wing. I snuck him sweets from my kitchen to make him feel better. After leaving here, he endured such tragedy. Yet, he overcame it and grew into the finest man I have ever known. He took you under his wing to protect you. And then you betrayed him."

Zoe gulped. She hadn't realized Amelia and Professor Chao had been so close. She should have come to speak with her immediately. "I'm sorry," she said again. "I'd give anything to do it all over again, but all I can do now is honour his last wish, from his final moment—that I protect his wife and daughter. And I'm trying to, I really am. But I don't know how to other than by stopping Ragnar and Marduk and . . . I'm not strong enough."

The head housemaid regarded her for a long time. "What is it you want from me?" she asked.

"To tell me where you take Marduk's food. And to let me put something in it."

Amelia shook her head. "I cannot help you."

"Please," Zoe begged. "I don't know what else to do."

"We do not feed him."

"What? But . . . how's that possible? He *must* eat. Is he getting takeout three times a day?"

"Food goes missing from the kitchen. We assume it is him."

So, he was still up to his old tricks, lurking around the castle unnoticed. "Still, you must know where he sleeps."

"I do not. Every suite is occupied."

Zoe felt defeated all over again. She should never have allowed herself to hope, even for a moment.

"I am sorry that I cannot help. But thank you for telling me about Ling's last moments. It seems he must have forgiven you, so . . . I will try to honour his wishes and do the same."

Zoe nodded, afraid her voice would break if she tried to speak. Suddenly, Amelia wrapped her in a bear hug, and Zoe began to sob.

"There, there, *mein Liebchen*. It will be okay."

■ ■ ■

Zoe hid in the kitchen, dressed in black, crouched and unmoving for hours. Eventually, Ethan would come for his late-night snack, and when he did, she would follow him and learn where he was hiding. Maybe it was in the cavern.

Do you think he'll spot us? Zoe asked.

I don't know, Tiamat said. *I can make us unnoticeable to Typicals and most Telepaths, but Marduk is a god, and I am only a shade of my former self. This is very dangerous, what you are doing.*

It's worth the risk. I need to know where he sleeps if we're to have any hope of capturing him for Professor Sharapova. Besides, he might be angry if he catches us, but I can't see him actually killing me for this. He wants to earn my trust.

The kitchen door opened and closed without a sound. Someone walked slowly through the shadows and stopped, looking around cautiously. Something was wrong. Why would Marduk be so careful? He was the most powerful Telepath in the world. The figure took a glass from a cupboard, filled it with water, and drank. Then, they washed the glass and put it back in the cupboard. What was going on here?

The figure removed a plate from inside their shirt and placed it quietly on the counter. They opened one of the refrigerators, and the light illuminated their face.

Zoe gasped. It was Fasil.

He froze and stared directly at her for a full ten seconds before rummaging through the fridge for leftovers. As he put them on his plate, Zoe crept from her hiding spot. Once again, he froze and looked at her before continuing with his business.

Amazing, Tiamat said. *He's a Typical. He should not notice us at all.*

Once Fasil had loaded up his plate, he then raided a cupboard, stuffing his pockets with as many cans of food as would fit before leaving the kitchen and heading down the dark hallway. Zoe followed. Every now and then, he would stop and look back, probably hearing her footsteps—though she tried to walk in step with him. Eventually, they reached the custodian's office. He opened it with a key and slipped inside, and Zoe carefully manoeuvred through, too—nearly touching him. She pressed herself against the wall and held her breath; she could literally see the hair rising on the back of his neck, as though he were sensing a ghost.

He made his way to the back of the office and into a large storage closet. He placed his plate of food on a shelf, picked up a broom, and swept the floor. Then, he pushed on a brick and pulled on a shelf, revealing a secret doorway. He took his plate and entered, Zoe creeping behind him. He closed the secret door with a click and made his way down a flight of stone steps that opened into a large room, where he had obviously been living since his "escape." He sat at a table and ate his cold dinner, while Zoe examined what could only be the legendary hidden chamber.

It had clearly always been intended as a hideout—a secret living quarters for the castle's original owner. It was tastefully decorated with expensive rugs, paintings, and furniture from the 1800s. There was a large bed, a couch, a dining room table and chairs, and shelves upon shelves of old books. There was even a washroom with a sink, tub, and toilet, as well as a small kitchen. There were no windows or electrical outlets, but an extension cord ran from a gap in the brick wall. A few more extension cords ran off of it, powering several lamps and a space heater.

Tiamat, you can let us be seen again.

"What are you still doing here, Fasil?"

Fasil jumped a foot in the air, knocking over his chair as he scrambled to grab a knife from the kitchen. When he realized it was only Zoe, he relaxed. "Oh, it's you," he said. "How did you find me? Why didn't I see or hear you come in?"

She ignored his questions. "Why are you here, Fasil? I thought you'd be long gone and back with your family by now."

He put down the knife and took his seat at the table again. "I was afraid your plan to get me out wouldn't work. It seemed easier to just break out on my own. I took that guard's phone, and once I was over the wall and far enough away for it to work, I searched for my wife and daughter." He took a deep breath. "And found their obituaries."

Zoe dropped into a chair at the table and placed her hand on his. "*'Ana hazina min 'ajlik,*" she said, expressing her sympathy.

He seemed surprised to hear his native tongue and smiled sadly. "*Shukran laki.* They were my life. Without them, I have nothing to go home to. No reason to go on living—save one." He looked her in the eyes. "Revenge."

"So, you've been hiding here ever since?"

"Yes," he said. "Waiting for a chance to kill Ragnar."

"How did you even find this place?" Zoe asked. "No one else ever has."

"I imagine that there was never another trained operative spending his days in the custodian's office. I doubt the new custodian will find it. I only come out at night for food, and I always sweep the floor, so the secret door swinging inward leaves no trace."

That made sense. "You know you can't beat Ragnar, right?"

"Not in a duel," he said. "But anyone, no matter how powerful, can be assassinated—so long as you don't care about dying in the process, yeah?"

"He's a Telepath, Fasil. A strong one. You're a Typical."

"Well . . ." To Zoe's surprise, he levitated a book up off the table.

"What? How?"

"I found a cache of godling drugs in the basement. I have my Abilities again. And I've been working hard to improve them and grow stronger."

"Wait," Zoe said. "Does this room connect to the rest of the basement?"

Fasil pointed to the far wall near the electrical cord. "Through that wall is a secret exit to a supply room."

"I was *in* that room!" Zoe cried. "I pushed on every brick, looking for a secret door, but I couldn't find anything."

Fasil nodded. "It can only be opened from this side. So, I'm very careful not to let it shut behind me whenever I use it, which is not often."

"So, that extension cord," she said, pointing. "You hooked into a power outlet on the other side?"

"I did," he said. "Without anything showing on the other side. This room was clearly built before electrical wiring was installed in the castle."

The wheels were turning in Zoe's mind. This was perfect. She could get into the basement without needing to sneak past the guards, and she could rescue Harrington, Lafleur, and Grant and bring them here to recover until they were ready to escape. She filled Fasil in on what she was thinking.

"Of course I will help," he said. "I owe you my life. I will be forever grateful to you for releasing me from Ragnar's mind control. Just tell me when."

"I will," she said, standing. "Are you okay here? Is there anything you need? Would you like me to bring your meals to you?"

Fasil shook his head. "No, I'm fine. I've made it this far without being discovered, yeah? Until tonight, of course. Did you follow me from the kitchen?"

She nodded.

"I should've known someone would notice food going missing eventually, but it couldn't be helped."

"Take care, Fasil. I'll let you know the plan as soon as I can."

. . .

"I can't believe you snuck out without me!" Lin said in the morning after Zoe had told her about Fasil.

"It seemed more like a one-man operation," Zoe said. "And I figured I'd be hiding in that kitchen every night for a while."

"You still should've told me," Lin grumbled.

"I'm sorry. But this is great news, right?"

"Yeah, it's great news, but I'm still mad at you, Zoe."

They got ready and went down for breakfast, and on their way to their first class, Professor Yeoh motioned for a private word with Lin.

Zoe went to find her seat, and a minute later, Lin arrived.

"Everything okay?" Zoe asked.

"Yup, she just wanted to know if I'd like to have dinner with her tonight." Lin rummaged through her backpack. *Listen, my mom just told me something really important.*

What?

She did it. She managed to switch the pills this morning.

Zoe did her best to appear calm. *Really?*

Yup. She said it took a while to figure out where the pills were stored and when they're given to the prisoners each day. It's every morning and evening, apparently. And then all of a sudden, an opportunity presented itself, and she just . . . swapped this morning's pills with something that looks the same. The prisoners should be starting to wake up.

"Class is cancelled!" Professor Martinov yelled as he strode into the classroom, clapping his hands. "Everyone, make your way to the auditorium for a surprise assembly!"

"What's going on?" Kyle asked from the back of the room.

"I don't know, but I love surprises, don't you?" Professor Martinov said with his usual childish glee. He seemed so normal most of the time, Zoe could almost forget that a piece of Marduk was in his mind.

This is amazing! Zoe said, as they filed down the hall with the rest of the students. *It would've been horrible if it had happened any earlier, but now we know how to sneak into the basement and where to hide the prisoners!*

This shouldn't really be too hard, Lin said. *We can easily overpower the guards, grab their keys, and get Lafleur and Harrington and Grant out of their cells and into the hidden chamber. Heck, we probably could've done this even without my mom's help.*

Yeah, but I'm glad we won't have to drag them. Plus, if things go sour somehow, they can fight alongside us.

Paige and Priya had saved them seats. Makena, though, was sitting with some friends from her grade. "Do you know what this is about?" Lin asked.

"No idea," Priya said. "I don't think anyone knows."

"It can't be good," Paige said, shaking their head. "I can't imagine a single thing they could say or do that would be good."

My mom tried to make me promise that I wouldn't go down there, Lin said. *I think she just wanted me to pass the message along to you. She was pretty mad when I refused, but I already told her that I'm not a helpless child. Besides, I'm not letting you have all the fun. Beating up those guards has been the highlight of my year.*

Before long, Ragnar appeared onstage and crossed to the podium. "Good morning, everyone. It seemed past time I gathered you all together for an information session. Much has happened since this school was liberated, and for security reasons, I have had to keep most of it quiet. But today, I will share with you what I can. Actually, *I* won't. Someone else will." He stepped aside as Ethan approached the podium, prompting considerable chatter among the students. He gazed out at the audience, and Zoe could *feel* his commanding strength.

"You've all known for a while now that I am not the same boy many of you grew up with," he said to a hushed audience. "So, I would like to formally declare myself before you today. I am your lord and god, Marduk. I am many thousands of years old, and my body was finally near its end. So, with the help of modern science, I revived the Igigi. I created children—*my* children. I call you the New Gods because you are literally my children. Each of you has my blood running through your veins. Well, all save one of you." He glanced at Ragnar.

The eyes of every Igigi kid widened in shock as they realized Zoe had been telling the truth—that they actually were siblings.

"One of my children was always going to become my vessel, and ultimately, I chose Ethan. My ancient body is now gone, but all that I ever was lives on in this youthful body. It has been a *long* time since I had this much power, and I intend to make good use of it."

He wandered from the podium as he continued. "Time is of the essence, my children. For decades, our planet has been at risk of utter annihilation—within a matter of minutes—by intercontinental ballistic missiles equipped with nuclear warheads. All it would take is one world leader with an erratic personality or cognitive impairment—and we have several leaders that fit that description right now. Or a high-risk game of chicken, like the Cuban Missile Crisis in 1962. Or a computer glitches and claims it sees incoming missiles. That actually happened in 1983 and the only reason we're still alive is because the Soviet officer on duty was suspicious that it might be a false alarm. He disobeyed protocol and refused to pick up the phone and inform his superiors, knowing they would launch their missiles and end the world. False alarms have happened at least twice in the U.S, too. And now we have artificial intelligence being used everywhere. How long until AI gets inserted into a defence computer system and makes a bad decision? And the Anunnaki just *let* this happen. It's unfathomable."

He shook his head. "To those of you in the audience who we liberated and brought into our Igigi family, I want you to know it's not your fault. You were taught to believe in this ridiculous notion of non-interference and free will, and you were never in charge to challenge it. But children today—not just us but Typicals, too—*are* challenging the accepted norms. They realize it's just a matter of time until some madman launches those missiles and destroys the world. They understand that climate change will make the world unliveable—not in generations but possibly in *this* generation—unless we *do* something. They grasp that greed and hate and lust for power are at the root of everything that is wrong with the world. They desperately *want* to have a future!"

He paused. "But Typical children have no power. We, on the other hand—" He clenched his fist in front of him. "*We* have power. And we are going to use it, starting now."

The auditorium erupted with applause and cheers—not just from the Igigi, Zoe noted, but from most of the others, too.

"Our first order of business," Marduk spoke above the uproar, "is to nullify the most immediate threat: nuclear weapons. This means infiltrating every level of government within nuclear-armed nations, mindbending our way up from the bottom until we reach the top. And I am pleased to announce to you all here today that I have succeeded in doing exactly this."

Zoe gasped. Already?

"Please turn your attention to the monitor as the leaders of the world make their joint statement!" The lights dimmed, and the giant screen at the back of the stage showed a live news event. A CBC reporter stood outside the Parliament Buildings in Ottawa, one hand holding a microphone, the other touching an earpiece. She nodded.

"To those of you just joining," the reporter said, "this is an unprecedented event that seemingly came out of nowhere. No one knew until just hours ago that the leaders of the United States, Russia, China, the United Kingdom, France, India, Pakistan, Israel, and North Korea were gathering in Ottawa for a surprise announcement. It hasn't escaped anyone's notice that these are all countries possessing nuclear weapons. No sooner did speculation begin that some sort of nuclear disarmament treaty was in the works than the actual text of this treaty was made public. And it is nothing short of astonishing. This treaty that—again, came out of nowhere—does not just scale back the proliferation of nuclear weapons, but will completely dismantle the *entire* nuclear arsenal of every nuclear state in the world."

Bullet points began to appear on the screen as the reporter read aloud from a piece of paper. "'Under the terms of this treaty, all nuclear weapons of any kind are henceforth banned. Representatives from each nuclear state will supervise the destruction of each nation's nuclear arsenal with the deadline being just one year from today'—which I'm told by experts is an unbelievably short amount of time, given that, in their estimation, it should take a full decade to dismantle the estimated 12,500 nuclear weapons that exist in the world. 'Any nation caught keeping its nuclear weapons or engaging in research into nuclear weapons will be dealt with *swiftly and decisively* via a joint military operation conducted by the current nuclear states and any other nation wishing to join, with the goal of capturing—and executing—that nation's leader and anyone else who was in a position of authority that led to the illegal pursuit of nuclear weapons technology.'"

She looked up from her paper. "That is the exact wording of this treaty, which is . . . difficult to believe, given its almost childlike simplicity. I think it's safe to say that there has never been a treaty like this in history." The reporter put her hand to her ear. "I'm being told that the world leaders are making their way to the podiums in front of Parliament now."

Zoe watched in disbelief as nine world leaders stood before the world and announced that no one would have to live in fear of nuclear destruction any longer. They said that nuclear weapons would never again be allowed to exist. They spoke of peace and cooperation and harmony—and absolutely zero tolerance for anyone who would break the treaty. They expected every nation—no matter how small—to sign an agreement promising they would never pursue nuclear weapons.

As they gave their speeches, Zoe closed her eyes and tried to extend her consciousness to the basement, looking for any minds to communicate with. She had experimented with this during her incarceration but had only found the guard outside her cell. After a minute, she found a mind. It was a guard. She looked through his eyes and saw two other guards with him. She left his mind and moved toward the nearest cell. She thought she could see a mind nearby, but it was faint.

Headmaster? Headmaster Harrington? Are you awake?

Zoe?

Headmaster! Thank goodness. Are you okay?

I'm . . . confused.

You've been drugged, Zoe said. *For a very long time. Ragnar told everyone he executed you, but then Lin and I found you in the basement. Lafleur is in the cell next to yours. And Grant is two cells down. Professor Yeoh swapped your drugs this morning so you can all wake up. Today is our only chance to get you all out of there before they drug you again this evening.*

I see, he said. *Do you have a plan?*

This is all very last-minute, but yeah, I think I do. Just last night, I discovered the famous "hidden chamber" where a friend is hiding out.

There's a secret entrance to it in a supply room in the basement, but it only opens from the other side. I'm going to try to move you all there tonight. You can spend a few days recovering there, and then we'll get you out of the castle. I assume you know about the secret tunnel in the cavern?

Ha. You've been busy.

Give me some time to figure out the details. I'd like to turn off the cameras somehow. Otherwise, they could discover your hideout. I'm not sure if I'll come get you or if you should take out the guard when he comes to drug you again, but I'll let you know soon.

Don't put yourself or anyone else in undue danger, Zoe. If you can handle the cameras, that would be most appreciated. We can do the rest, provided we can somehow let your friend know to open the supply room door. How much time do we have before the guards return to administer our nightly drugs?

I don't know. But Professor Yeoh might. I'll ask her and get back to you. Meanwhile, there's a camera watching you, so just act like you're still drugged. And if you can communicate with Lafleur or Professor Grant—

I am already doing so. And Zoe . . . I'm sorry.

Headmaster?

I failed you. I failed all of you.

Headmaster, no! It's not your fault. If it's anyone's fault, it's mine.

No, I know you called in the attack. Don't trouble yourself about that. Ling and I knew what you did and tried to use that knowledge to our advantage. And thank you for siding with us, by the way. But I am—I was—the headmaster. The safety of the Academy and all of its students and staff was my responsibility. I thought we were prepared, but I failed.

No, Headmaster, you did everything you could. We had no chance. The Igigi were just too powerful.

Tell Lin and Mei that I'm sorry about Ling. He was truly the best man I've ever known.

I will, Headmaster. Rest now. We'll talk soon.

On the screen, the world leaders were now sitting together and signing their names to a paper. Then, they laughed and hugged each other as people clapped and cheered.

The screen went dark, and the room brightened. Ethan spread his arms out wide and grinned. "And that, ladies and gentlemen, is how you make history."

The room erupted. Everyone was laughing and crying. Zoe just sat still, shocked by how quickly this had all happened.

When the applause died down, Ethan spoke again. "But there is still much to do. And I am not a man blessed with patience. So . . ." He sat on the edge of the stage and dangled his legs. "I need your help. And I hope that after what you just saw, you are all eager to do your part. The next imminent threat we must neutralize is climate change. And believe it or not, this will be a much more difficult task." He looked at each member of the audience.

"Typicals are like a disease. They have short little lives, during which they compete to gather as much wealth as possible, and they don't care what happens after they die. Unfortunately, fossil fuels make people *very* wealthy while also ruining the planet. With wealth comes power, and the fossil fuel companies use that power to keep everyone dependent upon their product while convincing them that climate change is a hoax. And then there's the agricultural industry, which convinces people that it's perfectly fine to destroy the rainforests in order to give a billion cows room to graze and burp and fart their methane into the atmosphere. Well, climate change *is* something to worry about. It will make the planet utterly uninhabitable, even for us. We need to do everything we can to stop it. *Now*. And absolutely *nothing* is off the table. I will do whatever it takes—no matter how draconian—to ensure our survival."

He stood. "So, go back to your classrooms and start talking with your professors and each other about this. Start coming up with ideas. Start coming up with plans—in which *you* take part. You have one month, and then your plans will be put into action. Dismissed."

He earned a standing ovation.

"Zoe," Lin said, tapping her on the arm as students started filing out of the auditorium. "Let's go."

Zoe followed her out in a daze.

"So . . . *that* was unexpected," Lin said.

"He infected the most powerful leaders in the world," Zoe said.

"And did what no one else in the world could have done."

"The students love him, Lin. Are we the only ones who think what he's doing is wrong?"

"You are," Ethan said, appearing out of nowhere at her side. Zoe jumped.

"You've been busy," she said, trying to hide her surprise.

"You've no idea," he said. "And there's still so much to do. But right now, I need your help. Both of you. And bring the rest of the Valkyries. Meet me out front in fifteen minutes." He turned down a side hall. "We're going on a road trip!"

Zoe and Lin looked at each other. "To where?" Zoe yelled at him.

"Ottawa!"

He disappeared into the crowd of students. "What are we going to do?" Lin asked. "We were supposed to rescue the prisoners downstairs."

"I don't think we have any choice but to go with him," Zoe said. "Can you find the others? I need to tell your mom what's happening."

"Wait, why don't I tell her? She's my mom."

"Because I have to tell her what Headmaster Harrington told me."

"What? When did you talk to him?"

"During the assembly," Zoe said, starting for the infirmary. "Come say goodbye to your mom after." Lin nodded and hurried off, and Zoe soon found Professor Yeoh at her usual desk.

"We have a problem," she said. She relayed her discovery of the hidden chamber and her conversation with Headmaster Harrington.

"But now Ethan says we have to go with him to Ottawa. Right now. All of us. Me, Lin, Makena, Priya, and Paige. He didn't say why. What do we do?"

The professor clenched her fists and shut her eyes. She stalked away and stared at a wall, before striding back. "I don't want Lin to go—no matter what the purpose is. But I can't control her any longer. She made that *very* clear to me earlier this morning. Please, Zoe. Watch out for her. She's angry and headstrong and reckless. She's strong, yes, but nowhere near her full potential. Whether she wants to admit it or not, she is still a child. I know you are, too, but . . ." She put her hand on Zoe's shoulder. "Please, watch out for her, will you?"

"Of course, Professor," Zoe said, feeling a lump in her throat. "I swore to your husband that I'll protect Lin with my life. But what about Harrington, Lafleur, and Grant? They need our help. It's now or never."

Lin entered the infirmary. "Mom? You okay with this?"

Professor Yeoh nodded and hugged her. "Be safe." She looked back at Zoe. "I will take care of the prisoners in the basement."

"Wait," Lin said. "Are you sure? What will you do? How will you turn off the cameras?"

"I don't know yet, but I'll think of something. I'll find the entrance to the hidden chamber, and with Fasil's help, I am sure we can handle this." She smiled. "Don't worry about me."

"Okay," Lin said. "If you're sure."

Professor Yeoh nudged them out the door. "Go now. Be careful. Both of you."

19

LAST RESORT

"Ottawa is the other direction," Paige said, breaking the awkward silence in the limousine. In addition to the Valkyries and Ethan, Ragnar had also come along.

"We're going to the airport. It's faster to fly than to drive," Ethan said.

After another long silence, Zoe had had enough. "Why are we going to Ottawa?"

"I thought you'd never ask." Ethan grinned. "As you know, the most powerful leaders in the world are currently gathered there."

"Leaders you infected," Zoe said.

Ethan nodded. "And now, I need to . . . debrief them."

"What does that mean?" Makena said. "You're already in their minds. Why would you need to debrief them?"

"It works like this," Ethan said. "I put shallow copies of myself into the minds of Telepaths. They spread shallow copies of me to government officials. But because those officials are Typicals, they can't spread me any further. So, instead, they give my Telepaths access to government officials higher up the chain. They spread me again, and the process continues until I get to the top. But I don't have some vast network that allows me to access their minds from anywhere in the world. So, I arranged for the treaty to be signed in Ottawa, so I could meet with them all in person and learn every one of their secrets."

"Cool," Lin said. "Why are *we* here?"

"You're here because I am a teenager and it might arouse suspicion if I am seen meeting world leaders. But a contingent of students in matching school uniforms? That's clearly some sort of organized event. Also, I need bodyguards."

"*You* need bodyguards?" Makena blurted.

"I will be deep inside their minds and not paying attention to the outside world. That will leave me vulnerable. You can be my royal guard."

Lin leaned forward. "Zoe and I tried to *kill* you not too long ago, remember?"

"You *threatened* to kill me. And it wasn't me, really, but my old husk. So, I don't take it personally."

"I don't get it," Zoe said. "What's your game? You have your own operatives, infected Telepaths, plenty of students who worship you, plus Ragnar himself here. Why us?"

"Naturally, Ragnar would have been my preferred bodyguard. However, he will, unfortunately, be indisposed. He needs to take care of a nuisance. Your old friend Gabriel—who I thought we had handled already—is apparently in Ottawa. I can only assume it has something to do with the gathering of world leaders."

Wait, how was that possible? Gabriel was infected, she'd thought. Did that mean it was possible to rid someone of Marduk's influence?

"I could use one or more of my other operatives," Ethan continued, "but you all have to get out into the field eventually. And honestly, I prefer to have someone I trust watching my back."

"Trust? Why would you possibly trust me?"

"I've known you my whole life, Zoe."

"*Ethan* has known me his whole life. You're not him."

"Yes, I *am*. It's still me, Zoe." He sighed. "Do you remember when

Lin made you open your brooch and read that codeword that reactivated Zoe 2.0? For a while, you had two distinct personas that were struggling to integrate. During that time, you were confused, yes, but you were still *you*. It's the same with me. Both Marduk and I struggled for a bit, each of us instinctively clinging to keep our personas whole, each one taking control for brief periods of time. But bit by bit, we merged. Just like you did."

"You really expect me to protect you?"

Ethan gazed into her eyes. "I guess we'll see."

■ ■ ■

An hour after takeoff, their private jet arrived in Ottawa, where Ragnar's men were waiting for him.

"What are you going to do to Gabriel?" Zoe asked.

Ragnar raised an eyebrow. "What will I do to the man who launched rockets at me the last time we met?"

"Please don't kill him. He's a good man."

"So was Professor Chao," he said. "We all think we're good, and yet we wind up on opposite sides nonetheless." He got into a waiting car and sped off.

Ethan pointed toward the open trunk of their limo, and they all peered inside at five katanas and five long school uniform capes. "If you're to be my royal guard," he said, "you need to both look and be able to play the part."

They drove up the Airport Parkway toward the Parliament Buildings. Zoe was restless. She was just sitting here, doing nothing, while Gabriel was in grave danger. She needed to help him. But what could she do? She could strike Marduk in the throat right now. He'd never expect it. But how fast was he? What if she missed? What if he survived? Would he kill her? Or worse, would he kill one of her friends?

And what if she succeeded? Ethan would be dead. Looking at him now, it was easy to forget that he wasn't the same boy she had always known.

"Weird, isn't it, Zoe?" Ethan said, looking out the window. "The last time we were here, we were trying to get close to that Russian diplomat's kids. Our first mission. It wasn't that long ago, but it may as well have been a lifetime. Look at us now. We literally just saved the world, and now we're on our way to do it again. After I debrief the world leaders, I'm going to make them all agree to make fighting climate change their next priority. That'll get the ball rolling. But leaders only have so much power. They need the support of the people, so that's still our biggest challenge."

He looked at Zoe, as if the others weren't even there. "Think about what we can accomplish, Zoe. We can turn the world into a paradise. And eventually, we won't even need to hide our true nature anymore. People won't fear us—they'll *worship* us. Like they did before." He gazed out the window again, lost in his musings. "It's all happening."

Before long, they arrived at the Office of the Prime Minister and Privy Council on Wellington Street. The four-storey building was directly across the street from the Parliament Buildings. The sidewalks were a media frenzy, with reporters covering the historic treaty. A man in a dark suit and sunglasses leaned down to speak to Ethan through the window.

"Welcome, sir. As you can see, there's a lot of media attention here right now. Would you prefer to use the back entrance?"

Ethan nodded, and the man motioned for the driver to circle around the block, where they found a contingent of more men in dark suits and sunglasses waiting for them.

"PPS?" Zoe asked as they walked down the pedestrian-only street. Ethan nodded.

"What's that?" Priya asked.

"Protective Policing Service," Zoe said. "They protect the federal politicians, diplomats, and visiting VIPs."

"Ooh! Are we VIPs?" Paige asked, excitedly.

"Very," Ethan replied.

"So, they're all yours, then?" Zoe asked.

"Oh yes," Ethan said. "Canada's government was the very first I infiltrated. Not everyone here is under my influence, though—just those who need to be."

They entered the nondescript doors of the ten-storey Blackburn Building and made their way up to the sky bridge that connected to the Office of the Prime Minister and Privy Council. After a few turns down opulent hallways, they entered the prime minister's office. All conversation ceased as the world leaders looked up and then abruptly dropped to one knee, hanging their heads in obeisance. Zoe was stunned.

Ethan smiled and spread his arms wide. "My friends. It is so good to finally meet all of you in person. Rise. We have much to discuss. But first, let me introduce you to my associates. This is Zoe, my most trusted friend. And these are her friends, Lin, Makena, Priya, and Paige. Powerful Telepaths, all of them."

The most powerful men in the world eagerly gathered around to shake their hands. The entire thing felt surreal.

"You all did very well this morning," Ethan said to the men. "Your speeches were excellent. I trust you will have no trouble following through on this treaty?"

The president of the United States spoke up. "Actually, sir, I expect to encounter a *considerable* amount of resistance. Due to how quickly we moved with this, we don't have all the political pundits on board yet, nor all the members of Congress. We're seeing a lot of outrage right now from people saying this is reckless and even treasonous—that if we get rid of our nukes, there is no guarantee that other nations will."

Ethan nodded. "As expected. My operatives will locate the most vocal and influential pundits and bring them into the fold. I would ask you to coordinate with my liaison in your office to bring your most vocal critics from Congress and the Senate into the fold, as well. I would like this done as soon as possible. The same goes for all of you. Coordinate with my liaisons to convert all opposition—whether they be in government, industry, or media. The people need to be told how to feel about this."

Murmurs of consent filled the room.

"Now, on to business. We are going to do great things together, gentlemen. We will remake the world, and you will all go down in history as those who made it happen. But first, I need to know everything that each one of you knows. All your secrets, big and small. Anything that I should know and that could be of use to me." He turned to the president of the People's Republic of China. "Mr. President," he said in Mandarin, "Let's begin with you. The rest of you . . . go about your business. I'm sure you have important things to discuss."

Ethan ushered the Chinese president to a seat in the corner of the room. "Ladies," he said to the Valkyries, "I don't anticipate any trouble, but we know the rebels are here somewhere. So, I'm counting on you to protect me." He paused to look them each in the eyes. "No matter what you may think of me, I want you to remember that we have done the impossible here today. No matter what you may think of my methods, *nothing* else could have accomplished this. These men here . . ." He gestured at the huddled world leaders. "These men are horrible people. Some more than others, but all of them despicable. It's virtually impossible for a good person to rise to the top as they have. But they are better people now than they were before. I'm *making* them better people, so that they will do right by those they are supposed to represent. The entire world—eight billion people—will now be safe from nuclear annihilation. At the expense of what? The free will of these terrible men? Surely that is a small price to pay. So, I . . . beg of you . . . don't jeopardize all the good we've done here."

Without waiting for a response, he placed his hands on the Chinese president's head and closed his eyes. Zoe and the Valkyries looked at each other awkwardly.

So . . . now what? Paige asked the group via mindlink. *Do we just, like, kill him?*

An uncomfortable silence followed.

I mean . . . we could, right? Lin said. *Or just bonk him on the head or something? But then, how would we get him back to the Academy for Sharapova to examine?*

We'd never be able to go back to the Academy, Priya said. *We'd be fugitives. Or dead. This is so weird. He's acting like we're on his side. Saying he trusts us.*

It's a test, Makena said, frowning. *It has to be. The moment we attack him, he'll kill us.*

He's not wrong, though, Paige said. *We can disapprove of his methods all we want but this was the only way this treaty would happen.*

My dad wouldn't have approved of what he's doing, Lin said.

I know, Paige replied. *I get the whole free will thing. But so far, he's just making them do what they should have done anyway. Getting rid of nuclear weapons is a good thing. You can't argue with that. And I don't know about you guys, but I want to live in a world that doesn't become a desert where nothing can survive, so I think reversing climate change is also a good thing.*

He won't stop at that, Zoe finally piped up. *I saw him, back in Babylon. He wants to be worshipped like that again. His motives aren't altruistic. He doesn't care about creating a paradise for people. He just wants a paradise for himself.*

Well, we're all living in the same place, Paige said, *so maybe we should wait until he actually starts doing evil stuff before we take him out?*

Lin looked at Zoe. *What do you want to do, Zoe?*

But that was just it. She was torn. Paralyzed by indecision. He had called her bluff and put himself at her mercy. *He knows full well I'm not going to stab him in the back, anymore than I was able to kill Old Man*

Marduk.

Well, that's it, then, isn't it? Lin said. *If we're not going to move against him even when we have the best opportunity we'll ever have, then let's not kid ourselves. We serve him now.*

I do not serve him, Zoe and Tiamat both said vehemently at the same time. Zoe was startled. Had Tiamat just spoken through her? Or had they both felt and vocalized the same thing?

Suddenly, Lin looked up and stared into space.

What's wrong? Zoe asked. Lin raised a hand to shush her. She was clearly listening to someone, but who else was here? It had to be—

Gabriel's in trouble, Lin said. *We have to hurry.* She snatched a vase from a side table and smashed it over Ethan's head.

Everyone froze.

"What did you do?" Makena whispered.

"He's fine," she said, turning to face the world leaders, who stared, slack-jawed. "Some help with this?" The Chinese president gazed at her in confusion. She touched his head, and he slumped to the floor, eyes closed.

Zoe held up her hand and entered the mind of the closest man, the UK prime minister. *Sleep,* she said, and he closed his eyes and lay down on the floor. The others followed her lead, and soon the room was full of napping world leaders.

"He says they're close," Lin said. "Somewhere on Sparks Street."

Zoe checked Ethan's pulse—still alive.

"Oh, he's going to be angry when he wakes up," Paige said. "We failed his loyalty test."

"But we didn't kill him, so maybe we still kind of passed?" Priya tried.

"Let's go," Zoe said, happy to finally have a clear course of action. They exited the way they'd come in and soon were back on Sparks Street, leaving a trail of sleeping PPS agents and office workers in their wake.

"He says they're two blocks away," Lin said. "Near the CBC

studios?"

"This way," Zoe said, racing toward Metcalfe. They ran as fast as they could, swords in hand, leaping over cars at the intersections. Zoe wondered just how many rules they were breaking and if they would end up on the news or social media.

Soon, she heard swords clanging, and panicked people ran past them. Ragnar and at least two dozen of his men had surrounded a smaller group in the middle of the pedestrian street. She had to assume Gabriel was among them. In the back of her mind, she realized she and her friends were about to cross a line. Fighting Ragnar and his men might very well get them killed. At the very least, they would never be allowed back at the Academy—not unless Marduk turned them into obedient puppets.

Lin suddenly sprinted ahead, face contorted with rage and apparently eager to be the first to cross that line. She had, no doubt, just decided that today would be the day she avenged her father's death. Ragnar spun just in time to block her strike. The power of her blow—amplified by her momentum and her newfound telekinetic strength—sent him sliding backwards as the rest of the Valkyries engaged his men.

It was utter chaos. There had been no time for a plan. Luckily, they had trained and fought together as a team for Doom, and they had all experienced actual combat during the Battle. But they were still kids, and they were far outnumbered. Lin pressed the attack on Ragnar like a wild thing, moving faster than Zoe had ever seen her. She had somehow grabbed another sword and was slashing and thrusting like a whirlwind—attacking high and low, determined to end the fight before Ragnar could get his footing and mount an offensive. Zoe suspected, though, that Ragnar was simply reluctant to kill his star pupil.

As Zoe fought her way to Lin's side, Gabriel shouted in her mind, *Hold them off! Buy me some time!*

What will you do? she shouted back.

I have a plan!

He ran into the CBC studios while the Resistance fighters—along with Makena, Priya, and Paige—kept the enemy from following. Zoe had no time to wonder what his plan was, though, because Ragnar suddenly stepped inside Lin's attack, grabbed her wrist, and backhanded her so hard that she dropped to her knees. Dazed, Lin's swords slipped from her fingers, along with her dreams of revenge. Ragnar grabbed her by the hair and brought his sword to her neck. He looked at Zoe, absolutely livid.

"Surrender. All—"

But Zoe had already flung her sword at him. He was forced to swat it aside with his blade, and Zoe rushed in and feigned a kick, then superman-punched him in the face hard enough to stagger him back and put herself between him and Lin.

"Don't touch her," she said. She willed her katana back into her hand. Electricity sparked across its blade.

Ragnar spat blood and rubbed his jaw. "She just tried her best to kill *me*, remember? *I* was defending myself. If I'd wanted to kill her, she'd be dead. Why are you doing this?"

The question took her aback. "Gabriel called for help," she said.

"Do you even know what's going on here? Do you know what he's planning to do?"

"I don't care," Zoe said. "Whatever it is, it isn't good for you and Marduk."

"It isn't good for *any* of us," Ragnar said, stepping forward. "If your beloved Professor Chao were here, he'd be trying to stop him, too."

"I doubt that."

"He's exposing us," Ragnar said. "To the world." He pointed at the large windows of the CBC studios. "Right now, on live television. He didn't just run in there for safety. This was his *plan*. God knows what he's saying or what he's already put out on the Internet or who he's already told."

Zoe's eyes widened. "You're lying."

"He's decided to sacrifice us all rather than let Marduk win. Nothing will ever be the same again. We'll be hunted down like animals, enslaved, experimented on, killed."

"Sounds kind of like what you've been up to," Zoe said. "Hunting down the Resistance, turning them into little Marduk clones."

Ragnar scowled. "I won't let him do this. I don't want to hurt you, Zoe, but I will if I have to." He started for the studio doors, but Zoe blocked his path.

"I won't let *you* do this," Zoe said. "I trust Gabriel. I have to assume he knows what he's doing."

"You *trust* him? You barely know him." Ragnar shook his head. "How can someone with such potential have such poor judgment? One side wants to save the world and the other wants to start a war that will likely kill us all." He took a deep breath. "I'm done talking. Stop me if you can."

Zoe put herself in an Aikido ready stance, her back foot perpendicular to her front, her weight balanced equally on both feet, her katana raised in front of her. She realized then that she had never fought a *real* opponent—someone who presented an actual challenge—in a life-or-death duel. She had seen Ragnar fight Professor Chao and was under no illusions that she was any match for him yet.

But before Ragnar could close the distance, Ethan suddenly plummeted out of the sky. He landed between them with such force that he made a crater and sent both her and Ragnar staggering back several steps. Ethan rose to his feet, and Ragnar's anger was nothing compared to his. Ethan looked like a wrathful god, electricity crackling all over his body.

He had his fear-inducing field on full strength, causing everyone around him to drop to the ground. Ragnar, though, dropped only to one knee, making it look like a bow of respect. Zoe found herself on both knees, trembling and struggling to maintain her grip on her sword. Ethan looked down on her.

"I trusted you," he said. "I did everything I could to prove to you that I can be the benevolent god this world needs. I wanted you to grow into adulthood with me and rule this world at my side. Forever. I put myself in a position of utter vulnerability, hoping you would finally choose to be with me. Instead, you betray me and attempt to undo all my plans."

"Ethan—"

"Don't call me that," he snapped. "Not anymore. There's no point. I tried so hard to be the Ethan you knew, the person you wanted me to be. I wasn't trying to trick you. I genuinely wanted to be good, to have Ethan be the dominant part of my merged personas, because he loves you—has *always* loved you, thanks to the mindbending of the man kneeling behind me."

Ragnar's eyes widened at the realization that Marduk knew what he had done all those years ago.

"He thought it would protect you, no doubt, should I choose Ethan to be my host. Ironic, isn't it, that his attempt to protect his daughter will ultimately be what kills her? Does anything foment hatred like being betrayed by someone you love?"

"Ethan," Zoe began again, struggling to form words amid her violent shaking.

"You will refer to me as Marduk now. The boy Ethan serves no further purpose, now that you have made your decision. I won't just relegate him to the background—I will destroy all traces of his memories and personality, so that nothing of him survives. And *you* are the reason."

"We could have killed you," Zoe barely managed to say. How could she fight back if she was paralyzed like this?

Tiamat! Zoe shouted in her mind. *I need you!*

"You should have," Marduk said. "You're consistent, though, aren't you? Forever indecisive, lacking the fortitude to do what needs to be done." He knelt and leaned in close, taking her chin in his hand. "When you stab the devil in the back, it's best not to miss."

I'm trying to rewire your brain to allow you to overcome the fear, Tiamat said in her mind.

Zoe nodded. "I've heard that saying," she said, trying to stall. "But I never wanted to kill you. I wanted to save you. I want my Ethan back."

Just inches from her, he whispered, "You will *never* have your Ethan back." He stood up and surveyed the chaos around him for the first time. "Who was it that hit me over the head?"

"Me," Zoe lied, deliberately not glancing at Lin.

"Hmm. I doubt that." He looked down at Lin, who was starting to regain consciousness. "It seems more in line with something your friend here would do."

"It was me," Zoe repeated, slowly shaking her head. *Tiamat?*

Almost there.

"It doesn't really matter. You allowed it. So, now I'm going to play the part of the malevolent god that you choose to believe I am. I'm going to kill you, Zoe. But first, I'm going to kill everyone you care about."

"No!" Zoe yelled, forcing herself to stand. *Tiamat! There's no more time. Decompress!*

No! I almost have this.

Marduk stretched out his arm, and pulled Lin through the air until her neck was in his grip. "Starting with this one."

"Let her go," Ragnar said from behind him.

Ethan turned his head. "Excuse me?"

"We don't kill children. Especially not this one."

"'We?' You are telling me what I can and cannot do?"

Ragnar stepped forward and gripped his sword tighter. "Let her go," he repeated.

Zoe abruptly felt all fear leave her. She straightened, stepped in, and punched Marduk with all her strength, channelling every ounce of telekinesis into the blow and making her fist as tough as iron. Marduk dropped Lin and staggered. Zoe gave him no time to recover. She tackled him to the ground and pummeled him, trying desperately to knock him unconscious.

Then she was flying backwards—along with everyone else—smashing through the windows of the CBC studios. Her ears rang as she rose to her feet amid the broken glass. It looked like a bomb had gone off. Everyone was bleeding—both Typicals and Telepaths. She saw Gabriel getting to his feet, still talking urgently into the camera.

Outside, Marduk stood alone in an even deeper crater. His fists were clenched, his face bloody and contorted in fury. He lifted his arm, and Zoe flew toward him. Spotting a sword on the ground, she summoned it into her hand and tried to skewer him as her neck reached his outstretched hand. He brushed her sword aside and grabbed her wrist, forcing her to drop the blade.

He lifted her off the ground, and she couldn't breathe. She flailed wildly.

Immune to my fear field now, I see. That's quite a trick. I must know how you managed it before I kill you.

He forced himself into her mind, and Zoe screamed in rage. She tried everything she could to push him out, but he was simply too powerful.

Incredible. You have no fear anymore. None at all. I knew you had an uncanny ability to heal your mind—ever since that day in the alley when you almost immediately overcame the memory wipe I'd placed on you. But this isn't healing. You rewired your own brain while we were speaking. I've never seen anything like it.

He casually stretched out his free arm to stop Lin in her tracks, a split second before she ran him through with her sword.

"You do inspire loyalty, Zoe, I'll say that for you. Not many friends would dare to attack a god. Take a look."

He beckoned, and all of her friends floated up behind him. Like her, they were hanging in the air, kicking their legs frantically and struggling to breathe.

Tiamat, it's last resort time.

"My fear field is as strong as ever, and still they came running, in a futile attempt to rescue you. I'm going to kill them one by one as you watch, as punishment for your betrayal. And then I'm going to kill—"

He looked down in astonishment at the sword protruding from his gut. Zoe and her friends dropped to the ground, gasping for breath. Ethan turned his head, and Ragnar pulled his sword free.

"They're *children*," Ragnar growled. He stepped forward and stabbed Ethan again. "And *she* is my daughter." He twisted his sword, and Ethan winced. "You think I will let you take her from me?"

Ethan placed his hand on the hilt of Ragnar's sword. "You've made a mistake, old friend." He slowly pulled the sword from his own gut, as Ragnar apparently struggled against paralysis. "When you attack a god, you have one chance."

Freed from Ethan's grasp, Zoe grabbed Lin's katana and tried to stab him from behind, but an invisible hand stopped her in her tracks and forced her to her knees.

Tiamat, we're out of time. Decompress or we all die!

"Attacking the body is almost pointless, except as a diversion," Marduk continued, grasping the blade to wrench it all the way free. "We can heal ourselves almost instantly, you see. That's why, when we gods fought among ourselves, we knew to attack the head. The heart might suffice, but what if you miss?" He moved faster than Zoe could see, impaling Ragnar with his own sword. "No, when trying to kill a god, you always go for the head."

"Like how you killed me?" Zoe said, slowly getting to her feet. Long-forgotten memories from thousands of years ago exploded into her mind. She had been a passenger for so long, a shell of her former self.

Now, she felt all of her power returning. She stretched and took a deep breath, savouring the smell of the city, the feeling of muscles responding to her will. "Firing an arrow into my head from a distance, like a coward?"

Ethan turned to look at her. "What did you say?" He tried to force her back down to her knees, but Zoe just cocked her head. He tried to enter her mind and bounced off her shields. His eyes went wide and Zoe smiled.

"Hello, Marduk. It's been so long." She hit him with telekinetic force so strong that he flew into the building across the street, smashing through it like paper. Her friends stared in disbelief.

"How did you do that?" Paige gasped, looking at the shattered building.

Lin looked up at her in horror. "What did you do?" she asked.

"Last resort, remember?" Zoe smiled and offered Lin her hand. "It's okay. It's still me. More than me, but . . . I'm still here." Lin tentatively took her hand, and Zoe helped her up. She saw movement in the dust of the shop across the street. "Can you guys deal with all of this?" she asked, indicating the chaos behind her. "Get everyone to safety. I'll deal with Marduk."

"What are you going to do to him?" Lin asked.

"I'm going to kill him, of course," she said, striding forward and willing two fallen katanas into her hands.

"He's still Ethan, though!" Lin yelled at her.

Zoe paused and looked down at Ragnar, who was on his knees with a sword through his belly, afraid to remove it lest he bleed out. He stared at her, perplexed. "How?" he asked.

"You've done so much evil in your lifetime, haven't you, Father? Do you ever wonder what your life would have been like had you never met him?" She knelt and looked Ragnar in the eyes. "Still, I do owe you for creating me. And you did just save our lives." She yanked the sword out of his gut and placed her hand on the wound. "Time enough to judge your sins after all this is over." She concentrated on his wound and healed the tissue, starting from his insides and working her way out to the skin.

Then, a figure emerged from the shop, and she placed her hand on Ragnar's head. "You are too dangerous to have running around unsupervised," she said, putting him to sleep.

She stood and threw one of her swords to Ethan, who caught it by the hilt. He looked unnerved.

"You always were a pathetic god," she said, as they slowly circled each other. "So *needy*. Needing to be loved. To be feared. To be worshipped. I truly pitied you."

"How are you here, Tiamat? I killed you thousands of years ago."

"I remember. Not from my original body's vantage point, but I was still there to witness it. I knew you were planning to move against me, but I stupidly thought you would be brave enough to challenge me directly. I never expected an arrow while I was sipping tea. You were clever, though, I'll give you that. I never saw it coming. How did you manage that anyway?"

"How did you survive?"

"Rude. If you're not going to answer my questions, I'm certainly not going to answer yours. Suffice to say that I *did* survive, and I have reluctantly returned because of you, and now you have to face me directly—and you are doing your best to pretend you aren't terrified."

"I've never been scared of you," he said.

"We both know that's not true. You hid in the trees and killed me with an arrow, remember?"

"We don't have to fight. I wanted Zoe to rule at my side. That can still happen."

Zoe snorted. "Me? With you? Please. You are my descendant. Besides, I have no intention of being another Sarpanit—a goddess relegated to the position of consort, forever remembered only as the spouse of Marduk."

"Then don't be my spouse. Be my partner. Rule this world with me."

Zoe shook her head. "No, Marduk. That will not happen. I can't allow you to rule. I can't even allow you to live."

"I'm trying to save the world," he said. "You would jeopardize all my work just for revenge?"

"Oh, I'm sorry. Does that make me shallow?"

"It does, actually. This world needs a benevolent god. No one else could have accomplished what I've done, and I'm only just beginning. You are risking the lives of eight billion people for your own petty vengeance."

"Maybe the world does need a god right now. But it certainly doesn't need two. And we both know you've never been benevolent, Marduk."

"Well," he said, twirling his katana. "I guess that's it, then. You and I were never especially skilled with the sword, but Zoe and Ethan certainly are. I wonder, though, who is better? They were always evenly matched, but they usually fought alongside each other, not against each other. They would be so displeased with us."

Zoe fixed him with her gaze. "I *am* Zoe, you fool. Every bit as much as I am Tiamat. It was a merging of equals, which I asked for as Zoe and which I granted as Tiamat—and only as a last resort. I would never take someone against their will or subjugate their persona as you have."

"He's still in here, Zoe. I haven't destroyed him yet. If you kill me, you'll kill him, too."

"Listen to yourself. Begging like a coward the moment you come up against someone you can't dominate. You're right about one thing, though. Ethan, if you can still hear me in there . . . I love you. I'm sorry I never said it before." She stopped circling him. "And I'm truly sorry that I have to do this."

She rushed in with a lunging thrust to his midsection. The moment he committed himself to stepping forward to meet her attack with a block, she pushed his sword to the ground with telekinesis. This caught him by surprise and almost ended the fight immediately, but he managed to twist awkwardly and avoid her blade. She didn't give him time to recover. While he was off-balance with his sword behind him, she grabbed his neck and pushed him even further off-balance while pulling her sword back to stab him. Ethan switched sword hands behind his back and threw his right arm over his left shoulder, kicking her with both feet to break her grip on his throat and flipping backwards. She tried to press the attack, but he slashed upward as he completed his flip, forcing her to jump back.

Ethan charged at her with a series of thrusts and slashes that she parried and sidestepped while dodging debris that flew at her from all sides. After getting hit by a brick, she began to redirect the debris in classic Aikido fashion, allowing it to enter her sphere, blending with it, and then redirecting it toward her opponent. Her thoughts went back to the first time Professor Chao and Ragnar had fought, in that restaurant, moving faster than she'd been able to follow, using their telekinesis to throw each other off-balance and attack with every object at hand. Were she and Ethan at that level now? Or had they surpassed it? She now had two sets of memories from that fight—from the perspective of a teenage girl, and from that of Professor Chao in whose mind she had been a passenger. Indeed, she had memories of his entire life. All of his training, all of his fighting experience.

When Ethan charged her again, she mixed it up by hitting him with as much electricity as she could manage. He stopped in his tracks, paralyzed. Zoe tried to close the distance—to finish him off while he was incapacitated—but was struck by electricity herself.

You think I don't know this trick? Marduk snarled.

She had never been electrocuted before. All of her muscles contracted and spasmed. She could feel the damage it was causing to her nerves and blood vessels and organs. She tried her best to repair the damage as it was happening while also increasing her electrical output, hoping to outlast him. Soon, though, she found it hard to breathe, and her heart started beating arrhythmically.

Mutually assured destruction, Marduk said. *Unless you wish to reconsider this tactic?*

It wasn't looking like she would outlast him, so she relented. *Fine. We release in three.*

Two, he said.

One, she said.

Release! they said, simultaneously stopping their electrical attacks and taking a moment to recover, panting, their hands on their knees.

"Drop your weapons!" someone shouted. Zoe and Ethan both paused to take stock of their surroundings. Dozens of police officers had guns trained on them. "Drop your weapons!" the officer shouted again, a moment before streaks of yellow light appeared all around them. Rather than dodging the streaks, Zoe stretched out a hand and stopped the bullets in midair, then made the officers in front of her drop to the ground asleep. She turned to see that the police in front of Ethan were dangling twelve feet in the air, clutching their throats.

"No!" she yelled. He smiled and let them drop as he resumed his attack upon her. She released a burst of telekinetic force in all directions, pushing him away and launching herself into the air, giving herself room to slow the officers' fall and put them gently to sleep.

Ethan pointed at her. "*That* is why you are weak. You always cared so much about them. The Anunnaki I can understand, but mortals? How could it possibly matter if they live or die?"

"Spoken like a true *benevolent* god," Zoe said.

Their swords flew again. Sometimes their blades would find their mark and send blood spattering, but both healed their wounds quickly as they fought. It would take a more significant blow to finish this fight. Marduk had nearly decapitated her several times already, and Zoe realized she *wasn't* going for the killing stroke. Such hesitancy was a sure way to lose this fight. What was holding her back? She knew the answer, of course. Despite her bravado, she didn't want to kill Ethan. None of this was his fault. He didn't deserve to die. He was an unwilling host.

An unwilling host!

Ethan, she said, using their familiar mindlink. *I need you to fight him.*

"You know I can hear you, right?" Marduk said, slashing at her head. "He might still be in here, but I'm the one in charge."

Ethan, she said again, ignoring Marduk as she parried his attacks. *I need you to summon all of your strength and do one thing for me.*

"You're wasting your time," Marduk said, slashing at her midsection now. "He can't help you. And once I've killed you, I will destroy what's left of him."

One, Zoe said, parrying a thrust.

Two, a voice from within Marduk's mind said. His eyes widened in surprise, then narrowed again as he pressed the attack in an all-out blitz to keep her on the defensive.

Three, she said, suddenly closing the distance between them. His sword found its mark, and she saw both her sword and the hand holding it fly through the air in a graceful arc. Ignoring the pain, she grabbed the back of his head to bring herself inches from his face. She looked into his eyes. *Let me in, Ethan.*

His shields dropped for a split second, which was all Zoe needed to enter his mind. She immediately severed the nerves to his spinal cord, causing him to drop to the ground, paralyzed from the neck down. She straddled him, her hand on his head, staring into his eyes, her other wrist pumping blood everywhere. She could feel him frantically trying to repair the nerves to his spinal cord and succeeding momentarily, causing him to flail briefly before she severed the nerves again. She quickly stopped the flow of blood from her wrist and tried to put him to sleep, but he resisted. Unable to move, he used the full force of his telekinetic power to blast her away, but she wrapped her arms around him and held on, using her own telekinetic strength to pull herself to him as he unleashed one telekinetic bomb after another. When he finally tired out, she tore ruthlessly into his mind.

She quickly realized that he had lied. He had barely merged with Ethan at all. Maybe he lacked the skill and finesse, or maybe he just didn't see the point. Regardless, she could clearly see two distinct personas, and she began ripping apart the areas of his brain responsible for his powers, preventing him from fighting back.

"Don't do this!" Marduk shrieked.

Because he hadn't tried to augment Ethan's powers and instead just added his own, she felt confident that Ethan should still have his Abilities when she was done. Next, she focused on ripping out Marduk's personality, his values, his memories.

"Please don't do this," Marduk whimpered. "I don't deserve this." She could feel his panic.

"You *completely* deserve this," Zoe said, relentlessly continuing her decimation of his mind. The more she destroyed, the more she could feel Ethan emerging.

"I don't want to die," Marduk said.

"You never cared about anyone else dying," Zoe said. "You never cared about taking Ethan's life from him. You said you would destroy every part of him, remember?" Half of Marduk was gone now, and he was trying frantically to push her from his mind and reconnect the nerves to his spine. But she could tell that even he knew it was useless. She had him now, and nothing he could do would stop her.

"I take it back! I promise. I'll leave him alone. He and I can be equals. A true merging, like you have."

Ethan? Do you want to be merged with Marduk?

I want him out of me, Ethan gasped. *I want him utterly destroyed.*

"Sorry, Marduk," Zoe said, continuing to rip his mind apart. "A true merging comes from two willing partners. You *took* Ethan against his will, to extend your own life. You had your time in this world. Thousands of years. And you have nothing good to show for it. Because it was always just about you."

"I . . . I don't remember. Was I not a good person?"

"You were a horrible person."

"I'm sorry. I don't know what's happening. Who are you?"

"It doesn't matter. Just relax. It won't be long now."

"I don't . . . know who I am."

"It's okay. You're almost gone now."

"I don't want to go." Marduk stopped speaking, and the panic left his eyes.

"Zoe?"

"Hello, Ethan." She smiled.

"I've missed you," he said.

20

BRAVE NEW WORLD

"It's almost over," Zoe said. "I've destroyed most of him. I'm just searching for any last remnants. Try to remember anything that isn't from your life."

Ethan did so, lighting up memories that Zoe immediately destroyed.

"I can't think of anything else," he said.

"That's good. Now, think of everything you can from the time you were Marduk's passenger."

"But . . . those are my memories, not his. You're going to remove those, too?"

"Your memories of his thoughts and actions will reactivate the motivations behind them. I need to find and remove all traces of his values and personality."

"But you'll leave those memories?"

"No, Ethan. Trust me, you don't want those memories. They'll haunt you. I'm going to make you whole again. It will be like he was never a part of you."

"Okay. If you think it's necessary."

She followed his memories of the past few months, removing all remnants of Marduk from his mind and then removing those memories themselves. His mind looked . . . clean. Tidy. The way a normal mind should look.

"Zoe? Where am I? What's happening? I can't move."

"It's okay. Your paralysis is temporary. I'll fix it. But first, what's the last thing you remember?"

"I . . . it was shortly after our mission in Toronto. I was telling you that I would go see Professor Sharapova about something. And then . . . I have a vague memory of sitting on my bed in my room and you were on the floor curled up in a ball."

Zoe nodded. "Marduk took control of you. But it's okay. He's gone now. I've erased every last trace of him from your mind."

"What? How were you able to *do* that? He was so powerful."

"It's a long story," she said. "I'll fill you in on everything, but first, let me get you fixed up." She repaired the connection to his spinal cord and stood up. She offered him her remaining hand and helped him to his feet. But he stared at the stump of her right wrist.

"Oh no. Zoe . . ."

"Don't worry," she said. She searched the debris nearby and found her severed hand, still clutching her katana. She placed it on her wrist and closed her eyes to concentrate. She undid her makeshift cauterization, causing the blood to begin pumping from her wrist again. Only for a moment, though, as she began to reconnect the severed blood vessels, repair the broken bone, and reconnect the nerves. She moved her fingers again and made a fist. Much better.

"Okay," Ethan said, slowly. "I can't wait to hear this story." He surveyed the chaos around them. "We're in Ottawa," he said. "Did we do all of this?"

"We did."

Helicopters flew in overhead. More police in tactical gear positioned themselves around them. Reporters and cameramen had come as near as they dared. Lin ran out of the decimated CBC studios, followed closely by Makena, Priya, and Paige. They all looked like they'd just been through war.

"Are you okay?" Lin called, racing up to Zoe. "Your hand."

"All good, Lin," she said, holding up her hand and moving her fingers.

"And you're still you?"

Zoe smiled and hugged her. "Still me."

"That is messed up," Paige said, pointing to her reattached hand.

"What about him?" Priya asked, eyeing Ethan warily.

"Marduk's gone," Zoe said. "For good."

Makena nodded and clasped Ethan's hand in camaraderie. "It's good to have you back," she said.

"I guess I've been gone a while, then? I hope I didn't cause too much trouble."

Paige snorted. "You have no idea."

"How did you do it, though?" Priya asked. "You were more powerful than Marduk."

"I'll explain it all later," Zoe said, as Gabriel emerged from the CBC studios and walked over.

"I don't know how you did it," he said, pointing at Ethan, "but nice job. Marduk's gone, I assume?"

She nodded. "How are you even here, Gabriel? We thought Marduk gained control of you a long time ago."

"Oh, he did," Gabriel said. "Luckily, someone noticed and was skilled enough to eradicate him from my mind. I'm me again."

"Interesting," Zoe said. "I need to meet this person."

"All right, then," Gabriel said, asserting command and facing the police. "Everyone just keep quiet and let me do the talking."

"No, Gabriel," Zoe said. "You've done quite enough talking. Your little stunt with the press may very well get us all killed. I'm in charge now."

Gabriel regarded her with a raised eyebrow. "I know you're strong, Zoe, but you're still a child. I was Professor Chao's right-hand man, and I'm the leader of the Resistance. *I'm* in charge."

"You're a fool who has always underestimated the threat Typicals pose to us. Professor Chao said so himself. And now you've recklessly exposed us all. I have merged with the oldest, most powerful being on the planet, and I am now our best hope for surviving your folly. *I'm* in charge, and that's that."

Utterly baffled, Gabriel started to protest, but Makena slapped him upside the head. "I don't understand what's going on yet, but she's in charge."

"So, what now?" Lin asked.

Zoe looked around. "Things are going to get bad. *Really* bad. The whole world knows about us now. There's no closing the box."

"A lot of mini Marduks are still out there, too," Paige said.

"We'll find them," Zoe said, "and remove his influence from them. It will be seen as a gesture of goodwill. It's important that the Typicals learn as quickly as possible that there are two factions among us and that the good guys just won. Our primary concern right now is the safety of all Telepaths. The kids back at the Academy. The adults out in the world. We're far away from all of them, so the best way to ensure their safety is to make the Typicals understand that we are friends, but we are also not to be trifled with."

"And how do we do that?" Lin asked.

Zoe thought about this. "Can you stall the police? I just need a few minutes."

Without waiting for an answer, she flew up into the air—to the gasps and shrieks of onlookers—and within seconds was back at the Office of the Prime Minister and Privy Council. This time, she entered through the front doors. She made her way to the prime minister's office, putting anyone who tried to stop her to sleep. She entered to find the groggy world leaders highly guarded and in the care of medical staff. She put the security guards and medical team to sleep and locked the door.

"Marduk is dead," she said, simply. They stared at her in horror, realizing their Marduk personas were about to cease to exist. Then, they bolted for the door. She stopped them in their tracks, and one by one, she placed her hands on their heads and removed all traces of Marduk from their minds. She left all their memories intact, though, so they would remember being his puppet and know that she had just saved them. When she was finished, she examined everyone else in the room and removed Marduk from some of the security team as well.

"There," she said, at last. Everyone looked bewildered, like they had all just woken from a long dream. "You're all free of that evil little man now. You should remember who it was who infected you. Detain them, and one of us will help you remove Marduk from their minds, as well. We'll work our way down the chains until we have freed everyone from his control."

"You're Zoe," the prime minister of Canada said. "I remember . . . there are more of you. Thousands."

Zoe nodded. "We're not a threat," she said. "We have always been here. We've kept ourselves hidden and never interfered with you . . . until now." She looked each of them in the eye. "Remember what I did here today. I could have joined Marduk. I could have usurped him and ruled over you myself. Instead, I have released you from his influence and exerted none of my own. You are free men again. I am under no illusions that you are *good* men, though. You will be tempted to wage war upon us or to capture us to use for your own purposes." She shook her head. "Don't. I would be a formidable enemy."

She left them and walked briskly back out onto the street. She flew back to Sparks Street, where her friends were surrounded by shouting police with raised guns. She landed in the centre of them.

"Where have you been?" Lin exclaimed. "That was not cool!"

"Sorry," she said. "I had to free the world leaders from Marduk's control before they all took off on their jets." Zoe stepped toward the police. "Lower your weapons." When nobody did, she tried again in a stern voice, "Lower your weapons *now* before someone accidentally gets hurt."

A yellow streak of light was suddenly on her chest. She instinctively flicked her fingers and sent the officer's gun flying up into the air.

"Wait," Ethan said. "We saw the streak but . . . the bullet was never fired. You changed the future. I didn't know that was possible."

Interesting. There was no time to ponder the broader philosophical implications, though, because yellow streaks erupted everywhere as the police began panic-shooting. Zoe erected a shield around them and waited for the police to stop. When the streaks finally disappeared and the street was quiet again, she lowered the shield.

"What is wrong with you?" she shouted. "You're shooting at *children*! I'm sorry, but I've lost my patience with the lot of you." She waved her hand and all of the police closed their eyes, curled up on the ground, and went to sleep.

Zoe peered into the CBC studios where a terrified cameraman was filming them. She walked toward him. "Are we live?"

He nodded, taking a step back.

"Good," she said, breathing deeply. "My name is Zoe. I have so much to tell you."

TO BE CONTINUED IN BOOK 3 OF TELEPATH

ACKNOWLEDGMENTS

Thank you to my daughters, Breana and Belinda, who inspired me to write this series back when they were little, and who provided their input for this book as beta readers. This novel took a little over two years to write, edit, and publish, which was longer than I had anticipated—but still better than the 17 years it took for the first book!

Thank you to my wife, Jennifer, for her love and support of my dream to be a writer.

Thank you again to my editor, Constance Renfrow, for her excellent insights and suggestions in the editing of this book.

Finally, thank you to my cover designer, Stefanie Shaw, for another amazing and distinctive cover.

www.ingramcontent.com/pod-product-compliance
Lightning Source LLC
Chambersburg PA
CBHW020649120726

47906CB00001B/195